Yellow Dog Red

Patrick Moran

Yellow Dog Red

Yet-Another-Non-Commercial Endeavor
by Sweet Pea & Company
A Barely Hanging On Enterprise
First Edition 2016
Published by Sweet Pea & Company
Glen Ellen, California
Front Cover Photo by Patrick Moran
Back Cover Photo by Patrick Moran.
Library of Congress Catalog Number: Pending
For information address Sweet Pea & Company, P.O. Box 644, Glen Ellen, CA 95442, email: pat.k.moran@gmail.com, website: www.patrickmoranbooks.com
Author's Page Lulu: www.lulu.com/spotlight/sweetpeasite
Author's Page Amazon:
www.amazon.com/Patrick-Moran/e/B000APSXLI/ ref=dp_byline_cont_book_3

This is a work of fiction. The people, events, circumstances, and institutions depicted are fictitious and the product of the author's imagination. Any resemblance of any character to any actual person, whether living or dead, is purely coincidental.

ISBN: 978-1-329-66623-8

Yellow Dog Red

For Cassie, Dina, Lollie, Tortilla, Sadie, Kellae: our girls

Yellow Dog Red passed away in November. The eighth to be exact. She was a Yellow Lab, eighteen, blind, snaggle-toothed, and hobbled by arthritis. She was a good old girl, and precious to her owner, Parker, who died two years later after never leaving his best friend's side.

Yellow Dog Red is buried in the pet cemetery at the base of the oak and eucalyptus grove above the vineyard at the end of Dotty's road. Parker's ashes are spread around her headstone. Both owner and pet were known for their loyalty and perceptiveness, as well as for their persistence. All three qualities play prominent roles in their story. The latter—persistence—begins it. Perceptiveness sustains it. But it is loyalty that supports it at every turn from start to finish, and it is for this quality that the memories of both man and dog are treasured.

Dotty's road was unofficially called Dotty Lane. But a year after Yellow Dog Red died people started calling it Memory Road, owing to its peculiar power to evoke long hidden memories in those who walked its length. In itself Dotty Lane, or Memory Road, is a nondescript strip of decomposing macadam that twists lazily through the wine country in an elongated thumb-shaped valley surrounded by forested hills on three sides and wetlands on the other. The road was once a stagecoach route that connected San Francisco with points north, before horse-drawn conveyances were replaced by railroad cars carting excursionists. Dotty's house, just a half-day coach-ride from the city, was its first way-station, where worn horses could be switched, men's thirsts quenched, and ladies' toilets attended to. Dotty's place is a pretty, somewhat fussy, Swiss-inspired gingerbread-trimmed house on a creek paralleling the quaint road that is really still only a muddy buckboard trail capped by a modern surface of ancient origins. Both road and creek are overhung with maple and oak, buckeye, locust, willow and eucalyptus that in the damper hollows are laced with Spanish Moss and mistletoe in a profuseness rarely encountered outside of mangrove swamps. The road's carrying capacity was never meant to convey anything larger than the four-wheel horse-drawn coaches and, later, the six-wheel motorized lorries that ferried redwood to the cities to the south. It was most certainly not designed for the diesel-powered eighteen-wheel behemoths sloshing with grape juice that some would presently have had it transport.

The road, like the vehicles it was designed to carry, is peopled by a mix of the eclectic, but surely not simple misfits, who came from near and far to hide, or to seek refuge, from whatever it was about society they found dispiriting. In the scheme of things, most of Dotty's neighbors until recently would have been adjudged outliers rather than suburbanites—eccentric common folk—whose lives were lived a few degrees south of the more frigid latitudes of quiet desperation that encircle the lives of most in-dwellers.

Before this band of intrepid characters came, bands of equally dauntless wanderers passed through for the soporific qualities imparted by the waters, which are unnaturally warm, and by the air, which is lush and unusually sweet. Like all of the plucky vagabonds, including Dotty, who came with her husband Max to flee the blackball, Parker, an ex-Army Intelligence Officer who had seen too much war and kept too many secrets, sought refuge here in order to find solace from a world gone viral with violence and technological miracles, both of which Parker believed killed the spirit in equal amounts. In this regard, one of the few sentiments Parker, in being an unvoluble man generally, was fond of espousing was that he did not envy God for having a mind that was unable to forget even the smallest of His creations lest it negate all His other creations. Which is to say, by Parker's reckoning, it was impossible for God to be of two minds about anything.

Unlike Parker, a select number of the newer folk who came to this place were indeed of two minds and did not seem in general to have migrated here seeking either refuge or solace; instead, they came to fatten their social brands in pastures clothed in grapevines, and to extend those same brands into newer pastures sown green with dividends. A few of these people for whom earning a living was the least of their worries are the ones who took umbrage with Parker over a matter that, to them, was paltry, but which, for Parker, was the stuff he would die for.

The pet cemetery, like the road it is on, is unimportant in the overall scheme of things, an artifact of simpler, mostly forgotten times really, when the road was first paved and used by bootleggers and G-Men alike to get to and from wood-fired stills that spilled out "sacramental" wines in such absurd quantities that the tax men could finally no longer ignore that the stills' outputs could have redeemed twice over the number of pious confessors that then existed on the whole planet. Five acres in size, the burial ground was set uphill from the southeast corner of a 200-acre parcel whose owner was a horse doctor by the name of Gainsaid Pound. It is on land that, before Gainsaid Pound purchased it, was deemed worthless except as a dump-site for animal parts and as a feasting place for the vultures that fattened themselves thereupon, and also as a place where fly-by-night mechanics could dispose of used antifreeze that the vultures subsequently guzzled thirstily to their own demise.

The veterinarian—in being shrewder than the dictates his professional practice—or indeed his name—demanded of him, and more loving of his clientele than was emotionally healthy for a person who wept pitiably through every euthanization—was a man whose loyalty was unquestioned, and he saw to it through various legally binding and supposedly unbreakable covenants that after he was gone the cemetery he created would be kept intact in perpetuity by its designated guarantor: initially the International Humane Society, and then the Society for the Prevention of Cruelty to Animals. It is these covenants that Parker defended with one of his own: a compact with himself to keep vigil over his best friend's resting place until it was indeed secured in law as well as in deed, or until death should reunite owner with best friend.

The vigil, which the local paper *The Valley Observer*, came to call "The Yellow Dog Red Overlook," began in concept the day Parker placed Yellow Dog Red's headstone at the head of her grave. About mid-afternoon on that fine autumn day, a duo of surveyors entered into the cemetery from the direction of the vet's kennel, which adjoined the cemetery to the north. By nature a nonconfrontational man, and out of respect for Yellow Dog Red, Parker greeted the surveyors cordially and watched with interest and in silence as they went about setting up their laser level on the property line not far downhill from Red's plot. This was in the corner next to the ancient redwood split-log fence that delineated the cemetery's lower southern boundary from the almost equally neglected vineyard to the east, now overgrown with mustard and calendula, where Gainsaid Pound had tried to coax muscat grapes to grow in the company of marauding deer he didn't have the heart to shoot.

"You from the county?" Parker inquired finally, during a lull in the men's work; for he had heard the vet's property had been sold yet again, and he assumed the title company had demanded a new survey after the last owners, a troupe of actors out of Chicago, had let the property and the farmhouse on it go to what would be the next-to-last all-but-inevitable step above going to seed.

"Nope," tersely replied the one who was in charge. He then whipped off his cap to show Parker the logo sewn on it: Wine Country Civil Engineering.

"They outsourcing now?" Parker asked, again surmising that the county was using resources in the private sector to augment or supplant its traditional public service commitments.

The man, who was perhaps half Parker's age, faced him and, scowling, cocked his head. It was an expression and a gesture both gauche and dismissive, which Parker, who, as part of his duties as an Intelligence Officer investigating corruption in the Army Corps of Engineers, received magnanimously and, instead of being offended by it, he gave the man the benefit of the doubt, ascribing his rudeness to the type of social awkwardness—geekiness it is called now—that both the data gathering and engineering professions seemed to esteem.

"Look, sir, if you don't mind, we're on a tight schedule here," the surveyor said, casting a disdainful glance at Parker's attire, which consisted of his usual, admittedly neglectful work clothes: an ill-coordinated wardrobe of faded, grease-stained jeans, threadbare canvas jacket, a shabby tartan-green-and-yellow muffler, and a rumpled pink beret whose rim was sullied with perspiration. "The owners want to start preparing this land before the rains come and make it too muddy to work the soil for planting in the spring." He then turned his back on Parker and resumed adjusting his level.

"Why would they—whoever they are—want to work the soil in a graveyard?"

The man, whose jowls were in girth at least two decades ahead of him in years, and whose eyes seemed to flit fitfully like a squirrel's, sparked with impatience. "How the fuck should I know, old man?" he spat, facing Parker again, perhaps assuming by his attire that Parker was a derelict. "Use your imagination. They probably want to dig up the fucking animal bones so they can put their fucking winery and vineyards here. I mean, look around you," he said, gesturing harshly toward the vineyard downslope from the graveyard, "and do the math. In this appellation, those vines, if they were Pinot, could bring in twenty-thou an acre times two hundred acres—four million a year—easy, if anyone wanted to put in the time and money to take care of 'em. And this," he frowned, scanning in a glance that took in the dozens of lichen-covered headstones overgrown with horsetail and thistles, buckeye and poison oak, "are worth nothing. Not in this terroir."

Parker was too stunned at the man's rudeness to reply, other than to say, "They are worth everything to me. And she was not a terrier. She was a Lab."

Another scowl began to form on the civil engineer's face before he realized that Parker was standing above a freshly placed headstone and a mound of dirt of a new grave whose perimeter was outlined with chewed-over dog bones and tennis balls. "Oh. Okay. Sorry. I didn't mean it that way. I'm sure the new owners will let you dig up...um..." he eyed the headstone, whose words of etched marble he mouthed to himself: "Here at my feet, my friend Yellow Dog Red lies, waiting for me in peace, always faithful." Then aloud, he said, "I'm sure the owners will let you dig up Yellow Dog Red before they doze all this under."

Again Parker was left speechless and could only repeat the man's last word in the form of a question. "Under?"

"Leave him be," intruded the voice of the other surveyor, who was grappling with coaxing the surveying rod through a grouping of buckeyes whose sinuous lateral branches intertwined with one another to form a web made of wood. The man was swarthy and had a ruddy complexion that, coupled with the frustration that tinged his words, telegraphed to Parker, whose work in Intelligence had been to size up men in a glance, a history of manual labor and, more importantly, of apologizing for a life of debauchery and, possibly, abandonment. "Look at him. He's probably homeless," he said, as if Parker were invisible. But then he too noticed the headstone and winced. "Sorry about the dog," he said, then appraising Parker's garments, three-day stubble, droopy-lidded milky-blue eyes, leathery skin and general gauntness, he reached into his pocket, and added, "You know, if you need a place to stay, Redwood Mission is good. Been there myself once. Here, have a wake for your friend," he said, as he withdrew a five-dollar bill out of his pants and waved it in Parker's face.

To that point, Parker, beside being stunned at the men's impertinence, had felt magnanimous, and perhaps even sympathetic, toward the two, especially the man with the pole, who was, to Parker, clearly projecting his own shortcomings. But the sight of the money so offended him that he instinctively lashed out.

13

"Go! Go now!" He muttered, lips tightened and blue with anger, and as he pushed aside the money he took a step forward and grabbed the surveying rod away from the man. He then heaved it like a javelin backwards over the fence line into the thicket of poison oak that grew along the water course lined with vulture bones and rusted radiators.

"Whoa! Okay! Okay! Now...now...cool it, Howard. You're getting us into a situation here," the jowly one interceded, motioning for Howard to stand back after he had advanced a retaliatory step toward Parker. "Just go and get the fucking stick."

"Fuck this, Bill. Get the fucking stick yourself. And fuck this tard," he spat, venting his anger on Bill rather than Parker. "I'm not going into that poison oak. Not this close to Thanksgiving, anyway, fuck you very much. Not after I spent all of last Christmas scratching my balls and dick to shreds."

Parker slid sideways so that he stood in front of Yellow Dog Red's headstone and between it and Howard who, he surmised, was prone to acting on his anger. He then picked up the shovel lying on the mound of earth in case Howard had any other ideas; for it had become clear to Parker that Howard had the type of pathetically short fuse and incendiary temper that characterized so many of the serial alcoholics he had encountered in the Army. Meanwhile, the one named Bill took out his phone and placed a call. He quickly and emotionlessly explained the situation, and after a minute or two he terminated the conversation.

"Okay, Howard, let's go," he said, then turning to Parker his tone modulated into overly unctuous politeness. "The owners said they'll get their lawyer to call the sheriff. They said we can come back after Mr..."

"Parker."

"After Mr. Parker has had some time to grieve for Yellow Dog Red and think about what he wants to do with him."

"Her."

"With her. Sorry. Look, Mr. Parker," Bill said, sincerely now it seemed, "I'm sorry for your loss. I love dogs. I even had a Chihuahua. And I'm sure everything will work out. But you have to know that there's too much money, big money, riding on this for a little bump in the road to prevent it from going forward." He gestured toward Yellow Dog Red.

Having had enough, Parker snapped, "Yellow Dog Red is not a little bump in the road. She was my best friend. And it is time for you to go."

"Look, just go and get a shower and a shave, and things will look a lot better for you tomorrow," inserted Howard, attempting to be conciliatory in his condescension.

"Young man," Parker said, enunciating his words slowly while lowering his head so that, to Howard, he looked, with his stubble and homeless mien, like a lunatic about to ram his head into his chest. "I am not homeless. And you are a rude jackass for assuming so. I also suggest that you work on your critical assessment skills if you want to go any higher than being a dickhead twizel-stick-bearer. Now, leave me with my dog." And to Bill, he added hesitantly, more as an afterthought he could no longer suppress, "I'm sorry your wife left you, Bill. Believe me, I know that loneliness in a man your age is a bottomless pit. But you must know that neither resentment nor work will fill it."

Bill's eyes bulged and his jaw dropped, causing his jowls to jiggle. "How the fuck do you know about my wife?"

Parker shrugged. "It used to be my business to know these things," he said, prepared to say no more than that. But when he saw tears welling in Bill's eyes, he felt compelled to explain further. "When a man feels he must take off his cap to say who he is, it tells me: there is a man who has given up trying to explain himself after losing too many fights with those closest to him. And," he appended, "the white band on your ring finger tells me you only recently took off your wedding ring, so I assumed that that person was your wife. Or ex-wife. And that she is also the one with whom the Chihuahua is now living."

"Shiiiit!" Howard exclaimed.

Bill shook his head and as he wiped away his tears a steely glint replaced them. "You should mind your own business, Parker." Whereupon he hastily boxed up his laser level and, striding off in the direction he and Howard had come, called out over his shoulder, "We'll be back. Bank on it. And if you're smart, Parker, you won't be here. And neither should your Yellow Dog Red."

"What about the pole?" Howard yelled, undecided whether he should follow Bill's lead or remain.

"Leave the fucking twizel-stick. We'll get it next time."

Howard shrugged and turned to Parker. "I tell you, Parker, a shower and a shave will do you a world—"

"Go! before I tell you about your daughter," warned Parker, from which followed a look that combined cocky bemusement tinged with fear to settle on Howard's ruddy face.

"What kind of business did you say you were in? Voodoo?" he persisted, in a manner that Parker adjudged was the type of self-punishing over-confident patter common in a man well-versed in the narrative of repeated failure.

Parker let a small smile escape, which Howard stupidly mistook to be one of accord. "I didn't say. But most assuredly it wasn't voodoo. Try science. Psychology to be specific. For your information, Howard," intoned Parker, in a fashion that totally belied his unkempt appearance, "I was a Captain in Army Intelligence. Retired twenty-two years ago. It was my job to ferret out weaknesses in our enemies and to spot crooks in our ranks. And as for your daughter, I would guess she's given up on you yet again, and that you are headed for detox in a few—"

"Okay! Okay! I don't want to know. I'm going," Howard yelped, as real fear spread across his continence.

Parker came down with a cold the next day. Nonetheless he was well enough to make it out to check up on Yellow Dog Red. Thankfully, there was no sign of any vandalism or such, and when it began to rain late in the afternoon, he went over to Dotty's for tea. She put some brandy, lemon rind and honey in it, and as he sipped it and ate four of the lemon tarts he prized so, he told her of his encounter with the surveyors and asked if she knew the new owners of The Pound House (which is how the locals have referred to it among themselves for over forty years), which she confessed she didn't, although she had heard at her quilting bee that they were of some nationality that began with an I, either Iranian or Italian. She also said she doubted he needed to worry too much; since the new owners would, like all the rest, probably not last any longer than had any of the others; all of whom had come in, remodeled, then either flipped the house immediately or lost interest in it after a few years and then sold it. The Pound House was just one of those places, Dotty and Parker agreed, that every neighborhood has, which is bought and sold again and again within a span of a few years while those of their neighbors' are held in the family for decades if not forever.

Having been exposed to the same sort of poison gas they dusted the jungle with in Vietnam, which had shortened Dotty's husband Max's life by decades, Parker, like Max, was prone to have his colds go into bronchitis or, worse, pneumonia. But as usual Dotty couldn't convince Parker to stay with her past tea, even if only to rest for awhile on the couch; not as long as his wife Sylvia, who sadly no longer recognized Parker or anyone else, was still alive. So, Dotty sent Parker home to his house up the hill from the market in town with more of the tarts, which she still made twice a week for Max's and her old delicatessen—Dotty's Deli.

It rained for the next few days and Dotty didn't see or hear from Parker. The next time she did see him he was much improved, with no sign, other than a few sniffles, of the pulmonary problems she had so feared. The rain had let up, and he was pulling behind his new pickup the ancient teardrop trailer that he and Sylvia had used for camping in Yosemite every summer until, at fourteen, their son Tad was overcome by hypothermia in Lake Tenaya and had drowned, and which hadn't been used since. Dotty's thought was that Parker had brought the trailer over in order to move it onto her property so that he couldn't be accused of sleeping in the same house with Dotty. Cheered at the prospect, she decorously said nothing of it, of course, because she didn't want to seem too eager. She then fixed Parker lunch while he played with her spaniel, Princess, growling and feigning on the floor with her in the manner he always did, which is to say like he was himself a dog. But as soon as he and Dotty sat down, as if to dispel her eagerness he told her right off the bat that the trailer was going into the cemetery so that he could keep close watch over Yellow Dog Red.

"You can't live in that! You'll catch your death up there in it, Parker," Dotty said in exasperation, truly alarmed at the prospect, which made it easy for her to hide her disappointment. "Leave it here, with me. It's only a short walk from here to the cemetery." Dotty looked imploringly into Parker's eyes, and in his gaze saw the love and friendship he held for her. She also saw a determination she knew would be impossible to shunt aside.

He said, "I'm over eighty, Dotty. Death is going to catch me soon enough anyway. And now that Sylvia is gone from me. And Yellow Dog Red is gone, I—"

"It's no wonder I always thought you and Max were blood brothers," she blurted, not wanting Parker to finish his thought, and also to remind Parker, ten years Max's senior, that he had promised on his friend's death

18

bed to look after Dotty when he was gone. "You are both as stubborn as Edgartown clammers at low tide. And if you do this thing, you're just asking for that tide to come in and get you."

"That may be," nodded Parker, and to Dotty's relief he did not see—or chose to ignore—the guilt on her face at her mention of being overtaken by the tide. "But Max was as loyal as I am stubborn," he said, "and so I think he would approve. He loved Yellow Dog Red as much as I did."

"And so did I. She was one game dame," Dotty admitted, knowing that Parker's old Lab was one of those once-in-a-lifetime companions—an avatar almost—one who had been able to provide Parker with the strength and endurance he needed to go on as Alzheimers inexorably excavated Sylvia of memory, leaving her and him with only the thin verdigris of the present to measure their decades together. And there was one other thing that tied her and Max and Parker together; Max was the one who had found Yellow Dog Red for Parker after his other Lab, Kitty, had passed away.

The Yellow Dog Red Overlook began simply enough that same day when Parker pulled the trailer up the dirt access road, which skirted the vineyard and ran parallel to the poison-oak-bone-radiator-clogged seasonal waterway, into the cemetery, where he parked it beside and just to the north of Yellow Dog Red, in-between the neighboring grave in which a German Shepard named Queenie lay at rest. He had brought some cement pavers in the back of his truck, which he stacked atop each other on either side and under the screw for leveling. Having had a fifth-wheel with Max, Dotty helped Parker by letting him know when the bubble in the level had split the black line. When he was satisfied the trailer was as good as it was going to be, he then wrapped a chain, which he had been keeping on his property for forty years just in case he should ever need it, around the trailer's axle and a huge valley oak that grew out of the poison oak. Being that it was a chain off a tugboat, whose individual links were each six-inches long and an inch thick of case-hardened steel, Parker felt sure that no one could come in with a bolt-cutter and cut it; that it would take a blowtorch, a bomb and a team of lumberjacks to get the job done.

A blustery storm—the second rainfall of the season—blew in that same night, downing numerous trees in the valley, including two diseased locust trees and an emaciated willow lining the driveway of The Pound House, which was itself located smack-dab in the middle of the property, mid-way between the road and the crest of the hilltop property lines. The next day a tree-cutting crew showed up at mid-morning and, since the ground was not yet close to being saturated, went about cutting and splitting and mulching the three trees before the crew broke for lunch.

Parker thought that that would be the end of it; that the men would move on to dispense with other fallen trees in the valley. However, after lunch the crew began working their way uphill from the kennel behind the house, felling, cutting, and then mulching every tree and shrub in their path, leaving only stumps large enough for a dozer to push over and uproot. By day's end they had cleared an acre of land, and it was apparent to Parker that they had no intention of stopping until all of the land outside the cemetery, from the crest of the hill to the old vineyard, was cleared of trees in preparation for the grapevines that were theoretically planned to replace them.

By week's end the tree removal team had worked their way to the uphill leg of the split-log fence boundary of the cemetery on the side opposite from Yellow Dog Red's grave. To that point, Parker had interacted with the cutting crew only minimally from a distance, choosing to spend his days to himself, grooming the grave sites nearest Yellow Dog Red's, reading, listening to the radio, writing in his journal, and resting his eyes by gazing out over the valley, whose trees and vineyards were in their full-on agog-with-autumn-color mode.

Parker had put down an indoor-outdoor carpet outside the trailer, upon which he had placed a camping table and four directors chairs, as well as a portable propane heater, an Army cot, and a futon sofa. Dotty had been his only visitor that first week, sharing tea and sandwiches (and of course a supply of Dotty's World Famous Lemon Tarts) with him on those afternoons when it wasn't too cold for her to be outside; for the trailer itself could realistically hold only one person, unless, that is, they wanted to lie or sit in bed together (She did. He wouldn't.). But Dotty's visits were perforce short ones—since Parker had only a portable, solar-powered water closet that she refused to use, despite that it was quite clean and modern, and he had gone to the trouble to set it up out of sight between two boulders and a makeshift screen constructed of woven bay laurel branches next to the grave of Queenie's lifelong companion, a German Shepard named Quagmire.

Parker and Dotty were sharing a glass of beer on the evening of the day the tree removal team had come to the edge of the cemetery. The crew had left for the day, but the supervisor came up to the trailer from the direction of the Pound House, calling out his approach across the graveyard with a series of loud hellos. Like most in his profession, Parker noticed he was muscular and had an air of fearlessness to him that bespoke years of dodging falling trees, broken chainsaw blades, and bankruptcy. In his mid-forties, he was a man who spoke plainly and who saw the world in the same dimensions as he did a cord of wood. After identifying himself by name as Roper, he genially informed Parker his crew would be cutting through the graveyard the next day, clearing away all trees and brush, and that Parker would need to move his trailer first thing that next morning.

Before replying to this, Parker gestured for the man to have a seat. "Why don't you have a beer with us so we can talk this over," he said.

Roper frowned, but after a moment of indecision and obviously exhausted from a day of bucking fifty-to-one-hundred-year-old trees, he fell into the canvas chair opposite Parker's, with a view toward Yellow Dog Red. "Just one."

"Coors okay?" Parker replied, flipping up the lid of the cooler he had brought with him, which was filled with beer and bottled water in the crushed ice Dotty had had delivered from the market.

"Perfect. Nothing like a cold beer on a day like this," he said, glancing appreciatively out over the valley, "when the first rains have washed away the dust. To me," he continued, with an ironic nod toward his own dusty clothing, "the land shimmers with a radiance that seems to come from within the land itself. Like there is a movie projector underground."

Parker nodded in appreciation of the sentiment as he pulled out a bottle and twisted off its cap. He then handed the beer to Roper. "To your health!" he toasted.

"And to the ethereal," Roper added, as the three clinked their bottles together.

After taking a big swig, Roper extended his bottle toward Yellow Dog Red's headstone. "Is that the dog all this fuss is about?"

Parker shrugged. "I don't see there's any fuss. But, yes, that's where my dog is buried."

"I heard she was a Lab. Had one of 'em myself," he said. "A chocolate. Named him Chewbaca. Turned out to be a good name for him too. Because he ate his way through a couch and a car seat. But he was a good dog after he grew up."

"Three years?"

"Nope. Five. Chewed everything in sight till then. Then just stopped and got fat and barked a lot at gophers and deer."

Parker smiled. "Males can be chewers. Bones help."

Roper shook his head. "Didn't with Chewbaca. But the biggest problem wasn't the chewing. It was that that dog just wouldn't stay home. If I wasn't watching him, he'd go off roaming through the sloughs. Get himself all covered with mud, come home and roll on the rugs to dry himself. Drove my girlfriend crazy. We'd get a phone call: 'Roper,' they'd say, 'I got Chewbaca over here. Covered with mud. Want me to throw him in the back of my truck and bring him back?'

"I really loved that dog," Roper continued, pensively peeling off strands of the label with a fingernail. "Early on, when I was cutting on burned-over land outside Groveland, I was out on a job and Chew started roaming round and round like Labs do. Going back and forth with his nose to the ground. Then he started barking. The first couple of times I yelled at him to quiet down, saying I wouldn't be able to take him with me anymore if he was going to make such a nuisance of himself. That did quiet him down—more the tone than the words—but the third time it happened he was only about ten feet from where I was bucking a gnarly two-hundred-year-old live oak by myself, and he wouldn't let up. I had

23

finally had enough. I shut off my saw and went over and kicked him in the side. Hard. Steel-toed boot too. You never want to kick a dog on the nose," Roper added, having by then peeled off the entire label. "But I wanted to teach him a lesson. He looked at me like I'd shot him. Then the crazy dog started barking again. Not at me but at the tree I was cutting. I thought that maybe he had distemper, or had eaten a mushroom, or even that he was trying to out-bark my saw or something like that to gain attention.

"That's when I heard the rattling. If you're like me," he continued, glancing at Parker, "once you've heard a rattler close by, you know your body is going to react without you even having to think. And I must've jumped ten feet back and two feet in the air. If it hadn't had been for Chewbaca," he said, rubbing his chin with the back of his hand, "I know for sure I wouldn't've heard that rattler, because he was coiled inside a void I wouldn't've paid any attention to until I was on it. And that would've been too late. I would've been bitten. And being that we were alone, probably ten miles from the nearest town, I might've died, or lost a leg at a minimum."

Roper sighed and his gaze grew distant. "It was a rattler that finally got Chewbaca. He was nosing around in a gopher hole on the back of my property. I didn't find his body until the buzzards had picked it clean.

"I'm sorry," responded Parker, furrowing his brow.

"Sometimes a dog just isn't happy unless it's free to roam," said Roper, with a tone of irony shadowed with sadness in his voice. He had come to the end of his beer, which he stood on the table. "So then," he said, bracing his hands to the sides of his knees, "do we have an understanding? You'll move the trailer tomorrow? I can give you till noon. To get this cleaned up, I mean."

"Parker's brows shot up. But contrary to his expression his voice betrayed none of his surprise. "My understanding is that this is sacred ground that is not to be disturbed. As you see, I am simply observing that that is indeed the case."

"You mean you're staying here? In that?" He gestured toward the trailer.

"That is correct. Until there is no longer any danger." He spread his arms to indicate that he was referring not only to his trailer but to the whole of the cemetery.

"What about sanitation? You can't just...you know..."

"I know," Parker said, while with his gaze he directed Roper's attention toward the two rocks separating Queenie and Quagmire. In the lichens on the rock nearest to them the letters "W.C." were etched. "I've taken care of it."

"Food? How do you eat?"

"I'm taking care of that," Dotty said.

Roper nodded, then he leaned back in the folding chair and clasped his hands behind his head. He remained in this pose for almost a minute, then in a subdued tone, said, "I've heard that the owners, some of them at least, are not nice people. So, it might be best for you if you just do as they ask, and hope for the best."

"And would that also be what's best for Yellow Dog Red?"

"A backhoe could have her out of here and into a new spot in an hour."

Parker eyed Roper with a look that bespoke not only skepticism but suspicion. "You never had a dog named Chewbaca, did you?" he said, but again without even the slightest hint of accusation.

Roper unclasped his hands and dropped his arms to his side as if they had been suddenly untied. "What do you mean? Of course I had a dog."

"Whose name was Chewbaca?"

Roper hesitated a moment, then, sourly, replied, "Yes, whose name was Chewbaca."

"No, respectfully, I doubt that very much, sir," Parker said, with a wave of his hand but without any hint of rancor in the tone of his voice. "I also doubt very much your story of how Chewbaca saved your life."

"Why? Why do you doubt me?" sputtered Roper. "I swear it's true."

"I'll leave you to swear to truth at another time, preferably to your confessor," Parker replied. "But for now I doubt your truthfulness for two reasons. The first is that you have demonstrated that in peeling off the Coors label you are a man of superficial impulses. One who thinks only in ways that are skin-deep. The second reason—and really the most telling—is that a man who truly loves his dog, a dog who saved his life, a dog who was faithful after being kicked by him with a steel-toed boot, would never be able to wait to find him until his bones were clean. Furthermore, in combining these two observations, it is my assumption that you have come here to put an earthy face on a lie in order to fatten your own wallet."

Roper stared at Parker in confoundment, but could find no words to respond before Parker went on.

"Here is what I would suggest. I suggest that you continue with your tree removal project, but that you leave the cemetery intact. As you can see for yourself, there are more than enough trees left to fell outside the cemetery to keep you busy for months, especially if the weather holds out like this. The other thing I'd suggest is that you go back to whoever is paying you for your work here, and tell them that I told you they or you will have to cut me in half with one of your chainsaws before I will leave Yellow Dog Red's side if her final resting place is in danger."

Roper placed his hands on the arms of the chair and pushed himself to his feet. His own arms, despite their muscularity, shook, but not from the effort to raise himself to standing but from the anger seething in him that he was barely able to contain.

"Look here, asshole," he hissed.

"I beg your pardon. Watch your language, young man," interjected Dotty, with unaffected injury glossing her voice.

"Sorry, Ma'am," Roper said, blushing, and his voice, like his arms, were shaking. "Look, Parker, you were right about Chewbaca. Truth is, I've never even had a dog. I was only saying it because I wanted to do you a favor. Like I said, these are not nice people. I meant it when I said they won't let two old coots get in their way. They could hurt you."

"Was it money they offered you to warn us off?" Parker said.

Roper shrugged. "No, not in so many words. They just said I would find it profitable if I could convince you to leave without them having to call in the sheriff and evict you. They're sensitive to how they'll be seen."

Parker rubbed his eyes, which were more bloodshot in the aftermath of his cold than was usually the case. "Well, look, Roper, I can see you're not a bad sort. Yes, you bent the truth a little, which is in bad form. But I can forgive you for that, because I can tell it doesn't come naturally to you, a sharp man with a good head on your shoulders. So, why don't we just say your blade hit a spike and got a little dull, and let it go at that. Deal?"

Parker extended his hand for Roper to shake. Roper's jaw muscles bulged against his urge to lash out for having been caught in a lie and then humiliated by the forgiveness extended by this old man. But being a man whose outlook on life was bundled into cords of perspective that almost always matched clean boundaries of right and wrong, Roper realized the wisdom of Parker's suggestion.

"Deal," he said, taking Parker's hand. "No cutting, for now, in the cemetery."

"Good! Now, go and tell whoever it is you're dealing with what I suggested about cutting around the cemetery, and what you have just agreed to. And tell them that I don't intend to be a bump in the road for anybody. Tell them my intention is to change the route of their whole road. In other words, tell them they will have to cut me down first before I let them disturb my friend Yellow Dog Red."

Roper's tree cutting crew did not show up for the next few days, and during the lull in the deforestation project Parker asked Dotty to go in to the county seat and visit the recorder's office in order to search out the deed, and to see if it was indeed true what he and she had always heard, but only secondhand, that there was a stipulation in the vet's original that the cemetery was to remain a pet cemetery in perpetuity. Parker also asked a lawyer friend of his to check out the deed and, also, to connect with the animal support group's national office to see if they supported such property covenants.

The deed was soon located and copies were made and given to Parker and to Dotty. It was an odd document, in that, although the intent by Dr. Pound had clearly been to treat the cemetery as a separate parcel in order to protect the animals buried therein, there was also enough ambiguity in its wording—because whoever wrote it was clearly not well-versed in the subject—for any good property law lawyer to drive a locomotive through. Which is what the Humane Society also told Parker: that the legal grounds for keeping the pet cemetery intact were wide open to debate.

Moreover, in such cases where the language was ambiguous, it meant that the ones who usually won such legal debates were those whose money spoke the loudest. The SPCA and the lawyer's advice to him, therefore, was to get a lawyer who specialized in real estate law to represent the animals buried in the cemetery; animals who were now animals in the memory of their owners only—most of whom existed only in memory themselves—and because of this there would probably be no one of legal standing to press the issue in court.

Having been a man whose profession had required him to spend far too many hours holed up with military prosecutors looking for loopholes through which to convict hapless dupes and imbecilic crooks, Parker took their advice with a grain—no, a ton—of salt, saying something to the effect that "venom-spewing perjurers had ruined the law," the gist of which meant that he would rather take a bath with rattlesnakes than to have to resort to depending on a lawyer to represent his beloved Yellow Dog Red. Dotty wasn't the least bit surprised by Parker's antipathy; for she herself had a jaundiced view of the legal profession after getting an unfair shake after Max died, when her lawyer not only did poorly, to the point of malpractice, in representing her in a suit Max had brought against a conglomerate that was infringing on Dolly's Deli trademarked lemon tarts, but who then managed to get himself hired on by that same tart-stealing firm. Dolly felt that she had probably lost several million dollars on account of that lawyer. Therefore, the word stubborn did not begin to do service to either hers or to Parker's aversion when it came to the possibility of litigation. In the end, though, this persistence—or obstinacy, as some would call it—would prove to be of pivotal importance in the battle to save the Gainsaid Pound Cemetery; for it was a battle which from the beginning was enjoined based on the law of love rather than on the love of the law.

Roper returned early in the morning a few days later, and before his crew commenced cutting down trees, he made a beeline straight across the graveyard to see Parker, who he found basking in the morning sun with a cup of steaming tea in his hand. It was a cool morning, with the thermometer hovering a few degrees above freezing. The hoarfrost had yet to evaporate, and, as Roper approached, his footfalls left dark prints across the icy carpet. Upon seeing Parker, he raised an arm in greeting, then quickly placed it across his chest.

"Hail, Parker!" he called out brightly, using a form of greeting Parker found oddly anachronistic as well as welcoming. Roper was wearing a beige lambskin coat with a white fur collar, both of which were drawn tightly about him against the cold, and which struck Parker as peculiar vestments for a tree cutter. His expression was one that Parker mistook at first for a grimace; for Roper possessed one of those austere Nordic mouths that stretched when he smiled from side to side rather than bowed up, although, as he drew nearer, Parker saw that Roper was in fact smiling broadly. There was also a spring in his step where before there had been only fatigue, which Parker attributed right off to Roper's having had a few days off.

"Good morning," Parker said, cocking his head warily at the goofy grin Roper wore. "What's up?"

With that, Roper carefully pulled open his lambs-wool lapel to reveal another mass, or rather a small roll, of beige-colored fur on which were affixed three black markings. Only after a second had passed did Parker realize that the round bundle Roper cradled in his arms was a puppy.

"What on earth?" were all the words he could summon.

"It's a Lab. A Yellow Lab!" Roper exclaimed, and he carefully pulled the small dog out from beneath its woolen cocoon for Parker to see.

"Oh my! I can see that!" Parker exclaimed in turn. Then his expression clouded. "I hope you didn't bring that dog to me as a peace offering," he said, "not the least because I'm too old for another dog, especially a puppy. But because it's so cruel a trick to tempt me, that I couldn't ever even begin to forgive you for doing this to me before I've had time to grieve for Yellow Dog Red."

"Hold on, Parker," Roper responded, still smiling despite Parker's rebuke. "I swear, it's not a bribe. This is not for you. This is my dog."

Parker furrowed his brows. "I don't understand."

"She came to me yesterday. Out of the blue. Becky, a longtime friend of my girlfriend found out three days ago she got a job as head winemaker in Otago, in New Zealand," he added, "and she had just gotten the puppy less than a week before. Hadn't even named her yet. And couldn't take it with her. So Becky asked me if I would take her."

"And now she's yours?"

"Can you believe it? Three days ago I was making up stories about my dog Chewbaca and..." He shook his head. "And I have you to thank for this," he added, with a note of gravity. "I don't know how you did it, but I think it's because of you that she came to me."

"I doubt that very much," answered Parker. "I may be able to pull a few strings occasionally to get something done. But I'm hardly in the business of interfering with how people live their lives."

Roper shrugged. "Well, whatever you think, it happened, and I've gone and named her after you."

Baffled, Parker said, "You named your dog Parker? What kind of name for a dog is that?"

"Here," Roper said, extending the puppy toward Parker, "would you like to hold Parker?"

A short pause ensued, then Parker placed his teacup on the table and reached out hesitantly for Roper's puppy, which he quickly drew against his down jacket for warmth. Then, directing his words to the headstone, he said, "What do you think, Red? Should I trust this man and his new little puppy? A man who lied about those who would be his best friend? No? Yes? Ah!" he said, tilting his head theatrically in acknowledgment. Then, to the puppy, "Well, hello, Parker, my friend Yellow Dog Red has just told me I would be an old fool not to trust you." He then lowered his voice so that it was barely above a whisper. "She also told me," he added, as Parker-the-dog bit down harmlessly on his thumb, "I would be an even older coot to trust a puppy that didn't bite me." Then, to Roper, "How old is she?"

"Twelve weeks."

"Purebred?"

"Got her AKC papers."

"Joints okay?"

"Guaranteed. And eyes too."

Parker nodded. "Looks like a good dog. Sharp teeth. And I guess I like the name too," he added, as Parker-the-dog wriggled to free herself of his arms. "I think she has to pee."

"Here, I'll take her out of the cemetery," Roper inserted. "Don't want her to desecrate it."

"Nonsense," responded Parker, lowering the puppy to the ground. "A dog peeing on her ancestors is like you and me putting flowers on our own's graves."

Roper nodded and, tipping his head in amusement, watched as Parker-the-dog scampered over to attack the dew on a tuft of soapweed, then to pounce on Parker's shoelaces, then to run lickety-split back over to Yellow Dog Red's headstone, where she batted at the letters etched therein, and then finally squatted to pee.

"Parker!" yelped Roper as he bent to fetch her. "Bad girl!"

"No, let her be," inserted Parker, resting his hand on Roper's arm to keep him from interfering with the puppy's business. Then, as she was about to finish it, he added, "Now, tell her what a good girl she is."

"Really?"

"Really. Better that she learns to run off to pee than to pee on your foot, or in your shoe when you're not there."

Roper nodded in recognition. "Good girl, Parker," he said, although the tone of his praise was more suited for one of his workers than for a twelve-week-old puppy. He then looked down at his watch. "I should be going," he said. "I just wanted to come over and apologize for last week. I can't believe what a jerk I was. I don't know why I let people talk me into doing stupid stuff like that. Some character flaw, I guess. My girlfriend says it's from a need to want to please people."

"That's why you need a dog. To help keep you honest," Parker said, as a grin spread across his face at the alacrity with which his namesake had begun chasing her tail. "And to bark at those who would want to do harm to you."

"Suppose so," Roper said absently, also smiling at his dog's antics. "The problem is," he added, "those who would want to do harm to me are sometimes the same ones who are paying me."

Parker shifted his gaze from the dog to Roper whose mouth had stretched into a rueful smile, and, in it, he saw that Roper was not really a shallow or a weak man, but one who, because he had not allowed himself to reflect too deeply, was put at the mercy of those who saw they could box him in and get away with it without much, if any, of a fight.

"That's exactly the reason why a dog will keep coming back to someone who kicks them, as long as it's the same one who's feeding them."

"You know, the truth is I would never kick a dog," Roper confessed. "I was just being dramatic the other day because I thought it would be an effective way to show you I knew what I was talking about, about dogs, I mean."

Parker shook his head slowly from side to side as he picked up his teacup and drew a sip of the hot liquid into his mouth. After a moment he said, "I disagree with what you said about never kicking a dog. But I'm not really sure we're talking about dogs now, are we?" Parker added. "Because in my experience, a man who lies about brutality toward an innocent being to make another man's point is a man who has experienced both in his own life. What goes around comes around is how the saying goes. My guess, if you want to hear it," he went on, as Roper shrugged in uncertain assent, "is that perhaps you yourself have been subjected to too many kickings and lyings of a kind. And that someday when Parker does something you don't like, like peeing in your shoe, you might be tempted to do what others did to you."

Roper had averted his eyes to his dog again, who was pawing earnestly at the soft earth beneath the headstone, but just as he was about to yell at her to stop, he caught himself. Instead, he retrained his eyes on Parker.

"I think you may be right, Parker," he sighed. "My old man was harder on me than he needed to be. Way harder. Because his own pa had been so hard on him. Couldn't help himself, he said. But what can I do? It's just the way me and my brothers were brought up."

"Do you still love your dad?"

"Of course. Hate him too." He frowned.

Parker shook his head. "Like I said, it's not my business to tell people what to do. I was in intelligence not psychoanalysis. I only observed how people behaved and, if what they were doing was against the law, call them out on it and let the lawyers play God with their lives. But let me tell you, there is one thing I've learned from my forty years of working inside peoples' heads: no man or woman, even the most evil one among us, deserves to be treated cruelly; because when we are cruel to others we are being cruel to ourselves, even if we think we're doing it in the name of love. No," Parker said pensively, while watching as his namesake rolled herself into a neat little ball in the depression she had dug, and fell immediately asleep, "the only way to stop cruelty is to stop being cruel. Just do it. It's as simple as that."

Roper's eyes flashed momentarily in anger. "Just do it! What the hell makes you think you can...you can..." he sputtered, before his words tailed away quickly into a contrite silence which Parker ended a moment later.

"What makes me think I can tell you how to act towards others?" he asked, to which Roper nodded feebly. "First," Parker went on, "I don't. Do you really think I—look at me, I'm old and I'm sitting in a cold graveyard with my dead dog—can presume to think that I can tell you or anyone else how to be? And, second, on the other hand, what makes you think it is wrong of someone like me to put myself in another person's place in order to understand him and, if I can, communicate what I know of it to him? Roper," he said, taking another sip of tea, "I'm not telling you anything about yourself you don't already know."

Roper cringed, and Parker motioned for him to take a seat. Parker then offered to pour him some tea from the teapot that was warming on a Sterno burner off to one side, which Roper declined, and after Parker had refilled his own cup, Roper said, "I didn't mean to say I think it's wrong for you to sit by your dog's side. On the contrary, I think it's touching. I'd like to feel the same way about Parker when her day comes. It's just that to stop doing something when it's all you know isn't as easy as making a slogan about it. Christ! If it was that easy, we'd all be saints, and dogs would always pee outside."

Parker drew his lips tight. "You're right," he said. "I overstepped myself. I was wrong to give you the impression that I diminish the difficulty in making changes in one's way of doing things. God knows—and Dotty will tell you—I have ruts and routines of my own that cripple how I interact with the world. But please do not believe for a moment," he went on, "that I was belittling you. I was merely stating my belief—sharing my own experience with you—that changes in myself have come about in the same way that I see them coming about in nature; by actions, not by thinking. And just by looking at you, I know you are a man of action. A man who prides himself on doing rather than being. Is that not right?"

Roper nodded doubtfully as if his feelings had been hurt. "I guess so," he said, and added, "But I'm not stupid."

Parker winced at Roper's response. "No, of course not," he said, "I'm sorry. That's not what I meant at all. And I apologize if you think I was inferring it. In fact, in the short time I've known you," he went on, "I have come to genuinely appreciate that you are highly intelligent. I have also come to see that your intelligence is projected onto things rather than ideas. In another life, I can see you as someone who designs and makes things, like a...like an architect perhaps."

"What?" Roper's face lit up. "I'm six credits away from my online Bachelor of Architecture Degree. How did you know that?"

Parker shrugged. "A good guess."

"In fact," Roper continued, "my goal is to design buildings that minimize the use of wood. You see," he said, gesturing toward the trees outside the cemetery, "I really do hate killing trees. But I'm good at it. Very good, I think. Third generation. And I'm kind toward them. But I also think I must be doing some sort of penitence for something me or my family has done in past lives."

"We all do things for reasons," Parker replied. "And we all pay a price for doing those things. The trick is to turn a profit," he added, "by keeping the price low and the reasons high-minded."

Before Roper could respond, a man's voice from the direction of the old kennel intruded in on their conversation. "I'll be right there!" answered Roper. Then, to Parker, he said, "Look, Parker. We'll cut around the graveyard like you suggested, and if the owners want the trees in here logged, we'll just say we're busy on other jobs. That's the best I can do."

"That's all I can ask of you," Parker said, then after a moment, added, "Why don't you leave Parker with me while you work? It'd be better than leaving her in a crate or in your truck." When Roper looked skeptically at the puppy, still sound asleep, Parker appended, "The fact is, Roper, we could both use a little disciplining."

"Oh, you don't have to train her."

Parker shook his head. "I wasn't talking about the dog Parker. I was talking about the man Parker—me—and Yellow Dog Red. We both need some help on how to go on now that we aren't together."

Roper smiled and looked down at his watch again. "Okay, if it's not too much trouble. She's eaten, but I'll bring over some kibble before we get started. I'll check in on our breaks, and if she's a problem anytime, just come over and get me, and I'll bring her back with me to the truck," he said, just as little Parker began to whimper and run in her sleep.

Parker poured himself the last of the tea. "Go about your work, Roper. Parker will be fine here with me. As a matter of fact," he yawned,

"I didn't sleep well last night. So, I think I'll catch up with Yellow Dog Red and Parker while they're running through the forest of their dreams, because that's where the air is always freshest, the trees are always greenest, and their barks are always loudest." Whereupon Parker stood and shuffled over beside Yellow Dog Red's headstone. He then lowered himself to the ground and leaned against the marble stone so that his arm was curled around Parker-the-dog.

"Away we go, girls," he said, as he returned Roper's wave and shut his eyes.

Early the next morning Parker was awakened out of a sound sleep when he heard heavy grunting and the sound of someone running down the hill past his trailer. By the time he was able to pull on his slippers, throw his robe on over his pajamas, and gather up his flashlight, there was no one to be seen in the direction that the animal or person had departed. However, when Parker directed the beam of his light in the opposite direction, toward Yellow Dog Red's headstone, he saw that it was gone. A moment later, still groggy and unsteady on his feet, he stumbled over and found that, rather than missing, the stone had been tipped over. Moreover, there were boot prints in the soft dirt of the grave. The intent of whoever had pushed it over was not lost on Parker: to intimidate him into leaving.

But that person, and perhaps even the ones who had put him up to it, if they were different, had miscalculated badly; for, if anything, the event sealed Parker's resolve as none other could have to keep him to his vigil. It also worked to galvanize the support of others who knew Parker, and of those who would in time come to know him, to help him maintain his overlook. He would meet the first of this latter coterie, a girl named Angwin, late that day just after he had reset Yellow Dog Red's stone in the ground, buttressed by a ring of bocce-ball-size stones.

Angwin approached Parker from the dirt access road through the vineyard that paralleled the seasonal creek, carrying a skateboard under her arm. This quirky conveyance alone, as well as her studied saunter, served to identify her to him as one of the group of five or six adolescents who regularly skateboarded up and down the road, often to Parker's trepidation over their acrobatic antics, which he was sure would land at least a few of them on crutches or—since none wore helmets—with neurological deficits. The young girl drew opposite the split-log fence at the southern edge of the cemetery, then flicked off the earbuds in her ears. She didn't say anything right off, even though Parker was only twenty feet away and gazing directly at her. Instead, she simply peered in every other direction but his, in what seemed a systematic surveillance of the perimeter of the area. Finally she let her gaze fall squarely on Parker.

"A friend of Dotty tweeted me about the headstone," she said, gesturing with her eyes, which were brown and almond-shaped and set in an oval face that Parker placed as of Middle Eastern lineage. "Bummer. My name's Angwin. You can call me Angie."

Having nephews and nieces of his own, Parker decided against asking for clarification about what bird-call it was that Dotty's friend had communicated. Instead, he replied, "Hi, Angie. I'm Parker."

"I already know that," she said, and lifted her iPhone as if it were self-evident that Parker should know his name was in it. "Can I come in?"

Parker shrugged. "Sure. I don't own this. This is a cemetery. It's public property."

"Thanks," she said, whereupon she vaulted over the fence like it was a pommel horse. She drew up beside Parker and without saying another word bent down to look closely at the headstone. "Yellow Dog Red is trending, you know," she murmured. "I like the epitaph. Can I take a picture of it to tweet?"

Parker could only shrug at the meaning of her words. "Why not."

Of less uncertainty to Parker than the peculiar lexicon of Angie's speech was the look she conveyed in her posture, which, to Parker, suggested a shallow earnestness, the type of which he had come to associate with con artists. In Angie, however, there was a countervailing optimism in her manner that, if she did not suppress it, might lead her to develop the kind of savvy suaveness that any actor would be proud to possess.

Angie snapped the picture with her phone, and after typing in a few hurried keystrokes, she put the oblong black object into the backpack she had just taken off her shoulders. She drew out half a dozen cubelike objects before zipping the sleeve closed, each the size and shape of a deck of cards, which she let fall onto Yellow Dog Red's grave.

"That's one thing I don't get," she said, without looking at Parker, and twisting around so that she could sit on her skateboard. "Why do adults always say Why not? when it would be easier just to say yes?"

Parker raised his eyebrows, more in appreciation at her curiosity than in surprise, and said, "I guess it's because saying yes gives outright permission. Saying why not leaves it open to supposition and conjecture. And many adults—like me, I confess—have learned that giving permission is the same as taking responsibility, while conjecturing isn't."

"So it's a form of evasion. That's what I thought," Angie responded, crossing her legs and arranging the cubes in a circle atop Yellow Dog Red's mound of earth.

"Then why did you ask?" riposted Parker, without annoyance.

"Because I don't want to be treated like a child."

"What would you like to be treated as?"

Angie paused. "That's a good question, Parker," she said, inspecting one of the objects, although, to Parker, it was clearly a perfunctory inspection meant only to buy time. "I guess I'd have to say I would like to be treated with respect."

"Done."

Angie nodded and a grudging smile escaped her lips. "I brought you these," she said, offering the cube in her hand to Parker. "They should deter anyone from coming in here and vandalizing things. Or from hurting you."

Parker was surprised by their heaviness. "What are they?"

"Go Cams." She handed one to Parker. "These are night cams." She pointed to four of the cubes.

"Ah! Far different than in my day," he said. "When I..." he let his breath slip into a sigh in the realization that Angie probably didn't want to hear how he had used cameras ten times the size of the one he was now holding for surveillance thirty years earlier.

"I think we should put them in this pattern," she said, gesturing to the circle of cameras. "Up high in the trees," she continued, motioning toward a number of the taller eucalyptus, bay, and oak trees ringing the inside of the cemetery. "So nobody can reach them without having to climb into a tree."

"Or cut them down with a chainsaw," offered Parker.

"Right. I have a friend who sleeps in trees. Says it grounds him," she said without irony. "He'll do it for me. And once they're up I can connect them to my LAN. That'll give me and my friends a record of anybody who comes in here anytime night or day."

"Very nice." Parker nodded, not wanting to short circuit her enthusiasm, and not even bothering to ask her what a LAN was.

"Do you have a laptop?" To which Parker shook his head. "A tablet?" To which Parker shook his head again. "No, I didn't think so. So, here, I brought this," she said, extracting a black, much larger object from out of her pack and extending it to Parker, "this is an old Toshiba laptop. I don't use it anymore."

Parker took the device, which appeared to be almost new, reluctantly. "Oh, I can't," he said. "It's too valuable."

"Valuable? Are you kidding, Parker? It's worth less than this backpack my Mom got me at Target," she said. "And, anyway, don't you think it's better to recycle it here than send it off to China where it'll sterilize a hundred Chinese girls younger than me?"

Abashed at Angie's reference, Parker raised an eyebrow, then nodding doubtfully toward the trailer, he added, "Thanks. I appreciate the offer, but I haven't any room."

"Time to press the reset key, Parker! That's a really lame excuse. Look at it. You could put it under your pillow and you wouldn't even know it was there." Seeing that Parker was still undecided, Angie tried a different tack. "Okay, how about if I loan it to you? Will that work?"

"I would feel better about that," acknowledged Parker, "since I don't even know you."

Angie tightened her lips in satisfaction. "Good! Then I'll set it up on me and my friends' LAN. It's name is 'the-dash-edge.' The password is 'Dubliners.' I live right down there," she added, pointing across the road at the base of the vineyard, toward the winery Parker knew had recently been bought by some Iranian advertising executive. "It's only a half mile. So, if I need to, I'll get another cheap Belken directional and..." Her voice trailed off as she finally came to see the look of bewilderment on Parker's face. "You don't have any idea what I'm saying, do you?" she said, tilting her head pointedly.

"I get some of it. I do," he said, trying unsuccessfully to suppress the defensiveness he had begun to experience at being essentially clueless about what this adolescent was saying.

"There's no fault in that," she said, and she reached out and let her hand fall to the sleeve of Parker's jacket. "You know, Parker, I've grown up with this one and that one since I was in a crib," she said, nodding first toward her iPhone and then to the Toshiba. "So it's probably like you trying to explain to me how only a half-century ago a few ugly men with swastikas could get a whole country to kill six million innocent people."

Parker drew his lips into his cheeks. "I couldn't even begin to explain it to you," he said, shaking his head.

"Exactly. That's what I'm saying too. Different times, different experiences. Both good, both bad. So, as Dotty likes to say, 'Don't let your panties get all tied in a knot.' It's just different. In fact," she added, "I can explain in one word why thugs killed six million people."

"Hatred?"

Angie shook her head. "Nope. Disrespect."

"You're a very smart girl, Angie," Parker said.

She shrugged modestly, but the sudden coloring of her cheeks told Parker she was flattered. "What do you do for electricity here?"

Parker pointed to the solar panel atop the water closet boulder."

"Cool. I have another one like it that I took to Everest," she said, "so I could vblog the trek to my friends along the trail. You can borrow it for the Toshiba. I'll have my friend come climb the trees to replace the cams' batteries if it's needed."

"Cool," Parker replied. "But may I ask you a question, Angie?"

"Why not?" she said, with a coy smile.

Parker chuckled at her response. "Why are you doing this for me?"

Angie's eyes darted back and forth a few times. "It's not for you entirely," she answered after a few moments. "It's for me too."

"How's that?"

"For respect."

"For respect from your parents?"

"Maybe. But they already respect me."

"From your friends?"

She shook her head, but with less certainty. "You know, Parker, I don't think it's a good idea for you to be interrogating me," she said. "Either you trust me, or you don't. Before I came here, I had already made up my mind to trust you. I mean, how stupid would it be of me if I couldn't let myself trust someone who's willing to keep watch over his best friend so that no harm will come to her? For me it doesn't get any more real than that."

"Mea culpa," replied Parker. "Forgive me. It's an old habit."

Angie nodded. "I know: old habits really are like old dogs," she said. "They bark a lot but their teeth aren't of much good anymore for chewing on bones."

Although he doubted that it was original, Parker found himself smiling at the homily nonetheless. Then he said, but without any hint of accusation, "You haven't said why you're doing this."

"That's because I'm clearly evading you," Angie said. "The truth of the matter is that I don't think I could respect myself for just sitting by and letting someone Dotty considers her best friend to be treated so disrespectfully. I mean, I have a whole life to live, and if I start making excuses now for not doing things I think I should, I'll be hosed when the time comes for me to make really big decisions."

"Very noble. But does that mean I'm a charity case?"

She scowled. "No, it means I am," she said, "in thinking that I can help take on dragons with nothing but a Go Cam and a computer illiterate."

"You sound like Don Quixote."

"Who?"

"A Spanish dreamer. He jousted with windmills he thought were dragons."

"Isn't that on X-Box?"

"What's an X-Box?"

The two stood mute for many seconds as each sounded beneath the surface to the profound diversity of their two universes. Finally, Parker said, "I do it out of respect too. I couldn't live with myself if I thought I had let Yellow Dog Red down."

Angie's phone made a chirping sound. Reading the device's display, she said, "It's Squirrel. He says he'll come by after school tomorrow to hook up the cameras. Till then, I'll just lay a few around on the ground and leave them on, just in case. Then I gotta go. Dad is Skyping Slag. He said I could sit in for it and maybe, if there was time, ask him a few questions for the vlog I'm doing in school on third world debt relief."

"Ah, debt relief! That is one thing I do know about," Parker said brightly, feeling he was finally on more secure footing. "Kleptocrats are

45

like termites; they bore into a country's wealth and eff them over till the country falls apart." Angie furrowed her brows, unsure if Parker was teasing her. Seeing her uncertainty, Parker added, "No, it's true. My work brought me close to their workings. Slag's done a good thing in bringing the problem out into the open. Say hello to him for me."

"You know Slag?" Angie's eyes widened so that for the first time she looked to Parker like the pre-adolescent she was.

Parker nodded. "I think I can safely say we respect each other."

"I gotta go," Angie said, throwing her backpack over her shoulders and hoisting her skateboard under her arm. And as she trotted across the vineyard down to the road, Parker could hear her saying "OMG! OMG! OMG!" over and over into her phone.

ngie returned the next day after school with the boy named Squirrel. It took only a short while for Parker to see why he was called this, for Squirrel had an uncanny ability, for someone without a tail, to make his way up into and through the crown of the forest as effortlessly as if he were walking on a sidewalk. He was very thin, as one would expect from someone who liked to climb and sleep in trees. But more than his thinness, it was his agility that was heart stopping; for his dexterity when he was in among the branches was as deft as any Parker had seen outside the big top of the Cirque du Soliel.

It took Squirrel only about forty minutes to place, via Angie's directions, the dozen Go Cams in the trees, as well as to hang and wire the solar charger. It required an equal amount of time for him and Angie to get the cameras oriented correctly so that the entire area around Parker's trailer and Yellow Dog Red's grave was covered seamlessly. It took another hour for Angie to connect to the Edge and to show Parker how to access the network and, if necessary, how to Skype to her and Squirrel and the other members of the LAN, who numbered ten or twelve, as near as Parker could figure.

Dusk was beginning to fall as Angie, finally satisfied with the setup, took off, leaving behind Squirrel, who had earlier strung a nylon hammock in the crown of a eucalyptus in which he was planning to spend the night. Dotty passed Angie on her way up through the vineyard, and from out of a wicker basket she handed her a small plastic food container filled with lemon tarts. Parker met Dotty at the split-log fence and helped her climb over it, taking the basket from out of her hands. The two, who hadn't seen or communicated for several days, then walked hand-in-hand over to the trailer, where Parker introduced Dotty to Squirrel.

"My, what a lovely name!" Dotty offered. "Is that your given one?"

"No, ma'am," he answered shyly and rose from his chair to shake her hand, stiffly she thought. "It's Peter von Brandt."

"Then why do you call yourself Squirrel?"

"Because my great-great-grandfather was a naturalist who first identified flying squirrels," he said flatly.

Squirrel, besides being tall and lanky, possessed one of those faces on which was written every thought that crossed his mind. Oppositely, his eyes were a jolting shade of gray, which in their intensity managed to capture others in such a way that made them feel reassured rather than caught. It was the type of aspect Parker had encountered in a few men and women who, when the characteristic had matured in tandem with wisdom, commanded respect, and when it had acquired neither commanded aversion in greater measure.

"Look at this, Dotty," Parker said, flipping open the laptop, which was on the camping table next to where he had put the basket. He then typed in the word 'Dubliners'; whereupon the screen was sectioned into twelve different views of the cemetery. Parker brought the cursor to one near the center, and clicked on it, which brought up a close-up image of Dotty, himself, and Squirrel.

"How...? Where...? she sputtered, gazing in the direction from which the perspective was formed, which was into the crown of a spindly bay tree not to far to the south of Red's grave.

Parker nodded toward Squirrel. "Squirrel and his friend Angie, who I guess you know, did it."

Dotty furrowed her brows. "But, why?"

"For safety," answered Squirrel. "It was Angie's idea. There are twelve cameras in the trees. I put them there today myself," he said proudly. His voice then rose and fell a half-octave in an ungoverned yodel, as it reverted momentarily to a younger timbre and then back. "And they're motion-activated," he added, "so they'll capture any movement day or night."

48

Dolly turned to Parker. "This must have cost you a fortune," she said, with less disapproval than incredulousness.

"Not a penny," replied Parker.

Perplexed, Dotty could only shake her head at his blasé attitude toward what was surely a technological marvel that must have cost a lot of money, despite his denial. "Are either of you hungry?" she said, dismissing the snarl of thoughts clogging her head. "I've brought enough lamb stew and buttermilk biscuits for an army."

"And lemon tarts?" piped Squirrel.

"Why, of course," replied Dotty. "Have you had them before?"

Squirrel nodded. "Tons. My third foster parents use to buy them by the sheet from Dotty's Deli out on the highway," he said, and added, "They said they were the best in the world."

"Oh, how sweet of you to say that," Dotty murmured; whereupon she opened the basket and began taking out containers, bowls, and utensils and placing them on the table. The last item out was a LED flashlight. "Do you mind if I join you? For dinner, I mean," she said, and added sheepishly. "I've brought my lantern."

"Happily," said Parker. "And when we're done I'll walk you down to your car." But it was clear to him by Dotty's smile of resignation that that was not the answer she had wanted to hear.

Parker came back after escorting Dotty to her car to find Squirrel sitting in the crotch of the huge eucalyptus that grew behind the latrine in a line beyond Yellow Dog Red and the trailer. He was ten feet off the ground. Thirty feet above him was his hammock.

"Dotty's a really good cook, isn't she?" Squirrel said, by way of welcoming Parker back.

"She is," acknowledged Parker. "She's also a loyal friend."

Squirrel nodded. "She said she's gonna bring us things to eat for as long as we need it."

Parker tilted his head. "I didn't hear her say that."

49

"No? Well, that's what she told me when I took her over to show her how I get into the trees."

"She did?" To which Squirrel nodded again.

A gibbous moon had risen over the peaks of the mountain to the east, and it cast the eucalyptus and Squirrel in a light that was a cross between pumpkin and pewter, which reminded Parker of the Maxfield Parrish painting in the Pied Piper Bar at the Palace, in front of which he had downed far too many Manhattans when he had been stationed at the Presidio. Those two memories, of the painting of the children's exodus from their parents' hamlet, and of the many lonely nights he had squandered drooped over empty cocktail glasses, both of which bespoke loneliness and addiction, prompted him to ask Squirrel why he liked trees so much. To which Squirrel only shrugged.

"Is it only because of your great-great-grandfather?" inquired Parker, although he knew beforehand what the answer would be.

"Not really."

"Then why did you say it was?" he responded, trying to sound confused rather than inquisitorial.

Squirrel repositioned himself in the V of the crotch, then said, "Because it's an answer that most people believe."

Parker blinked in recognition but remained quiet as he watched Squirrel idly peel off a loose piece of eucalyptus bark and wrap it around his wrist and then fasten it by twisting it ingeniously back on itself. The yip of a coyote high in the hills to the east finally broke Squirrel's concentration.

"The reason I like trees is that they make me feel free when I'm in them," he stated, again plainly, as if it were self-evident.

Parker shook his head slowly from side to side. "Are you sure it isn't the danger of falling out of them that gives you the sense of freedom you feel?"

Squirrel cheeks reddened and he let his gaze rest on Parker's, and, through it, appraised him. "Yes, I'm sure," he said finally. "The truth is I do like the ability to let go of a branch. But it is not because I find it dangerous."

"But it is dangerous," Parker replied.

"It's also reassuring."

"Reassuring?"

"Yeah, reassuring. Like, when I let go of a branch I know there will be another one for me to grab onto."

"Ah! Got it," responded Parker. "You like the order and continuity of trees."

Squirrel shrugged. "I guess trees are dependable that way. More dependable than people, anyway."

"If you don't mind me asking, What do your mother and father think about you climbing and sleeping in trees?"

A frown spread across Squirrel's face. "Are you a social worker?" he asked.

"Me? Hardly," Parker said, smiling broadly. "Just the opposite, I think you could say. I worked in Army Intelligence. Now I volunteer twice a week at the Animal Shelter."

Squirrel's eyes expanded, and in the moonlight the grayness of his irises took on a silvery sheen. "You were a spy?"

Parker shook his head. "Nope. Internal intelligence. I looked for thieves and swindlers in the ranks."

"Did you look for Nazis?"

Taken aback, Parker twisted his mouth into his cheek. "A few times. But not as a general rule. Why?"

"My mother's parents survived the death camps in Germany during the war."

Parker glanced away just as a jackrabbit scurried out from beneath the bramble of poison oak, then, upon seeing Parker, scurried back the way it had come. "I'm glad they survived but sorry for their suffering," he said, noting that beneath the curiously challenging tone of Squirrel's declaration, there was an opposite one of personal dispossession.

Squirrel leaned forward and draped his arms around the trunk of the eucalyptus, letting them hang limply, as if around the neck of a huge horse. He then laid his cheek against its smooth surface and continued in a barely audible voice.

"When I was three something happened to my mother. I don't remember any of it, but my father said she stopped talking and cried all the time. She was a big rig driver and went on the road for weeks. And then one day my dad said she called and said she wasn't coming home." His tone ascended as if it were questioning itself. "When I was eight, my father left and I became a ward of the court. Before going away he told me she pushed me away because the camps still had a hold over her," he went on, "even though she hadn't been in them herself. Maybe he was right. And maybe my mother just couldn't bear to be in a family without also wanting to destroy it. Maybe it's survivor's guilt, like my foster parents say, or something like that."

"I see," said Parker, shaking his head both in sadness and in the knowledge that there was more to Squirrel's tale than he was either letting on to or knew. "Sometimes it isn't easy for families that have been broken by the past to let go of it, even when they try. Tell me," he added, "do the trees heal you?"

Squirrel started to smirk at this, but then nodded in acknowledgment, and said, "They're my family. And that's what families are supposed to do, isn't it? Give you roots so that you can grow, and if you're wounded, heal you?"

"Unless they're so broken they can't."

"Don't you think everybody is broken by the past?" To which Parker shrugged. Squirrel then said, "What heals you?"

"Sylvia used to...until she was broken," Parker answered, letting his eyes go out of focus in remembrance of the week when he and Sylvia, in their early forties, had camped out inside a huge lightning-gutted redwood on the beach along The Lost Coast as a way to heal themselves after they had lost their son.

"Was she a dog? Sylvia, I mean," inquired Squirrel.

Parker shook his head. "No. Sylvia was—is—my wife. She has Alzheimers. She hasn't known who I am for ten years."

"Oh, shit. I'm so sorry. I... I didn't know."

"It's okay," replied Parker, scuffing the soft earth at the foot of the grave with his boot. "Yellow Dog Red heals me now. Dotty too. And Sylvia...."

"She must've been a good dog," Squirrel said, leaning back and stretching his arms while gazing down at Yellow Dog Red's headstone.

"A great dog. And irreplaceable. Sylvia too."

"See? That's what I mean. When a friend dies or a wife or a mother goes away, trees are good to be in because they can catch you when you fall," Squirrel said. Then looking up into the crown of the eucalyptus, he added, "Look, Parker, I'm sorry, but I have to get some sleep. I have a test at school tomorrow."

"Sweet dreams," Parker said, then added, "In what subject?"

"Calculus."

"Oh, boy. By all means, get some sleep."

"Likewise."

The next morning Roper showed up with his puppy shortly after Parker was finished with his grooming and just as Squirrel was climbing down out of the eucalyptus. As soon as the puppy saw Squirrel, she ran straight over and rolled over onto her back and began pawing his tennis shoe laces and squealing happily. Beaming brightly in delight, Squirrel bent down and lifted Parker into his arms, and, bringing her close to his face, let her lick him.

"Squirrel, meet Parker-the-dog," Parker said, in bemusement, as his namesake lavished Squirrel with gobs of puppy saliva. He then introduced Squirrel to Roper, and after explaining the unusual choice of name, informed Squirrel of Roper's occupation.

Squirrel recoiled as if bitten by a snake, and in the process he let Parker slip from out of his grip. Only Roper's quick reaction in catching Parker in midair prevented her from hitting the ground headfirst.

"Jesus! Did I do something wrong?" Roper cried, as he righted, then gathered Parker close to him. Squirrel just glared.

"You're an assassin! You butcher trees for money! That's what's wrong," Squirrel bleated finally, his voice again modulating higher and lower as if yodeling, and his own saliva spraying onto Roper.

Roper glanced in dismay at Squirrel, who turned away, and then at Parker. "Is he all right?" he said, touching a hand to his temple and directing his words to Parker as Squirrel stalked off toward the road.

Parker nodded. "He's fine. He—"

"You're not my parent. Don't tell me how I feel, Parker. I'm not fine!" yelled Squirrel. His eyes welled with tears. "The truth is I feel my heart is being ripped from me. And I...I...I just gotta go." And with that,

Squirrel sprinted down to the road where, after a few moments, a van stopped and, after he had climbed in, drove off.

"Wow! What was all that about?" Roper said, taking the seat Parker offered him.

"Family problems, I guess," replied Parker. "And a true lover of trees."

Roper grimaced. "Oh no, I didn't realize."

"There's nothing you could've done," Parker said, striking a match to his Sterno stove and placing his teapot on the burner. "He's just one of those kids who bleeds sap. Lives in a foster home, I was told."

"Ah, Jesus," Roper said, lowering Parker to the ground. "I know the kind. My brother was almost the same at Squirrel's age when my father wanted to start introducing him to the business. Loved trees."

"What happened?"

Parker shrugged. "He became a soldier. Turns out he didn't mind cutting down people with a gun nearly as much as he did trees with a chainsaw. Got so good at it, he was pretty damn scary to be around after he got out."

"Hmm, predictable, I suppose. Sounds like PTSD to me," ventured Parker, not bothering to hide the deflation in his voice. "Fact is, I've seen it go undiagnosed so often I can't even begin to count. Squirrel too, I fear."

"Well, it worked out all right for my brother, I guess," he shrugged. "The Army put him through school, and he's a dentist now. Loves pulling teeth but still can't stand to prune trees. And he has a wife—his fourth—whose mission in life seems to be to make her tits big and his bank account small."

Parker winced as he placed two teacups on the table, remembering the innumerable divorces he had witnessed, as a consequence of honor in uniform being transformed into sadism in marriage. He sat down opposite Roper, and the two watched in silence as Parker's namesake sniffed around the headstone, then chased after a butterfly, until the teapot began to whistle, at which point she ran over to investigate, before becoming distracted with the interior lining of one of the boots Parker had yet to put on.

"Is there any chance you can be done cutting by the time Squirrel gets out of school?" Parker voiced, pouring hot water into their cups. "If he even comes back, that is," he added.

"What time is that?"

"I think about four."

Roper shrugged. "Not a problem. Mulching too?"

Parker winced again. "I'm not certain that that wouldn't be even worse for him," he said, remembering from his own experiences the way mulchers brutalized vegetation.

Yeah, I can see that," agreed Roper, and as he dipped his tea bag up and down in his cup he silently weighed his options. After a while, he said, "It's doable. We'll make our composting run early and sharpen our blades afterward."

"Thanks," Parker said, and, opening the laptop, he added, "Would you like to see what he's done for me?"

"Sure," Roper said, squeezing the last of the infusion from the bag and swirling two teaspoonsful of sugar in the cup.

Doing as Angie had instructed him, Parker brought up the wi-fi network and clicked on the camera icon, which she had named "Peepers." A few seconds later the screen filled again with twelve boxes, two of which were recording him and Roper. All the others were dark, but a blinking light indicated that they had all captured movement since their reset the day before. Parker clicked on the view that looked at Yellow Dog Red's grave from the east.

The infrared camera had caught some mice scurrying this way and that, an owl swooping like a specter, a possum, a gang of raccoons, and any number of bats careening about. Then something much larger and warmer strolled into view, and only after several moments passed were both men able—since the infrared resolution was low—to make out that it was a mountain lion.

"I'll be darned," Parker whistled, and like Roper he was unprepared for what happened next; for after snuffling around Yellow Dog Red for several minutes, the cat stretched out luxuriantly atop the mound of earth, and, without disturbing any of the dirt, began grooming herself.

After ten minutes of licking and of running her paw over her head and body, the cat lay on her side and gazed back in the direction she had come. A moment later two lion cubs, at some unseen signal, came bounding into view. They homed in directly to their mother's teats, onto which they affixed themselves.

"I hear them in the hills when I'm cutting sometimes. Mating I guess. But I've never actually seen one, much less three," Roper said, leaning closer to get a better look. "Phew! What a beautiful cat! What time was this?"

Parker glanced at the real-time register at the top of the video. "About four-thirty."

He then fast-forwarded the camera, as Angie had shown him how to do, till one of the cubs stood and squatted to pee. This action was met with a swift reaction from the mother, who batted the cub off her feet with her paw. The lioness then rose and led her offspring through the split-log fence at the edge of the cemetery, where only then did she and her cub squat to pee. The second cub was not far behind, and it too left its spoor atop a flat rock just outside the fence. The three then disappeared into the budding brilliance of an infrared dawn before fading to black.

"What was that all about?" Roper said, noting that his crew had arrived and were heading his way.

"Looks to me like the lioness didn't want her cubs peeing on Yellow Dog Red."

"Think so?"

"Why not? Animals sense that sort of thing," Parker said. "Kids too." Parker was relieved when Roper, unlike Angie, did not take note of his question in answer to Roper's.

"What sort of thing?"

Parker remained silent in thought for a moment, then stated succinctly, "Veneration. And that they need to extend respect."

Roper's expression turned doubtful. "Only when it's deserved. Respect, I mean."

"Yes, of course," Parker parried, having realized from Roper's response that veneration had perhaps become a dirty word for him. "Otherwise," he went on, "it's a disingenuous gesture. A curtsy to dignity. Which is an affront to honor."

Roper nodded, then as one of his men called out to him, sighed, "I guess I better get going." And downing his tea in a gulp, he added, "But I'd rather stay and talk."

Parker nodded. "I'll watch Parker, if you'd like."

"Thanks, Parker. I can't tell you how much I appreciate your doing this for me. And I can tell she's mellowed out already from being around you."

Parker shrugged in acknowledgment of the compliment, but even more gratifying to him was his recognition of the sincerity revealed by Roper's voice. This, in turn, led him to choose to deflect his own part in both. "Thanks," he said, "but the truth is it's not me. It's her. Yellow Dog Red. Parker knows she's in the presence of a good dog, even one in death."

Roper tilted his head as if trying to hear something far away, then, almost at a whisper, said, "Trees are like that too, I think." And when Parker drew the corners of his mouth into his cheeks in question, he added, "I mean, trees seem to show respect for their elders somehow. At least that's what I feel when I cut down an old one; that the trees around it feel the loss. I can't say how I know this, but I definitely know I feel it.

That's the way my grandfather felt, too, so he taught me to always say thank you to a tree before I harvested it."

"Makes sense to me," Parker responded, as both men smiled at the puppy trying to climb into Squirrel's tree. "If there's one thing I've learned in my time on this planet, it's that life is a circle formed out of respect and trust. Break either one and things go all to hell in a handbasket."

Roper nodded in agreement, and with that he joined his men. Meanwhile Parker finished his tea and made some toast over the Sterno burner. He wrested his boots from out of Parker's jaws, then he began busying himself with a project that would take him through the rest of that day and many more days: grooming the cemetery's long-neglected grave sites back to the dignity they deserved.

In total, there were almost two hundred graves. The earliest ones dated back seventy years and were located in a ring radiating out from the veterinarian's farmhouse. A small portion were marked only with cairns, which Parker surmised marked the end of the road for various beasts of burden. But most of graves had plaques or headstones indicating that the animals buried therein had been pets. Parker had already decided he would start with the newest; that is, those immediately surrounding Yellow Dog Red: Bounder, Robby, Charlie, Orix and "C", whose name had broken off the stone tablet. All five had headstones that were discolored and were leaning over as the result of kids using them for paint-ball targets.

Of the five, only Charlie's site contained evidence of recent visits, presumably by his owner, as was indicated by a well-preserved mosaic food dish embedded in concrete inside of which a relatively new bone was affixed by a heart-shaped bolt sunken into to the bottom. By the bone and the bowl, Parker inferred that Charlie had been a small dog and probably one with a hardy appetite and possibly a stubborn streak; a Jack Russell, perhaps. From the dates on the headstone, Parker saw that Charlie had lived for nine years, and had died only six years earlier, making Charlie the newest of the newcomers, and also among the youngest to die.

Parker also surmised that Charlie's owner was probably a fastidious person who paid attention to details—a bookkeeper, a librarian, a deliveryman, or perhaps even a gardener—who had lost Charlie unexpectedly.

Among Yellow Dog Red's neighbors, only C's headstone was made of slate, and its engraved inscription read: "He was a good boy. My protector demon. May he run and sleep with the big dogs." The only indicator of who C's owner might have been, and of what C's full name was, came from the remnant of some circular floral motif engraved on the remaining half of the headstone that Parker thought he recognized. His best guess was that C's name was Cookie.

Roper's puppy was at Parker's heels every step he took that day: shredding and swallowing weeds Parker pulled up, then upchucking them minutes later; chasing dirt clods and falling all over herself when they disintegrated; getting underfoot and then curling up in Parker's lap whenever he sat down to rest. Roper, meanwhile, made quick work of some of the oldest trees on the property, which were located atop a knoll in the northwest corner, on land farthest removed from the pet cemetery. True to his word, Roper and his crew knocked off early and were packing up to leave before either Squirrel or Angie appeared. Before Roper departed, he came to retrieve his pup. He met up with Parker as he was finishing his own workday by bringing C's headstone to vertical.

"Here, look at these, Parker," Roper said, extending to Parker, who was still kneeling beside the headstone, an obsidian arrowhead and a spearhead his crew had found inside a crude circle comprised of moss-covered serpentine boulders at the peak of the knoll, from which they had harvested a century-old bay laurel.

"Nice," Parker said, taking the sleek objects and inspecting them in the oblique rays of the late afternoon sun; for he was indeed impressed by the quality of workmanship that had gone into the artifacts. They were of the type he himself had acquired over the years, mostly along the old railroad and stagecoach routes that had been footpaths frequented by Wappo, Ohlone, and Pomo hunters and gatherers making their way through the valley. Even after a hundred years had passed, the razor-sharp edges of the weapons glinted in the light, and the symmetry of their scalloped cuts told Parker that the artifacts would probably fly as straight and cut as deep now as they had then.

Parker handed the elegant items back to Roper with an appreciative nod. Roper, in turn, inserted them between a sheet of folded paper before depositing them in a sleeve of his computer satchel.

"The owner will need to show these to the county," Roper said, to which Parker nodded; for, like Roper, he knew that developers and those who worked for them were obliged by state law and county regulations to report any findings of potentially historical significance, even though most would be routinely dismissed as irrelevant.

"Probably won't be happy about it either," Parker responded. "Developers aren't too keen about having archeologists snooping around their projects."

Roper shrugged. "I don't think it'll be a problem. Doesn't seem like a significant site to me," he replied. "I've seen dozens just like it in the valley. Places where there was obsidian that the Indians could camp at to shape arrowheads, shuck acorns, and drink their wine." He paused. "Have you ever had any of that stuff? I forget what it's called."

Parker nodded. "I've had it a couple times. Pulque, I think it's called. Made with honey and wild plum from recipes given them by the missions. Sometimes it's made with agave too, I think."

Roper moaned in remembrance. "Yeah, sweet and wretched...killer stuff. Anyway," he went on, "I and my crew won't be here tomorrow or the day after. I have a conference call with my school advisor, and my top cutter has a Christening to go to in Salinas. And then it's the weekend. So, unless it's pouring rain, we'll be back Monday. Then Thanksgiving is coming. In other words, I'm saying progress will be slow. Which I thought you might appreciate..." His voice trailed off.

"Well, good luck with the call," Parker said, filling the pause and letting a smile escape.

Simultaneously, from a short distance behind him, he heard Angie talking baby-talk to Roper's Parker, who responded by rushing headlong and then slamming into her at full speed. Angie howled in laughter at the collision. Roper frowned; he was not looking forward to another confrontation. Angie picked up the puppy in her arms and, like Squirrel, beamed as the dog licked her face. Parker rose stiffly to greet her, but as he did so he felt himself growing dizzy, which prompted him to plop back down in his chair.

"What a great dog!" Angie giggled, as she drew up beside Parker. But then, seeing the color—or lack of it—in Parker's face, she said, "Are you okay, Parker?"

Parker nodded. "I'm fine. Just winded from setting this headstone is all."

"You shouldn't work so hard," she admonished, sounding uncannily like Dotty, but then noticing Roper for the first time, she said, "Hi, I'm Angie. This your dog?"

"It is. Her name is—"

"Parker," inserted Angie. "Squirrel told me. He doesn't like the name. But I think it's cool."

"How is he?" Roper asked. "Squirrel, I mean."

Angie eyed Roper appraisingly. "He said he felt bad about yelling at you. You're the tree-cutter, right?" To which Roper shrugged in a manner that was more noncommittal than he intended. "Don't worry about him," Angie continued. "He'll be okay. He's just moody. He's going to spend the rest of the day in the redwood down by the church. They're his family now. The redwoods, I mean. They always calm him down."

"Me too," Roper said, again surprising himself at the frankness of his response.

Angie furrowed her brow doubtfully but let her questions pass for the time being. Instead, she turned to Parker. "Did you see the lions?"

"We both did," Parker said, nodding toward Roper.

"Weren't they rad!"

"Very rad," Parker replied.

"Want to know what else is rad?" Angie fairly yelped out. And before either Parker or Roper could answer, she cried, "I uploaded the cat video onto YouTube before I went to school. I just checked. Guess how many hits we've had?"

"What kind of hits?" Parker said in alarm.

"She means viewings on computers," Roper inserted, then ventured the number one hundred.

"Nope! We've already had forty thousand," she exalted. "In only six hours." Parker-the-dog now began to whine and to struggle to break free of Angie's arms.

"I think she wants to go to the bathroom," Parker said.

"Whew!" Roper blurted in astonishment. "That's a lot."

Angie smiled, then lowered Parker to the ground. The puppy immediately began to sniff in earnest around Yellow Dog Red. A second later, however, she reared back as if slapped on the muzzle, and raced in a straight line over to the fence, where, wiggling her way through it, she lowered herself and peed.

"Hmm. Just like the cats," Parker remarked quizzically. "It seems now Parker too doesn't want to pee in the cemetery. The lion must've left a message..." he added, squinting in thought.

"Guess what else?" Angie said exuberantly, disregarding Parker's confusion. "Remember I said I was going to sit with my dad when he Skyped Slag?" To which Parker nodded, although still clueless as to what a Skype was. "Well, after my dad was done talking business stuff with him, I talked to Slag. Me! And I told him about Yellow Dog Red." She opened her eyes so wide that they seemed to grow to almost twice their size. "He said he wants me to tweet him about how it's going. Guess what else?" she said, barely able to contain her excitement and not bothering to wait for an answer. "He said he thought it was a good name for a song. Slag and Dash singing about Yellow Dog Red! I can't believe it!"

64

"You can't, or don't, or won't believe it?" Parker said, purposefully redirecting Angie's exuberance, which he found so endearing that he himself wanted to yelp out gleefully.

The bait left Angie speechless, and it took her looking into Parker's rheumy eyes to see that they were twinkling mischievously before she caught on. "Why not?" she said, after several seconds had passed. Her own voice had assumed a teasing quality.

"Wouldn't the simplest answer have been yes?"

Angie feigned a pout. "I'm glad all old people aren't like you," she said, smiling broadly despite her efforts to affect the opposite attitude.

"Why is that?"

"Then it wouldn't be as easy to take advantage of them."

"Ah!" Parker said. "You mean you would like to pull the wool over the eyes of unsuspecting old people so that whippersnappers like you can take the reins of power away from us."

"It's only a theory."

"That's because you don't have an army. Once you've got one of those, theories don't count."

"What counts then? Respect?" Angie's eyes sparkled in victory.

Parker shook his head. "No. Power."

While Angie pondered this, Roper, having been left in the dust by this intimate exchange from which he was clearly excluded, was glad to gather Parker up in his arms. "Is there a hashtag I can tweet?" he said.

"You're almost standing on it," Angie replied.

Roper looked down at the headstone, which was vertical again. "Yellow Dog Red?"

"Yep. Hashtag Yellow Dog Red."

Roper shook his head appreciatively at Angie's perspicaciousness and at her companionship and, mostly, at the obvious camaraderie she was affording Parker. He doubted very much the veracity of her story about Slag, but he decided against saying anything, on the assumption that she was probably just being a young girl with conflated fantasies brought on from playing too many video games.

"I like it," Roper said. "Might even be a good name for a song." After a second, he added, "When you see Squirrel, will you tell him for me that I probably revere trees as much as he does. And that just as it's his job to honor trees as family, it's my job to honor their lives in a way that lets others share in their strength and wisdom."

"Doesn't that mean you're in business with them to turn a profit?" Angie said. Roper's eyes only widened in answer. Angie lowered herself to the ground and sat down cross-legged on Yellow Dog Red's grave next to Parker, and added, "Do you ever consult the trees about whether they want to be in business with you?"

"I thank them for the gift of their lives, if that's what you mean."

Angie shook her head. "I think it's good you thank them," she answered. "That's respectful. That's good. But don't you think the trees are in business with you only because you made them? I mean, I doubt you gave them the choice. And don't you think that if they were people not trees, they would be called slaves?"

Roper did a double take and was left wordless until Parker intervened.

"Sir, you'd better go and make your call to your advisor," Parker said, and added sympathetically while nodding toward Angie, "before this one fells you like you yourself are a tree."

"Good idea," Roper said, nodding in agreement. Then, as an afterthought, to Angie he said, "Are all kids your age like you?"

"Like what?"

"As smart as you."

Angie thought on this for a few seconds, then offered, "We're not really all that smart. We're just faster than a lot of older people because everything in our world moves faster. Your world moves at the speed of things like machines. Ours moves at the speed of light." She held up her iPhone.

66

Parker shook his head wearily. He then reached out and placed a hand atop the headstone. "Did you hear that, Red?" he consoled. "According to our friend, now that you're moving at the speed of light you're young again..." Parker's voice trailed off.

"Does Yellow Dog Red answer you?" Angie asked, unsure if Parker was still teasing her.

"She does," answered Parker, and by the somber look that spread across his face, Angie realized he was sincere. "She does," he repeated. She says 'Hurry up, Parker!'"

The weekend came and that next week saw a series of storms blow in off the Pacific. At the first sign of rain Parker installed a tarp over his living area, which he anchored by lengths of nylon rope affixed to trees. He also dug a diversion trench that sufficed to keep his outdoor living space dry. The storms lasted for ten days, dumping almost ten inches of rain in the valley before moving on. They were followed by a cold snap, and then by Thanksgiving, which Parker celebrated with Dotty. Parker did not want to leave Yellow Dog Red unattended, so he and Dotty dined in the cemetery, sitting so that Yellow Dog Red formed the third corner of a triangle. Dotty had baked a small turkey and all the regular holiday fixings, including lemon bars. Then she kept vigil at the trailer while Parker paid a late afternoon visit to Sylvia in the convalescent facility.

As always, Parker was a mess after seeing her; for Sylvia had long since forgotten him, their marriage, their child, and even her own name. Moreover, she viewed Parker's visits as menacing, and wailed disconsolately over his intrusion into the comfort of her ever-shrinking routines until long after he departed. Thus, when he returned to the cemetery, Parker asked Dotty to come with him into the trailer where, sitting side-by-side on the bed, he shared an after-dinner Port with her, reminiscing about the past mostly, with both weeping silently over better times. Soon Parker fell asleep. Dotty, barely awake herself, removed the half-empty glass from his hand and drew a blanket over him. She then found her way to her car on her own—or, rather, she found her way while Squirrel and Angie looked on through their remote connection to the infrared cameras.

A month after Thanksgiving still saw no activity of any sort on the Pound property, other than Parker's methodical housekeeping of the many plots in the cemetery, and the regular nocturnal visits of the mountain lion and cubs whose presence, it seems, had discouraged all other interlopers from venturing through the graveyard at night. During the month of December Parker was visited almost every afternoon by Dotty, who, wearing Wellingtons, a Burberry insulated raincoat, muffler, and wool cap, brought him comestibles and clean clothes, and shared a meal, conversation, and an aperitif, all under the tarp. During one such meal, Dotty pulled from out of her basket a copy of a slick local business magazine's Christmas issue. She then read to Parker a short piece about the new owners and their plans for the Gainsaid Pound property.

According to the piece, there were three brothers. All in their sixties and all bachelors. The youngest two, Enzo and Marco Zinni, lived in Turlock, where they farmed their own grapes—Zinfandel and Petite Syrah mostly—on two different ranches, and from them made lackluster wines under the Zinni Brothers Vineyards label. Rocco, the eldest, and head of the endeavor, lived in Rio Vista where he had a trucking company that specialized in mobile bottling and bulk wine transportation.

The Zinni's new venture, of which Rocco was reported to be the leader, aspired to be a re-creation of their family's legendary winery that had operated out of an Etruscan cave, in a cliff below an Italian hill town, for two hundred years before the cliff and the cave fell away in an earthquake. In homage, the winery's name was slated to be Etruscan Estate Vineyards. It was scheduled to produce ten thousand cases of ultra-premium wines—a paltry amount and a small operation as wineries went in this part of the world. An artist's drawing of the proposed facility showed it to be a scaled-down replica clearly inspired by a Las Vegas style casino, only with a tiny Umbrian hill town replacing a Venetian palazzo. Nowhere in the schematic was there any sign of the cemetery, which, as near as Parker and Dotty could figure from the small picture, was replaced by a theme park devoted to truffles, wild boar, and Etruscan pottery.

Dotty later forwarded the article to a lawyer who owed her a favor. But all written attempts the lawyer made to contact any of the principals went unanswered. When she did finally get ahold of them through Rocco's trucking firm, they reluctantly agreed to meet her at a truck stop north of Stockton, where she was to confer with Rocco, Enzo and Marco. Rocco was absent, but the two brothers, one of whom—Enzo—was corpulent and bullying, and the other—Marco—corpulent and effeminate, took a single nonnegotiable position that, besides shocking to the lawyer as a negotiator, was so unyielding that it seemed more a product of inbred recalcitrance than business logic. Essentially, they said that all anybody needed to know could be found in the public record. Period. Non-negotiable. End of interview. Furthermore, they maintained they would put nothing in writing unless legally required to do so. They even went so far as to deny the lawyer the courtesy of giving out the name of an attorney she might contact.

What was most disconcerting about the meeting, however, was not that Enzo's churlishness and Marco's leering had been offensive to Dotty's friend personally, for both had clearly so disrespected her as a woman for doing what they thought was a man's work that she was left feeling sullied and denigrated by the encounter; rather, it was what happened after the meeting was over and they had departed. That is, as she went to use the restroom, she found the floor littered with half-a-dozen business cards—Enzo's, which he must have tossed in there hoping for...what? That some lonely woman in transit to L.A., having stopped to fill her gas tank and take a leak, would be so horny that she would actually give Enzo—a complete stranger, not to mention a fat bully—a call in order to schedule some sort of opportunistic tryst?

Stunned and disgusted and frankly boggled by the bald scourge of misogynous brutality that such a stratagem intimated, she began to wonder

70

what sort of troglodyte would even begin to think that such a ploy would bear fruit? Even more pertinent and perplexing than that for her was, What sort of wine could such a family hope to make and market to the type of high-end clientele who could afford to pay a few hundred dollars for a bottle of California Pinot Noir?

Around Christmastime it was discovered that because the Zinni winery was in full compliance with zoning regulations and the proposed production was well below the amount allowed, and was unopposed by either the county Planning Department or by members of the community the plans had sailed the through Design Review. Furthermore, the brothers Zinni had received a simple Negative Declaration Report—meaning that their project was deemed to have no significant detrimental impact on the environment—and consequently the site plan and building plan were approved without opposition. In short, all the necessary paperwork was in place, and the time to have submitted an appeal had passed.

In the month spanning Thanksgiving and Christmas, Squirrel came by only when there were breaks in the weather, and he kept his contact with Parker minimal. He refrained from sleeping in the cemetery's trees—although he did leave his hammock aloft—and chose instead to spend his time shuffling about through the logged-over portions of the property consoling stumps of trees that had been harvested. His form of solace was always the same and consisted of placing his right hand on a stump while kneeling and with his left forefinger touching the ground. After meditating in this pose for a short period, he withdrew a seed from out of his backpack and, using a dibble, planted it beside the stump. As a final act Squirrel would locate an uncut tree of similar variety and, wrapping his arms around it, press himself against the trunk in an act of commiseration for its fallen brethren.

Squirrel's tributes were more touching to Parker than even he himself admitted; for despite the obligations of his earlier career that had obliged him to view such ceremonial deeds largely as acts of subterfuge that often unconsciously masked more ambiguous motives, Parker was also as unabashedly sentimental a human as any that had ever existed. He was one for whom the goodness of others was simply a natural outgrowth of being alive, for whom evil was an unnatural outgrowth of denying goodness, a poor relation of truth inculcated through lack of information. Moreover, it was clear to him that Squirrel, if nothing else, was a good-hearted misfit, and, like himself, an outsider, a loner who coped with the harshness of reality by falling back on the comfort of beings who accepted him unconditionally. In Squirrel's case that meant trees and Angie. In Parker's case it was dogs and Dotty.

Despite the holidays and the inclement weather, Angie continued to stop by almost every day with reports about her tweets and her YouTube videos, which, she proudly showed Parker on her phone, were going gangbusters in the virtual world. The Monday before Christmas saw a break in the weather, and inasmuch as school was out for the holidays Angie and four of her skateboarding friends, who she brought up to meet Parker, were skating up and down the road with what seemed to Parker reckless abandon, whooping and hollering when one or another of them accomplished some amazing airborne feat that would have maimed a person of lesser dexterity.

At dusk the skateboarding band made a final run southward toward town and out of Parker's view. A third of a mile later the closely packed group rounded a tight curve on one of the more challenging portions of the road just north of Dotty's. The road was wide enough at that spot, though steep, for the skateboarders to pass unimpeded past opposing traffic. But on that day a van was parked, its lights extinguished, behind a hedge of ornamental quince on their left. Angie was in the lead. She rounded the corner and was suddenly confronted by the vehicle, which had only just then turned on its lights and pulled onto the road.

Rather than tracking to the right side where there was plenty of room, the van swerved instead to the center of the road, cutting off Angie's progress. Angie and her friends, traveling at close to 20 mph, were blinded by the sudden illumination. With no time to react, they could do nothing to avoid hitting the van head-on other than to steer to their right.

That maneuver, while it saved their lives, propelled all five off the pavement and straight into a two-foot-deep ditch that was backed by a dense thicket of blackberries. Before the boarders knew what was happening, their skateboards were planted nose-first in the rain-softened bank and they themselves were catapulted head over heels into the quarter-acre bed of thorns. In the meantime the van disappeared around the curve.

Christmas was now upon Parker, and he ascribed Angie's absence in the preceding days to the holiday. He and Dotty, as they had on Thanksgiving, ate Christmas dinner together. Likewise, afterwards Dotty kept vigil at the cemetery while Parker visited with Sylvia. Again the results of the visit were predictable. But on this night Parker came back even more devastated than before; for without explicitly saying as much he let on that he was certain this Christmas would be Sylvia's last.

Parker again invited Dotty into the trailer after dinner for a glass of Port and consolation as he had on Thanksgiving. Sitting side-by-side on the bed, their space lit only by one solar-powered light and warmed only by their proximity to each other, the two sipped their drinks and reminisced quietly. As night fell Parker began to recount his and Sylvia's fortieth anniversary, which they had spent in Paris, until suddenly his jaw clenched. At once it became locked in place and ceased to move altogether, although his lips continued to shape words he could not bring himself to say. Unable to speak, he turned to Dotty, who had only just then realizated that Parker's silence was unintentional.

Barely above a whisper he managed to implore, more with his eyes than with words, "May I lay my head in your lap?"

Dotty's first reaction was stunned surprise; for the profound sadness that was echoed in his breathless voice, and the sorrow lines that were etched into his face as deep as knife wounds spoke of unbearable suffering. But then there came a counter aspect which she recognized at once; for in his eyes was a look that imparted kindness and goodwill, something Dotty had also seen in her husband Max at those times of duress late in his life when he had known time was short and that he was doing what was right even though it was unspeakably painful.

That same quality of charity was inherent in Parker's request, and Dotty understood that he was asking her to help him release Sylvia from Parker's desire to keep her with him. Wordlessly, Dotty grasped the truth that, rather than feeling guilty or even resentful toward Sylvia that their life together was over, Parker had finally arrived at a place where he now wanted only to express, through the surrogacy of his friend's presence, the love he felt toward Sylvia for having shared her life with him. And through this love he was setting her free.

"I would like that," Dotty answered. Little was said afterward. Both wept on and off, but their grief, in being measured out in equal amounts of forbearance and suffering, was contained, and soon both, spent but unburdened, started to nod off.

Rather than getting up to escort Dotty down to her car, Parker instead drew the covers over her. Thus the two spent their first night together, with their companionship gifts that each gave to the other for having been able to say farewell to Sylvia.

The next time Parker saw Angie was late in the day after New Years. He at first did not recognize her, since she was not carrying her skateboard and was limping. In fact; he thought she was the bothersome woman who came to his house regularly on Saturdays to proselytize her religion. Additionally, even as Angie drew nearer to Parker and he could see her more clearly, he had trouble identifying her; for her face was misshapen and colored by a massive bruise in the shape and shade of an eggplant. Her

74

lips were also swollen, and her forehead was crisscrossed by an irregular lattice of ugly black lines consisting of partially healed scratches. In short, she looked to him like one of those troll-like Smurf dolls that had been put into a microwave to dry.

"Mother of mercy! What in heaven's name happened to you?" was all Parker could say when he finally did recognize her.

"Skateboard accident," Angie replied thickly, throwing herself into a chair. "I'm grounded for a month," she added glumly. She then went on to recount the incident, in which one of her friends had sustained a broken clavicle, another a broken wrist, and all had suffered severe lacerations to their heads and hands. She concluded by saying that none of the skateboarders were able to identify the make, the model, the driver, the color, or the vehicle's licence number, and that the sheriff was treating the accident as a felony hit-and-run.

"Good luck finding him," Parker replied after she was finished.

Angie shrugged. "My dad thinks it was some kid who pulled onto the road at the wrong time, then got scared. But that's not what I think," she said, shaking her head vehemently. "I think whoever it was did it on purpose."

"Why on earth would you think that?" Parker said, knitting his brows at the likelihood of anyone purposefully trying to run down four children on a quiet country road. "I mean, who would knowingly aim to run over a pack of kids on skateboards?"

Angie shrugged again. "Dunno. But it's what Squirrel thinks too. He came over to see me after the accident and said Ethel, the redwood tree he hangs out in, told him to look out for himself."

"The redwood tree Ethel told him that?" Parker said, restating Angie's assertion less as a question than as an exclamation. He slid the plastic container out of which he himself had just withdrawn a lemon bar across the table to Angie.

"That's what Squirrel says. I know, it sounds lame to me too," she said, twisting her mouth in a half-scowl, half-frown that was meant to be a smile. "But is it any more lame than Yellow Dog Red talking to you? Or a woman named Isis tweeting me from Egypt?"

Although Angie had said this without any hint of insolence or dismissiveness, Parker flinched nonetheless. Then, laughing aloud, he said, "Touche!, my friend. I guess when it comes down to it you could say we're all talking through our hats."

"Uh, huh," she said, pushing a square awkwardly past her swollen lips into her misshapen mouth, and in the process coating her lips with a rim of confectioner's sugar. "Do you know what else the tree told Squirrel?"

Parker shook his head, as much in question as in sympathy for Angie's injuries and for Squirrel's need to communicate with a plant instead of people.

"Ethel said she was worried that if Yellow Dog Red is lost, then Squirrel was going to be torn from his roots."

Parker responded with a furrowed brow. "What does that mean?" he said, and he wondered to himself if he shouldn't have a talk sometime soon with Squirrel, and perhaps even his foster parents, about letting himself get drawn too deeply into other people's—and other trees' for that matter—business. After all, Yellow Dog Red had not been Squirrel's dog, and other than for the trees that were being harvested on the property, he had no real skin in Parker's game.

"Dunno," shrugged Angie. "I think maybe it's because first his mother and then his father dumped him. You know how people are sometimes. They say they're worried about other people when it's really themselves they're worried about."

"Projection," replied Parker, nodding.

"Yeah," Angie said, squeezing another lemon bar past her swollen lips, releasing a puff of sugar into the air. "Just like me thinking I'm going to write a song with Slag because he Skyped with me."

At that moment Parker's attention was diverted away from Angie's little cloud of sugar to the base of the driveway leading to the vet's house, from which direction came the clanking of heavy machinery moving along the asphalt road. At a glance, Parker recognized it as a John Deere 850J track-layer. It had just backed down off the flatbed truck that had transported it, and was beginning to lumber off the paved road and up the gravel one toward the vet's compound.

Perplexed, Parker said to himself more than to Angie, "What the heck are they doing?" and he glanced down at his watch. "It's New Years Day. And it's too late for them to start anything today anyway."

"Way too late," Angie agreed, and drawing out her iPhone she typed in the name of the company logo stenciled onto the cab of the bulldozer. It came up as a construction firm operating out of Stockton. "Let's go check it out," she said, rising to her feet, "And ask them what they're up to."

Parker shook his head. "Probably better that we don't," he said, and when Angie shot him a questioning look, he explained, "That's private property. This cemetery is in the public domain. If we break any property laws, like trespassing, then the owners might be able to use it as an excuse to evict Yellow Dog Red and me, or to prevent me and you from gaining access here again. And anyway," he said, gesturing toward Angie's injuries, "you're in no shape at the moment to be chasing after windmills or dragons or bulldozers."

Angie nodded reluctantly, but then, defiantly, declared, "Let them try to stop me from tweeting a picture of their dragon to hashtag Yellow Dog Red." Whereupon she pointed her phone toward the bulldozer and took a number of pictures, including a selfie of her and Parker. "So we have a record at least."

Ten minutes later the bulldozer drew parallel to the vet's house. Its driver brought it to a halt but kept the engine idling. Parker and Angie had by then walked over to the side of the cemetery nearest the house. From their vantage they could see the driver calling someone on his phone. A few seconds after the call was placed, a dark cloud of diesel smoke from the dozer's exhaust indicated the conversation was ended. The operator then veered sharply away from the Gainsaid Pound house and cemetery, and headed obliquely up the knoll on which Roper had made his last cuts.

The sun had long since dipped behind the mountains to the west when the track-layer attained the crest of the hill, casting it in shadow, which made the dozer's actions hard for Parker and Angie to make out. What was clear to Parker immediately, however, was that the driver had lowered the dozer's blade and had begun to butt it again and again against the stump of the ancient bay tree around which Roper had found the Indian artifacts.

"What is he doing? I can't see," Angie said, and after placing a call to explain her tardiness to her parents, she laid her phone in annoyance down on the split log fence against which she and Parker leaned.

"They're destroying evidence," he remarked sourly, then told Angie about the arrowheads Roper had found, and the rules governing their handling and the treatment of the location at which they were found.

"But isn't that illegal?" she sputtered when he was done.

Parker shrugged. "Where's the body? There's no crime if there isn't any evidence of it."

Angie stared at him as though he had just told her he had murdered his best friend. "Isn't there something we can do? Call the sheriff? Call the governor? Call Slag?"

"It's New Years Day," sighed Parker. "None of the offices are open. And the sheriff isn't..." his voice trailed off into another shrug.

"Isn't what?" Angie said.

"Isn't going to be interested in workmen going about their business. Anyway," he added, "by the time anybody gets here there won't be anything to see except for a chewed up hill and an uprooted stump."

The work of attaining this last goal, though, proved less straightforward than might have been expected; for the soil, which was mostly adobe, had been softened to such an extent by rainfall that the dozer's tracks were getting coated with clay and having trouble finding traction. Thus the relatively minor task of uprooting the stump took a good hour-and-a-half to accomplish, on a job that, on firmer ground, would have taken less than a quarter of that time.

Darkness had, in fact, fallen by the time the task was completed and the driver had departed, leaving his vehicle atop the knoll. Nightfall, given what had happened to Angie and her friends, also made it necessary for her to call for a ride. Angie's ride met her down at the road, but instead of driving off, the person who had come for her returned on foot to the cemetery.

"Is something wrong?" Parker said, after Angie and the other had drawn close.

"My father wishes to meet you," she said, gesturing to the man a step behind her who, like herself, was using his phone as a flashlight.

"I am sorry to disturb you," Angie's father said, extending his hand to Parker once he had climbed over the fence. "I'm Bahram. My daughter is spending so much time here that I insisted she introduce me to you."

Of slight build, Bahram wore a stylish, almost debonair suit, a white silk shirt, and a charcoal-gray tie that matched his hair color. He looked to be in his early fifties, but for a man of that age his dark eyes were placid and twinkled like those of an adolescent. They were also set too close to each other, which gave him a look of confusion. Combined with clear skin and a lineless complexion, a crop of wavy hair and a thin nose, he presented a look of blithe, impeccable augustness, which Parker had become all too familiar with in his years in Intelligence; wherein boys, usually of upper-class European or Middle Eastern descent, born into wealth and stature in the world of the diplomatic corps, ofttimes grew into men who were urbane and charming to a fault, but who were

79

unaccomplished in anything other than spending money and wasting other peoples' time.

"I'm Parker," Parker replied tentatively, not knowing quite what to make of Bahram.

He took Bahram's hand in his. A firm but noncommital handshake, it confirmed to Parker what he had taken in at a glance; that Bahram, not unlike his daughter, was well-bred, kind and also manipulative. That is, in that Bahram had held Parker's hand a beat or two longer than would have been expected from a complete stranger, especially one of such evident refinement, it told Parker that Bahram was one of two things: either an opportunist, a financier, or a wheeler-dealer of some sort who maintained tactile contact in order to assess and possibly exploit another's station for his own purpose; or else he was an empathic sort who held his grip in order to convey a sense of familiarity so as to instill a perception of trust, such as a minister might. In Bahram's grip, as well as in his gaze, Parker was pleased to ascertain that both were extant, just as he would have expected in an artistically inclined diplomat's son.

It was in Bahram's voice, though, that Parker heard the precautionary tenor of confused priorities that could presage either misplaced blissfulness or downright befuddlement, and, in the worse case, the kind of blissful befuddlement entertained by those who wore their internal chaos as a medal and who sowed disorganization as though it were a victory over misrepresentation. These were loveable rascals, as Parker had come to know them, and they had been by far the hardest for him to weed out in Intelligence operations; for in their likability and chamaeleon-like ability to be subsumed seamlessly into any number of environments, they were hidden from easy view. That is, their motives could be ferreted out only when the shear volume of contradictions and the mass of nonsequiturs they employed, to disguise that they were unable to think more than one step ahead, finally collapsed around them, always with confusing results and often with disastrous repercussions.

Normally, Parker would have been reticent to warm quickly to a person of such conflicting characteristics; for, in his experience, trust was by far the easiest asset to exploit for personal gain once it was extended, and the hardest to recapture once it was lost. But in having come to know and trust Angie, and in general willing to give others the benefit of the doubt, and finally, figuring there was small risk associated with it, Parker summarily gave his trust over to Bahram.

"Would you like some tea?" Parker said, gesturing toward his living area.

Bahram glanced down at his watch. "One cup," he said. "I'm expecting a Skype. And Angwin has homework to do."

While Parker prepared a pot of tea, Angie showed her father Yellow Dog Red's grave and pointed out where she and Squirrel had placed their cameras, and where Squirrel had hung his hammock. Bahram read Yellow Dog Red's inscription to himself, then read C's aloud. "'He was a good boy. He was my protector demon. May he run and sleep with the big dogs.' What do you think possessed C's owner to put that about the protector demon on his headstone?" he said, addressing his question to Parker while lowering himself into the chair Parker had pulled out from the table for him.

"Maybe the owner was Buddhist or Hindu," Parker replied. "It's a common theme in Eastern religions."

"Hmm," Bahram said, taking a sip of tea. "Perhaps. But I think not."

"I Googled it," Angie inserted, having just pulled the tab off one of the boxed fruit juices Dotty had brought up the day before, which Parker had offered her. "Protector demons are like guardian angels. They're supposed to look fierce in order to scare away the real demons. So C protected his owner from demons."

"Isn't that what all dogs are supposed to do?" her father said. "Protect their owners from danger."

"Maybe C's owner had a lot of trouble with robbers and muggers and other things like that," Angie replied. "Maybe C was a watchdog."

Bahram shrugged. "It could mean that, Apple," he said. "But it could also refer to the more general condition of domestication. What do you think, Parker? You must have had had some time, I presume, to think on what it means."

Parker shrugged, then said, "I think your daughter is right in thinking C was a watchdog, whose owner I also think is a woman." He extended the box of lemon bars to Bahram, who took one. "But I don't actually think C's owner was referring to a Buddhist entity. I think she was referring to his breed. A small dog. A fierce dog. A dog like a Jack Russell."

Bahram nodded in agreement. Then, glancing down at his watch, gestured with the lemon bar toward Yellow Dog Red's grave. "Tell me about your dog and the vigil you are keeping. It has captured my daughter's imagination like nothing else ever has. She and I have a musician friend, and even he has expressed interest in your endeavor."

P arker nodded. "I know your friend," he said. "If it is the person I am thinking of, he was better than I in figuring out where African kleptocrats hid their money. Perhaps because he's Irish and is used to such shenanigans at home." But when Bahram lifted his brows in surprise, Parker, seeing that his words had been taken more literally—and negatively—than he had intended, hastily said, "I am only joking. But the musician of whom you speak did meet Yellow Dog Red once, although I am certain he has forgotten her.

"We—Yellow Dog Red and I—were playing fetch at Crissey Field, in San Francisco, on a very windy and foggy day," he continued. "One time, instead of bringing her tennis ball back to me, she brought it straight over to this other person who was walking down the beach toward us. I did not know him or anything about him then. In any case, he was so bundled up against the wind and the fog I wouldn't have recognized him if he had been my twin brother.

"Yellow Dog Red was probably about eight years old then. In her prime. The thing about her that made her so special was that she was sensitive to people in a way that made her seem clairvoyant. That day when she went up to the man and dropped her ball at his feet it was because he seemed, even to me, like the loneliest person in the world.

"It's hard to tell why she or I thought this," he said, after pausing to draw his collar against the cold and to ascertain whether or not to delve too explicitly into the matter, on the chance, albeit a slim one, that in baring himself to Bahram his candor might be used against him later. But when his eye caught Angie's and he saw the same sense of belonging of which he was about to speak, he decided to go on. "Other than to say people, especially creative people, sometimes send forth their feelings like shadows that walk ahead of them. Dogs can sense these shadows easier than people can, and that day Yellow Dog Red saw before I did that the man, maybe the most famous person in the world I learned later, had a shadow surrounding him so completely that he could have been an alien from another planet in his isolation."

Parker paused again and glanced across the table at Bahram to see if he was interested in what he was saying, or if he was just feigning to listen in order to be polite. Adjudging that both Bahram and Angie were indeed paying close attention, Parker continued.

"Long before I had Yellow Dog Red, I was in Army Intelligence. In my work, I was trained to spot potential suicidal tendencies in people before they could be acted upon with destructive results either against themselves or organizations. Usually it was the emotional dissonance of their bearing or their voices versus their expressions that I counted on to flag the bubble of isolation overlying their actions. Yellow Dog Red smelled or saw that same inner conflict that day. Or, as I believe, she was able to utilize her innate sense of belonging in order to adapt to the man's suffering, so she could penetrate through the hard crust of loneliness into his core being. Into his soul if you will.

"Like all good dogs she did what she did best," Parker shook his head and smiled fondly in remembrance. "She shook off right in front of him. Soaked him through and through to the bone with fifty-degree San Francisco Bay water. And then she wouldn't take no for an answer from him to play fetch. Finally the man relented, and by playing fetch with her he befriended her, and by being befriended by him she gave herself over to him, and he to her. And it was with that one simple unquestioning shared extension of unconditional devotion that the shadow in the man was lifted. His playfulness allowed him to reattach himself again to the unconditional acceptance of the virtue of his own existence, that sense of belongingness which every person hankers after and deserves. These days people call it 'being grounded'. Back then, though, it was just called being true to oneself.

"I have seldom seen a man or a woman change so dramatically or so swiftly from morose to mirthful as I did on that day. The process of clarification he went through was truly astonishing. One moment he was a man on the brink of self-annihilation. The next he was romping around on the beach like a kid without a worry in the world. He hardly said a word to me, except to say as he went his way finally that I had a really good dog."

Parker's gaze drifted over to Yellow Dog Red's headstone. To himself he mouthed the words written thereon: "Here at my feet my friend Yellow Dog Red lies, waiting for me in peace, always faithful."

"Most people underestimate the cathartic effect playing fetch can have," Parker resumed. "But every day with Red was like that. A catharsis. Every day, whether it was playing fetch, hiking in the hills, or going swimming, I saw or felt something new. Or, more often than not, I saw something familiar that I re-experienced in a new way. For me it was like wearing a pair of colored glasses that let me see behind ordinary every day reality. In fact, all things considered," he shrugged, "she was probably a better Intelligence asset than I could have ever aspired to be."

"That sounds like your Google-Glasses, Dad," Angie piped up. But when Parker cocked his head and Angie realized that he had no idea of what she spoke, she explained. "Google-Glasses. They're glasses with a built-in computer in them that let people connect to the Internet. My dad has a beta pair that Sergei gave him. They're really cool. They let him search for things as he's doing them. Except," she added, "my friends think it's creepy when he videos them while they're talking to me and uploads them to YouTube. Show him yours, Dad."

"Apple, I am certain Mr. Parker does not want to be bothered with exotic gizmos," demurred Bahram.

"No, I'd like to see them," said Parker. "I mean, your daughter has already surveilled the whole cemetery with technology I can't begin to understand."

Bahram shrugged. "Very well," he said, and, reaching under the lapel of his suit, he withdrew a pair of what looked to Parker like the protective goggles he wore when operating his chainsaw. "Would you like to try them on?" Bahram said, extending the clunky-looking object to Parker.

Parker took up the glasses and inspected them. Then he handed them back to Bahram. "Maybe some other time," he said. "But I think I might have liked to have had them a while ago..." His voice trailed off as a pained expression dashed across his face.

"Why?" Angie, her curiosity piqued, inquired. "I mean, why did you need them a while ago?"

Parker let a sigh escape in reply, which he hoped would express his reasoning far more than any words could and leave it at that. Taking note of Parker's reluctance and also the pain in his face, Bahram nodded and replaced the glasses in his suit. Then he lifted his hand to Angie's shoulder. However, if his intent had been to squelch his daughter's inquisitiveness, it only exacerbated it and, shrugging him off, she persisted until, a minute later, Parker sighed again, this time in acquiescence.

"I was only speaking wishfully when I said that I could have used them a few months ago," he said, "in order for me to be able to see behind ordinary every day reality when, one day, Yellow Dog Red came up to me and pawed at my foot like she wanted me to do something for her. Mind you, this was at a time when she could hardly walk and was close to death. Dotty and I were looking through some old boxes in my attic for a Boy Scout Backpacking Merit Badge, because it was the one and only thing my wife Sylvia—who, if Angie hasn't told you, is in the last stages of Alzheimer Disease—had said that same day she remembered about our son. Even though she didn't even remember who our son was." Parker shook his head and shut his eyes, letting his gaze turn inward as he spoke.

"Yellow Dog Red was completely blind and almost deaf," he continued. "But she wouldn't stop pestering me. 'What's up, old girl?' I said finally in exasperation.

"I don't know how to explain this exactly without it sounding made-up," he enunciated slowly, with his eyes still shut, "because it still doesn't make any sense to me. Not unless I believe animals can contact spirits and transcend time and space. But that day," he continued, "it was like Red had heard a voice that led her, with me and Dotty following behind, out of the house and across the field to the shed where I keep my tools.

"When Red got inside she went straight to the mulcher at the back of the shed. Like I said, she was as blind as a bat. But it seemed she could see exactly where she was going. Then she started whining and pawing at a metal plate I had put over the floorboards forty years earlier to catch oil from leaking into the ground. Thinking that she had smelled a bone there from long ago, I moved the mulcher aside and lifted the pad expecting to see one. Instead there was a plastic sandwich bag. Tad's badge was in it, and a note written in his hand." Parker fell silent.

He had opened his eyes when confiding this last part. But although they were open and his gaze was directed at Bahram, it was clear to the latter that Parker's gaze was focused not on the present but to another time far removed. Bahram squirmed uneasily and, having already grown disquieted in the telling of such a personal story, he redirected his gaze to the bottom of his teacup. "Perhaps we should go, Apple," he murmured.

Angie ignored her father's remark. "What did the note say?" she inserted, her voice quivering with anticipation.

Parker blinked his eyes in rapid succession to clear his visual field of the past. He then refocused his gaze onto Bahram and tilted his head in question, to which Bahram shrugged as if to say, "Might as well go on."

Parker nodded. Then to Angie, he said, "It said, 'Dad, in case I'm gone Yellow Dog Red is the password you'll need to get past the tree spirit who protects my tree fort.'"

"What's so odd about that?" asked Bahram. "I myself had many secret passwords to get past jinns when I was a boy."

Parker nodded in acknowledgment, then said, "It's odd only because my son died forty years ago. The note was dated three days before he drowned in Yosemite. And I named my dog Yellow Dog Red fifteen years ago. Fifteen years before I even knew of the note and the password's existence."

Angie's eyes opened wide. "How did Tad know he wasn't coming back? How did he know you would name your dog Yellow Dog Red?"

"I asked Yellow Dog Red those very same questions."

"What did she say?"

"Let's play fetch. She had this tennis ball with bells in it that she could hear wherever I threw it. It was the last time we played fetch. She died the next day..." Parker's voice trailed off into a wince.

"It's too sad," Bahram sighed, then added, "My father, who was Ambassador to Luxembourg, had a similar experience when he discovered his great grandfather had written a note on the back of a picture that was taken of the exact spot in front of the hotel where my father was assassinated forty years later. It said, 'A very bad place to stay.'"

"You never told me that about Grandpa," Angie said.

Bahram shrugged. "It is not a child's tale," he replied.

Angie stretched her arms and rubbed her eyes, which, rather than excitement, showed the real fear of a young girl. "All this is making me tired. I better go do my homework," she said.

Stifling a yawn, more to demonstrate nonchalance to Angie than to express tiredness, Bahram looked down at his watch. Then, to Parker, he said, "And how long do you plan to stay here with Yellow Dog Red?"

"Until the owners of this property acknowledge that the cemetery is sacred ground that can't be disturbed."

"For my daughter's sake, I hope that happens before hell freezes over."

Parker nodded. "It could be a long winter."

"Not if my daughter has anything to do with it," he said. "Let's go, Apple. I do not want to miss my Skype."

Angie perked up. "Is it with Slag?"

"It is."

"Can I talk to him?" And when Bahram frowned, she added, "I only want to ask him one question about if he remembers meeting Yellow Dog Red in San Francisco."

Bahram sighed. "One question only." Then he turned to Parker. "I am sorry for your losses, Parker, and for your wife's condition. May God go with her and your son. And with your dog. Life sometimes rains down burdens as well as partnerships on us for purposes only God can know. I am only glad for my daughter, now that I have met you, that she has made your acquaintance. I can think of no better use of her time in learning how to become fully human than by keeping vigil with you over Yellow Dog Red." Then he winked. "Know that I am also your ally. But for many reasons I must stay out of it."

"Of course," Parker said unsurely, for he was uncertain if the wink had been conspiratorial or friendly.

Shortly after daybreak the next day, activity on the Pound property renewed with a vengeance. The first to arrive on the scene was the bulldozer operator who had uprooted the bay tree the night before. Additionally, he had brought with him a 10-yard dump truck and a truck hauling a Caterpillar excavator. After unloading the Caterpillar, he motored it up the driveway to a point opposite the veterinarian's house not far from where the bulldozer was parked. The dump truck, backing up the whole way, followed behind.

The excavator operator dismounted his vehicle as did the dump-truck driver and, along with the bulldozer operator, gathered in a circle to confer for several minutes. Then at precisely 8:00am, just after the sun had risen over the mountains to the east, the three donned their hard hats and climbed aboard their respective rigs. The John Deere bulldozer took the lead. Starting at the northwest corner of the house, it began to bulldoze its way through the farmhouse, flattening, splintering, crushing and shattering everything in its path.

While this was occurring, the excavator went in the opposite direction to the uprooted bay laurel stump where, lifting the stump with a grappling attachment, it transported the remains of the bay over to the dump truck and deposited the stump therein. Then the excavator turned back toward the house, where it began grappling the demolished materials into the truck bed.

The next to arrive were the two surveyors, Bill and Howard. They steered clear of the cemetery and the demolition scene and, rather than beginning their survey from their previous starting point, they started from the southwest corner of the property at the crest of the hill, well west of the cemetery. It was then that Parker saw Roper and his crew at the opposite side of the property pull their mulcher and small dump truck up the driveway below the now mostly destroyed house.

Even from his vantage several hundred feet removed, Parker gathered from Roper's bearing and his earnest gesturings that he was displeased the bay tree's stump had been uprooted. This assessment was borne out a few minutes later when Roper, with Parker-the-dog loping behind him, strode with a purposeful gait into the cemetery. The first words out of his mouth after nodding a terse greeting to Parker were, "I can't believe those fucking assholes! I go away for a few days and the owners purposely destroy a potentially historic site!" he yelled in exasperation. "I told them personally that they needed to leave it intact, and they assured that me they would. But then...but then," he ranted, with spittle forming in the corners of his mouth, "they went ahead and had some clueless dickhead from out of county come in the middle of the night and uproot the goddamn stump and destroy the scene." He shook his head in disbelief and removed his blue and white baseball cap—a new one, Parker noted—that read, "Architects do it with pencils."

"Correct me if I'm wrong," Parker replied, "but weren't you the one who told me the new owners were not nice people?"

Roper nodded ruefully. Then, seeing the skeptical rise of Parker's brow, he added, "But the thing is they do pay well. Very well, in fact. And on time. That's not usually the case with a lot of wineries. If they don't stiff you altogether, they drag out payments for as long as they can. And anyway," he concluded, "once I finish with my degree, I'm getting out of this business, and, oh, marrying my girlfriend..."

While Roper was speaking this last, Parker became distracted as Parker-the-dog went over and stretched herself out on her back on Yellow Dog Red's grave. Seeing his namesake arrayed thus, a pang of sorrow seized Parker as he recalled the day fifteen years earlier when he had gone down to Salinas to pick up the puppy that would become Yellow Dog Red; for he only just now realized that the son of the breeder had been wearing a Boy Scout uniform that day on which was affixed the same backpacking merit badge of his son's that Parker had found in the toolshed fifteen years later.

The memory of the badge also suddenly brought back the conversation he and Sylvia—shortly before the onset of her Alzheimers—had had on that day, in which the breeder, a woman named Kelly, had asked them if they had picked out a name for the dog yet. Sylvia had ventured a few tentative names—Puddle, Lizzie, Violet—which, if they had stuck, would have become the dog's name. But Kelly, knowing the dog's nature better than Sylvia, had accepted each of the names with a doubtful shrug and a polite scoff. Then, addressing herself to Sylvia solely, she had said, "Before you give her a name, you need to look at your girl. Look at her closely. Find out who she is. Then tell me what you see."

Sylvia had then done just that. And what she saw was a very cute fluff ball of yellow fur with a drop of bright red blood from the index finger the puppy had begun to gnaw on while curled in the crook of her husband's arm. Her reply to Kelly had communicated those facts. And Kelly's reply had been to throw down in a single gulp the last slugs of beer from the can she had just opened and, crushing the can, to gesticulate stridently with the crushed can for Sylvia to finish her thought process. In response to Kelly's gesture, the first three words out of Sylvia's mouth had been, "Yellow Dog Red," at which point the puppy had suddenly stopped its gnawing and rolled over onto its back.

"That's it! That's her name!" both Parker and Kelly had exclaimed in unison before the words were even out of Sylvia's mouth.

And now, fifteen years later, Yellow Dog Red was about the only name Sylvia, out of the thousands she had once known, remembered; for despite that her past was sinking inexorably deeper into the murky plaque of tarry forgetfulness that was dementia, she never failed to ask Parker on his visits to her if Yellow Dog Red was house broken yet.

Parker was nudged from this momentary reverie when he heard Roper, with a note of urgency in his voice, ask him if he was okay.

"Yes...yes. I'm fine. Why?"

"You seem totally lost in thought. I thought maybe you were having a stroke."

Parker smiled and shook his head. "Thanks for your concern. I appreciate it. But I was just thinking about those kids who're helping me with the vigil," he fibbed. "Did you hear that Angwin, the little girl with the cameras, was almost run over on her skateboard?"

"Doesn't surprise me much," Roper replied, although with an almost pained expression. "I've had to drive past them on these skinny roads more than a few times. And my girlfriend had one of them actually grab onto her rear bumper and draft for over a mile down the road behind her. So, I'd say they're pretty reckless. Inviting vegetative brain death, all of them."

"Speaking of recklessness, what's your plan of attack today?" queried Parker, for Roper's tone had reminded him of both Angie and Squirrel's expressions of fearlessness in the face of insuperable odds.

A spiritless smile spread across Roper's face in appreciation at Parker's attempt to buoy his spirits. "We're going to clear the area above the knoll and work our way west to the ridge and back south this way. Why?"

"Just wondering. Do you remember the boy, the one they call Squirrel?"

"The one who lives in trees? And who hates me? Sure. How could I forget him? But why do you ask?"

"I guess because the way you just said something reminds me of him."

"What! He detests everything he thinks I stand for."

"I know. But while you were away, he went through the area you logged and had some sort of ceremony at each stump."

"Oh yeah, I was wondering what those symbols were as I was coming over to see you," he said. "All the stumps have them. Written in mud.

Looks like the number 30 inside a circle." He then picked up a twig and drew the design in the dirt beside Yellow Dog Red. Parker-the-dog then instantly took the twig into her mouth and began chomping on it.

"30?" Parker tilted his head inquisitively. Then he took the twig from out of the puppy's mouth and drew a curved line, like a smile, and a dot, above the number Roper had drawn: ॐ.

"Is this what you saw?"

"That's it. Do you know it?"

Parker nodded, and handed the twig back to Parker-the-dog. "It's a symbol for a sound used in mantras. I'm sure you'll know it when you hear it." Parker then pursed his lips as if to speak the letter "O" and emitted instead a resonant, elongated nasal tone, which he let dwindle until his breath had been extended into a soundless "M."

"Sure, that's 'OM.' Sam—Samantha, my girlfriend—chants it after doing her yoga."

Parker nodded again. "Hindus believe that consciousness took the form of a vibration as creation began. OM symbolizes in Sanskrit the reflection of the absolute reality without beginning or end, and embraces all that exists."

Roper scratched his head then replaced his cap. "So, you think Squirrel was just wishing the life force, the consciousness, or whatever is in those trees godspeed or something?"

"Something like that. Paying them respect for their sacrifice, I'd say."

Roper nodded his head slowly. "I do something like that every time I cut down a tree. Seems only right to pay respect to something I'm about to kill."

"See what I'm saying? The same but different."

Roper knitted his brows, then bowed his head uncertainly. "Got it. But I still say he hates me."

Parker shrugged. "As an aspiring architect, you probably already know that repulsion and attraction are generated from the same antecedent and are equal to each other, only in reverse. So, in a Newtonian universe, tension supports underpinning, and underpinning supports tension. And in a human universe hate supports love, and love supports hate... Aha!..." Parker blurted suddenly, as he diverted his glance from the drawing in the dirt, to the engraving on C's headstone, then back again. "So that's what that fragment is. It's the bottom half of that." He poked his boot into Roper's drawing and then pointed his hand at the design on C's marker."

"Hmm...I think you might be right," Roper said, examining both. So, C's owner was either a Buddhist or a Hindu?"

"So it would seem," Parker said.

At that point, Roper's foreman, a tall gangly Mexican who couldn't have been over eighteen, called out to Roper and pointed to the knoll where the bay had stood. Roper nodded, then, to Parker, sighed. "Gotta go," he said, and, raising his voice to be heard above the din of the bulldozer and excavator, added, "By the way, Parker, I plan on proposing to my girlfriend in March."

"Congratulations," Parker replied.

Roper nodded. "Yeah. It's long overdue. We've been with each other for four years."

"Are there any kids? I mean, from previous marriages?"

Roper shook his head. "No such luck, and she can't have kids. But we're planning to start working with an adoption agency soon after we're married." Donning the extra hard hat that his helper had brought over with him, he began to make his way across the cemetery. Before he had gone ten steps, however, he turned back. "I'd like you to come to the wedding, if you're interested."

"I'd be honored," Parker said, and to him it felt like the truest thing he had said and felt for many a day. "When is it?"

"A month after I become an architect, which should be pretty soon."

The next couple of weeks were taken up with the demolition of the Gainsaid Pound house and kennels, and the only thing that remained of either by the middle of the month was the concrete pad that had underlain the kennel. That was then taken care of in short order when the bulldozer was affixed with a rake that obliterated every last trace of any fixed structures and underground plumbing. Additionally, the dozer uprooted the stumps Roper's crew left behind and, with its rake attachment, scraped the existing vineyard of its old vines, as well as the hillside from which the trees had been cut of all but the smallest shrubs, in preparation for preparing the land for Pinot Noir grapes.

Each morning Roper came by with his puppy, and each evening he trudged over to fetch him. It was in the evenings that Parker the man could see most clearly the progressively damaging toll the job was taking on Roper; for by the second week Roper eschewed almost all conversation with Parker and did not bother to come by during his lunch break or during other breaks in the workday to play with his dog. Furthermore, Roper's bearing at the end of the day had begun to take on the characteristics of someone who was in the process of being flattened by a heavy burden; that is, his demeanor grew more gloomy with each passing day, and the optimism in his step evaporated inversely in the face of the arboreal carnage he was overseeing.

It was Parker's estimation that what was occurring in Roper was that the fulcrum balancing his professionalism against his morals had suddenly shifted, and he had begun judging his actions more harshly as being less morally justifiable than they had been before the owners had shown themselves to be less than moral actors themselves. Parker suspected that this was so, based not on anything Roper said but on his own experience when just such a shift had occurred in himself when Army Intelligence's political atmospherics began to supercede their on-the-ground facts, leaving him with having to choose between doing what he thought was politically convenient or what he knew personally to be right.

Nevertheless, or perhaps because of this internal conflict and its resultant withdrawal into depression, Roper and his crew made exceptionally fast work of the rest of the forest of trees, and thus by the third week of January all the trees, as well as all the stumps, had been removed, save for those inside the perimeter of the cemetery.

Normally in this part of the world with its Mediterranean climate January is the wettest month. But this year only half an inch of rain fell. So, by the beginning of February the whole two hundred acres, minus the five in the graveyard, was dry enough to have been scraped and tilled and generally made ready for the winery buildings and for the planting of the vines.

Parker himself had gone about his regular routine of grooming the cemetery's graves and making the pathways through them passable, paying as little attention as was possible to the surrounding carnage. Keeping his head down so to speak, he had neither sought nor heard anything from the land's new owners, their lawyers, or any local officials about eviction, and he began to wonder if, in fact, the void in contact was actually part of their plan; that is, to move ahead with their project and leave the development of the cemetery until last, in the hope that if they waited long enough Parker would lose interest, become isolated, succumb to some illness, or simply die outright of old age. Of these possibilities, only the last, to Parker's mind, held out any promise of being realized.

Dotty continued to come by every other afternoon bearing food and drink and, lately, a back rub; for Parker's back, being that he was so tall, not to mention that his spine had buckled predictably beneath eighty years of gravity's unrelenting pull, was barely holding up under the task of landscaping five acres of neglected forest land. Early in February while sprucing up a large marble headstone he knew he should not have attempted to move alone, he threw his back out.

The day afterward Parker stayed down with back spasms, and Dotty arrived late in the afternoon to find him stretched out flat on his back on the futon sofa. His arms were extended into the air and he was staring upward at the screen of the cell phone he held in his hands. The contours of his face were twisted in pain as though the phone had bitten him. Dotty guessed instantly that he must have received a call concerning Sylvia.

"Parker, is something wrong?" she said, before she had had a chance to lower her basket of food and clean clothes to the table.

Saying nothing in reply at first and unable to raise himself to sitting to greet Dotty, Parker rolled over onto his hands and knees and, grabbing onto the nearest chair, pulled himself with great difficulty into it. Beads of sweat glistened on his brow, and his breathing was labored from the effort. His eyes were glazed and his gaze peered unfocused into the distance.

Although alarmed by his silence and the inability of Parker to raise himself to standing, and seeing how uncomfortably erect he was sitting, Dotty held her tongue; for she was well aware that he did not like to be badgered about his health.

Only when he was situated more comfortably on the chair did Parker finally respond to Dotty's presence. "Sylvia...is...gone," he murmured softly, elongating each nearly breathless word as though it were too precious for him to release.

A vacuum formed around her and Parker, and all Dotty could do was sigh. And once the rarified meaning of the words Parker had spoken sank in, "Oh, no," was all she could finally manage to say. Then, putting the basket aside, she skirted around the side of the table and knelt down beside Parker.

"Did you just find out?" she said, laying one hand on his knee and with the other lifting the phone Parker had left on the futon onto the table.

Parker nodded absently and cringed in pain from the motion. "Less than a minute before you arrived."

"I'm so sorry," whispered Dotty, whose eyes filled instantly with tears. "How?"

"Aspiration...during her afternoon nap. There was nothing they could do. Sylvia made sure," he continued, wincing in pain sheathed with grief at each word, "that before she could no longer decide for herself, she wanted to have a DNR directive in place so...so..." The barrenness of Parker's tone did not begin to match his expression, however, for Parker's face was ravaged by a look of abject sorrow. "But it was a good way for her to go," he added. "Butterscotch pudding was her favorite."

"Mine too," Dotty blurted, before she realized how imbecilic the remark was.

Parker managed a wan smile and nodded. "Mine too, it so happens."

"Is there anything I can do?" Dotty said, glad Parker had let her anxious response pass.

Parker shook his head. "Don't think so. Thanks. All the arrangements are in place." He raised his eyes and focused his gaze for the first time to meet Dotty's. "Unless you want to go view her."

She shook her head sharply. "No. I don't want to. I can't. I want to remember her as she was," Dotty replied, dabbing her eyes with her fingers. "A vibrant, happy-go-lucky woman."

"Yes, a vibrant woman," echoed Parker. But as he raised his arm to wipe away a tear, his breath caught and his expression caved in upon itself beneath the pummeling of an upwelling back spasm.

Seeing the pain seize his face, Dotty decided Sylvia's death couldn't be entirely the cause of it. "What did you do to yourself, Parker? You look like you've got the world's worst toothache."

He shook his head. "Back spasms."

"Did it happen just now? When the hospital called?" she said.

He shook his head again and winced at the pain incurred by the movement. "No, yesterday afternoon."

"Well, I think we need to get you to a doctor," she stated. "Do you think you could have a slipped disk or a pinched nerve? Can you walk? Or do I need to call an ambulance?" she asked, in quick succession. But when Parker tilted his head in a gesture Dotty took to be one of appreciation mixed with mild annoyance, she caught herself from asking more questions.

"No doctors," he said firmly, which was an answer, stopping just short of crossness, Dotty knew would be forthcoming the moment she had made the proposal; for, like Max, Parker was of a generation of self-contained men who, having seen far too many VA medical practitioners, disdained seeing doctors of any ilk under all but the most dire circumstances.

"I'll be all right in a day or two. A week at the most. I'm taking aspirin, which usually does it for me. But," he added, "if you can, could you bring me some ice the next time you come? That would be helpful."

I will. I'll bring ice tomorrow," Dotty said, noting that Parker's clothes were rumpled and that he had not shaved for several days, both of which gave him the grizzled-old-man look favored by the self-described survivalist, MacLamore was his name, who lived at the end of the road. She didn't really know the man, but she disliked him and how he looked nonetheless, mainly because, she supposed, every time she ran into him he was wearing camouflage clothing and tried to engage her in talk of black op helicopters and of a conspiracy by the Federal Reserve to take away her right to bear arms. She knew it was not her place to say anything to Parker about his own appearance, though, especially since he was injured and was probably having trouble even getting dressed or shaving, and instead she said, "What about Sylvia?"

"What about her? She's gone," uttered Parker, in a tone whose sparseness startled Dotty; for it was really nothing more than an echo of a sorrow that had reached its zenith years earlier and had come around finally to roost on numbness.

"Well...I mean...You have papers to sign. Make arrangements...Go to the mortuary...Tend to..." She found herself stammering, for despite her longtime friendship with Parker she now felt like an intruder infringing on a wholly private moment.

The contours of Parker's face suddenly began to relax as the current wave of spasms was finally loosening its grip on his spine. "Most were made five years ago," he said, exhaling tentatively in relief. "The Neptune Society will take care of the rest. If worse comes to worst, I could get a notary to come out and have me sign things. And the memorial...I think it can wait until I can safely leave Yellow Dog Red."

Unexpectedly Dotty found herself frowning and her face growing hot, and before she could censor herself, she blurted indignantly, "Your dog is more important than your wife? They're both dead, you know. What do you want? To be a hermit?" Parker furrowed his brows as much in surprise as in aggrievement at Dotty's outburst. "Oh, I'm so sorry, Parker," she cried, shuddering in regret. "You know I didn't mean that. I'm just too sad..." And as her voice trailed off she lowered her forehead to his knee and began weeping. "I'm just too sad," she repeated.

Parker rested his hand atop the back of Dotty's head, matching her tears with his own. Nothing was said between them for many minutes as each traversed independent paths along a diaphanous plateau of intermingled sorrow and grief. Finally, their tears spent, Parker patted Dotty's head.

"Yes, I know they are both dead," he murmured. "But the difference is that Sylvia is safe in death. And that her soul is at rest. I know that you know this is true because you are her friend. It is Yellow Dog Red's soul," he went on, "that is in danger of losing its resting spot. Like me with my time spent with Sylvia, and you with your time spent with Max, I cannot leave my friend until I know I have done all that I can to help protect her.

101

Otherwise, I have been unworthy of her friendship. It may be an old-fashioned sense of honor," he shrugged, "but you and I are old-fashioned. And you know me well enough to know I make no apologies for this."

Free from excruciating back pain for the moment, Parker was breathing easier, and he leaned back into a more relaxed position, as Dotty had by then also leaned back. "It is who I am," he resumed. "It is who I always wanted to be even when I did not know I wanted it. It is who I always will be. As for what I want," he concluded, taking a deep breath and gesturing toward Dotty and then to Yellow Dog Red's marker, "for myself it is only the friendships that I have formed. I consider them to be the only fortune I care about taking out of this life into the next. Into death. For these alone are, for me, the measure of my character and of the meaning of my life."

Dotty stood and, wiping her eyes and blowing her nose into one of the freshly washed tee shirts she had brought for Parker, glanced around the graveyard. It looked different to her somehow, in that she saw now what she had not seen as keenly before: that, in tending to the physical memories of these forgotten loved ones, Parker had maintained the dignity of the love he himself had brought to this life, and that he was, in effect, sustaining the loved ones' rightful honor. She recognized that Parker's vigil was not a protest against an injustice, as she had at first believed, but was an obligation—one he held sacred—he had taken up solely in the service of witnessing and upholding the honor due his best friend, Yellow Dog Red.

In realizing this fully for the first time—that is, in realizing its sacredness in her own heart—it explained to her finally why Parker had been able to draw the interest of the pre-adolescent children of the town to his cause; they had seen in him the idealism of their own innocence expressed in adult actions that were, like their own ideals of innocence, righteous in their tactics and selfless in their goals. That is, in the world into which they were entering, where hustlers of every stripe posed as Pied

102

Piper's, he was to them honorable. The real deal. Not a phoney. Which is what Dotty realized she had always known about Parker, and that it was what had drawn Sylvia to him in the first place, but which she, in knowing Parker mainly through Max, had never really had the chance to see in isolation from everything else.

Dotty stood and looked down at Parker. His gray whiskers and rumpled clothing seemed more dignified now, and she realized that while nothing about him had changed, much in herself had, in particular her sense of loyalty toward him had redoubled. And for this she acknowledged to herself the debt she owed Sylvia; for it was Parker's loyalty to Sylvia that had made it possible for Dotty to take on Parker's vigil as her own. The Yellow Dog Red Overlook was no longer his vigil alone. Now it was hers too.

Dotty knew better than to address the coupling of these realizations and feelings directly, however; for to do so would only make Parker uncomfortable and put him in the position of having to downplay his importance. Instead, she said, "If you're okay here for awhile, I'd like to run back and get some ice right now. Tomorrow or even the day after seems too long to wait."

"That would be great," Parker replied. "And perhaps you'd like to share a glass of Port with me when you return. If I can sit up for that long, that is, and drink to the love of my life, our Sylvia."

"And to our Yellow Dog Red."

"And to our Max."

"And to us."

Parker's face lit up in a smile that was so full of light, and so diametrically opposed to his pained expression of only minutes earlier, Dotty almost didn't recognize it to be a smile until she remembered that it was the selfsame expression of appreciation she so looked forward to seeing at those times when he came into her dining room for his lemon bars; for it did indeed cast the room into light.

"I'll be right back," she said, and scooted down the hill.

The next day Parker's back, with help from Dotty's ice, felt good enough to him that he decided to limber up with a walk around the perimeter of the cemetery. On the second leg of the boundary, midway along its northern edge, at the opening that had marked the original entry to the grounds, he surveyed the expanse of tilled land where once had stood a house and kennel. As he looked to where a stand of locust and willow trees had stood, Parker happened to look down and notice a thin, pie-shaped slate rock sticking up from the disturbed earth. With his back barely flexible enough to bend, he hesitated to make the effort to inspect it. But since the rock was painted and there was some writing on it, he did so nonetheless; perhaps, he thought, it might have some value if it were to be the original sign designating the cemetery's entrance, in which case it could possibly be a marker establishing the time of the graveyard's inception. Instead, after straightening up very deliberately and brushing the dirt off with equal deliberation, he saw that the object was roughly quarter-circle-shaped, with a radius of eight inches. Forest-green in color, it contained six letters above its bottom border—"hester"—which themselves were punctuated with four bullet holes. Additionally, below the letters there was a half-circle with figures inside.

"Chester!" he murmured. "Chester. C's name is Chester," he repeated, trying it on for size several times; for he had realized, if only by the shape and color of the rock, that he had indeed come upon the missing part of C's headstone.

Summarily inspecting the depth of the bullet holes, he surmised that a .22-caliber had probably been the cause of them and of the breakage. A kids' game of target practice, he guessed, in which the kids, to hide their vandalism, had tossed the fragment aside. In any event, its discovery gave Parker a feeling of comfort in the knowledge that it closed the circle of Yellow Dog Red's closest neighbor.

Later that same day, shortly before Angie was scheduled to show up, Roper came by for the first time since he had finished with his work on the property. His arrival was preceded by Parker-the-dog, who, now that she was two months older and had reached the fall-all-over-herself-at-full-speed stage of puppy development, literally rolled to a stop at Parker's knee while he was temporarily taping Chester's missing portion back in place with duct tape and wooden braces. Roper, although not as loose-limbed as his dog, also seemed as he approached Parker to be far more at ease than he had been the last time the two had spoken. Parker also noticed that Roper's shoulders sagged under the weight of a seemingly full backpack.

Roper's greeting showed no signs of strain, however, and took the form of the cheerful injunction: "Say hello to the world's newest architect, Parker!"

"You passed your exam!" responded Parker with equal gladness.

Roper beamed. "I did. A week ago."

"Congratulations!" Parker said, but winced at the effort it took for him to stand and extend his hand for a handshake.

"Bad back?" Roper said, after taking Parker's hand and noting his grimace.

Parker nodded. "A landlubber, in way over his head. Wrenched it jumping down to tie a hawser to a dock in Panama... Long story," he added, shaking his head, "the price of misplaced enthusiasm in my misspent youth."

Roper drew his lips tight in empathy for Parker's pain, and said, "Well, I think I can safely say I've given my own back a reprieve. There'll be no more backbreaking tree-felling for me. I signed the papers yesterday that give my portion of the tree business to my brother."

Parker's brows rose, less in surprise to Roper's news than to the incongruous tone of amazement with which it had been delivered. "You don't say," he said, and because Roper's intonation had put him on guard, he added tentatively, "I would also think that makes Samantha happy, now that she won't have to worry about marrying someone whose back could go out any day."

Roper screwed his lips over to one side of his face in a gesture Parker recognized to be one of self-inflicted complicity. "Well," he said, twisting out of his backpack and placing it upright on the ground, "that's probably true. But not because of my line of work. You see, Parker," he spelled out while still conveying amazement, "The engagement is off. Roper and Sam are not going to happen. If anything, Sam and Becky are going to happen."

"Becky? Who's Becky?"

"Becky is Parker-the-dog's original owner. Remember? The woman who went to New Zealand to make wine."

Parker nodded. "Ah, yes, now I remember."

"Well, it turns out Becky has had a secret crush on Sam since college. And when I became licensed and there was nothing standing in the way of Sam and me getting married, Becky called Sam to congratulate her and confess to her..." Roper's voice trailed off and he shrugged. "The long and short of it is that the two of them decided to try and make a go of it together down under, in Queenstown. No pun intended," he added hastily.

"I'm sorry," Parker said, missing the pun. "It must be hard on you."

Roper shook his head. "No, not really. Relieved is probably closest to how I feel, I guess. Because I see now that there was actually a good reason why Sam and I were together all that time and never got married. She was in love with Becky and didn't know it. And," he said, acknowledging the presence of his backpack, "I'm out of work for the first time in fifteen years. Don't have a girlfriend. Don't have a place to stay. Don't—"

"And don't forget," Parker inserted, glancing down at Parker-the-dog who had begun to growl at and tug on the waist-strap of Roper's pack, "you have a friend."

Roper grinned drolly. "In other words, according to you I'm right where I need to be. Right?" he quipped.

Parker shrugged. "That depends on what you will make of it," he replied. "But if it's any help, I don't see any good reason why you and Parker can't stay here. I mean," he added, sweeping his arms in a gesture that took in the whole of the cemetery, "There's plenty of room. And what can they do? Evict us?"

Roper considered the offer for a moment, then said, "You know, I came here hoping that you'd take care of Parker for me for a bit until I found a place that'll take us. But hanging out here might be just what I need to do with myself right now. At least until you have Yellow Dog Red settled for good."

"*We*, you mean," Parker responded, pointedly correcting Roper. "Until *we* have Yellow Dog Red settled."

"Yes. *We*," answered Roper, and his face colored in acknowledgment of his assimilation into Parker's vigil. Meanwhile Parker-the-dog had yanked with all her might on his backpack, toppling it to the ground and sending her scurrying for refuge and to pee spontaneously between Roper's legs.

"It turns out," Roper said, tugging affectionately on Parker's ears, "I brought a backpacking tent intended for Parker to sleep in. But now that our residency is settled for the time being, how about if I pitch it for the two of us?"

"Over there would be good," Parker suggested, as he pointed toward two eight-foot-round boulders behind the WC that were enclosed within a copse of scraggly toyon. "You'll be hidden from view unless someone looks down from directly above."

Roper took Parker's suggestion and set up camp. As it happened, his residency couldn't have come at a better time; for Parker's stiff back was making it difficult for him to manage on his own the tasks that living in such rudimentary conditions brought to bear, the most important of which, to Parker at least, was seeing to it that the cemetery's grounds were tidied up. Thus the first thing Roper did after pitching his tent and throwing lunch together for himself and Parker was to screw a wooden brace onto the back of Chester's broken headstone, making the repair more or less permanent.

While they we savoring their handiwork over a cold beer, Angie came by, and as she approached the eastern boundary of the cemetery from the road both remarked at how Angie walked with a lightness to her step that made it seem like she was about to break into a skip. Upon their greeting, Parker was pleased to see that her wounds had healed, and that she seemed to radiate an intense happiness more in keeping with her age than with the premature adult seriousness she had brought to his vigil. No sooner had she come up to them and knelt down to take Parker-the-dog into her arms than the reason for her buoyancy became known.

"It's a song!" she blurted, shaking her head from side to side amid Parker's kisses.

"What's a song?" asked Parker, thinking she had referred to Squirrel's skateboard, which he thought he had overheard her say to Dotty was named "Kong."

"*Yellow Dog Red!* Slag wrote it. It's a song," she cried, stroking the downy belly Parker-the-dog had exposed to her. She then pulled her iphone from out of her day pack, as well as a round blue-plastic object about the same size and shape of a large muffin, the latter which she balanced atop Chester's reconstructed headstone. "Want to hear it?"

Without waiting for an answer, she tapped the glass panel of her phone several times, and a moment later a lustrous, almost milky melody emerged. The song, a lullaby it seemed, was carried across the cemetery on the wings of the dreamy lilting minor chords that Parker had come to associate with Irish female vocalists who sang soulful Celtic ballads as easily as they breathed. Except in this instance the lead vocalist's voice was unmistakable as belonging to Slag.

When after a minute or two the tune wound down into the wispy lapping of an Irish harp, Angie tapped her phone's screen again triumphantly. "Wow! Can you believe it! Slag did this!" she cried, unable to contain herself. "He e-mailed it to me last night. He says he wants to use it on their next CD. And he says he wants some of the money they make from it to go to the fund my dad wrote to him he would set up for us to keep Yellow Dog Red safe. He says—"

But when Angie paused a moment to catch her breath Parker interrupted her. "He says. He says. Does it matter only what Slag says?" His tone, though edgy, was devoid of any hint of stridency. Nevertheless, Angie, thinking Parker was rebuking her, was taken aback by it.

"What do you mean? It's Slag's song. He wrote it."

"Yes, Slag wrote it, but what I mean is, Does Yellow Dog Red have a say in it?"

Angie furrowed her brows in confusion. "You don't like the song?"

"No, I like it very much actually," responded Parker. "But the song isn't about me. It isn't about Slag either. How would you like it if Slag wrote a song about you that you didn't like?"

Angie shrugged. "Not much, I guess. But Yellow Dog Red is dead," she went on. "She can't say whether she likes the song or not."

Parker nodded and grimaced at once. "Yes, our friend is gone. But our memory of her does live on..." His voice trailed off and he shifted his position to a more comfortable angle of repose. When he spoke again into the awkward silence that ensued, his tone was exacting yet sympathetic. "Tell me, Angie, how would you like it if your father died and Slag came out with a song about him, saying that he was a swindler?"

"My dad's not a swindler," Angie replied, and by the heat in her reply Parker knew it was not the first time she had heard such a charge leveled against Bahram.

"But if Slag sang that it is so," Parker went on, "that your father was a swindler, then millions of people who don't know your father would believe that what Slag sang is true. That Bahram had been a swindler."

Angie's enthusiasm, having slowly collapsed under Parker's comments, now turned to sullen frustration. "So you're saying I should go e-mail Slag and tell him not to sing about Yellow Dog Red," she said glumly, "because she's dead and can't defend herself."

"That's not what I said," Parker replied, and seeing that Angie was growing sulky, and realizing that he had been too austere, his tone became paternal. "First off, I think it's a lovely tribute by a lovely man to a lovely dog. And I would like him to know that, as Yellow Dog Red's best friend, that is how I feel about him and his song. But the second thing is something I have thought about throughout all my professional life: What might be the unintended consequences of an act, or in this case a song, however well-intentioned it is?"

"People will love it. They'll download it. We'll use that money to save the cemetery."

Parker nodded. "Yes, those are the intended consequences. But how will the new owners of the property react, especially if they are blind-sided by it?"

At this Angie rocked back on her haunches to consider Parker's concerns. It was only then that she noticed that her bluetooth speaker was atop C's now repaired headstone. "C is Chester?" she said, as much to buy time as to recognize the change in the cemetery. "Where did you find the missing piece?"

"Over there," Parker said, frowning in pain as he pointed to the spot. "It was unearthed by the bulldozer."

"What's wrong with you?" Angie said, noticing Parker's discomfort for the first time.

"Too much gardening for an old man," Parker replied, and nodded to the grave of the dog named "Pixie" he had been grooming when his back had gone out.

"Why don't you let me help you with that," Roper said, but not as a question. "It'll bring up the property values."

"Me too," Angie said. "I love to garden." To which Parker tilted his head uncertainly. "See, that's your problem, Parker," Angie said. "You think this is your job." She gestured to encompass the graveyard. "But it's not. It's become my job too. And Squirrel's. And Slag's. And Dotty's. And my skateboard friends'. If you'll let us, we all want to help."

"But only if you ask us," Roper inserted.

Parker sighed. "I confess that one of the hardest things for me to do in life has been to ask others for help," he said. "Because I was taught that to be self-sufficient was the highest calling for a man...but..." His words failed him as he tried to go on, and his shoulders drew up around his ears and his chest caved inward. But no more words came. And his eyes miostened with tears until finally he nodded and, in response to some inner voice, said, "Yes, I need your help. And I want your help."

"Does that mean you want Slag to sing Yellow Dog Red?"

Parker nodded. "But first I want you to help me groom these graves so that Yellow Dog Red's memory lives on in a nice place. And before I say yes to the song, I'd like to write or talk to Slag myself. I also want to get in touch with the property's owner and let him know what we're doing."

"That's probably a good idea," Roper nodded. "Because my sense of him tells me that if he thinks there's a potential he'll be caught off-guard by a lot of publicity, he might just initiate trouble for you...for us, I mean. In any event, once the song comes out it's probably going to go viral," Roper said.

Parker tilted his head questioningly. "How can a song get sick?"

"He means the song will sell like hotpies on itunes," Angie explained.

"Hotpies? Itunes?"

"Hotcakes. It'll sell like hotcakes on the Apple music store. On the Internet."

At that point, Roper stood and walked around the boulder to where his tent was hidden from view, followed closely by Parker-the-dog. When he came back a few minutes later, he was bearing a food dish filled with kibble and another filled with water. With each of Roper's steps, Parker-the-dog bounded backwards in excitement and then tumbled over onto her back only to scramble immediately to her feet again. To Angie's quizzical expression, Roper informed her that he had given up his job, his fiancee, and that he had moved onto the property until things settled down for him. The commiseration in Angie's response to Roper's litany of travails was quickly replaced by a smile when she realized what Roper's residency meant; that Parker-the-dog would be there when she came to see Parker-the-man. But then the smile sank immediately into a frown.

"Squirrel is not going to be happy about it," she said, directing her gaze toward Roper as he told Parker to sit. "He's really depressed about all the trees being chopped down."

"I know. He thinks I'm a butcher," Roper said, shaking his head. "But maybe by helping Yellow Dog Red I can make it up to him...Parker, sit!" he intoned gravely after Angie had raised her brows skeptically at the suggestion. Then, when Parker had obeyed, Roper chirped, "Good dog, Parker! That's sit." And he laid down the dog dishes, which the puppy attacked as though she hadn't eaten in a week instead of the five hours it had actually been.

"Good dog, Parker!" Angie repeated, then said, "Squirrel holds grudges. He gets along better with trees than he does with people. So it'll take a lot for him to change. And as long as you kill trees..." She shrugged.

"Killed trees. Past tense. Remember, I said I quit. Perhaps you could tell Squirrel when you see him," he continued, "that I said people can forgive a tree when it falls on them. So why can't he forgive a person when he fells a tree?"

"That doesn't make sense to forgive a person who fells a tree. A tree doesn't decide to kill a person when it tips over. It happens by accident. The roots rot or the wind pushes it. But a person who fells a tree does decide to kill the tree. It's no accident. It's a choice." Angie crossed her arms in a manner that communicated the certainty of her moral high-ground.

"Felling trees was my job. And having a job means having to kill something, whether its only the time you have left to live, or, in my case, trees. Look at it this way," he said, watching as his puppy flipped over her food dish with her snout in search of more kibble. "I have to pay my workers, and they have mouths to feed. What if I decide to not cut trees and, because of my decision to save the lives of the trees, I can't pay my workers' salaries, and then they can't buy food, which incidentally has also been killed by someone in order to make it into food, causing their children to die of starvation? Would the trees I saved from death think I was doing my job? Or would they think I was murdering children?"

"Hold on you two! Too much talk of killing, whether by design or chance," intoned Parker, whose voice conveyed an appeal more than a reproach. "Death is the same door to all those who have passed through it. And we all do pass through it sooner or later. And so we the living should have more respect for those who have passed through before us and are buried here. The least we can do is close the door behind them." He brought the palms of his hands together as though he were closing leaves in a book. "And it's the least they deserve from us for the lives they led only so they could make ours richer."

Together Roper and Angie nodded sheepishly in recognition that their quarrel was at best banal, and that Squirrel's problems with trees were of his own making, not theirs.

"That settles it then," Roper said, gathering up Parker's dishes. "If it's all right with you, Parker, I'm going to get to work right now and go set Pixie upright. The way that headstone leans over has bothered my sense of order from the first day I came in here."

"I'll help," chimed Angie. "Pixie was probably as good a dog to her owner as Yellow Dog Red was to Parker.

"They were all good dogs," Parker replied, and waved his hand toward Pixie's grave in a gesture of thanks.

Whereupon Roper and then Angie sidestepped the now slumbering puppy in order to get over to Pixie's grave. Once there, they lowered their shoulders to the headstone that had betrayed Parker's back and, using their legs to propel their combined masses, they put their backs into it. With this leverage and their combined energy, the headstone gave way with an abrupt release of resistance, and a few minutes later Angie and Roper had shored it up with stones and dirt so that it stood plumb again.

"There, that should improve the neighborhood," Roper said, turning to Angie, who was already in the process of replaying *The Yellow Dog Red Lullaby*, as it would come to be called, on her bluetooth speaker, whose first stanza—"Here at my feet my friend Yellow Dog Red lies, waiting for me in peace, always faithful, always true..."—wafted sleepily into the air.

The following weeks saw winter return with a vengeance, as storm after storm passed through, dumping another ten inches of rain. This kept Angie and even Dotty away, and Parker had to rely on Roper to transport his laundry and Dotty's cooked meals and their spent containers back and forth. Roper's presence also made it possible for Parker to leave the cemetery on three occasions in order to make the unexpected but necessary last minute arrangements for Sylvia's body to be cremated, and for her ashes to be placed in the urn she had picked out for herself before her dementia had set in. On that same occasion he swung by his house and removed their son Tad's ashes from its repository in an alcove off to the side of the fireplace and brought it and Sylvia's urn back with him to the trailer.

It was during the last and the most violent of the storms during that rainy period that an equally violent storm lashed Parker from within, as he wrestled all night with the decision of whether or not he wanted to—or should—spread Sylvia's ashes and their son Tad's in the same spot he had determined over the last month that he wanted his own; that is, admixed into the dirt atop Yellow Dog Red's grave. The major decisions he needed to make for himself were: Would it be sacrilegious of him to inter their ashes with a dog's remains? And, Would Tad or Sylvia have wanted that for themselves? knowing, as Parker did, that Sylvia and he had designated their chosen resting spot to be the place where Parker had proposed marriage to her: Drakes Bay.

It was only shortly before sunrise after the rain had let up following a long sleepless night of indecision, that he did finally make up his mind; he decided that two-thirds of his family's ashes would be laid to rest right there where they could be together with Yellow Dog Red. The remaining thirds would be combined when Parker himself died, into one urn whose contents would go into Drakes Bay. Thus resolved, he gathered one urn under each arm and opened the door of the trailer with the intent of taking them to Red's grave.

Parker had expected it to be stormy, but once outside he was greeted instead by a cloudless sunrise, the first one in weeks. Bending over gingerly from his lack of activity and sore back, he extracted from out of the bucket beside the trailer in which his gardening tools were stored a three-pronged digging trowel. He also pulled out a rolled up three-foot-square of plastic to place on the ground to keep his knees dry. He surveyed his surroundings in the budding light and was pleased to see that the overnight monsoonal rains had brought out the buttercups in such sudden profusion that their yellow flowers, having sprung open all at once, floated above the carpet of new grass and supplicating milkmaids like happy little cherubs in the fledgling dawn. In a word, the view was inspiring, and to Parker it was a sigil signifying that his decision had been the right thing to do by Tad and Sylvia.

He wanted the disposition of the ashes to be a private occasion, and because of this he moved as soundlessly as was possible from the trailer to Yellow Dog Red's side, in the hope he would rouse neither Roper or Parker. He lowered the trowel and unrolled the tarp onto the ground so that they fell without a sound on the grass beside Yellow Dog Red's headstone. He then let down the urns, and, once he was satisfied they were stable on the wet surface, he lowered himself to kneeling. He then picked up the trowel and dragged it slowly across the longitudinal surface of Yellow Dog Red's mound in order to furrow the earth without making any scraping noises. Then he picked up Tad's urn and unscrewed the lid.

The tarnished brass was cold against his palm, yet when he laid the lid aside the imprint of moisture the palm and his fingers left on the rounded top was a comforting reminder to him that despite its hardness the metallic barrier separating himself from the remains of his loved one was yet only another form of light, and as such was capable of being impressed by the film of life's dreams no matter how far removed in time or space or composition. Thus Parker was more than a little surprised to find that, when he reached into the urn to extract a handful of Tad's ashes, the ashes had clumped over the years and were as warm in his hand as if the life they had once held was still extant in their now sterile mixture of chemicals.

Parker sprinkled Tad's ashes evenly into the eight four-foot long, two-inch-deep furrows that retained their shapes in the wet clay soil. Then he removed two more handfuls and did the same with them before twisting the lid back onto the urn, leaving it one-third full. The removal of Sylvia's ashes from her urn proved infinitely more difficult for Parker, however; for unlike Tad's, hers were as cold and clammy as damp mortar, and he wondered if perhaps the undertaker hadn't mixed some sort of embalming compound in with them in order to keep them from clumping. In any case, it caused a frisson of fear to seize Parker, which unlike the comforting warmth of Tad's ashes, produced an unwelcome shudder of recognition in him—that death's imminent nearness was as yet too close for him to be able to form a perspective upon the visage whose most prominent feature was terror.

Thus, panic gripped him, and Parker found he could neither withdraw his hand from the urn, or breathe. He had always been a man insusceptible to such attacks, but now death seemed disconcertingly near and Parker was all of a sudden faced with the abrupt reality that he was himself dying. He moved his lips in an effort to shout out that he wasn't ready to die, and his eyes darted from side to side seeking a handhold on which to keep himself from sinking into the earth. He felt the tips of his fingers grow numb on Sylvia's urn, while oppositely, he felt shame for being afraid to let go of the inevitable. Simultaneously he heard his name called out from above. "Parker?" And for a split second Parker thought the voice was that of God calling him home.

When Parker did not—indeed could not—respond to this ecclesiastic summons, the voice repeated his name, only this time with a note of urgency. "Parker!"

"What?" Parker finally managed to croak, after inhaling the first air into his lungs in over two minutes and after deciding it was not God's voice he had heard.

"Are you okay?"

Parker craned his head upward so that he was looking directly above him to where, forty feet up in the crown of a eucalyptus tree, stood a person on a limb. In the blaze of dawn's first light he saw it was a boy and that the youth stood, legs apart and hands on hips, beside a tube-tent, both of which were just catching the first rays of the morning sun. If Parker hadn't known better, he would have thought he was seeing Peter Pan. Instead, he queried, "Squirrel?"

The boy waved. "Hi, Parker! Are you okay?" he repeated.

Parker nodded, but then, owing to the fact that his was no longer a private ceremony, he reacted impulsively. "Want to help?" he said, surprising himself with his own request.

"Sure!" Squirrel said brightly, whereupon he jumped and bounded and shinnied his way down the wet tree trunk faster than Parker thought was humanly possible. When Squirrel was on the ground, he said, "I hope you don't mind, but I've been watching you." Then, pointing to the urns, he added. "Those are your family, aren't they?" To which Parker only nodded, still feeling the need to inhale deeply in order to catch his breath. "Angie told me about your wife. I'm sorry. But at least your family is with you..." He said, and his voice, which modulated in a seemingly haphazard manner between mournfulness and cheerfulness, tapered off, and his eyes fell again to the urns.

"How long have you been up there?" Parker asked.

"A couple of nights. Two. I didn't want to bother you, though. There's nothing like sleeping in a tree when it's raining," he said, lowering himself to his haunches on the opposite side of Yellow Dog Red and visually inspecting the urns Parker had just put there. Then, in answer to Parker's knitted brows, he added, "I know you'll think this is silly, but when I'm in a tree and it's raining the sound reminds me of how I felt when I heard my mother laugh. Before she left, I mean. Maybe it's the sound of the raindrops on the leaves," he said. Then he made a staccato sound with his lips that did indeed sound, to Parker, like drops falling on leaves, or, even more to his ear, like the sound of bemusement made by someone for whom amusement was a foreign language. Someone, that is, whose laugh only accentuated their suffering. "Dunno." Squirrel shrugged.

At that point, their conversation was interrupted by a loud squealing sound from behind them, followed a moment later by the hiss of a zipper. A second later Parker-the-dog emerged from behind a boulder. Seeing Squirrel she yelped happily. She then scooted over at breakneck speed only to crash broadside into him, bowling herself and almost him over. Squirrel, in turn, howled with laughter.

A few seconds later, Roper emerged, wearing only a tee shirt and underwear. He yawned and stretched his back and arms stiffly, and then waved desultorily while muttering a sleepy good morning.

Squirrel rose to his feet and glowered at Roper in reply. Then glancing down at Parker he mumbled, "I guess I'll go now."

"Nonsense. Stay right where you are. You only just a minute ago said you wanted to help me," voiced Parker, in a tone containing equal amounts of incredulousness and authority.

"And we have breakfast," Roper inserted, with forced amiability, as he approached after donning a down jacket, pants, shoes and a wool cap.

As Roper drew near, Squirrel backed away a few steps from Yellow Dog Red. "My foster parents will worry if I don't check in for breakfast," he said.

But it was such a lamely delivered excuse that Parker could only shake his head and exclaim, "Are you telling me that your foster parents let you

120

spend the night in a rainstorm in a tree, and then they get worried if you're late for breakfast!?"

Squirrel shrugged noncommittally. "I have to get to school."

"It's Sunday," pointed out Parker.

Roper looked down at Parker, who was still holding Sylvia's urn and kneeling. He shifted his gaze to Squirrel. "Can we—you and me—talk?" Roper said.

"What's there to talk about?" replied Squirrel, pointedly gesturing toward the acreage now stripped of trees outside the cemetery. "You killed my family."

Parker and Roper winced at this, both momentarily stunned by the unfairness and by the vehemence of the accusation. Roper gave reply first.

"I'm sorry you feel that way," he said, in a measured tone. "Really, I am sorry. And the fact of the matter is I am now even more sorry for having done it. What can I do to make it up to you?" he added, to which Squirrel only shrugged. "Does it help that I quit doing it?" Roper went on. "Cutting down trees, I mean."

"You mean once you had butchered them all, you got fired," he spat.

Roper's cheeks flamed and his eyes narrowed in resentment, but having heard the true degree of aggrievement in Squirrel's words, he sighed and said, "I mean, I gave away the arborist business. And as soon as things settle down here, I am going to find work in architecture. The truth," he went on, as he turned and walked over to and behind the eucalyptus to take a pee, "is I could no longer forgive myself for killing innocent living things so that people, most of whom don't care one way or the other about what they do, could make a fast buck."

Squirrel remained silent as he processed Roper's words.

Meanwhile Parker pulled his hand from out of Sylvia's urn, and with her ashes, coarse and white, cupped in his palm, he leaned forward and let them fall atop Tad's. By the time Roper reappeared, Parker had let fall two more handfuls and was in the process of replacing the cap. Squirrel had in the meantime lowered himself to his haunches again and was stroking Parker-the-dog's side as she gnawed on the handle of the trowel.

"You really quit cutting trees?" Squirrel asked, as Roper reappeared behind Yellow Dog Red's headstone and began stripping the bark from a twig he had picked up.

"I did."

"What about these?" queried Squirrel, gesturing to the dozens of trees still standing in the cemetery.

"What about 'em?" Roper said, using the end of the twig as a toothpick.

"They're supposed to be cut down too, you know."

He shrugged. "Not by me, they won't," he said. "And, as a matter of fact, if I have anything to say about it, nobody is going to cut them down."

Squirrel said nothing in reply and, instead, focused his attention, along with Roper's, on Parker, who had taken the trowel away from Parker-the-dog and was drawing it latitudinally at right angles across the furrows that contained Sylvia and Tad's ashes, effectively forming a crisscross pattern that covered and combined the ashes with the dirt. After completing the last pass with the trowel, Parker laid the tool atop the now completed fusion of ash and dirt.

Roper watched Parker enviously as he stretched his back and extended his arms over his head; for he wondered if, after having been a lumberjack for so long, he had any chance of being that limber when he was Parker's age, especially after enduring a week of back spasms. When Parker had finished, Roper said, "Made any coffee yet, Parker?"

Before Parker could answer, Parker-the-dog, seeing the idle tool, bounded onto the grave and, pouncing on the trowel, began pawing it into the dirt.

Squirrel jumped to his feet. "Parker! Stop that!" he cried.

Roper stood too, stiffly and with a mortified expression on his face. But in the instant before he went to pull his dog off the grave, he glanced down at Parker and was taken suddenly aback; for expecting to see disapproval, he saw instead a smile of delight as broad and as luminous as any he had ever seen lighting Parker's face.

"It's okay," Parker blurted, stilling Roper's reprimand. "Leave her be. She's only doing what Sylvia and Tad would have wanted done with their ashes. To have them laid to rest in a place where happiness lives on."

And, indeed, no sooner had Parker spoken than Parker-the-dog grabbed the trowel in her teeth and began to career with it as fast as she could in tight circles round and round them, as if she were engaged in a delirious game of inner tag. Her reverie was itself infectious, and instantly brought expressions of unvarnished joy to each of the three men's faces. More pertinently, though, Parker's gamboling served to form a single tentative bond of gratitude between the three, one which was interrupted only with the bleating of a horn from a van at the base of the hill.

At the sound, Squirrel's smile turned to a frown. "Uh oh, gotta go. Time to get ready to go to church," he said, rising to his feet. He extended a hand, along with Roper, to help Parker also stand.

"Which one?" Roper said.

"Lutheran," Squirrel replied. "The one at the south end of the valley."

Roper nodded. "I used to go there myself. Then I decided that the best place for me to pray was in places like right here. No walls. No dogma. Just life." He gestured in a fully encompassing circle.

"I like going to church," Squirrel responded, shaking his head, although his attempt to sound enthusiastic was betrayed by his whole being, whose voice Parker gave franchise to.

"Who are you kidding, Squirrel? If ever before I saw someone more in awe of nature, I couldn't name him. No, young man, there is your church," he said, nodding to the eucalyptus in which Squirrel had spent the last two nights.

Roper looked up and saw the tube tent for the first time. "And how many people are lucky enough to be able to say their bed is their church?"

The van's horn bleated again. Squirrel waved his hand and held up two fingers to signify two more minutes. His cheeks reddened at his being caught in feigned shallowness, and as he averted his gaze from Roper's he saw for the first time that Chester's headstone was repaired.

"Chester? That's C?"

"It appears so," Parker replied, as another long bleat of the van's horn rent the morning air.

At once, Squirrel turned and began to lope down the hill, but not before Parker saw the color drain from Squirrel's face after learning Chester's name.

Parker spent the next week drying out and keeping vigil over Yellow Dog Red's grave, mostly by himself and with Parker-the-dog during the day, and with Squirrel in the evenings; for Roper was called away for a pair of interviews with architectural firms, one in San Francisco and one in Los Angeles; and Dotty came down with bronchitis and didn't venture out further than to soak up the late-winter sun in her yard. Meanwhile, Angie had gone away with her parents to vacation in Aspen, which caused her to miss the first real yield from her online handiwork.

The early fruit of this harvest came to the cemetery around noon on Wednesday of that week in the person of a rumpled, lanky, and balding man in his twenties with tousled hair and an academic air who strode up to Parker as he was absorbed in writing in a bound journal while sitting beside Yellow Dog Red.

"Hello, Parker," he intoned, in accented, if somewhat formal English that was rounded down almost to a sough by the guttural vowels of a Germanic accent. The man spoke in such a congenial manner that it caused Parker to think that the two had met before, and his own reply gravitated naturally to the other's affability. Parker-the-dog, sleeping at Parker's feet, seeing and hearing no cause in the man's manner or in his mellifluous voice to bestir herself, rose her head only reluctantly in greeting.

"Hello!" Parker chimed. "How are you?"

"I confess I am tired," the man answered, wiping his brow of sweat with the back of his bare forearm, which extended from the rolled-up sleeve of a navy-blue, hopelessly wrinkled muslin shirt that was almost equaled in rumpledness by his beige linen trousers. Had it been less

125

mussed, Parker thought, it would have been a wardrobe that he would have considered dapper. As it was, however, Parker assessed that his visitor was either a local homeless man or a tourist who had lost his luggage.

Gesturing to Parker-the-dog, the man added, "And that must be Parker." Then he glanced at Yellow Dog Red's headstone and his expression brightened. "May I have the honor of sitting down with you next to Yellow Dog Red?" he said, in a tone of punctilious solemnity that belied his expression and also the possibility that he was a homeless vagrant.

"You may indeed," Parker replied, and as he did so he noticed that the young man was in possession of the type of finely-boned, delicately-hewn features Parker had come to associate over his years in Army Intelligence with the kind of inborn genotypic sensitivity that could be relied upon in most instances to express either artistry or debilitating fragility, depending on how the phenotype responded to its environment.

"Danke," the young man said, but when Parker motioned for him to bring over the canvas chair from beside the trailer, he added quickly as if alarmed at the prospect, "Oh, no! No thank you! I would much prefer it if you would permit me the honor of sitting on the same earth under which our friend is buried." He then swung the day pack he carried onto the ground and lowered himself onto the still moist grass.

Confused by the man's familiarity Parker said, "Have we met before?" as he watched the other open his pack and pull out an iphone. "If so, I am sorry to say I have forgotten your name." The thought crossed Parker's mind that perhaps they had met in one of his investigations, which he dismissed summarily because the man's youthfulness put him at least a decade beyond the time Parker would have worked with him.

The young man shook his head. "Nein. Not in person anyway," he said, and after a few seconds of swiping his iphone, he handed it over to Parker. "But we have already been introduced on Dubliners through Twitter and Instagram by Zand."

Parker recognized Dubliners as being Angie's network name, but tilted his head in question at Zand. "What is Zand?" he said, then took the phone from the other's hand.

On first glance he saw immediately what the youth had meant; for the phone's little screen was filled with an image of him and Squirrel standing to each side of Yellow Dog Red's headstone, which was a picture that must have been transmitted to this person's phone, he surmised, via Angie's.

"Zand is the name of a Persian princess."

"And what is your name?" Parker asked, after realizing, in that Zand was a Persian name, that it was probably the name Angie had used for some purpose on Dubliners.

"Oh! I am called Danquin," he said, his face reddening in the realization that he had not told Parker his name. "I am German and I live in Dusseldorf," he added, then hastily reeled off his bona fides. "I go to university there, but this semester I am attending the University of California at Riverside. In Germany I live with my parents, who are mechanical engineers for Mercedes. My undergraduate degree is in Sociology, and I am embarked on a graduate program in Evolutionary Sociology."

Parker furrowed his brows. "Evolutionary Sociology. What is that?"

Danquin nodded eagerly at the opportunity to answer him. "It is a course of study that examines long-term cycles and stages of societal and inter-societal development; the rise and demise of world-systems; evolutionary psychology; and the biological basis of human behavior, interaction, and social organization. My specialty is cross-species comparisons and analysis of human behavior and organization. From this," he went on, "I hope to acquire my doctorate. My dissertation is about human interaction with domesticated animals as a template for strategies to circumvent violent conflict."

"Ah!" Parker responded, which caused Parker-the-dog to perk up. "And so," he went on, "I suppose it is your research that brings you here to gather data?"

"Yes, exactly..." Danquin's voice trailed off and he added, "but not entirely. Not now, at least. You see...Parker—May I call you Parker?" To which Parker nodded. "You see, Parker, when I began to hear about Yellow Dog Red on Twitter, my first instinct was that of a scientist; that is, to remain detached and come and study why a man such as yourself would remove himself from his society in order to pay homage to his deceased pet; to pay homage, that is, to the ideal of loyalty rather than to the object of loyalty itself which no longer exists.

"There are, of course, many recorded instances of a pet doing such a thing for years beside its master's grave," he continued, "and of ancestral veneration in some contemporaneous Oriental and in ancient Levantine and Mesopotamian societies, and even with some animal organizations such as exist in pachyderms. But the contemporary literature on the opposite is very thin, other than to report on those yearly candlelight vigils, such as the Day of the Dead, that last for one night only, and on those proscribed periods of mourning, such as exist in many cultures. My thesis," he concluded, "states that an advanced and highly developed society can utilize extended acts of primitive reverse devotion to a pet as a way to diminish that society's need to resort to violence to resolve both inter- and intra-societal conflicts."

"Replace aggression with devotion...good idea," Parker said absently; for Danquin's earnestness combined with his accent had left Parker barely enough time to grasp more than the rudimentary meaning of his words.

"Exactly," Danquin replied, smiling humorlessly before his smile faded to a frown. "But then as I read through the thousands of the Yellow Dog Red tweets, I saw the inescapably personal nature of the pet owners' suffering for their own pets, and against my better judgment and my professional training I too began to empathize with their suffering. In a short time," he went on, "it was my own suffering for the owner—that is, for you, Parker—that caused me to realize that there exists an enigma at the center of my hypothesis.

"The dilemma is that I believe human interaction with pets is indeed a template for defeating the urge for violent conflict. But as a template it does not, I now also believe, lend itself to strategies that can be applied widely to society, because it is a personal template that can only be experienced directly between closely related beings, not between a being and a society at large. That is," he went on, "devotion to a pet does not scale up beyond a certain point of social organization from the personal to the abstract, at least not without the imposition of an intermediate and impersonal mechanism of attachment, such as exists in a religious dogma or in an adherence to patriotic doctrines. In my homeland we sadly know better than most people that such expansions of dispersed devotion can be manipulated by unscrupulous people to further their own prejudices.

"Nevertheless," he concluded, gesturing toward Yellow Dog Red's headstone, "I am certain I can gain insight into resolving this dilemma if you will allow me to take part in your vigil, and assist you in any way I can."

Parker was taken aback by this request, and his initial response to it was to politely decline Danquin's offer; first, on the basis that his hypothesis was itself flawed, but more importantly because additional company would only prevent him from doing what he wanted to do most: sit alone with Yellow Dog Red until her resting place was made safe.

Danquin nodded finally that he understood Parker's position. But then as he stood to go, he added, "I will of course honor your privacy, Parker. But when the others begin to show up, I hope you will also reconsider my request in that light."

"What others?" Parker replied, as Danquin took back his phone.

After replacing the phone in his backpack, Danquin brushed off his pants and said, "Did not Zand tell you? Many of Yellow Dog Red's followers have said they are planning to come to help you with your vigil. And," he added encouragingly, "I have read tweets from Zand saying there may very well be a paean in the works by a well-known recording artist."

"How many?" inserted Parker, unable to hide his abashment at the prospect of the cemetery becoming crowded with strangers, none of whom had actually known him or Yellow Dog Red.

Danquin shrugged. "If you believe the tweets, which I am inclined to do, I would say hundreds at least. Maybe thousands, if there is really a song as Zand said there is."

The color drained from Parker's face and an image of lemmings running toward him flashed before his eyes. "Here? They're coming here? To the valley?"

"Why, of course. Where else would they go?"

"But, but, why?" Parker stammered in bafflement.

Danquin shrugged. "Well, my guess is because they, like me, want to be part of a noble cause. A majestic call to action in a world were such causes are used only to sell things or to do harm to others."

Parker's eyes drifted over to the headstone where for an instant in his mind's eye he saw not the cold hard stone but the warm soft gold-rimmed brown eyes of Yellow Dog Red locked with his own gaze as they had for fifteen years. Eyes that met his gaze somewhere far beneath the retina or even inside the optical cortex; it was a gaze that met his own in a timeless place, a place where to look was to understand the connection between the same love and devotion that transfuses the aura of a newborn, that permeates the embrace of a partner, that saturates the laughter of a child.

"I only want Yellow Dog Red to lie in peace," he murmured, knowing as he spoke that he was in fact talking not to Danquin but to those not there except in spirit.

"But that is no longer the only issue," Danquin responded, hoisting his pack onto his shoulders. "Because the issue has grown. We live now in an age where the Internet can water the potted plant of one man's

130

devotion, such as yours, so that it can spread to become a global tree." He gestured first to the bruised and scarred landscape surrounding the cemetery, then to the tree in which he now noted Squirrel's hammock and tent. "Through social media your issue has grown from one concerning property rights only, to one that has become an issue concerning how our veneration of those we love can become a model for the stewardship of living in peace with the whole planet."

"I can't believe this," Parker said in astonishment, although he also recognized that Danquin's words contained more than a grain of truth. "I am only doing this because I want to be with my friend and keep her safe. That's all I want. That is all I ever wanted. To take her home."

"It no longer matters what you *wanted*," Danquin shrugged again, placing emphasis on the last word. "Like it or not, Parker, your devotion to the memory of your friend Yellow Dog Red has for many like me who have read Zand's tweets personalized our connection to our planet. It has come to symbolize a personal yet also universal reverence for Mother Earth. And for the others and for me," Danquin went on, "it is easier for us to see that the way to save the earth from the ravages of thoughtless human activity is through saving small things, rather than trying to save whole ecosystems at once. Ten million people doing one thing is a better way to change something than one person doing ten million things. But it's hard to scale up devotion without changing the original inspiration into something that can be manipulated...even to the point of hatred..." Danquin's voice trailed off and his whole body seemed to deflate. "I'll be going, then," he added, and patting Parker-the-dog on her head, he strode off. "Good luck, Parker. I will do what I can to help you from afar," he called back.

Parker pondered Danquin's words as he watched him walk away. Were they accurate? he wondered. And if they were, did they augur an onslaught of evangelically inclined fundamentalist eco-voyeurs—overzealous tree huggers and their ilk—overrunning the cemetery with fervency in order to be part of something they scarcely knew about? Would his private vigil become just another media spectacle, one that could possibly jeopardize the very purpose of his original intent? Would someone want to make a movie from it? Unable to get his mind fully around these questions, in part because the forces—such as Twitter, Instagram, and Facebook—that were bringing people like Danquin to him were beyond his ability to comprehend, he felt compelled to call out to Danquin.

"Wait!" he shouted, just as Danquin was straddling the split log fence. "Come back. I would like to talk to you a little more about this."

Doing as Parker asked, Danquin returned and sat by Yellow Dog Red again. When he was settled, Parker-the-dog came over and flopped herself down between his crossed legs.

"Where are you staying?" Parker-the-man continued.

"At the motel in town."

"For how long?"

"I can stay through August. Then I must go back to Dusseldorf."

Parker mulled this over for a moment, then said, "If it is true what you are saying about visitors, I'm wondering how hard would it be for you to help me organize a way to keep my vigil from becoming a zoo attraction?"

Danquin's expression brightened and he stiffened his back in order to both sit up straight and to bask in Parker's extension of trust. "I do not think it would be hard at all," he said. "I will just send out tweets describing your concerns."

"Will that stop people from coming here?"

Danquin shook his head. "Nein. Not all. But it will stop some. Perhaps most. But if I am any judge, from the tweets I have read I think many, most of whom have lost pets themselves, will come anyway, if only to bear witness to something they deem is important to honor: your pain and suffering. Many have also tweeted that they have already begun to undertake their journey here."

"What would you do if you were me?" Parker said.

"If I were you?" Danquin murmured. "I guess I would try to limit in an organized way who comes here and when."

Parker nodded. Then looking Danquin in the eye, he said, "Would you do that for me?"

Danquin's face lit up, and Parker realized for the first time since Danquin had come that when he wasn't frowning or looking distracted he was actually a quite handsome man. "I would be delighted to assist you in this," Danquin said, rolling Parker-the-dog's ears with his hands, one in each palm, an action which prompted her to roll over on her back. "Through my tweets I will instruct visitors of your concerns, and with Zand's help I will set up headquarters in town where visitors can check in before they come here to pay their respects. I do not know if this will stop all people from intruding unexpectedly on your vigil, but it may be the best that can be done." Warming more to the task with each word, he said, "Now, where does Zand live? Perhaps she and I could even rent an office in town. In any event, I would like to meet her so she and I can talk more about this."

Parker nodded in agreement with each of Danquin's proposals, but then raised his brows in surprise at the last. "Then you have not met Angie?" he said.

"Who is Angie?"

"Angie is Zand."

"Ah!" Danquin said, then added more hopefully than if he were asking only for information, "Is Angie single?"

Parker tilted his head questioningly, trying to ascertain if Danquin was being sincere, then answered, "Angie is eleven. She is in the seventh grade."

Now it was Danquin's brows that rose in surprise. "Eleven? She organized all these threads and all the videos and...and she is only a...a school girl?" he sputtered.

"A precocious one I would say."

"Indeed. When can I meet her?"

"When she gets back from visiting someone named Ted in Aspen. I think she said a friend of hers is a presenter at some school conference there this year."

Danquin's eyes opened wide again in surprise. "Zand is at Ted? In Aspen?"

"Yes, I think that's what she said. That she's talking to Ted," replied Parker, dismissing as an error in translation Danquin's apparent misuse of prepositions.

"Do you know the topic?"

Parker glanced into the eucalyptus tree, where the tube of blue nylon on Squirrel's tent rippled like snake skin across a cat's paw of wind, trying to recollect what Angie had said about her vacation plans. "She only mentioned in passing about going to talk to someone named Ted. Something she wanted to hear from her friend about using social media to foster something like crowd sourcing...or flashing communities."

"Ah! Flash *micro*-communities," Danquin replied. "Makes sense Zand would want to hear about that."

"What are they? Are they something I should know about?" queried Parker, rolling his eyes; for he was again feeling hopelessly out of the loop with all the newest technologies he had not much interest in learning about, but which also seemed to be impinging on him in ways he couldn't avoid. "When Angie told me about it, I just assumed she was talking about her community of skateboarders."

Danquin rolled his head back and forth as if to loosen his neck muscles, although Parker recognized the movement instantly as being a device by Danquin to keep himself from smiling at Parker's cluelessness. "No, they've nothing to do with skateboarding. They're spontaneous gatherings that come together for a single purpose. Here," Danquin said, when Parker furrowed his brows; whereupon he pulled out his phone again and keyed in a few words on the keyboard, "look at this and you'll see what I mean."

Parker took the phone and watched as a video began to play. It showed the crowded plaza of an old European city, into which began to enter, first, one, then another, then another, and another musician. Each entered from a different direction, each was dressed casually, and each toted an instrument—a base, a violin, a trumpet, a bassoon. Soon the musicians had assembled in one corner of the plaza as a quartet and began to play Beethoven's *Ode to Joy*, much to the delight of the surprised onlookers. With each passing second more and more musicians entered the plaza with their instruments and, like the others, began to play. In short order a whole symphony orchestra numbering nearly a hundred, including choir, had assembled and were playing and singing a full-blown version of Beethoven's 4th Movement. When it ended ten minutes later, tears filled Parker's eyes as they did most of those in the video. Then the musicians simply stood up and, to the applause of the stunned onlookers, dispersed in different directions across the plaza.

"That is called a flash mob," Danquin said, as Parker handed him his phone. "That is what your friend Angie has caused to happen here with Yellow Dog Red. And just as those musicians did, she and I and the others will come and play our small part, then we will fade from here and go back to our lives when we have played our own *Ode to Joy*."

"Got it," Parker sighed, wiping his eyes. Then, to Yellow Dog Red, he added, "I hope you'll be okay with more visitors, girl." To which Parker-the-dog, having fallen asleep on Danquin's lap, wagged her tail.

That very next morning while Parker was eating his breakfast, two groups of men descended on the vineyard: one was a fencing crew; the other was a fumigation crew. All, including the fencing men, wore white bio-hazard jumpsuits, caps, and carried face masks. One of the men, a handsome Hispanic man in his mid-forties, with a shock of salt-and-pepper hair and the chiseled countenance of a Basque shepherd and who, Parker noted, transported himself with a courtly yet wary bearing, approached Parker. In a cordial tone he introduced himself simply as Armando and inquired, "Are you Mr. Parker?"

Parker-the-dog, having heard her name, scampered down from behind boulders and ran up to greet Armando. In turn, he raised his hands to ward her off. Being still a puppy, she mistook his defensive motion to mean it was playtime instead, and lifted her front paws to Armando's white suit in an effort to reach his hands. Armando recoiled and Parker hopped playfully after him.

"It's not mister. It's just Parker," Parker replied, and wiping his mouth with a napkin he commanded Parker-the-dog to sit, while gesturing for Armando to also take a seat. Both complied in unison, and as Armando brushed the dirt off his pant leg, Parker noted that Parker-the-dog's back was streaked with some brown substance, some of which had been transferred to Armando's white pant leg.

"Ah, yes, Parker, of course," Armando nodded, as he sank into the futon sofa. "I am sorry to intrude on your meal. The reason I am here is to tell you we are putting up a fence around the cemetery today. When we are done with this job, which should take us two days only, we will begin to put up a fence around the vineyard."

Parker did not respond at first, but instead looked eastward where the two crews—all of whom he noted were of Hispanic origin—were assembled on the dirt access road, perhaps fifty feet from the split log fence, making preliminary preparations, finishing off cups of coffee, or throwing down the last of their breakfast burritos. Then he let his gaze linger for a few seconds on Armando. His first appraisal of him was that, in his wary yet polite hesitancy, he appeared to be uncomfortable in his role as a go-between for the owners of the property, as had Roper. And also, like Roper, he exuded an aura of competence. Taken together, the contradictory qualities produced an air of dissonance whose two facets came into focus in Armando's hands; for it was with and through them that Armando revealed himself most succinctly to Parker.

"So you are working for Zinni?" Parker said.

"Yes," Armando replied tersely, seemingly taken aback by the abruptness of the question.

As he spoke he flexed the fingers of both hands and repositioned himself on the sofa while tugging in a strange jerking motion at the inseam of his jumpsuit, apparently to straighten it of a bothersome gather in the crotch. Parker knew from past experience in working with people who were being less than forthright that this was not simply an awkward wardrobe adjustment, but rather a nervous tic, an indication perhaps if not of outright fearfulness or contempt, then of the same type of apprehension which in the right circumstances could cause a man to lose control of his bladder. Perhaps, Parker thought, Armando endured some sort of neurological, or even epileptic, condition.

"You don't like him very much, do you," declared Parker, but not as a question.

Armando blinked four times in reply, then shrugged stolidly, then blinked again three times in rapid succession as if to emphasize the first barrage. "It does not matter what I think. I have been hired to prepare this vineyard for planting."

137

Parker-the-dog, her game with Armando having been thwarted, now came over and threw herself down at Parker's feet. It was only as Parker took in a breath that he realized that the source of the brown swatches on the dog's back and on her paws was some sort of animal's spoor, which Parker-the-dog must have found to roll and dig in. It took only one more breath for him to identify the odor—sweet yet putrid—as being of porcine origin, which answered for him the question he had been pondering about what was disturbing the soil behind the boulders by the grave of a dog named Buster.

"Is putting a fence around a publicly owned pet cemetery a usual part of your preparations?" inquired Parker.

"Not usually," Armando admitted. "But when we spray methyl bromide we must take precautions."

Parker's eyes shot open. "Methyl Bromide! I thought that was banned."

"There is no better fumigant," Armando answered in reply, with a wave of his hand that Parker would have thought was dismissive but for its sinuous quality, which he realized was accentuating something Armando didn't himself believe while also being uncontrolled. "And it is not yet illegal if one has an exemption," he added, halfheartedly.

"What about 1,3-D?" Parker questioned, having learned of the latter through Dotty's husband when Max was looking to convert an acre of his land over to a vineyard and was denied the use of methyl bromide.

"1,3-dichloropropene does not spread well in clay soils such as this is. Yes," Armando went on, "it will kill nematodes. But the owner will need to followup every year with herbicides for the weeds that will grow. And the multi-layered tarp we will be using here will trap ninety-percent of the methyl in the soil, where it will break down harmlessly."

Parker ran his palm down the stubble on his cheek, trying to recall the problems Max had encountered when planting his little vineyard. "What about a steam rig? If I recall, it supposedly kills soil pests as effectively as methyl bromide. Or mustard seed meal. I heard it sterilizes soil but isn't toxic to people. My friend Max finally used something called 'anaerobic soil disinfestation,'" Parker continued. "All he had to do to make his soil good for grapes was to increase its anaerobic microbes by feeding them rice bran and keeping them wet."

"Glad to hear it worked for your friend," Armando replied laconically. "But those other methods are not yet commercially viable. So we're doing methyl."

"Then go to it." Parker responded tersely, in a nod to his assessment that he was confronting a lost cause; for besides contradiction in Armando's voice, he had also heard the sort of conviction inspired by exposure to years of listening to product propaganda, which from Parker's own experience with converted true-believers was as difficult to expunge as was the notion that the sun rose every day instead of the earth rotating beneath it.

He bent to lift the coffee pot from the propane burner. "Coffee?" to which Armando shook his head in a stop-and-start motion, and as Parker emptied the coffee into his own cup, Armando's hands, involuntarily it seemed, mimicked Parker's hand movements.

"What I have come to tell you," Armando said, "is that in order to be safe you should vacate this place for at least the time we are spraying. You can come back when the tarp is in place."

"How long will it take to spray?"

"We will do it in sections. It should take four days to spray and cover."

Parker pondered the offer for a moment. "Will I be able to come back to the cemetery after those four days?"

"That is none of my business."

"Whose business is it?"

"Mr. Zinni's."

"What about the fence around the cemetery? Is there going to be a gate in it?"

Armando winced and then lifted his arm and ran his fingers through his hair. Again, the movement caught Parker's eye; for instead of using a continuous combing motion to keep his hair in place, Armando used what Parker could only describe as a crabbing motion, one which made it seem as though Armando was scraping furrows into his skull rather than straightening hair follicles. "There are no plans for a gate," he admitted.

"Then how do you propose I or anybody else enter into the cemetery once the fence is up and we want to get back in?"

Armando shrugged. "Again, it is none of my business. I have orders to build two fences and to fumigate the land outside the perimeter of the inner fence. You will need to talk to Mr. Zinni to change the plans."

Parker nodded. "Then do what you must. But I'm not leaving."

Armando blinked in disbelief, and he flexed his fingers again. "You could be affected by the spray if a wind comes up before we can spread the tarp."

"Then spread the tarp before one does. I'm not leaving." Parker rose to do the dishes.

Armando shook his head and then pulled out his cell phone. Punching in a few numbers, he said, "Let me see if Mr. Zinni wants to talk to you. He's in Italy." Then after identifying himself and describing the situation, Armando handed the phone over to Parker.

"This is Parker," he said.

"Parker, this is Rocco Zinni. I'm the new owner of the property on which you are trespassing. What can I do for you?"

It was a bad connection and the static prevented Parker from fully hearing the tone of Zinni's voice. His first impression of it, though, was that Zinni was a man of few words and even though his voice was fuzzy it confirmed Parker's earlier take on the man from what Roper had said:

that he was a bully used to using intimidation to get his way. Therefore, Parker responded sparsely in kind, with no affect whatsoever in his voice.

"Keep the cemetery open," he said flatly.

Parker heard what sounded to him like a chuckle. "A cemetery!" Zinni replied. "Is that what you call that toxic waste dump where an alcoholic animal quack who failed medical school ditched dead animal parts and paint cans? Look, Parker," he continued, "it's my property and I can damn well say whether it is or it isn't a cemetery. And to me it is a vineyard that has the potential to be one of the best Pinot wineries in the country. And you are a trespasser. Period."

"This has been a pet cemetery for a hundred years, Mr. Zinni," persisted Parker, "and I have made a pledge to the memory of my pet that I will stay here with her until I have an agreement to keep her resting place as it is."

"Are you some kind of PETA lunatic?" erupted Zinni. "Agree with you! I wouldn't honor the memory of you, your dog, or any other animal for that matter, even if I was told you were the reincarnated body of Christ."

"Then we have nothing more to say," Parker responded, and handed the phone back to Armando, who listened to Zinni rant on for a minute before signing off.

"He's a man of few words," Armando said apologetically. "He said he'll talk to you personally when he gets back. In the meantime, he said he'll have his lawyers get an eviction notice and a restraining order to kick you off the property."

"Few words or not. He's boorish and he's crude," Parker replied, casting a jaundiced eye at Armando.

He had made up his mind from that single interaction that Zinni was a crass churl and the type of man he had thankfully encountered only a handful of times previously in his life; sociopaths, such as murderous fundamentalist religious fanatics, serial rapists, and corporate raiders who

141

understood only two things—power and the incontrovertible correctness of their power. In his experience, men like Zinni were driven to win at all costs. For them, negotiations were never a vehicle for accommodation, only one for eliciting complete surrender. Men, in other words, for whom compromise was as antithetical to them as was justice to a malignancy. Thus Parker, feeling he needed to be uncharacteristically blunt, added, "And therefore I have no interest in talking to him, or to any of his lackeys if they will not think for themselves..."

Parker's voice trailed off and he paused a moment in order to weigh what he would say next; for he was not quite sure if Armando, who had seemed a reasonable, if not damaged, man to Parker, fit the bill of a pigheaded subordinate. He decided it was worth a try. "It does make me ask myself, though, why would someone with what are most probably chemically induced neurological issues want to work for Zinni."

Armando blanched, and his skin took on a waxen green hue. "You don't know him. Mr. Zinni can be very persuasive," he said, blinking rapidly, which was accompanied by a curious jabbing movement of his hands that reminded Parker of how the junco birds pecked for seeds in his feeder. "Especially," he added hesitantly, "when he holds your debts."

"Ah!" Parker said. "Now I see."

"See what?" Armando responded, making a fist after realizing he had revealed more than he had intended.

"I see now why you continue to work with him," Parker said evenly. "And despite what you may think, Armando, the fact is I do know Mr. Zinni, or at least I know his type. And I think if you were being true to yourself, you would admit you're torn in two working for Zinni, because you owe money to the very same man whose chemicals you know are destroying your nervous system."

Armando stared at Parker for a full twenty seconds, then loosed a deep sigh as he leaned back on the futon and brought his hands together in his lap, where he began to twiddle his thumbs. "It is not as simple as

142

that," he murmured, and for the first time Parker detected that the notes of truthfulness outweighed those of distressed duplicity. "I know my work is hurting me, and that I am working for a bad man," he confessed. "But I have eight children. The oldest two are gang-bangers, and my youngest is autistic. My wife has MS. My home was underwater, and only last year I walked away from it. My family now lives in a two bedroom shack that is really a chicken coop."

He raised his eyes to meet Parker's, who saw in them now the bitter resentment mixed with ambivalence and desperation of a man who resented feeling trapped while also feeling responsible for having walked willingly into an ambush of his own making. One of Armando's co-workers called out in Spanish to him, and Armando raised five fingers to indicate minutes. Then he turned back to Parker.

"It is true, as you say, that my neurological issues," he continued, "are destroying my nervous system. My doctor has said in another year I will no longer be able to work the vineyards. But I do not know how to do any other kind of work," he went on, nodding to the gang of men impatiently awaiting his return. "And if I cannot work, then who will pay my debts? And if I cannot pay my debts, where will my family go?" He shook his head. "There is only one place that will take us. The streets."

Armando fell silent and his hands returned to their twiddling, albeit in an altered pattern. Several dozen seconds passed in silence, then Parker, noting Armando shifting his weight in preparation to standing, said, "Are all your debts owed to Zinni?"

Armando's thumbs stopped revolving and he stared frigidly at Parker. But again, it was from Armando's hands that Parker had taken his cue; for rather than continuing to twiddle his thumbs in a circular motion, Armando had begun to hammer them against each other, an indicator to Parker that Parker himself had entered an area of inquiry where he was treading on the thin ice of a man's soul.

"What business is that of yours?" Armando growled, his whole continence having suddenly grown livid.

"None," Parker admitted, knowing that he had better be careful; for he was beginning to infringe too deeply on Armando's pride, without which Armando would have nothing left to buttress him from falling into what Parker recognized was the pit of a very bleak future. "But I'll offer my guess anyway," he said. "Gambling."

Armando sprang off the futon. "Look, Parker," he said, as Parker-the-dog also sprang to her feet, "I was trying to be nice to you. My mother used to say it was always better to bet on people who are nice than to do what people like Zinni do to others."

"Push people around, you mean?"

"Exactly. So be forewarned. Zinni will push you out of here to get what he wants, and when he's done with you he won't blink an eye if someone gets hurt."

"Is that supposed to frighten me?"

"It should worry you."

Parker lifted himself from his chair and turned to face Armando, who was almost a foot shorter. Armando's hands were balled into fists but his arms swayed gently as if they were kelp fronds undulating in a tidal current.

"What worries me, Armando, is that the movements of your hands and arms and your eyes are indicative of lesions on the brain that may not be reversible. I have seen similar athetosis in drug-induced Huntington's Disease, so it is nothing to take lightly."

Now a number of the vineyard workers began shouting in Spanish at Armando. He raised only one finger this time, in an obscene gesture, and turned back to Parker.

"I do not take it lightly, Parker. I am frightened by it. But there is nothing I can do but do my work. I am sorry if I have taken up your time..." his voice trailed off. "But I will do what I can with a gate."

anquin arrived at noon while the fencing and fumigation crews were having lunch by a food wagon that had parked down on the road. He himself was bearing a boxed lunch he had picked up from Dotty on the way over.

"Guten morgen! What is going on here?" He said worriedly, after he had slipped through an opening in the partially erected chain link fence.

"Boxing us in, I reckon," replied Parker, who was tending to the weeds on the grave of a cat named Colton just inside the perimeter of the new fence.

"Ah, *gut*," Danquin nodded approvingly. "To keep out uninvited visitors."

Parker shook his head. "Nein. To keep uninvited trespassers in." He then went on to relate his conversations with Armando and Rocco Zinni.

After Parker had explained the chemical situation, Danquin asked, "Is it very bad this methyl bromide?"

"I wouldn't want to take a bath in it," Parker said, as, with Danquin's help, he stood and, after stretching the stiffness from his back and neck, took the plastic food container from him. He then nodded toward the crest of the hill, where the applicators to either side of the fumigant tank could be seen spraying their nefarious load into the soil. The dispenser was followed closely by the tarp crew, in their full hazmat regalia, as it sealed the seams of the white plastic swaths which were unrolled off a vehicle made for that purpose.

"Are we in danger?" Danquin asked in alarm.

"Not me. I'm too old for anything like that to have any effect before I die of other causes," Parker said. "But you might want to leave. Or at least borrow a mask for a few days."

Appalled by either prospect, Danquin blanched. "Nein! I will never wear such a mask," he rejoined, then inhaling deeply twice, said, "Who is in charge here?"

Parker pointed to Armando, who was walking back up the hill from the food truck, holding a burrito in one hand and bottled water in the other. "But I've already decided he's a lost cause."

"In any case, I will go talk to him," he said. Then, noting Parker's questioning expression, he explained, "When I was only a child, my parents took me to hear their friend, violinist Isaac Perlman in Tel Aviv. I was too young to remember it, but my parents told me the audience, including myself, was provided with masks, such as these men are wearing, in case an Iraqi Scud bearing chemical weapons landed in the city. They said I screamed when I saw everyone around me wearing them. That is probably why every time I see them now I feel I can't breathe. I will be right back," he said, whereupon, taking another deep breath, he strode off purposefully toward Armando.

While Danquin was engaging Armando in an animated discussion out of earshot, Parker sat alone at his table and ate the lunch Dotty had packed, a turkey sandwich that contained cranberry sauce, sweet pickles, and potato salad, all tucked between once-thick slices of Basque sourdough bread that had been compressed under a weighted breadboard—or a heavy person willing to remain seated on it for an hour—until it was now only an inch thick. It was a recipe Dotty had served at her restaurant, and which had been made famous by some visiting New York City gastronome or other. Sylvia, who had sat on many such sandwiches for Dotty, had coined them "Dotty's Railroad Sandwiches."

Meals were the hardest part of the day for Parker, particularly when they were taken alone, but also lately when they were shared with Dotty; for they inescapably reminded him of all the conversations he and Sylvia had shared over meals, and also of all the ones that he and she had missed since her dementia had drained her words and life of meaning. That day proved to be no exception as he worked his way through Dotty's sandwich, despite all the activity going on around him, and thus Parker did what he had done for the last few years when eating alone: he turned to Yellow Dog Red.

"Well, old girl, it looks like another perfect day in Paradise," he murmured, in a voice low enough that even a person sitting opposite him would have had difficulty in hearing. "Roper's puppy is going to be almost as good a dog as you were. I think. Not as good with tennis balls, of course, but pretty good at fetching sticks. And she minds well for a puppy. Remember how you used to love to roll in cat shit? Well, Parker rolled in pig shit today. Trust me," he continued, biting into the sandwich, which because of its compression was the consistency of quiche, "pig shit smells a lot worse than cat shit. Apart from that, though, I was happy for her, because she seemed so pleased with herself. Puppies need that, you know, or they get surly. But it also reminded me of the time you rolled in cat shit and then got sprayed by a skunk not a minute later. Remember that? Sorry I laughed so much at you, but you looked so miserable it was hard not to. Lucky for us we had plenty of tomato sauce in the pantry to make you presentable enough to let you back in the house for bed. Even Sylvia still remembers that day like it was yesterday..."

Parker's voice trailed off as a van pulled up and parked behind the food truck. Thinking it was an official vehicle of some sort stopping for lunch, he watched the driver get out and then go around to the back of the van. Half-expecting surveying equipment or some other such construction related device to be offloaded, he was surprised when instead a mechanical lift lowered a person in an electric wheelchair to the street. Then, without interacting with any of the workmen, the wheelchair-bound person headed off toward him, leaving his driver behind.

It was an electric-powered wheelchair, and progress up the dirt road was made far faster than Parker thought would have been possible, given the uneven terrain, the soil's residual dampness, and the slope. But no more than ten minutes later the wheelchair and its occupant had reached the opening that Squirrel had made in the split log fence, and then, with a deft bit of maneuvering, the chair and its driver were through it and into the cemetery. A minute later they rolled to a stop opposite the table at which Parker sat.

The driver was a wiry Caucasian man in his thirties, with short hair, a goatee, and bovine eyes sunk in a countenance torqued severely to the right. In a gesture of greeting, he lifted his right hand from the chair's joystick controller with a sudden lurching motion, and as the hand floated down in a much smoother, lilting motion to his lap, the man's face relaxed into what Parker realized was an almost sublime expression.

"Are you Parker, the owner of Yellow Dog Red?" the man said. His voice was thick with the unmalleable marbles of cerebral palsy and reedy with the spasticity of relentlessly taut vocal cords. But despite these impediments, his words were relatively easy to understand and possessed a penetrating quality that Parker had come to recognize as one that used honesty not as a weapon—as it was wielded by some people to disarm beforehand those who might become potential adversaries—but rather as an Archimedean lever to hold sway in a game against which unruly muscles perpetually guaranteed the deck was stacked.

"I am he," answered Parker, and added awkwardly, "And whom do I have the pleasure of meeting?"

"Keith," the other replied. A smile flitted across his lips but was lost immediately inside an involuntary grimace. Then, shaking his head as if to ward off a mosquito, he said, "Do you always talk like that?"

"Like what?" Parker said, but lamely; for he had realized as soon as the words had left his mouth that his response to being confronted by Keith had been unconsciously formulated to sound so formal as to be archaic, and accordingly he had already guessed what was to follow.

"Like you're a toady in an Edwardian novel talking with undo deference to the King of England, who you know to be a first rate prig.

Or," he added, as a mischievous smile crept across his face, "is it only when you're talking to someone who you've probably figured is too disabled to be as smart as you are?"

"Ho! Touche!" Parker laughed heartily, and then laid his sandwich aside. "I beg your pardon for my..."

"Stupidity? Or was it only simple arrogance?"

"Only stupidity," Parker replied, then added, "Look, it seems we might have gotten off on the wrong foot. Shall we start over?"

"Let's do," Keith said, mimicking Parker's earlier imperious tone.

"I'm Parker."

"I'm Keith."

"That's Parker-the-dog," Parker said, pointing to where she cowered behind the trailer, looking askance and growling softly at Keith's chair. "I don't think she's ever seen a person in a chair like yours," he said.

"Happens all the time. Animals think the chair and I are some sort of monster. She'll get over it."

Parker then gestured in the direction Keith had just come. "That one down there you passed on the way up is Danquin."

"I thought I recognized the other man. He's a vineyard manager, I think. Danquin, judging by his accent, is German. He was haranguing the Latino man."

"That's the one. He's come all the way from Germany to study devotion."

"He certainly seems devoted to getting something from the other guy."

"He's angling to get us some overalls." Parker gestured to the methyl bromide operation at the top of the hill.

"Methyl bromide? That can't be what they're spraying."

"It is."

Keith's mouth moved but no words came out. A moment later his right hand again ascended precipitantly as if jettisoned from the controller

149

panel. It rose to a point equal to the height of his head, and then sank to his lap. "How...How is that possible?" he said, after having regained control of his vocalizations. "My winery hasn't been able to use methyl bromide for at least a year."

"I was told these guys have an exemption."

Keith smirked. "Right. More like whoever is doing this has a friend in high places who owes him big time." He gazed up at the fumigators. "Well, at least they're doing it in compliance with regulations," he said, "and the workers look like they've been protected. Maybe," he added, "they told the state they were going to do strawberries or almonds, and got an exemption through the back door that way. Probably happens all the time," he shrugged.

"What winery do you work for?" Parker asked, his interest having been piqued by Keith's assertion.

"You've probably never heard of it. It's a small one. Paradoxum. Fifteen thousand cases is all. Mostly Pinot." He applied pressure to his controller, and his chair responded by making a quarter-turn and tilting his backrest backward, so that he was in a better position to see the spaying operation without having to crane his neck.

"What do you do for them?" asked Parker.

"I'm the winemaker and owner," answered Keith. "Surprise you?"

Noting the dare implicit in Keith's question, Parker shrugged. "No, not really. I have a cousin who's a paraplegic and who's a top commodities trader at Goldman Sachs. What does surprise me, though, is that you're here at all. I mean, what caused you to make the effort to come here?"

"Paradoxum. We were interested in buying this property until it was taken off the market. Unaccountably, we thought. We liked the idea of having a pet cemetery on it. Gives the wine a spiritual dimension, don't you think? Of course he does, you twit," he chastised himself, before Parker could respond.

"Matter of fact," he went on, "that's one of the things that has brought me here today. I know a man named Bahram, in advertising. He buys wine on the bulk market and has Paradoxum bottle it for his clients, who find that having the cachet of a vanity brand is a huge boost for their egos, as if they needed it," he added. "It was Bahram who forwarded his daughter Angwin's tweets. But it turns out that that's not the only reason why I want to help her keep the cemetery open."

He paused again to let his hand levitate as it had before. "The other reason is Twig. She was the best thing that ever happened to me," he continued. "She was my companion service dog at U.C.D. A Lab. And I wouldn't be here today if she hadn't helped me get through Oenology, Organic Chemistry, English, all the operations...and suicide." He brought his hand to his scalp and brushed it back and forth as if to dust it free of cobwebs. "Anyway," he went on, "I would like to honor the memory of service dogs like Twig. So, what can I do to help you with your vigil?"

Parker chose to not answer Keith's immediate question, but instead chose to refer to what Keith had said earlier. "As a matter of fact, I have heard of Paradoxum," Parker replied. "I went to something called Pinot Envy a few years ago. You weren't there, but I remember the name. And the wine. It was second only to Costa-Browne's Petaluma Gap Pinot."

"I can't do lots of people," Keith said. "Too much stimulus at things like that. They fire up my CP with rocket fuel, and I get locked down. Can't talk. Can't think. Not a very good poster child for United Cerebral Palsy." He clenched his jaw and hands to demonstrate. "See, it's not pretty, is it?"

Parker shrugged but said nothing, for Danquin had just then returned from his talk with Armando. He was carrying two gas masks in one hand, and two jumpsuits in the other. "Well, it looks like that went all right," Parker said, after introducing him to Keith.

"Nein. But not too bad," he replied. "He was not going to give me these," he went on, laying the gas masks on the futon as though they were mating horseshoe crabs, "until I started to tweet that Americans are gassing Mexican field workers in California."

With two notable exceptions to their original plan, and working methodically through the rest of that day and most of the next, the fencing crew finished enclosing the cemetery on schedule. The first exception was that, instead of fully sealing the perimeter, the crew left the last of the chainlink panels unattached on the untilled southern side, which was adjacent to the access road that paralleled the paint-can-filled draw across the property line. When asked by Parker if this lack of linkage was an oversight, Armando shrugged and pointed out to him, within earshot of his crew, most of whom had insisted on coming to pay homage to Yellow Dog Red, that he had faithfully interpreted Zinni's instructions to fully enclose the cemetery without installing a gate. But he had also interpreted those same instructions—correctly in his mind—to say that the enclosure need not be a continuous one. Thus he had merely exercised his professional discretion and left the last panel unattached.

To Parker this distinction between a gate and an opening seemed a dubious one, but in any event, even if Armando had gone ahead and used fasteners to permanently attach the panel, Parker saw that it would have taken only a bolt cutter or a monkey wrench to disconnect them.

The other exception to Armando's original plan was to not begin the erection of the proposed deer fence along the road first. Reasoning that it would be less disruptive to the fumigation operation, Armando instead began putting up the fence along the northernmost boundary, adjacent to the now bulldozed Indian camping site. Parker, however, saw this too as a dodge; since if the fence were erected along the county road first, it would have hindered egress, making access to the cemetery more difficult.

The methyl bromide crew had also worked apace with the fencers, and by the end of the second day they had sprayed the soil and covered, with a hundred-acre sheet of gleaming white plastic, the portion of the cleared land stretching from the western ridge down to the cemetery, and from the northern boundary to the draw on the southern one.

Parker eschewed wearing the overalls and the gas mask Armando had provided, as did Danquin, who alternately had gone and stuffed both overalls with rocks and weeds and then hung them, along with the gas masks, onto the fence, facing outward like armless death camp scarecrows. Before Parker had him take them down only minutes after they had gone up, however, the macabre images of the scarecrows in their masks had been sent forth by Danquin on Facebook, Twitter, and Instagram to detail the latest events.

But not more than five minutes after Danquin had done as Parker had asked, thousands of tweets began flooding in from the world over, all expressing varying degrees of indignation, ranging from mild rebukes against the vineyard's owner, to the sorts of vehement personal attacks that were usually leveled against animal abusers and war criminals. Although Parker was grateful for the number of supportive responses, a sampling of which Danquin read aloud to him, he found himself growing increasingly wary of the immense power of the Internet, whose workings he barely understood, when it was combined with mobile phones. That the two working in tandem could so easily incite such passions while also disseminating them around the world as though they were electronic wildfires made him more than a little uncomfortable. As the two men sat side-by-side beside Yellow Dog Red, Parker, after having mulled over the reason for his disquiet, decided to see if he could share his uneasiness aloud.

He began with a question. "Danquin, do you actually think the people who write back to you really care about me in the same way those flash-mob people cared about hearing Beethoven's Ninth?"

As he spoke he looked westward, out over the hundred acres of recumbent whiteness that seemed, to him, to contain the same sucrose-like sheen as did the ultra-white frosting on the carrot cakes Sylvia used to make every Saturday for her bridge club. At the thought of Sylvia's frosting, Parker could almost taste it on his tongue, and he glanced down at the soil of Yellow Dog Red's grave, whose adobe-brown clay had definitely been lightened several shades by the adding of Sylvia and Tad's ashes into it. He wondered if any of the ashes that had already been metabolized in the soil tasted as sweet to the fauna living within as had Sylvia's frosting.

"What do you mean by 'care'?" Danquin said, interrupting Parker's thoughts, as the former laid the now empty overalls behind him atop Chester's grave.

"I mean, you call the electronic vehicle that delivers the tweets a social media," responded Parker, keeping his eyes on the whorls of ashes in the dirt. "But I wonder," he continued, "if it is really social in the sense that the people who are writing me are really my friends, with values they share with me. Or if social in this case isn't more closely related to the botanical sense of the word, as a clumping together in a shared space?" he said, thinking aloud more than discussing it. "A friend cares for me because he or she shares some of the same emotional values with me. But a social class doesn't care about its peers' values, or their inner feelings, in the same way," he went on, not noticing in his introspection that the work crews, having stored their equipment, had departed for the day.

"The problem I am having with the enlistment of all these people to help me honor the memory of my dog is that it is beginning to feel to me more like the second kind of society, the clumping sort. And I do not think the devotion from that kind of society is the same as the kind I feel for old friends." He nodded toward Yellow Dog Red's headstone. "Theirs is more like the devotion of a pack against outsiders. It's not personal, it's political.

155

"And, frankly," he continued, "it scares me to think that my devotion to Yellow Dog Red is causing a lot of people to act like a pack whose primary devotion is not to me, my dog, or even to the idea of my dog, but to the desire to keep intact their interaction with a clump of similarly interested people. To act politically. To act like a mob. I know it's probably a quibble, but their devotion seems to me to be directed only outward against an adversary most of them couldn't even name, while mine is directed mostly in the opposite direction toward the specific one I do love.

"Does this make any sense to you?" Parker queried finally, noting that Danquin's gaze was still fixed on the screen of his phone rather than on him. "Or am I just prattling on like an old fart who's being selfish in not wanting to share the object of his grief with strangers?"

Danquin had in fact kept on reading the tweets while Parker had spoken, listening to him with only half an ear. But in response to Parker's direct question, he laid his phone aside.

"Yes, of course it makes sense to me, Parker," he answered. "Yours are the very same concerns which I am also wrestling with in my research; for they describe the paradox at the heart of such explorations, and therefore as a scholar I must ask myself: How is it possible for an objective researcher to keep detached from the objects of his research when his goal is to understand the depth of the objects' subjective attachment?

"For me," he went on, "devotion such as yours to Yellow Dog Red is closer to consecration than it is to dedication. It is in the realm of the numinous. Of the unseen. Of the holy. And because it possesses that quality of inward direction, devotion is incorporeal and hard to quantify. For my research, I have come to realize, through experiencing for myself the grief you and others experience with the passing of your pets, that dedication is an easier quality to quantify than devotion, because dedication is more often manifest objectively in the phenomenal realm and, therefore, can be measured with greater ease.

"For instance," he went on, glancing down at his phone across which a torrent of tweets continued to stream, "I am able to measure the time you have dedicated to sitting beside Yellow Dog Red's grave, and I can log the time you dedicate to speaking about her. I can even make judgments as to the content of those discussions. I can count tweets. But because my research methods cannot let me truly go inside your head I can only quantify the outward manifestations of your devotion.

"Even if I were to subject you to questionnaires or electronic eavesdropping with devices such as PET scanners," he continued, "I could not quantify the real depth of your emotions, because they are subjective. The only way I could begin to quantify those numinous qualities is to directly share in the experience myself. And that is what I have done. It makes for good feelings and deeper understanding, but I have yet to find a way to make those anecdotal experiences into good science without them seeming to be entirely discretionary."

Danquin's voice trailed off but his lips continued to move in silence as he had again redirected his gaze to the tweets on his phone. When he looked up, he saw that Parker, wearing an unsettled expression, had shifted his own gaze so that it was directed skyward. Following Parker's gaze, Danquin's expression likewise became worried, as he discerned that the object of their attention was a person in a grimy hazmat suit and gas mask standing beside a duffel astride a eucalyptus limb forty feet off the ground. His attention was not directed at them but at his own phone.

Knowing it could only be Squirrel, Parker shouted out and, after he had caught Squirrel's attention, he motioned for him to come down.

"That's Angie's friend Squirrel," he said, as Squirrel, having stored his phone in a backpack, bounded, with exquisite ease for one wearing such cumbersome garb, from limb to limb until he was on the ground.

Only then did Squirrel remove his gas mask. "I thought those guys would never leave," he said, after Parker had introduced him to Danquin, whose first response was to ask Squirrel how he had gotten up into the tree without either him or Parker or the workers noticing him."

Squirrel shrugged and dusted clumps of dirt off his overalls, the whole front of which was smeared with it. "I stole these yesterday afternoon out of their trailer when the workers went down to the taco wagon to have their break. Then, after school was out today, I swung from Angie's through the trees up to the top of the hill and crawled downhill under the tarp from up there." He pointed to a spot that was hidden behind the eucalyptus from which he had descended.

Upon hearing this, both Parker and Danquin's expressions mirrored the inner horror they felt in having to acknowledge to themselves the possibility that Squirrel had exposed himself to a toxic dose of chemicals. Seeing their concern, Squirrel nodded and said, "Don't worry. I Googled methyl bromide, and I was very careful. So, I'll be all right. Besides, it can't be any more dangerous than living in trees," he added, as he unwrapped the tape he had wound around his wrists and ankles to keep out contaminants, and then unzipped his jumpsuit. After the garment had fallen to his feet he stepped out of it.

Only then did Parker-the-dog, who had retreated again to cowering under the trailer the moment the alien-like being had touched the ground, recognize Squirrel. In turn, she scampered out from behind a wheel, whining giddily and dribbling a trail of pee behind her. Squirrel too let out a yelp, and lowered himself to a knee to greet her, and while she slathered him with dog kisses he hugged her and ruffled her coat with equal enthusiasm. When the two had had their fill of mutual affection, Squirrel looked over and saw that Danquin was yet again reading tweets.

"Did you read the curious tweet that came in a few minutes ago from Sedona?" he asked Danquin, nodding toward the limb from which he had descended.

"Ya. Just before you appeared. I was going to read it to Parker, but—"

"You *should* read it to him," Squirrel interjected, rising to his feet and looking down at Chester's reconstructed headstone as though it had said something aloud to him.

"Um...let's see..." Danquin said, fanning back through the tweets on the screen. "Here it is. It's from Tilly. Om. 'SS death heads a godsend. Kick-started memory after MIA 10 yrs. Chester is my dog. Coming with new friend to see old one and to thank YDR. OMG! OMG!'"

"'SS death heads a godsend'? What on earth could that mean?" Parker said.

"Maybe she is a neo-Nazi," Danquin answered matter-of-factly, as though it was self-evident. His expression, though, belied unmistakable anxiousness.

"A Nazi living in Sedona? I doubt it," responded Parker.

"But don't you see? It doesn't matter," Squirrel observed. "If owners like you and her come and make a stink, it'll probably help keep the cemetery open. And by the way," he added, turning to Danquin, "loved the death heads." He then shifted his gaze up into the eucalyptus where his duffel bag was leaning precariously to one side.

Parker followed Squirrel's gaze. "I hope there's nothing breakable in that bag."

Squirrel shook his head. "Nope, only clothes. All of 'em," he added, resentfully to Parker's ear.

"Do you really live in trees?" Danquin said, as he finally switched off his phone.

"Not all the time," murmured Squirrel. "Usually I live in a house. But..." His voice receded into an uneasy silence, then he added, "not always."

Having heard the bitterness edging Squirrel's voice, Parker commented with a question of his own. "Is there something wrong at home?" he said.

159

Squirrel shrugged. "I guess you could say that. My foster parents told me yesterday that they asked my social worker to place me in a group home."

"And you don't want that?" Danquin said, to which Squirrel shook his head.

"Not when it's one for 'troubled adolescents,'" he replied, scowling as he made air-quotes. "Just because I like being in trees doesn't make me a troubled youth."

"If it was assault rifles you liked being around, would that make a difference?" Danquin said ingenuously, without bothering to mask the lingering anxiety he still felt over the death head tweet.

"Assault rifles are used only to kill people," Squirrel responded. "I've never heard of anyone using a tree to assault or even kill a person. Have you?"

Danquin shook his head. "Nein. But before I came to America, my friends told me everyone who lived here had a lawyer and an assault rifle."

Parker raised his eyebrows at the line of associations Danquin had hit on, and frowned, as did Squirrel. He then said to Squirrel, "You don't seem troubled. To me you seem upset and also—"

"Free?" inserted Squirrel, finishing Parker's sentence for him. "That's just the problem," he went on. "My foster parents are worried they'll be sued by the state if I hurt myself falling out of a tree. They say their insurance agent told them that as long as they allow me to climb around in trees, I'm a big liability, and that they could lose their home, their license, or even go to jail."

"So, what are you going to do?" Parker said.

Squirrel eyed Parker with a look that told him the boy was in great turmoil despite his outer calm. "I'm not going to stop sleeping in trees, if that's what you mean," he said evenly.

"No, that's not what I meant," replied Parker, aware that he had slipped into a paternal tone. "Are you going to go to a group home?" to which Squirrel shook his head, prompting Parker to ask, "Then where will you live?"

Squirrel spread his arms in an expansive, almost devil-may-care gesture. "In the wild, I guess. Otherwise, I'd have to live with kids who are truly screwed up."

"Where will you get money?" Danquin said, assuming a grown-up attitude that matched Parker's.

Squirrel fidgeted with his phone. "I don't know. But I think if I fall into the homeless category, I can eat at soup kitchens and shelters, or out of dumpsters...look, I don't want to talk about this anymore," he said, and, changing the subject, added, "Has Angie come by yet?"

"I haven't seen her," replied Parker. "Why?"

"She texted me late last night and said she and her dad were flying home early today. Maybe her dad could..."

His thought remained unfinished, and after a moment of silence Danquin spoke up. "You could stay in my apartment," he offered. "At least until I have to vacate it in the fall, or until Parker's vigil ends, whichever comes first."

Squirrel stared at Danquin in disbelief. "Why would you do this for me? I...I don't even know you," he sputtered.

Danquin sighed. "I have only recently discovered that it has become a necessary part of my research on devotion... Oh, altruism, I mean," he added, after Squirrel had received his words with a blank expression. "I now believe it is probable that altruism, which is the unselfish concern for the welfare of others, is one of the invariable factors at the root of devotion. And so, if I have come here to study devotion, then I must explore it from within its parameters to understand it from the inside. And furthermore, I do not own any property. So I will have no need for a lawyer if you fall out of a tree and I am sued."

"You could be deported." To which Danquin shrugged. "Well," Squirrel continued, "I would prefer to stay in the tree here with Parker most nights, but I could use a shower every now and then."

Fresh lemon bars, anyone?

Dotty, who had approached the cemetery unnoticed, put an abrupt end to the conversation as she stepped through the narrow opening in the fence and came up to the others carrying a plastic container cradled in her arms. "I don't like this fence. Not one bit," she said unequivocally, while eying the ugly gray meshwork as she placed the box of confections into Squirrel's eagerly outstretched hands. To Parker, who had risen to his feet to intercept and assist her, she said, "My friend called this morning to tell me to give you the message that the Zinnis are planning to have the sheriff serve you with an eviction notice on Thursday next week. What should I tell her?" Her voice was thin while also husky from the remnants of her bronchitis.

Parker noted the lack of breath in Dotty's words. "You need to take better care of yourself, Dotty," he admonished. "You could've just called. After all, I do have a phone and the laptop computer Angwin loaned me. I can use them even if I don't really know how they work. So, I will talk to Zinni. Armando the job foreman has his number. And," he added, while helping Dotty lower herself into a chair, "we need you to stay healthy so you can keep us in lemon bars."

"You needn't fuss over me," Dotty said, waving away Parker's solicitations. "You're the one living like a savage."

"What if there are many yous?" Danquin piped up, directing his words to Dotty after having gobbled down a lemon bar in two bites.

Dotty's brows shot up. "Do you mean to bring in a flock of sheep?" And after a moment of rumination, she added, "I suppose that might give the sheriff some trouble."

Danquin furrowed his brows in confusion. "Flock of sheep?" Then he exclaimed, "Oh! No, I did not mean *mutterschaf.* A mother sheep. I meant y-o-u-s." He spelled it out. "Like many peoples."

"There is no yous. Y-o-u, you, is plural," Squirrel inserted absently, while he simultaneously typed on his phone.

"Yes, yes, of course. Y-o-u," Danquin replied. Then to Parker, "What I am saying is that with the help of Yellow Dog Red's Twitter friends we can maybe be many people here to be also served by the sheriff."

Parker's expression lit up. "A flash mob?"

"Ya! Maybe we can do that. We have almost a week to organize it."

"I can help with that," Squirrel said, speaking through a mouthful of lemon bar, his lips ringed white with confectioner's sugar. "Angie, too. I'm sure she'll want to help when she gets back. Look," he went on, and handed his phone to Parker, "we're already getting tweets from people who say they'll come on Thursday if we want them to."

Parker stared at the screen as tweet after tweet appeared. "You did this just now?" he said in disbelief, to which Squirrel shrugged. "Do any of these people have real lives?" Parker continued. "I mean, do they work? Do they have families? Or is all they do is sit around and live on their phones?"

"All three," answered Squirrel, as he took the phone back from Parker. He glanced down at the screen. "Hey!" he said brightly. "It's Zand. She's back online."

"Who's Zand?" Dotty said.

"What's she say?" Parker asked.

"Zand is Angie," Squirrel replied. "She says, 'Dad says online timeout over. Want to meet this Danquin at market at 8pm tonight to look with Dad at a place in town next to laundry for YDR office.' Does he know where the laundry is?"

Danquin nodded. "I know where it is. Is that all she says?"

"No, here's another tweet. 'YDR vigil set Thursday 8am. Need portable toilets and H20. Pay with bitcoins? Saw S in Aspen. Said will Skype with me and Keith if can. Oh boy!'"

"What's going on?" Dotty said, shaking her head at the rapidity and the unintelligibility of unfolding events.

"Keith is the winemaker at Paradoxum," Parker replied. "He came by and, among other things, said he makes wine for Angie's father. But," he added, "I haven't the foggiest idea how to describe to you what Skype is. As far as I can tell it's like closed circuit television that a computer has—"

"'Here at my feet my friend Yellow Dog Red lies, waiting for me in peace, always faithful,'" Dotty inserted as, having purposely lost the thread of Parker's explanation, she read aloud from Yellow Dog Red's headstone. "I wonder though," she added, shifting her gaze between Danquin and Squirrel, both of whom had moved off a few paces in order to confer between themselves over the incoming tweets, "if she really finds all this" she gestured to the fence, the white tarp, and to the electronic devices with which Squirrel and Danquin seemed to interact incessantly, "to be peaceful?"

Parker shrugged. "Peaceful, no. But she is *resting in peace*," he said, "like Max and Sylvia and Tad are, despite all the hubbub and confusion surrounding us the living."

Now another person, a woman in her late thirties, approached the cemetery. She wore a wide-brimmed floppy straw hat and a lime-green pantsuit belted with a cherry-red sash on which a yellow silk sunflower was affixed. Most notable, despite her flamboyant attire and jaunty gait, was that she was also drop-dead beautiful. "Hello!" she called out, waving a stenographer's pad. "Press here!" she yelled, in a voice whose brassiness was matched by a shrillness that might have been emitted from a steam pipe.

By her voice alone, both Parker and Dotty knew that it was Wili Wallenstock, the community activities stringer-cum-columnist for the valley's only legitimate newspaper, *The Valley Observer*, which was a rural bi-weekly that had devolved from its original charter as a second cousin to the *The Farmers Almanac*, to an unpitying tabloid devoted to propagating endless ultraconservative screeds on the virtues of untrammeled business, augmented by virulent polemics against virtually all tax policy, both of which dovetailed into nativistic tirades against immigrants and homosexuals.

Twenty years earlier Wili's beat had originally chronicled local community issues in what sufficed for the gentrified up-valley, winery-and-vineyard-studded suburbs. But in her overeagerness to please her publisher, she had embraced the paper's philosophical spectrum to a degree that was palpably fanatical even for a true believer like the publisher, and over the years Wili's column had passed seamlessly into the realm of gossip-mongering exposés that were more in tune with Hollywood tattletale publications than with a farmers' planting guide.

To further this image of an eccentric California-conservative-nut-job-Hollywood-insider, Wili had patterned herself after a local mattress saleswoman whose claim to fame was her flamboyant attire, along with an oleaginous, magniloquent personality. Many of the old timers in the community, especially older women, despised Wili. But the community itself had changed over the years; from one comprised of farmers interested in the weather and commodity futures, to one of landed gentry and the minions of winery-related wage-slaves enthralled by celebrity and by their connection to the exalted status and esteem their industry aggregated to itself, which Wili glorified to the hilt as being America's "New Burgundy." Despite this tectonic fissure that ran through the heart of the valley, Wili had shrewdly milked it to her professional advantage, as well as to her personal profit; for she had not only been kept on the payroll but also in an estate house; the latter was due in large part for the parochially mundane reason that she had been bedding the publisher for over two decades, to everyone's knowledge, including his wife's.

"Forget about resting in peace," Dotty cracked, as Wili drew parallel with the trailer and surveyed the scene.

"Hi, y'all," Wili chimed, in a cheerfully counterfeit Oklahoma drawl that copied to a tee the mattress celebrity's welcoming Sage County accent. "I've heard through the grapevine that there was a major make-over happening up *heah*. But I *rally* had no idea it was so far along," she said, while with her phone she simultaneously snapped a few pictures of the cemetery and the property surrounding it.

"Y'know, I haven't been to this pet cemetery in years," she said. "Ever since—" But she snapped her mouth shut abruptly and, opening her ipad, began scribbling some notes.

Her blonde hair, augmented with extensions to shoulder-length, did not hide, however, the blush that had rushed into her cheeks; for left unspoken had been that the first time she was on these grounds had been twenty years earlier when, as a cub reporter fresh out of journalism school, into her sixth month on the payroll and her second month underneath its contributor, she had been consigned to write her first ever front page feature on a case in which a cuckolded farmhand had slit the throat of his wife and their Chihuahua outside the cemetery. To make a long story short: it had not gone as well as Wili had hoped.

As Parker remembered it, the main problem had been that Wili could not overcome her inability to reconcile the stark reality of a crime of passion against her puerile, almost Machiavellian world view, borne out of a privileged life lived among plutocrats, that held that the world was nothing more than a proscenium on which people and events were stooges who acted out pre-rehearsed lines and actions, much in the same vein that classical theater actors portrayed humanity as dupes of the gods. Thus, every word Wili wrote about the murders dripped with an anachronistic, righteous moralism and innate prejudice that she could neither reconcile in herself nor surmount. All of which led to a situation wherein the pool of local jurors became so tainted by journalistic partiality through reading her stories that the venue of the trial was moved to Los Angeles, where Wili was unfortunately left out of the journalistic loop.

"Neither had we," Parker replied. "Not until a few months ago. Oh, by the way, I came upon Poco's grave," he said, referring to the murderer's deceased wife's Chihuahua. "It's in the weeds over there. I haven't gotten around to grooming it yet."

Her composure momentarily restored from her retreat into her writing, Wili turned her head in the direction Parker pointed, then scanned the whole of the cemetery. "From the looks of it you've already done a bang-up job of cleaning up the place," she responded, then with a flirtatious fluttering of her eyelashes, added, "My memory of it is that it was full of paint cans, beer bottles, shell casings, and condoms."

Parker nodded but did not fail to notice that her cheeks had flamed into color again. He responded by making a sweeping motion and saying pointedly, "But in the opposite order, judging from what I've cleaned up."

Wili smiled uncomfortably at the latent insinuation she thought she heard in Parker's comment; for she had undertaken a number of less than noble assignations among the headstones. "Yes, I've been told the cemetery was a regular Lovers Lane. It's always been a shooting range, though," she said, and before she could censor herself she added, "Same impulse. Different weapons." She batted her eyes again at Parker and then, turning her attention to Dotty, smiled pallidly.

"Hi, Dotty," she said stiffly, for the two had been at odds in recent years; Wili over Dotty's embrace of Parker's friendship during Sylvia's decline, which as a gossip columnist Wili naturally assumed was seedy and therefore newsworthy. And Dotty over Wili's inability to separate fact from fiction, and, specifically, for her wilful dismissal of people's wishes to keep certain unproven aspects of their lives out of the gossip column.

Dotty nodded a greeting, then said, "Are you going to write about this?"

"Brad—my publisher," Wili corrected herself, ignoring the disdain implicit in Dotty's voice, "thought it would be a good idea. He's right. Our Twitter, Snapshot, Instagram, and Vine accounts are all trending with Yellow Dog Red. *The Observer* is getting oodles of calls from wine tour agencies who want to know where the cemetery is so they can swing by here to see Yellow Dog Red. Oh! There she is! Right here," Wili blurted, seeing the headstone at her feet for the first time, and, squinting in the declining light, she read the epitaph. "Oh, how sweet. Did you write that, Parker?"

"I did."

"Can I quote it?" she said.

Parker shrugged. "Go ahead. I don't think epitaphs on graves, especially ones for dogs, are proprietary works of art."

"Was he a good dog?" Wili said, while she snapped a photo and then scribbled on her pad.

"He was a she," Parker replied. "And yes, she was an exemplary dog."

"Are you going to get another dog? I can Photoshop this later," she stated, while snapping a picture of Parker standing four steps removed from Yellow Dog Red's headstone, then typing out captions on her phone once more.

"I can't replace her," answered Parker. "And look at me, Wili. I'm over eighty. I'm going to die long before any dog I get would." He shook his head. "No, sad to say, my dog days are over. Yellow Dog Red is the last of the line."

"Oh, don't be silly. You don't look a day over sixty, Parker. But what about that one?" she said, pointing to Parker-the-dog, a barely visible lump in the shadows of the fading light.

"She belongs to a man named Roper. He's helping me keep my vigil," he said. "I'm just looking after her for a few days while he does some job interviews."

Wili's eyes opened wide, and in the gloaming light their greenness was startling. "Roper? Roper Welling?"

Parker shrugged. "I guess so. I don't know his last name."

"Roper Welling is the grandson of Scott Welling, scion of the Napa Welling Group. Their great-grandfather made a fortune lumbering redwoods and clearing forests for vineyards that his son parlayed into a wine distribution empire. What's Roper's angle here," Wili said, again writing earnestly in her notepad.

Parker furrowed his brows. "Angle?"

"Sure. Angle. People like the Wellings don't do anything without angles. That's how people like them make their fortunes. They play the angles. Work the percentages. You know, pit rich people against poor people, big money against little money. Vineyards against trees. Those sorts of things."

"He hasn't said a word about that to me," Parker replied, mildly surprised by Wili's harsh but, to him, apt assessment of the Darwinian workings of capitalism, given her well-known journalistic posture.

"Just the same, it wouldn't surprise me if he has some ulterior angle in mind for this place."

"Don't talk nonsense," Dotty inserted sourly, stepping over Parker-the-dog in order to stand beside Parker. "Roper seems like a fine young man. And for your information, Wili, not everyone in the world has an angle. Can't you believe that Roper—Mr. Welling—is helping Parker out of the kindness of his heart? Or don't stories of that kind of heart make for very good reading in *The Observer*?"

Wili glowered at Dotty with an expression that only strengthened each's firm conviction that there would be no love lost between them anytime soon. Dotty stared back in return, prompting Wili to blink and smile, then veer her attention away to Parker.

Without skipping a beat, Wili addressed Parker as if her conversation with Dotty had never occurred. "Have you ever been without a dog,

170

Parker? Because, if my recollections serve me right, it seems I've never seen you without one. Even after Sylvia went into the facility. Isn't that true?"

Parker blinked in rapid succession both at the question and at the shift toward frigidity in the atmospherics that had occurred between Dotty and Wili; for it was as though the two events had borne with them a sudden wind bearing a lifetime of memories connecting events in his life with the various dogs he had owned, eight in all. "Your recollections are right," he admitted, and he felt the icy breath of loss congeal on his lips as his words escaped him. "Sylvia and I have had dogs ever since I got out of the service."

Squirrel, who until then had been engrossed by his phone, interrupted Parker. "I wasn't sure you would want to read this," Squirrel said, as he extended the phone to Parker. "But Danquin didn't think it was right to keep it from you."

"What is it?" Parker said, taking up the phone.

"A tweet. Just read it," Danquin replied, and he extended a hand to Wili and introduced himself and then, when it appeared Wili didn't already know Squirrel, introduced him to her.

Parker had to hold the phone at arm's length in order to read it, which he did aloud. "'For every visitor to YDR 10 dogs will die. krul2dbone.' Who's krul2dbone?" asked Parker, with a look of disgust on his face, while handing the phone back to Squirrel as Dotty and Wili looked on in bewilderment.

"Don't know," Squirrel shrugged.

"Could be anybody," added Danquin, shaking his head in disapproval and frowning.

"Could be a joke," Wili said. "Can I see that?" she asked, and she took the phone from Squirrel. She lowered the device to her waist for a moment as though to get a better grip on it, then after rereading the message aloud several times, she said, "Best thing is to ignore it. Just some sicko wanting a minute in the limelight after something happened that moved people. I see it all the time. Unfortunately. A deviant who wants to stir shit into the kettle because it makes him feel powerful."

"It seems like something I might read in *The Observer*," Dotty inserted.

"Are you going to write about it in your newspaper?" Danquin said, squinting against the flagging light to read the tweet again.

"Probably not," Wili replied, scowling at Dotty as she passed the phone back to Squirrel. "I've got plenty of material already."

"Well, I have to get some sleep. Goodnight," Squirrel interjected, with a swiping motion of his hand. He then yawned and stretched, and taking three bounding steps proceeded to climb up into the nearby eucalyptus tree.

"Marvelous!" Wili exclaimed, as she watched Squirrel make his way adroitly into the crown. She then snapped a picture of Squirrel standing atop a limb before he grabbed his duffle bag and disappeared into his tent. Meanwhile, Parker had gone over and flipped the switch on the solar-powered floodlight, which cast his living area into dim and highly shadowed light.

"But why not? It's news, isn't it?" Danquin challenged, drawing Wili's attention back. "Why would you not use hateful words to tell people the larger part of the truth?" His voice was even but his tone contained an implicit taunt as he continued. "I have read your paper. It is a *boulevardzeitung* such as the ones in my own country, and I have seen that, like them, it specializes in printing the same kind of lunatic *geschwätz*—small crazy lies—as if they were big news."

Wili frowned and then took her hat from her head and lowered it in front of the sunflower on her sash, but not before Danquin noted that the knot that held the ornamental flower obscured a metal object too large to be a buckle.

"Truth?" Wili said, running her fingers around the hat's brim. "Okay, maybe I can write a note paraphrasing something to the effect that there has been some minor opposition voiced to Parker's vigil...The Yellow Dog Red Overlook is what I'm thinking of calling it."

Danquin sighed. "Paraphrasing. That is how truth was lost in my country by reporters like yourself. They lost truth through the paraphrasing of little lies, so that people did not see the lies for what they were until it was too late, and the crazy little lies became big lies that were confused with truth. Like on your lunatic-fringe talk-radio here in America."

"What is the truth then?" Wili said, startled and galled by this unknown foreigner's impertinence at likening her to a hate-radio host. She glanced down at her watch, for darkness was almost upon them.

"The truth is that powerful people use their power to create reality in their own image."

"And, in America, reality is the power that creates powerful people. Look," she snapped, clearly having grown ruffled with the course and the unexpectedly hostile tone to her visit, "I'd love to stick around and chitchat with you over Hegelian Dialectics and Supply Side Economics, but I've got poor night vision and need to get back to my car before it gets too dark, so that I can drive home and write up the truth of what I've seen here for tomorrow's edition."

She turned her back on Danquin, but after taking three steps she tripped over the sleeping dog Parker and fell heavily to the tarp. The impact with the ground, in turn, disentangled the tiny metal object and the sunflower from the knot in her sash and they and Wili's hat rolled across the ground. This startled Parker-the-dog awake, who yelped at being kicked and then, spying the saucer-shaped object bounding past her, bolted instinctively after it. A moment later and before Wili or anyone could say anything, Parker had pounced on the contraption and the attached sunflower and had begun chomping down on them like they were a chew-toy.

"Curb your dog, Parker!" Wili, her limbs still akimbo, cried hoarsely to Parker who, along with Danquin, had rushed forward to assist her.

But the shrill timbre of her cry only served to cause Parker-the-dog to interpret Wili's tone as one of excitement—of play, that is—and she reacted like any puppy would by scampering away with her newfound plaything in a sport that quickly devolved into a game of keep-away. By the time Parker was able to get Parker to give him her toy, she had so thoroughly macerated the gray metal object and the silk flower with her puppy teeth that they looked more like an utterly chewed-over rawhide toy than a metal box attached to masquerading apparel.

"What is this thing?" Parker said, handing the cube back to Wili, who Danquin and Dotty had by then helped into a chair.

"It's a camera. It's attached to a silk sunflower, can't you see that, you asshole?" she spat, grabbing the maimed contrivance from Parker.

"You were filming us?" Parker said, startled in equal measure by Wili's vehemence as by the fact that she had brought a hidden camera with her.

"It's S-O-P nowadays," she replied, but as she took her hat from Danquin, Parker-the-dog, thinking it was also—since it had been on the ground—a plaything, lunged at it, ripping a hole in its brim before Parker could wrest it from her and give her a command to sit.

"Can't anyone control this dog?" Wili shouted in exasperation, just as the puppy sat, and then a second later, at Parker's further command, lay down obediently on the tarp at his feet.

After praising Parker, Parker the man turned his attention back to Wili. "Standard operating procedure for a newspaper reporter is to film people without their knowledge?" he asked incredulously, handing her back her hat.

"It's for the blogs," she said. "And YouTube."

"You can do that without my permission?"

Wili shrugged. "This is public property. And besides, what's the downside? That you sue us? Nobody in his right mind would do that, because then that itself becomes more news we can use to critique you. And in the unlikely event you should spend a lot of money and win, which is even more unlikely, then all we would have to do is pay a fine, flip a switch, make a contrite retraction, and take it offline. You're the poorer for it. We've sold more advertising and newspapers. End of case."

"The downside," Danquin interrupted, after looking nervously at his watch, "is that people like you think your job is to spit out all the data you gather as if you are a computer. But if there is no one there to interpret it, most of that data is only noise. Yet, from those little noisy bits, you think you can form a big perspective. But that is the perspective from the bottom up only, not from the top down. That is a fine job for a non-thinking machine like a computer and a bottom-feeding life form. But it is not fine work for a human reporter. Such a mechanical perspective sees only small things on the bottom. It does not see big things on the top. To me," he continued, "it is like you telling me that Beethoven was inspired by the quill he used to write the score of his *Ode to Joy* rather than by his Savior.

"But," he sighed, "as you say, we do not have time to discuss Hegelian Dialectics. For I must go meet a friend. If you like, though, I can help you and Miss Dotty to your cars. I can also help fill you in, Miss Wili, on the big picture from the top down so that your story will be accurate." Then, as an afterthought, he added, "Perhaps you could write your story from the angle that Parker's vigil is a chorale of devotion in his symphony to Yellow Dog Red."

Wili's eyes narrowed and she trained her gaze on Parker. "Parker, does this lunatic truly speak for you?" she said. "I mean, *Ode to Joy*? *Yellow Dog Red Symphony*? Come on, Parker, that's pathetic. What I see we have here is a bereaved lonely eighty-year-old man who's lost his wife and dog and who can't think of anything better to do with his time. Period. Yes, I agree there is some nobility to it. And maybe even some pity. But with spokesmen like him," she pointed at Danquin, "if it's sympathy you want,

175

then the best you'll get is going to come from the mental health professionals who will be changing your bedpan and shooting you full of Atavan in the nursing home you've committed yourself to with this stunt. I'm sorry, but I can't support..."

Wili fell silent and Parker held her in his gaze until she shifted hers away. "Go," he said finally. "These lunatics, as you call them, are my friends. And if I'm pathetic, then at least we are pathetic friends together. Please, Danquin," he said, turning his back on Wili, "would you escort Miss Wallenstock and Dotty to their cars."

Thereupon Danquin gathered up three lemon bars and, using his phone as a flashlight, helped Wili to her feet and led her and Dotty through the vineyard to the street. When their car's taillights had passed out of sight behind a thicket of blackberries Parker, alone again, turned his attention back to Yellow Dog Red.

"Well, old girl," he murmured, lowering himself down in the chair next to her after grabbing Dotty's box of lemon bars, "I think we're at the point where I can safely say the proverbial lemon curd is about to hit the fan."

Parker then took a square from Dotty's plastic container. With each bite he revisited each of his eight dogs one-by-one, each of which was a Labrador, and each of which he considered to be his best friend. By the end of the lemon bar, the memories of his friends had melded into a single memory that had no particular name or face or even personality. Instead, his dogs became one sensation that suffused Parker with a calm assurance and contentment that leashed his soul to the endless love and loyalty of all of his friends, in whose company he was right where he wanted to be.

He was awakened sometime later that night when, from within the crown of leaves high above, a voice called out to him.

"Parker!" he heard Sylvia murmur from across four decades, "Go to bed. I'll keep an eye on Yellow Dog Red."

The next morning saw Armando's fumigation and fencing crews arrive half-an-hour before the sun was up, just as the taco wagon was pulling to a halt at the base of the driveway at the north corner of the property. By then, Parker had been awake for an hour, reminiscing with Yellow Dog Red in the custom of widowers who, no longer having a partner to share their memories, meander aimlessly through them like sprites flitting from eddy to eddy in the fast flowing stream of endlessness. At first glance, Parker thought the number of workers who had gathered seemed fewer than the day before, and Armando clarified this for him a few minutes later when, after buying himself a coffee and a confection, he brought up an extra coffee and a pan dulce for Parker.

"Had to pick up some day laborers down in town," he said wearily, confirming Parker's assessment as he sat down heavily opposite him, "after a few of my regulars called in sick. But tell me," he continued, taking a bite out of a donas and shaking his head, "have you ever known a Mexican laborer to call in sick? I sure as hell haven't. So something else is going on. Nobody said anything to me, but by the medallions around the necks of the ones who did show up today, and by the Madonnas on their dashboards that weren't there yesterday, I suspect the men are worried about desecrating a graveyard, even if it is only for pets. And frankly," he added, "the more time I've had to think about it, so am I."

Parker, who had already consumed a pot of coffee, blew across the surface of the steaming cup to cool it. He then dunked the pan dulce and took a bite.

"Are you?" he said. "Worried, I mean."

Armando shrugged. "I've worked in places I liked better. But it's not the places or even the dead I fear. It's the living." He then unzipped the collar of his white jumpsuit and brought out a tarnished Virgin of Guadalupe medal affixed to a chain. "My great-great grandfather, Jose Rodriguez Hidalgo, fought on Spain's side against the Americans in '98. He gave this to my grandfather who gave it to my father who gave it to me. Jose Hidalgo had a saying: 'God is for redemption. Gunpowder is for protection. Good intention is for justification.' And God doesn't need no justification." Armando replaced the medallion and unzipped his jumpsuit to the waist. He then reached inside and without brandishing it withdrew a pistol from a holster. "You never know which *patrone* is the *manzana podrida* whose poison will make you sick."

"That rotten apple wouldn't be Zinni, would it?" offered Parker, who noted that the gun was an old Colt with a mother of pearl handle; decorative rather than businesslike, it was the type of weapon that an equestrian would wear in a parade.

Armando shrugged again and replaced the gun in its holster. Once more Parker noted the sinuous movements of Armando's arm as he struggled to re-zip his jumpsuit. "Let us just say Rocco Zinni is a businessman," Armando resumed. "He does not suffer losses lightly. His brothers Enzo and Marco are the ones I worry about. Each one is a *manzana podrida perro rabioso*—a rotten apple mad dog—and unpredictable in his own way. Rocco is their boss, but he does not always do a good job of supervising them."

"Why are you telling me this?" Parker said.

"Because I like you, gringo. I admire you too, even though I also think you are incautious. And," he shrugged, "I do not want anything to happen to you."

"Thanks for your concern," Parker replied. "I like you too. But I think I can take care of myself. And besides, if you haven't noticed, I've attracted the help of a few young friends."

178

Armando nodded slowly. "Si, I have noticed. And so has my third youngest daughter. She showed me the tweeters that were sent from her friends," he said, barely above a whisper while pulling an iphone out of his pocket and glancing over his shoulder to make sure none of his crew had come up to the cemetery for him. "These are pictures of the masks and suits I gave you. My daughter said some of her Mexican friends who live here are frightened by the figures because they remind them of the *Zetas* who forced their parents to bring them to the U.S. It would not surprise me if some of my workers' children did not also show the pictures to them, and that they too..." Armando's voice trailed off, but by his implication of the ruthless Mexican drug cartel death squads, he had made his point clear to Parker.

"Today is Friday," Armando continued, as he stood to go. "We will finish with our fumigation today and come back next week to remove the tarp. The fence will be finished by next Wednesday. There will be only one opening and it will have a locked gate." Armando blinked in rapid succession and then resumed. "I have been told you will be served by the sheriff on Thursday. Rocco called this morning to tell me he is on his way home and has hired some *'friends'*," he said, making air-quotes, "to help with security. I was told by my daughter this morning that I should not come to work here that day, so I have decided to take my crew and work on another job."

Armando looked across the field toward the taco truck where his men were still milling about in dawn's shadow while the sun now lit the hillside opposite them. "Look at them," he sighed. "The sun is almost up and normally they would be shouting at me to get to work so they could make some money. But today," he sighed, "they only wait... Oh, I forgot. Pedro, one of my crew, gave me this to give to you," he said, placing his phone back in his pocket and retrieving a pliant, saucer-shaped object from the same. "He said it contains two Liberty silver dollars. For luck."

Parker took it up in his hand and saw that it was actually a bird made from a finely woven wool sock. On closer inspection, he realized it had been fashioned into the likeness of a falcon. "It's a falcon, isn't it?" he said, admiring the woven bird, to which Armando nodded. "I know it well from my son's Scout days," Parker continued. "It was Tad's favorite. In case you don't know," he added, "Falcon is a Native American talisman. To the leader of Tad's troop, who was one-sixteenth Wappo, it represents the elevated spirituality needed for leadership. He said Falcon is like what a friend of mine calls a protector demon, whose power is to perceive negative energy and make it its prey."

Parker looked down at his still sleeping namesake, knowing that if the talisman were left lying around, Parker-the-dog would surely find a way to get to it. He started to put Falcon in his pocket, but a flicker of light above him caught his eye and changed his mind; for when he glanced up for the light's source, he saw that Squirrel's blue tent was shimmering like water bedazzled by the rays of a sunrise over a mountain lake.

He said, "I think I'll give this to a friend of mine who might find Falcon helpful in turning a lot of negative energy around."

Parker then gathered from the table a two-foot-long length of baling string he had picked off the ground after it had been left behind by the fencing crew. He wrapped one end around Falcon's neck. Then he stood and walked over to Squirrel's eucalyptus and tied the other end to the top of a six-foot sucker emerging from its base. There it caught the first rays of sunlight as they poured through a gap in the mountains to the east.

Armando twitched as if bitten by a horsefly at the sudden illumination and hastily crossed himself. "Well, good then. Back to work," he said, squinting against the sudden burst of light. "Be safe, Parker. But I'd wear those hazmat suits if I were you."

"I'll think about it," Parker said, as, above him, he heard the sound of the zipper on Squirrel's tent.

Soon thereafter the methyl bromide and tarp crew fired up their vehicles. At the sound, Squirrel, already in his school clothes, emerged from his tent. Twenty seconds later he was on the ground, backpack strapped to his back. After stopping briefly to greet Parker and Parker-the-dog and to inspect the knitted falcon, he trotted hurriedly toward the water closet, followed closely by Parker-the-dog. Five minutes later both emerged.

"Too many lemon bars, I guess," Squirrel explained, grinning sheepishly while standing beside the eucalyptus looking more closely at the falcon. "Where'd this come from?"

Parker gestured down the hill. "From Pedro. One of Armando's guys. It's Falcon."

"I know. A good luck charm, right?"

Parker nodded. "Sort of." And he repeated what he had said to Armando.

"Nice. I like things that can see negative energy and make it its prey. Like Chester's OM," Squirrel said, "and Dotty's lemon bars." He then took out his phone and photographed the falcon. After he had attached it to a tweet, he turned his attention to the nearly empty box of lemon bars Parker had brought out from the trailer. "I suppose I should have something to eat before school."

"Go ahead. Liberate 'em," Parker said, "I'm sure Dotty will bring reinforcements to the barricades soon."

Squirrel smiled and then wolfed down the four bars that were left, then, looking down at the field operations commencing parallel to the road, he shook his head. "I'd better get going before they start spraying."

"Don't want to tempt fate again?" Parker said.

"Naw. I could do it again easily. Too easily. That's the problem. I don't like repeating things I've figured out. When I grow up," he added, "I want to try to do something new every day. That way I'll never stop being curious..."

Squirrel's voice trailed off and he shifted his gaze to Parker-the-dog, who had just toppled over on her back after standing on her hind legs trying to reach the talisman hanging from the sucker. From Squirrel's expression, Parker guessed that Squirrel was trying to decide whether or not to remove Falcon to a less tantalizing spot, or to call the puppy off. But then suddenly, Squirrel turned his gaze on Parker, and through clenched teeth finished his thought. "Like you, Parker," he said tersely. "I want to be like you. I want my life to have meaning. Even if it's only inside a cemetery."

Taken aback, Parker was left momentarily speechless by this unsolicited confession that seemed to have been wrung out of Squirrel unwillingly, in part because Squirrel's sentiment was so unexpected, but mostly because Squirrel had reminded him then of Tad, who, like Squirrel, had had just such an effacing knack for spontaneous truth telling that seemed to come from out of nowhere.

As Parker was about to acknowledge his appreciation of Squirrel's admission, both of their attentions were all of a sudden diverted when two deafening explosions rent the air. The origin of the detonations quickly became discernable as having come from the two tractors pulling the methyl bromide tank and the rolls of tarp; for, from out of their tailpipes shot two long tongues of flame. On the heels of these a staccato string of lesser belches, consisting of flame and smoky backfires, quickly followed. These fiery burps were, in turn, succeeded by a rapid series of spasmodic splutters and, finally, by a grim, drawn out duet that ended with a paroxysm of grisly exhalations and a final gasp into stillness.

"That didn't sound good," said Parker.

Squirrel nodded, and his jaw went slack in relief for the disruption that had precluded his embarrassment for having revealed himself. "I probably won't get back here tonight," he said, "but I'll get in touch with Angie and Danquin about next week." Before Parker could respond to this or to the other, Squirrel had already turned away and was loping down the hill toward the van that had just pulled up.

Now that he was alone with his thoughts again, Parker began his work day by clearing the grave of Poco, while in the field below work continued on repairing the quieted vehicles. Finally, as he was finishing up with Poco an hour later, Armando strode up to the cemetery with a lightness in his step Parked did not fail to notice.

"Done for the day. Done till next week at least," he said blithely, as if it were self-evident, while he held out an empty five pound sack of confectioners sugar for Parker to see. "Looks like someone sugared our gas tanks."

"Can't say I'm sorry," Parker said.

"Can't say I am either," Armando responded. "Those tractors are older than I am. If we're lucky, insurance will cover the rebuild of at least one."

"Can I see the bag?"

"Sure. But why?" queried Armando. "It's just an empty bag anyone could get in a grocery store. And besides, I'm sure whoever did this would've had enough brains to have worn gloves."

"Just the same," he said, taking the bag from Armando. "Got any suspects?" Parker turned the torn remnants in his hands.

"Yep. Twenty Mexicans," Armando replied, nodding toward the street, where Parker could see the workers were putting away their materials.

Parker handed the bag back to Armando, who blinked rapidly and raised his hand to fend off the object as though it might sting him. "No, you keep it," he said, and glanced at the empty lemon bar container on the table. "In the vineyards it is said by some who know more than I that it is better sometimes to walk away from what you know so that what you don't know can free the grapes to find their own truth." To which Parker nodded and, crumpling the bag in his hands, took out a lighter and set fire to the evidence.

Dotty appeared later that same day shortly before noon bearing lunch, dinner, and a copy of *The Valley Observer*. She showed little surprise that the tilled field hadn't been sprayed and covered with plastic, or that the equipment, which had already been towed away, had been sabotaged. Parker thought it prudent not to ask any direct questions about the monkey-wrenching of the tractors, and after she and he had eaten a pleasant, largely wordless lunch together, during which they contented themselves with watching Parker-the-dog scamper after butterflies, Dotty took the newspaper from her basket and slapped it onto the table in front of Parker.

"Here's Wili Wallenstock's screed," she said, crinkling her nose. "If you'd like to read it."

"I would," Parker said, not failing to note the challenge in Dotty's voice and the disdain in her expression. He put his plate down and unfolded the slim weekend edition to find Wili's article featured beneath the fold on the first page of the *Opinion & People Section*, accompanied by a picture of him standing beside what should have been Yellow Dog Red's headstone, but which was instead a composite picture of him and Danquin. Though put off at once by Wili's electronic legerdemain, Parker nonetheless raised his eyebrows in admiration at the expertise with which she had Photoshopped the two seamlessly into one, but he said nothing of it and read the headline aloud.

"'Controversy Over Yellow Dog Red Overlook,'" he read, with a tentative smile of approval forming on his lips. "'Local Man's Vigil Sheds Light on Lack of Community Resources for Elderly.' What!" he exclaimed, after rereading the sub-heading. "Where did she come up with that?"

"Read on," said Dotty, splitting her gaze between Parker and Parker-the-dog who had begun leaping for the sock falcon affixed to the eucalyptus. "It gets worse."

Parker cleared his throat and read on. "'The plight of the elderly in the twilight years of their lives to find emotional sustenance and safe environments in our valley has been highlighted these past months by an unlikely act of civil disobedience carried out by a man quite possibly in the early stages of the same debilitating dementia that recently killed his wife.'"

Parker lowered the paper and peered over his spectacles at Dotty. "You've gotta be kidding. Me? With dementia? Isn't that libelous?" he said in dismay, not bothering to hide his own disdain at Wili's audacity. "You've read through this already, right?"

"Of course. Twice actually, although I rarely read her anymore. I can't stand the style she affects," Dotty scowled. "And the liberty she takes with truth makes everything into tabloid smut."

Parker nodded. "Is it worth reading the rest? Or will it only make me angry?"

Dotty shrugged. "Depends. But if you want to get an idea what nonsense everybody else in the valley reads and maybe even what they think..."

Dotty's voice trailed off and Parker nodded in deference to her pessimistic assessment, then shifting his gaze, he noticed that a white van had pulled to a stop down on the road. "Okay, I'll read on then," he said, ignoring the van, and reluctantly he continued.

"'This improbable story, which has stirred many people across the globe, concerns Parker (he refers to himself with his first name only). He is eighty, a recent widower, and a long-time valley resident who three months ago illegally moved a ten-foot travel trailer onto the long-neglected pet cemetery adjacent to the old Gainsaid Pound property, supposedly to protest the burial ground's proposed closure to make way for the newly approved ultra-premium Pinot Noir winery: Etruscan Estates Vineyards.

"'The winery's owner, Rocco Zinni, of Turlock, is out of the country and could not be reached for comment in time for this article, but if it is publicity Mr. Zinni seeks for his new venture, he has acquired an embarrassment of riches without lifting so much as a shovelful of our valley's superior terroir. The instant notoriety for Etruscan Estate Vineyards is owed not to anything Mr. Zinni himself has done but solely to Parker and to a band of zealous, devoted, and some would say misguided followers, mostly young, who through their adept use of social media have come to view Parker's vigil as an online cause-celebre pitting the haves of the valley (Mr. Zinni) against the have-nots (everyone else). These so-called *Yellow Dog Red Riders* (i.e., an online cult) of fanciful social activists assert their participation in Parker's cause to be some sort of crowd-sourcing-flash-mobbing-action, whose call-to-arms is nothing less than a fanatical revision of *The Ode to Joy* in what they call *The Yellow Dog Red Symphony*.'"

Parker lowered the paper and stared speechlessly at Dotty, whose gesture in reply said, "I know." And shaking his head he resumed.

"'This comparison by Parker's erstwhile partisans with Beethoven's singular masterpiece about the maestro's adoration to his redemptive God is nonsensical and perhaps pitiable, even dangerous; as it highlights the elements of pathos, manipulation, grandiose delusions of grandeur, and false nobility that attend those mislaid beings among us, particularly our impressionable youth, who in their pursuit of meaning attach themselves to an unassuming yet cynically charismatic cult figure. And indeed, this reporter too found herself coming under the sway of Parker, who is both charming and nonthreatening. Some would say he is inspiring. I myself say he is wily and arresting. Which is why I am worried. And here is why I think our readers should also worry.

"'Parker has spent his working life in Army Intelligence as a domestic analyst—e.g. a spook. He has toiled incognito for decades in an agency invested with the knowledge and skills of how to covertly manipulate public sentiment to its advantage. To be fair to Parker, he does not seem Machiavellian in the least, for to be in his presence elicits only sympathy, which renders it highly unlikely that he himself would at his advanced age and decrepitude be capable of undertaking any type of subterfuge. Unless, that is, he is aided and abetted by younger, less than well-meaning lieutenants sympathetic to Parker only insofar as he serves their possibly nefarious agendas.

"'But, putting the crowd-sourcing-sharing-economy-cultist nonsense aside for the moment, the more pertinent truth here is that the Yellow Dog Red Overlook is neither a wholly homegrown subversive plot nor a paean to the sacred; rather, it is a more insidious hybrid that lies somewhere between the no-man's-land of societal disruption, and ennui. It revolves around a regrettably sad story: that of a bereaved man who has lost his wife of over forty years and who is predictably afflicted with a profound sense of loneliness and purposelessness. Unfortunately this existential aimlessness, born of boredom, bereavement and loneliness, is reflected in our elderly population at large. It is, in fact, rampant. And, as the Yellow Red Dog Overlook attests, it is easily exploitable; which can be explained by the fact that many of our community's limited resources have been diverted, by misguided liberal welfare policies, into mitigating the issues that have arisen in our schools and welfare system caused by illegal immigrants.'" Stunned and at a loss for words, Parker fell silent and shook his head.

Dotty said, "You needn't read any more."

Parker nodded, and, knitting his brows, muttered, "What is that woman's problem? Do you think she really believes my grief for Yellow Dog Red was caused by illegal immigrants?"

Dotty shrugged. "No, probably not, deep down. Nobody in their right mind would. But what can you say about a hack writer who's made her living lying on her back under her publisher? I mean, remember how shamelessly she flirted with you so that she could get a story to butcher?"

Parker looked over his glasses at Dotty, who blushed in embarrassment at betraying her own resentment. "Sorry. That was cruel of me," she said. "But I just don't understand how her publisher has allowed her to get away with stuff like this for decades."

"They're mercenaries. Both of them," Parker replied. "And mercenaries only have noses for money."

"Well," Dotty sniffed, "you may be right that Wili has a nose for money. But that pretty writer's nose of hers is filled with so much excrement after rooting around for so long in it that she can't smell the roses for the..."

Dotty's voice trailed off, and Parker, who unexpectedly found himself enjoying Dotty's indignation, said, "Then I'll hold my nose and keep reading. Even if it makes me ill."

"If you must," Dotty shrugged.

Parker brought the paper closer and continued. "'One offshoot of these policies is that daycare activities for seniors are bereft of sufficient community resources to adequately fund them. This has left people like Parker without anything better to do than spend his remaining days planted in a pet cemetery wallowing in grief while allowing people with ulterior motives, many of whom are foreign born, to stir up sympathy for him in the hope that their propaganda will generate publicity for their own causes of class warfare, income redistribution, and unconstitutional pathways to U.S. citizenship.'"

Parker took a deep breath and raised his gaze to Dotty, who again threw her hands up in a gesture of disbelief. "This is horrible," he muttered, his voice quivering.

"I know," Dotty said. "But you're almost to the end. Might as well read on."

Parker shrugged and resumed. "'But a graveyard does not provide Parker with the peace of mind, economic justice, or social safety net he or his reputed social media *followers* need most," he read. "Those needs can be administered best by mental health and criminal justice professionals who, working in conjunction with family, church, law enforcement, and private enterprise, can deal with the scourge of geriatric depression and victimization in a cost-efficient, business-friendly manner.

"'Nor frankly does the pet cemetery now provide the valley with what it needs most; jobs and prestige. To be sure, the publicity generated by the Yellow Dog Red Overlook has indeed attracted worldwide attention to our fair valley, but it has no hope in proving itself a practicable or sustainable financial magnet in the same vein as will Mr. Zinni's ultra-premium winery, which will continue to provide renown to the valley long after Yellow Dog Red, Parker, and his online denizens of discontent have faded into history like yesteryear's favorite cheap vintage.'"

Parker had come to the bottom of the column, which was continued on a back page. Rather than turn to it, however, he shoved the paper away and ripped off his glasses.

"What on earth?" he frowned. "Cults? Disciples? Illegals? Spooks? How can she get away with this kind of prolix propaganda? And just how dumb does she think the people in this valley are?"

Dotty shook her head.

"And not even one mention of the real Yellow Dog Red."

"No, not on the front page. But she does mention her in the last paragraph on the last page. One sentence about you burying your pet in the cemetery."

"And the picture," Parker said indignantly. "Look. She took out Yellow Dog Red and put in Danquin like he's the mastermind behind the whole thing."

Dotty glanced at the picture, and clicked her tongue disparagingly. "She's thinking there is more money in writing about old people with Alzheimers being manipulated by unscrupulous foreign handlers than about old people mourning their beloved pets," Dotty said. "And she's probably right."

"But she's gotten it all wrong," Parker muttered, and knowing that there was little he could do to try to correct or get the story retracted, he sighed in resignation. "I knew by the way she was fluttering her lashes that I shouldn't have talked to her."

"I don't think it was you that got her so wound up," Dotty said. "I think she actually likes you. It was me and Danquin she didn't like. She probably really does think he's an alien terrorist bent on the overthrow of capitalism in the United States, and that I'm a geriatric jezebel leading you around by the nose...and by these," she added teasingly, prying open a new box of lemon bars and sliding them toward Parker.

Parker laughed begrudgingly at Dotty's characterization of herself and Danquin, but his laugh was cut short when his attention was again averted to the van at the bottom of the hill, from out of which two men emerged, one holding a long cardboard tube. "Uh oh," he said. "Looks like we have uninvited guests."

The two men who approached wore identical gray overalls of the type worn by farmhands. Both were grossly overweight, and both were out of breath by the time they had climbed from the street and across the turned earth to the cemetery and had squeezed through the opening in the fence. Strangely, Parker-the-dog, resting her head on Dotty's foot, did not move a muscle to either greet or warn off the men. Likewise, despite their close proximity to Parker and Dotty, neither man stopped to acknowledge them. Instead, as if they were in a parallel universe, the two walked northward until they came to the intersection of the portion of fence that ran perpendicular westward to the one they followed. Facing into the interior of the cemetery, they took a rolled document from out of their tube, which they unfurled and began to argue over vehemently.

Though both men were at least a hundred pounds overweight and approximately somewhere in their fifties, from his vantage Parker noted that, of the two men, the one holding the document was of a completely different physiognomic body type from the other. That is, while the latter was built in the manner of a wrestler, whose weight was anchored by an ample musculature that gave to him a look of solidity, the former was built like someone whose weight was anchored only by a skeleton, which gave him a look of bloated viscosity. Furthermore, in the way each carried himself, Parker realized intuitively that it was the gelatinous one who should worry him most; for in his demeanor Parker detected an inwardly resentful defensive timidity he had come to recognize as one of the signatures underlying incipient cruelty in some of those he had investigated. A cruelty, that is, that was self-sustaining in those whose beleaguerment has been cultivated by self-imposed persecution and which, inasmuch as it was least expected and because it was manifested insidiously, was often the most destructive.

It was the other man, though, who seemed to be the one in charge as, after gesturing to something in the drawings, he poked the paper with his pudgy fingers and then gesticulated impatiently in all directions. On several occasions he was overheard to exclaim, "No, you idiot! That's not what it says!"

This pattern of inspection and impatience followed by abuse was repeated at the next two corners of the cemetery. At each intersection the two men stopped and, with seemingly little success, tried to coordinate their understanding of the graphics with the landscape. By the time they came to the final corner they still had not said a word to, or even acknowledged, Parker and Dotty's presence. The only concession that the men were obliged to make was that instead of shouting at one another they now lowered their voices and merely hissed their disagreements.

Dotty had almost immediately realized from her friend's unflattering description upon meeting them at the truck stop in Turlock months earlier that the men were Marco and Enzo Zinni, which Dotty communicated to Parker. Just as Marco and Enzo were preparing to exit the cemetery by squeezing through the breach in the fencing, Dotty suddenly called out to them.

"Hi there! Time for some lemon bars?" Whereupon, having gained their attention, she hastened over to them with her box of lemon bars in hand.

"Mr. Zinni, my name is Dotty. Care for something sweet? I made them myself," she said, extending the box toward the one nearest her who she thought was Enzo, for he was holding the cardboard tube.

"Have we met before?" the other replied instead, stepping forward and glancing austerely into the plastic container filled to the brim with three layers of lemon bars.

"You've met my friend. She's a lawyer," Dotty replied. "She went to see you to discuss keeping the cemetery open."

"I see. What can I do for you?" he responded dourly, after taking in both Dotty and Parker at a glance and disdainfully surveying the encampment.

Before Dotty could reply, the first one blurted, "Are those from Dotty's Deli?" His eyes were opened wide.

"They are. And I'm Dotty," she said, smiling in satisfaction that her signature confection had been recognized by a stranger. She extended the box to him.

"Marco, don't!"

"Enzo, we haven't eaten anything since breakfast, and I'm hungry," Marco complained. "So why not?" A bar was already in the grip of his hand.

"Because this woman is the enemy," Enzo rejoined. "And because when Rocco gets back he will kill us when he finds out we were fraternizing with her. So put it back."

Marco's eyes narrowed and darted from side to side, but, not to be deterred, he refused to withdraw his hand. Instead, he offered Enzo a proposition. "What if we were to take the whole box from this woman, since she's offering them, and eat all the lemon bars?" he said. "Wouldn't that be like we weren't fraternizing with our enemy but were taking something away from her so she wouldn't be able to feed our other enemies?"

Like Marco, Enzo's eyes narrowed as he considered this suggestion. But Dotty had already made his decision an easy one. "Here, take the whole lot," she said. "I can't stand to see hard-working men go hungry." She pressed the box against Marco's overalls and let go of it so that he was forced to grab hold or let it fall to the ground.

"I don't know, it feels like a bribe," Enzo muttered, simultaneously licking his lips and scowling as he glanced at the dozens of lemon bars now firmly in his brother's grip.

By then Parker had joined Dotty, and to Enzo he said, "I suggest you take the offering, Mr. Zinni. For the road. I'm sure you know that *Sunset Magazine* says they're the best in the west. Besides," he added, "it's me—and I know you know my name is Parker—who you have a quarrel with, not with the bars or Dotty. And in fact, Dotty isn't offering you a bribe, she's offering you an out-and-out gift. No strings attached." Considering Parker's words, Enzo tilted his head first to one side then to the other. Seeing that Enzo was wavering, Parker continued, "Look, there's no reason for us to tell your brother you accepted a bite of food from us. Isn't it true that if we were in Italy, like Rocco, we would be rude to not offer you something, and you would be rude to refuse our offer?"

"Yes, it is true," Marco answered for Enzo. "We have been to Sienna many times, and people feed us everywhere we go."

While Enzo pondered Parker's argument, Marco lifted the boxful of lemon bars to his nose and, breathing deeply of their scent, cast Enzo an imploring glance. Enzo's expression softened to one of longing. "Oh, all right. But we will only take a few," he said, and he reached into the box and took out six bars, with Marco following his lead.

"Thank you," Marco said, as Enzo nodded in acknowledgment. He then tapped Marco on the shoulder, signifying that it was time for them to go.

One after the other they squeezed through the narrow cleft in the fence. Before they had gone out of earshot, Parker called out to them. "Maybe you could answer just one question for me," he said. "What's so wrong with keeping a pet cemetery on this property?"

"Rocco hates dogs," Marco shouted in reply, not bothering to turn back. Then with a small puff of confectioner's sugar escaping his mouth, he added, "even more than I hate squatters."

Ten minutes later another car stopped at the base of the hill, and from out of the driver's side back door emerged Angie. Seeing Parker she waved and cried out, "Parker! I'm back!"

Then from out of the front passenger door Danquin emerged. And finally Bahram opened the driver's door. Both men lagged behind Angie, however, as neither one could keep up with her as she sprinted up the hill toward the cemetery. The instant Parker-the-dog had heard Angie call her name, she too dashed off to meet her from the opposite direction, despite Parker's efforts to call her back. At about the three-quarter mark, Angie, seeing that the puppy was bounding out of control downhill toward her, lowered herself to one knee and braced herself in preparation for the impact. And, indeed, unable to halt his headlong gallop Parker slammed into her with such momentum that he pitched her over backwards onto the ground, where for several seconds the two lay splayed out inertly on their backs.

Dotty caught her breath, thinking the dog had injured Angie, or worse. But then girl and dog sat up both yelping joyfully, and at least one dribbled a few drops of pee into the soil out of shear happiness. When Angie drew up to the fence with Parker-the-dog beside her, she was flushed with exertion.

"Guess what?" she cried exuberantly, dusting off smudges of moist dirt as best she could from her jeans and shirt.

At a loss at how to answer, Parker could only shrug, but then offered tentatively, "Your dad let you go online?"

Angie let a conspiratorial smile escape, and before answering him she peeked over her shoulder to see where her father was. "I never was really offline...totally...only officially," she whispered, although it wasn't necessary since Bahram was still out of earshot. "My father just thinks I was. Promise me you won't tell him," she added hastily, glancing at both Parker and Dotty as Danquin passed through the gap in the fence.

"Promise," affirmed Parker then Dotty, both of whom greeted Danquin and then Bahram a minute later.

They were saying their hellos when another car and, a second later, a van, pulled to a stop behind Bahram's car. From out of the car came Roper bearing a canvas satchel, and from the van emerged a wheelchair carrying Keith. Being that the earth was too tilled now for his wheelchair to navigate directly to the cemetery, Keith swung his chair southward along the paved road and headed up the dirt road that ran alongside the vineyard, with Roper rather than his driver at his side in escort. In the interim before their arrival, Parker informed Angie, Bahram and Danquin about the monkey-wrenching and the postponement of the preparatory work on the vineyard on account of it.

Both Angie and Bahram were delighted to hear about the delay, but Angie could barely suppress her enthusiasm about sharing what she'd heard at the Aspen Institute. But no sooner had she begun telling of her experiences than she was interrupted when Parker-the-dog, barely able to contain herself at the influx of familiar people entering into her home turf, started to whine and paw at her. Unable to ignore her and crestfallen at being unable to relate her story, she had no choice but to stop talking as Roper now entered into the cemetery ahead of Keith.

"Where's my sweetest little Parker-the-dog?" Roper cooed, lowering himself to let his dog lavish him with wet puppy kisses. Then, looking up at Parker and then into the tree at Squirrel's tent, he added, "And where's our favorite tree elf?"

"He said he won't be back for a couple days," replied Parker, as, pushing aside the futon sofa, he made room for Keith to maneuver his chair off the soft ground onto the firmer earth under the ground-cloth.

"That's too bad," Roper responded. "I was looking forward to giving him these." He pulled a pair of boot spikes out of his satchel. "I thought he might be able to use them, since I won't be needing them anymore."

"It's his foster parents," inserted Angie, frowning petulantly in disappointment that her telling of the Ted Talks had been circumvented. "Squirrel said they get more money putting a kid with special needs in his room than they get for him, so they're dumping him into a group home."

"Can I look at those?" Danquin said, gesturing to the boot spikes. Roper handed them to him. "These are for climbing into trees, no?"

"They are. And those are the best ones I've ever had. Case-hardened spikes. Leather leg wrappings. Oh, and here's a cinch," he said, pulling a coiled, well-used leather strap out of the satchel. "You can give it a go if you'd like," he said, pointing to the trees behind Yellow Dog Red's grave.

"Yes, I would like that very much," Danquin beamed, whereupon, with Roper's help, he managed to fit the spikes onto his legs and hobble over to Squirrel's eucalyptus.

"This is how you do it," Roper said, demonstrating for him how to thrust the spikes obliquely downward into the tree trunk and how to lift the cinch just enough to keep him secure while allowing him to ascend. "But be careful," he added. "Coming down can be trickier than going up."

In the meantime, Angie, having given up for the time being on the Ted Talks, was informing Parker that she and her father and Danquin had met the night before with the laundry owner and had arranged to use the defunct video store next to the laundry, which was used now only for storage, as Command Central for the Yellow Dog Red Overlook. With a distinct note of pride permeating her voice, she related that a link had already been enabled connecting the laundry's wifi network to the blog several friends had just posted online, which, she said, gave them easy access to the cemetery's cameras, so that when people came to pay their respects to Yellow Dog Red they could first watch the feed instead of heading out to the cemetery. But it was not the expansion of their ad hoc network, or the crowd control element contained implicitly within it which reignited her enthusiasm. Rather, it was a conversation with Slag that lit her eyes from within as she began to speak of it.

"From his tweets I didn't really believe he was really that interested in us," she said. "Until he walked up to me and father the third day and said, 'And so, lass, how is the High Priestess Zand of Yellow Dog Red today?'" Angie's eyes opened wide as if to take in the entirety of the meeting again. "Really, he did!" she went on. "That's what he called me: 'the High Priestess Zand.' I've never been called high priestess by anyone before. And he said it in his Irish accent, so I knew he meant it. And that wasn't even the best part," she continued. "The best part was that he took me aside and, holding my hand, sang me some of the song he's writing. And, oh my god, The High Priestess Zand of Yellow Dog Red was one of his lyrics. Really!"

At overhearing this, Keith, who had initiated a conversation with Bahram about bottling some of Paradoxum's newly released Petite Sarah, halted in mid-sentence, and, nudging his wheelchair's steering stick, pivoted the chair so he faced Angie.

"Really? Slag sang to you?"

"Really," Angie nodded solemnly.

"No way, girl!" Keith exclaimed. "That's like Yahweh talking to Moses through a burning bush."

Angie furrowed her brows in confusion. "No, he did," she insisted. "He sang to me, didn't he, Father?"

Bahram nodded. "He did. Really," he acknowledged. "And what's more," he added, "Slag himself said he is going to release it as a single on itunes sometime very soon." He then turned to Parker.

"Oh, and by the way, I have just today opened a bank account to receive direct deposits from the song's proceeds. They will go to my daughter's and your efforts to keep Yellow Dog Red safe. In fact we have already gathered five-thousand dollars." He glanced at Angie to whom he

199

now directed his words. "Although I encouraged Angie from the very beginning to do what she thought was right, I admit I was skeptical at first that her efforts would succeed. But after talking to Slag and hearing him sing his song, I must admit now that I myself am finding this all to be very exciting."

As Bahram was telling this, Parker had begun shuffling away to join Dotty, who had seated herself beside Yellow Dog Red's headstone. But upon hearing Bahram say he had opened an account and had gathered thousands of dollars on his behalf, Parker halted and wheeled around abruptly to face him.

"What will become of this money?" he said, leveling a withering gaze on Bahram and speaking in a tone that was excoriating. "And who will see how it's dispersed?"

Abashed by Parker's bluntness, and barely able to hide his shock over the implied insinuation of Parker's gaze, Bahram's cheeks reddened and he began fumbling for words. "Why...why, it will go to...go to pay salaries...for security, for crowd control, for portable toilets, for...for food, for accountants... Already," he went on, "my daughter has received commitments from thousands of people who say they will come here to pay their respects. Surely their needs will have to be accommodated...to be paid for... And as to how the money will be spent," he added, "I assure you it will all be dispersed on the up-and-up. That is why I have asked my friend Keith, whose credentials are more impeccable than mine, to be a co-signatory with me on the account."

"And what if people donate a lot more money than either of you can spend?"

"It will go to...go to...maintaining the cemetery. And..." His voice trailed off and he gazed imploringly at Keith for help.

"And we haven't gotten any farther in our planning than that yet, Parker," Keith interposed, his voice croaking through his partially paralyzed vocal cords. Then, after his arm had shot up and in the interim his voice had re-cocked itself, he added almost mellifluously, "But give us a chance. We're making this up as we go along. I mean, look at us," he said, throwing his head back and laughing, "Do any of us look to you like we know what we're doing?"

"No, in truth you do not," Parker replied. And although his glare softened, he did not bother to hide the lingering skepticism in his voice. He fell silent to ruminate to himself while letting his gaze fall on Yellow Dog Red's headstone. After several moments had passed he whispered, "'Here at my feet my friend Yellow Dog Red lies, waiting for me in peace, always faithful.'" Then, aloud and addressing the grave, he said, "What should we do, old girl? Should we trust these strange people to do what is best for you?"

Parker then cocked his head and listened intently, as did the others, all of whom had ceased their discussions during the confrontation. The only sound came from Parker-the-dog, who had begun to gnaw on a stick. When Parker resumed a minute later, his lips were drawn tautly into an expression of forbearance somewhere between monition and approval.

"Yellow Dog Red gives you her blessing to do with the money what you see fit." But then through clenched teeth he murmured, "But under no circumstances will I allow my vigil to be turned into a circus or anything like it that demeans Red's memory. If it does, then I swear I will dig up my sweet little girl's bones with my bare hands and leave this place to the profiteers, carnies, polluters and tweeting misanthropes you will have brought down upon her."

The silence that ensued was inexorable, chastening and complete; for none there had ever seen this aspect of Parker that made him a feisty and intractable foe with whom to reckon. The tension was broken only when Angie walked over from behind and slipped her hand into his. "I will never allow that to happen, Parker. I promise," she intoned solemnly.

"I promise too," Roper said.

"And me too," attested Keith.

"I as well," said Bahram.

"Don't forget me," interjected Danquin, who by then had managed to climb ten feet off the ground. "If there is anything my people know how to do, it is to organize crowds."

Parker nodded, both in relief and resolve. "Okay then, that's good we're agreed. Because if we're going to have company—lots of it, there is much work that needs doing, especially after our interesting visit today from two of the Zinni brothers," he said. "Interesting because they referred to us," he gestured to Dotty and himself, "as their 'enemies.' Normally I wouldn't be too concerned about cheap talk like that coming from people who are merely bullies. But in my day I worked with enough people who were very much like them to know they are not your run-of-the-mill garden-variety bullies." He shook his head as if to clear it of decades of cobwebs, then continued.

"No, they are of another, more remorseless type. Professionals you might say. Run of the mill bullies work from the outside and try to get their way by bluffing and by pushing people around. The others, though, are like flesh-eating bacteria, the kind that work to excavate their host from the inside."

"Ugh!" Angie frowned.

"Ugh is right," rejoined Roper. "And by the way," he offered, "I actually have some information about them in that regard. When I was in San Francisco last week I had a chance to talk to my grandfather. In case I haven't told you," he continued, "he owns the Napa Welling Group. It's a wine distribution company, although he doesn't run it anymore. I told him about your vigil, Parker, and asked him if he knew the Zinnis. When he heard me say their name he made a face like I've never seen on him before." In demonstration Roper drew his lips down into an exaggerated scowl and his brows into a ropy mass so that together they formed an expression not unlike one that might grace a gothic cathedral gargoyle.

"'Clod farmers' he called them. Which, to grandpa, means not only are they beneath dirt farmers, who are honorable men but who have no business making wine, but they are, as he called them, 'worthless, scum of the earth scoundrels.' He told me to be careful. Because they might be connected to the Mafia. And that if this wasn't my fight, to steer clear. I asked him to elaborate, but that's all he would say. It's like he felt so befouled in even talking about them that it made him ill."

"Befouled. That's it exactly," Dotty put in. "There was something actively unscrupulous and repulsive about both those boys that made my skin crawl."

Parker nodded reflexively. "Unscrupulous and repulsive, along with what I would call insatiable greediness," he sighed. "Those are the signatures of the kind of rapacious moral depravity that knows nothing other than its own craving for domination. The kind of dehumanizing lust for power that allows men to believe they are liberating their victims when they are in fact not only destroying them but are taking their humanity from them.

"When I was working once on a panel taking the testimony of war criminals," he continued, "I was struck again and again by how deeply and sincerely those men who committed unspeakable acts of genocide, rape, and societal destruction could not admit to being anything other than liberators of the oppressed and victims of their victims' retribution. Now that I have met two of the Zinnis myself, I am afraid I agree with your grandfather," he said, with a nod to Roper. "The Zinnis are made of just such stuff as nightmares are made of," he concluded.

Scanning those gathered around him, he then added, "That's why we have to be careful to not do anything stupid, or especially anything blatantly illegal. Because men with no scruples will usually have the best lawyers representing them."

"Are you trying to scare us on purpose?" Roper said, glancing worriedly up toward Danquin, who had almost attained the level of Squirrel's tent.

Parker shook his head. "The only thing I set out to do on purpose was to make sure my dog was okay," he replied. "Now, though, I am also trying to keep us safe. And the best way for me to achieve that is to not allow others to keep me from reaching my original goal."

A stretch-limo drew to a stop now behind Keith's van. Two men emerged from its rear doors and they soon entered into the graveyard. Judging by their attire, which were matching gray suits that clung so cleanly to their bodies that they had to have been tailored by an expert haberdasher, Parker at first guessed they were wealthy businessmen, perhaps Zinnis' lawyers. Although, by their dark skin, the headbands that both wore, and by their shoulder-length ponytails, they gave every indication of being Native Americans, which seemed an unlikely choice of attorneys for the Zinnis to hire to represent them. Nevertheless, Parker braced himself for what he expected might be forthcoming.

The first man through the fence strode up to Bahram. "Mr. Parker," he said, extending a hand, "I am Stanley White Shadow, and this is my associate Thomas Ant Lake."

Both men were in their forties, dark-haired, and in possession of an air of competence and command that gave a businesslike but also unlawyerly straightforwardness that was refreshing and also approachable. Bahram was about to correct Stanley White Shadow's mistake, but in glancing over at Parker he saw him shake his head imperceptibly, and Bahram reciprocated their introduction as if he were Parker.

After being introduced to the others, Stanley White Shadow turned to Bahram again and said, "The reason we are here is because our tribal council—we are Northern Paiute—and our executive council, which owns the Red Bud Casino up in Downland, called and asked me and Thomas, who is our tribal shaman, to come here today to see if there is anything we can do to be of service to the Yellow Dog Red Overlook." He handed Bahram a card, which Bahram passed to Parker.

Bahram knitted his brows. "Why would a Paiute casino up in Downland want to help us down here?" he said.

"Because the spirit of Falcon communicated through tweets that you needed help," inserted Thomas Ant Lake, in a dismissive manner that conveyed that his answer should have been self-evident.

"What I guess I mean," persisted Bahram, mimicking Thomas Ant Lake's air of superiority, "is what's in it for you to help us—people you've never met—keep a long forgotten pet cemetery open that's nowhere even close to Downland? Unless you're planning to open a casino..."

Thomas Ant Lake waved off Bahram's dangling insinuation with a shake of his head that sent his braid swinging over his shoulder. "What's in it for us," he replied, "is for our people to help Falcon breathe, so that we ourselves may breathe more easily. Which is the business of all of us."

"It is a received honor that came to us on the spirit winds from Aspen," inserted Stanley White Shadow. "And in being received, all we expect in return is to be of service."

"What about the Zinnis? The owners of this property," Bahram persevered. "Are you working for them?"

Thomas Ant Lake and Stanley White Shadow looked at one another and shrugged. "We do not know the Zinnis," Stanley White Shadow responded. "And as to who we are working for, we are working for you and those who are supporting you in your fight to keep this land a sacred burial spot for Yellow Dog Red."

Parker, having determined to his own satisfaction that the men had at least no direct connection to the Zinnis, cleared his throat and stepped forward so that he stood next to Bahram. "I'm sorry to have deceived you, Stanley, Thomas, but I'm Parker. I didn't know who you were, and I thought the better part of caution would be to be prudent," he said, and as he extended his hand he nodded to Bahram. "And this is my friend Bahram you are talking to."

Stanley White Shadow and Thomas Ant Lake nodded in understanding. Then, taking a deep breath and letting it out, Stanley White Shadow said, "Yes, I can understand your reluctance to trust us, for the earth beneath us is also suffering a loss of confidence," he said, and gesturing to the tarped earth, explained, "because she cannot breathe."

Thomas Ant Lake had meanwhile stepped aside to inspect the falcon sock affixed to the eucalyptus sucker. It was only then that, hearing a rustling sound above him, he looked up to see Danquin, who had gotten high enough into the tree so that, except from directly below, he was hidden from view by two low hanging branches to either side of Squirrel's tent. Thomas Ant Lake's reaction was amazed disbelief, which prompted him to shout out.

"What's the matter, Thomas?" Stanley White Shadow said, and as he and the others shifted their attention they saw that the color had drained from Thomas Ant Lake's face.

At just that moment the tree trunk splintered under one of Danquin's spikes. As the wood gave way, Danquin's foot, no longer anchored to the trunk, slipped free. A split second later, the other foot, having been twisted out of its mooring, also slipped free, and Danquin started to fall. But because he was holding tight to his cinch, as Roper had instructed, his descent was slowed so that he slid at a relatively controlled rate rather than in a free-fall.

Danquin's trajectory almost landed him atop Thomas Ant Lake, who only just barely managed at the last second to jump aside. Thomas Ant Lake could only stare.

"Sorry, sir," apologized Danquin, and added quickly. "I'm Danquin." Before Thomas could respond, Danquin, seeing the headband and braids for the first time, blurted, "Are you a real American Indian?"

Roper and the others had by then rushed to Danquin's side. "Are you okay?" he said, to which Danquin nodded. He then took the hands Roper and Bahram extended to help him to his feet.

"*Das macht freude!*" he beamed enthusiastically, dusting himself off. "I had no idea climbing a tree could be so much fun."

"Fun maybe. But you were very lucky, my friend." Roper said. "Nine times out of ten when a spike loses hold like that, the climber will end up spraining an ankle or worse."

"That was very cool," Angie said. "Can I try it, Father?" to which Bahram shook his head in such a sharp manner that Angie knew better than to challenge his decision.

Stanley White Shadow strode up beside Thomas and, to Danquin, he replied coldly, "In answer to your question, we are Native Americans of the Northern Paiute tribe."

Realizing that he had offended the men, Danquin apologized. "I'm sorry. It's just that I've never met a real American Ind—I mean, a Native American—before," he said, and he held up his right hand with his palm toward Stanley White Shadow. "Can I say 'How' in greeting?"

Stanley White Shadow shook his head and, smiling sourly, extended his hand to Danquin. "A handshake will suffice," he said.

"Oh, I'm so sorry," Danquin said, realizing he had committed another blunder. He then took Stanley White Shadow's and Thomas Ant Lake's hands in his own and shook each vigorously. "I didn't mean to insult you. I'm German. I...I mean, we don't have any Native Germans, like you have Native Americans here."

Stanley waved aside Danquin's apology. "Falcon has summoned us here," he said, "And for whatever reason, he has apparently chosen a very naive person like you to help your friends gain the vision they need to change into their prey the negative energy that is keeping Falcon and the earth from breathing."

"Me!" yelped Danquin, then in a considered tone, said, "Yes, I may be naive, as you say. But I am a visiting scholar from another country, so you must understand that I cannot let my preconceptions interfere with my research. You see," he went on, "I have come here to observe American phenomena. Yes, I admit I have also become a participant in the subject of my research, which may seem like naivete," he shrugged, "but that is only because I am learning that such scholarship requires that I compromise my objectivity with an amount of subjectivity in order for me to better understand the underlying motivations and dynamics of my subject. I also see that, as part of my research, I must quantify the struggle to retain my position as a neutral observer, or my work will be useless. Therefore," he concluded, "it is these people who must change the negative energy into their prey, not me."

"That of which you have spoken is probably true," Thomas replied. "But it is also true that Falcon has spoken to us here today through you. Not them. Therefore," he said, mimicking Danquin's tone, "as a scholar you are obligated to compromise your objectivity so that you may translate Falcon's words into deeds."

Thomas Ant Lake fell silent for a moment and tilted his head into the air as if to capture a scent. He then pointed toward the knoll, now covered with white plastic, along the northern border. "Tell me," he said to no one in particular, "what is over there on that rise?"

Roper, who had rolled up the cinch and was now inspecting the splinter that Danquin's spike had dislodged, replied, "That's where I found the obsidian artifacts I tried to have the county catalogue before the owners of this property turned all of the land under."

Thomas Ant Lake nodded. "A nut gathering camp. My grandfather has told me how his parents shucked acorns and made wine from plums that gave them dreams of Falcon, Coyote, Bear and Eagle. It is there," he said, "where you must go to help Falcon breathe. For there is where you will begin to help him change the negative into prey."

Monday morning saw the return of Armando with only four of his crew, all of whom came up to the cemetery in their white hazmat outfits, with two bearing coffee cups and two carrying bags of Mexican pastries.

"We can't get a sprayer or a tarp-layer here till next week," Armando told Parker with evident relief, as his men squatted against the trailer. "So, before the next rains come we're going to pull up the tarp, and I don't think we'll get back to doing the perimeter fence till then either." He gazed up into the sky, whose eastern border was blazing with rubescence. "And by the looks of it, I think we're in for a wet spell. Maybe a week or so, which will not help the schedule if the ground is too wet to handle the equipment. My guess," he concluded, "is that we won't be back to full speed for a couple of weeks."

Most of the men avoided making contact with Parker-the-dog, except for the one who Armando introduced as Bill, a slightly built, stooped and thin-boned man with sandy hair and hazel eyes whose coloring, Armando informed Parker, signified that Bill hailed from French ancestry in the state of Oaxaca. Whatever his lineage, Bill took on the persona of a Labrador puppy when Parker-the-dog trotted up to him and laid a well-chewed knotted-rope dog toy at his feet. For no sooner had Parker released the toy than Bill lowered himself to all fours and took up the toy in his mouth and began growling and shaking it like a dead rabbit. Parker-the-dog, in turn, latched her jaws onto the other end of the rope, dug in her heels, and began to tug against Bill. The tug of war and the accompanying canine verbal-human bombast that ensued soon brought tears of laughter to the eyes of even the other workmen who were clearly aghast at seeing Bill's mouth holding onto a dog toy.

When Bill finally released the toy signaling that the game was over, and stood to get a cup of coffee, Parker-the-dog followed him, and when Bill remained stationary she dropped the toy on his feet and lay down beside him. When Bill had finished his coffee, he picked up the toy and, motioning for Parker-the-dog to not grab it, carried it over beside Yellow Dog Red's grave, where he laid the toy, along with a tiny, handwoven straw figure that he drew out from the street clothes beneath his jumpsuit.

"Good luck, Yellow Dog Red," he murmured, in thickly accented English. "Your little friend has asked Coyote to guide you."

In the meantime, Parker had filled Armando in on his meeting with the Zinnis, to which Armando could only frown and shake his head sadly in acknowledgment. Parker also agreed with Armando that a rainy spell was likely, which, he said, was probably for the better as far as the the Yellow Dog Red Overlook (as even Parker now called it) was concerned; for in the day and a half following the meeting with Stanley White Shadow and Thomas Ant Lake, visitors had begun to trickle by, and if inclement weather was coming, Parker hoped that those numbers would diminish. As it was, the pilgrimage that began later in the day on Sunday and on into the evening numbered in the dozens, which was an amount that Angie and Danquin had thus far been able to organize so that the YDRP—as the Yellow Dog Red Pilgrims came to call themselves—came by one at a time.

To that point virtually all the visitors had brought pictures of their deceased pets, which they shared with Parker, and after reminiscing, most took selfies of themselves and Parker beside Yellow Dog Red's headstone. A few had brought lengths of butcher paper, which they spread across Yellow Dog Red's tombstone in order to make rubbings of the epitaph that they then had Parker sign. All who had brought pictures of their pets hung those pictures on the fence surrounding the cemetery. And virtually all of the pilgrims either sat on the ground beside Yellow Dog Red in silent vigil, or, for those too old or stiff to lower themselves to the ground, stood over her in silence.

Soon after having rolled up half of the white plastic and transporting it by hand to a flatbed truck on the road, which left only half-a-dozen strips immediately above the cemetery still on the ground, Armando and his men broke for lunch when their taco truck rolled to a stop on the road. At the same time Danquin, his voice reedy with excitement, called Parker and advised him that the first sojourner to come by Command Central that day was the woman named Tilly who had tweeted that Chester was her dog.

"She's come all the way from Sedona," Danquin fairly shouted into the phone. "She left the office fifteen minutes ago and said she would walk to the cemetery. So she will be there soon. I will come and ask her to let me interview her for my research," he added hopefully.

As Danquin was speaking, Dotty pulled her car to a stop behind the taco truck. "Why don't you come up for lunch yourself," Parker said to Danquin. "Dotty's just gotten here, and she usually brings too much food for the two of us."

"That will leave the office empty for three hours," he said. "Miss Angie does not get out of school till three."

"Leave a note on the door with your number on it," Parker said, and after Danquin hesitated, Parker added, "Dotty will have brought more lemon bars."

"I will come," Danquin replied.

Armando, having purchased lunch for himself, carried Dotty's basket of food up the hill for her, taking the long way round on the dirt road up the south side of the vineyard. They arrived just as Danquin drew his car to a stop beside a diminutive woman standing on the edge of the pavement and gazing up at the cemetery. A dog half her size sat at her side. Danquin greeted the woman, who was wearing a Tartan plaid wool coat and a matching tam-o'-shanter, and set out with her for the cemetery, although neither Danquin nor the woman spoke more than three words to the other during the five minutes it took for them and the dog to enter into the cemetery grounds. Parker-the-dog, having become interested in the scents emanating from Dotty's basket, now saw the other dog and, forgetting the savory scents of roast beef, made a beeline for the dog. The woman, in turn, tightened her grip on the leash, whose other end was affixed to a spiked choke-collar around the massive neck of a pewter-gray male pit bull.

"Weasel, sit and stay!" the woman enunciated crisply, her voice curiously strong, coming, as it did, from someone so small and frail-appearing. Weasel, doing as he was commanded, lowered himself to sitting and remained immobile as Parker-the-dog careened toward him.

Responding immediately to this, Parker the man shouted, "Parker, come!"

At the command, Parker-the-dog flinched when she was only four feet from the other dog. Then, after taking another step, she stopped altogether as if she had been garroted. She wagged her tail at the pit bull, voiced a friendly bark, then turned away and ran back to Parker, as he reached into his pocket and brought out a begging biscuit, which he let her take from his hand after she sat on her haunches in front of him.

"What a good dog!" the woman said in approval, to which the others nodded both in surprise and acknowledgment. Then unfastening the leash of her own dog, she patted him on the head and said, "Weasel, release!" Upon which Weasel scampered over to Parker-the-dog and the two of them got down to the business at hand of getting each other's scent.

"I'm Tilly Thomassock. That's Weasel," she said in a tremulous voice. "He looks formidable. But he's really a pussycat...unless he thinks I'm being threatened," she added. She then spotted Chester's grave, and her countenance, which till that moment she had held rigidly in a stern, if not apprehensive expression, softened. In fact, her whole person relaxed, and she looked ten years younger as she shed perhaps twenty years of something Parker could not quite ascertain, although her name alone did ring a bell for him. "Chester was my dog," she went on, "before

Weasel…long before." She then scanned the cemetery without, purposefully it seemed, making eye contact with anyone. "Where are the SS death heads?"

"We—I—took them down," Danquin said sheepishly. "They sent a message. A negative one."

"They were horrid. I hated them," Dotty interjected.

Tilly nodded. "Yes they were. And I hated them too. But they also sent a message to me, that's for sure," she replied. "Because that horridness broke through the door to my memory that's been locked for ten years."

Her voice was a curious fusion of flattened Midwestern coherence and optimism that alerted Parker's curiosity; the two divergent intonations gave her an emotional friability that was garbled, in the sense of an alien language being lost in translation. He stepped forward and introduced himself and the others with purposeful nonchalance; as he had become aware that in addressing her he perhaps needed to be careful to not be too direct lest something fragile in her shatter. "Where are you staying?" he said, and he motioned for her to take a seat on the futon sofa.

"I've borrowed a camper van from the Zen Ranch," she said, remaining on her feet and pointing toward the hills to the west. "And Weasel and I are at the campground in the mountains just north of here." She looked more closely at Parker's trailer and Armando's men. "The van isn't much bigger than that. There are more homeless neighbors up there than there are here, though, that's for sure." She fell silent as if embarrassed by voicing her assumption that Armando's men were homeless. Her eyes, which were nut-brown and mournful, darted around Parker's little compound and the cemetery restlessly again, seemingly unable to rest in one spot while taking in the surroundings in limited doses. After coming around to Parker, her gaze settled on him.

"Can I go be with Chester?" she blurted suddenly.

Taken aback by both the gravity inherent in her words and by the sadness in her eyes, the latter of which pled for linkage while simultaneously shunning it, Parker shrugged and shivered at once.

"Please. Feel free to do as you like. This place is as much yours as it is mine or anybody else's," he said. But it was not her request that had caused Parker to shiver. It was her gaze, for in it Parker saw now what had perplexed him initially about Tilly. It was the same look he had seen early on in Sylvia's eyes at those few terrible times when she realized she had irretrievably lost decades of memory: like a plea for help sprouting from a seed of sorrow planted in a substrate of confusion. It was the lonely desolation of seeing from behind the veil of shadows that when she was without memories she was a wraith.

Tilly nodded, then skirting Weasel and Parker-the-dog, who had begun pawing one another playfully, she went over to stand between and slightly behind Chester and Yellow Dog Red's graves. "This one is your dog, right?" she said, turning to face Parker while gesturing with her right hand, to which Parker nodded. Tilly then dropped to her knees and reached across her body to touch Chester's engraved epitaph, and as the others looked on she seemed for an instant to meld into a single entity with Chester's headstone.

Then choking back tears, she said, "The very first thing about my life—my old life, I mean—that came back to me, after the shock of seeing the death heads, was this: 'He was a good boy. He was my protector demon. May he run and sleep with the big dogs.' I remember now writing those words myself," she continued, her eyes brimming with tears as her fingers traced the letters. "Fifteen years ago. Then I forgot them. Forgot everything. Until I saw your tweet.

"The second thing that came to me then was that I had to come here," she went on, now making eye contact with each person in turn. "Because memory is where home lives, and once memory is gone, so is home." She looked up now and saw Squirrel's tent in the tree, which startled her so that she seemed unable to speak for a moment. Then she said, "And here—this county—is my home. Or it used to be."

Tilly fell silent as a torrent of tears fell to the ground. Her hand slipped from Chester's headstone and she bowed her head, and from some unfathomably place deep within her there emerged a guttural cry of such profound sorrow that Parker-the-dog and Weasel both put their tails between their legs and whimpered. Dotty went to Tilly at once, kneeling with one arm draped over her, her own eyes moist from Tilly's lamentation.

Several minutes passed with only the rhythmic distillate of Tilly's weeping and, in the distance, solicitous strains of mariachi music playing from the taco truck. Then Tilly straightened and, wiping her eyes, looked to the right of Chester's headstone, seeking out something that seemed to be calling to her from out of the past. After having found it, she nodded as if in answer and said, "I remember Chester now, but before now the only thing I could remember about my past was my name." She then pointed to a headstone in the next row over from Chester's, where one of Parker's freshly spruced graves displayed the name of Tilly Thomassock, whose epitaph read: "May my Tilly sleep till we meet again."

"I took her name, Tilly Thomassock, as mine."

"Ah!" exclaimed Parker.

"What did you say your last name was before that?" asked Danquin, who had propped his laptop atop a waist-high rock in order to take notes, and who was also snapping photos with his phone.

Tilly shook her head. "I didn't say, because I don't know. That part hasn't come back to me yet. Or what my first name was. Or where I lived. Or with whom. It's only been a week since I realized I wasn't who I thought I was. It's as if my old life is an onion whose layers are peeling off in slow motion."

"That's probably because those things about your previous life, whatever they were, are too painful for you to recall," Parker inserted, and as he spoke he saw that Roper had pulled his car up behind the taco wagon, and that he and Squirrel were at its window. "And if my own experience is any guide, at least part of the reason you contracted it in the first place was to suppress traumatic experiences."

Tilly nodded. "I know. That's why I'm here. To uncover who I am. And how I got here."

"I will tweet your picture," offered Danquin. "Someone in the tweetisphere will see it and recognize you."

"No! Please don't do that," Tilly cried, rising to her feet and facing Danquin. She then helped Dotty to hers. "I've tried. But now I'm afraid," she continued. "I worry that if the wrong person recognizes me, I could be in danger. I need more time to find out these things for myself."

"What sort of danger?" asked Armando, glancing down at his watch, which prompted his four workers to rise and, paying their respects to Yellow Dog Red, depart the cemetery.

Before answering him, Tilly went over to Weasel and pushed him away from Parker-the-dog who he was attempting to mount. "The sort of danger that I may find I don't like the person I uncover myself to be. Or that I might put other's I don't even remember in danger. That's what frightens me the most."

"If you had real amnesia, how did you know how to get to Sedona from here?" Danquin asked pointedly, his tone having suddenly become suspicious. "Doesn't that imply you had a plan? And, if so, doesn't that negate the idea of amnesia? And what about documentation? I assume you had none. So, how did you support yourself?"

"Danquin," Parker interceded gently in admonishment, "that's not being very helpful."

Tilly waved Parker's concern aside. "No, it's okay," she said, "I want to answer questions. It's the only way I will be able to find myself." She stepped over Yellow Dog Red's mound of earth in order to stand beside Danquin, and, lowering herself to her haunches, continued.

"The problem, sir, is until this last week I didn't remember how I got to where I went, or from where I started, other than I had been in a truck. I was told by the nuns who took me in only that I had hitchhiked out to their place, which was a Buddhist retreat outside of Sedona, where they put me to work as a janitor, for room and board. Till last week, that retreat was the only reality I knew. That means," she continued, "I must've eaten in food kitchens along the way and stayed in shelters, and then somehow got across the country on my own. Or somebody brought me to Sedona. And the whole time nobody must've questioned whether my real name was Tilly Thomassock or asked where I came from. And—"

"Are you working for the Zinnis?" Armando blurted suddenly, just as he was about to exit the cemetery.

"The who?" Tilly replied, knitting her brow, perplexed by the hostility in Armando's tone. And, alerted to the aggressive posture in Armando's voice, Weasel swung around menacingly and fronted Armando.

"What are you two talking about?" Parker said, confronting both Armando and Danquin.

"Remember, I work for Zinni. I know him," Armando said, "I know he's not a nice man. I know how he works. And it would not surprise me if he paid somebody you don't know well, like me, or him," he pointed to Danquin, "or this complete stranger, to gain your trust and pass information to him."

Tilly motioned for Weasel to sit and she reattached his collar as a precaution after he bared his teeth to Armando. "I am working for no one. I swear," she replied tersely, her voice again growing tremulous. "I know it doesn't make sense to you who know who you are that I do not know who I am or where I came from. But if you were in my place, I can tell you, you would surely be unable to rest until you found out who you were."

217

Parker went over beside Tilly and Danquin and looked over Danquin's shoulder at the script on his laptop's screen. After reading it, he said, "Erase that, Danquin."

"It's only a blog," Danquin protested. "To chronicle events here."

"A blog saying," Parker responded, frowning as he squinted at the screen, "that there is, quote, a suspicion gathering among the YDRP that a mole may have infiltrated the Yellow Dog Red Overlook, unquote."

Danquin shrugged. "Well, what if that is true?"

"True or untrue, I don't care," Parker said, shrugging sharply. "The only thing I care about is that those of us here who truly care for Yellow Dog Red will continue to care for her. All the other stuff," he said, gesturing to the screen, the plastic tarp, the fence, "is static. White noise. And if there is too much of the sort of static like the speculations you're writing, then the Yellow Dog Red Overlook is over, and faster than you can say Jack Robinson I'll take Yellow Dog Red away with me to a place where she and I can lie in peace."

"You are asking me to censor my research, no?" Danquin asked. His brows were drawn in quizzically and his voice was disbelieving.

Parker shook his head. "No, I am not asking you to censor yourself. I am asking you only to see clearly what you yourself have told me about your own research: that you are much more a part of this experiment" he said, "than you are apart from it. In other words, don't provoke discord in yourself, or you may sow dissolution elsewhere. Let doubt grow of its own accord where it will to the place where it belongs, but also trust that the truth of your devotion to truth is pure enough to drown out the static the discord produces. Otherwise, your research will mistake the static for its opposite."

Danquin leaned back and considered Parker's words for a few seconds. Then he rolled the cursor over the text and highlighted it. "You are right, Parker. I will not use this kind of material in real time. It is valuable only as a tool in retrospect," he said, "after our vigil is over and

I am able to reestablish some distance to form a more objective perspective for my academic work." He then saved the text to a different file and closed the lid on his laptop.

Armando passed Squirrel and Roper as they made their way up to the cemetery, and after cluing them in briefly on Tilly's presence and cautioning them to tread lightly with her, he shook his head as if to give weight to his unstated assessment that she was a mental case. He then motioned for his men to get to work, saying as he left, "There is a bird inside that woman that wants to fly. For her sake, I hope it doesn't fly into the jaws of people like Zinni."

When Roper and Squirrel reached the cemetery and saw Tilly standing beside Danquin, Roper went straight up to her and introduced himself. Squirrel, on the other hand, took one look at her, stopped in his tracks, then turned and went immediately up to his tent, without so much as a nod in greeting to her or any of the others, or even a welcoming pat on the head to Parker-the-dog when she bounded over to intercept him.

When Parker raised his brows over Squirrel's slight, Roper only shrugged and said, "He was fine until a minute ago."

For her part, Tilly had followed Squirrel's every movement from the instant she saw him come into the cemetery, and she watched in rapt fascination as he climbed up the eucalyptus with primate-like dexterity and disappeared into the tent forty feet above her. After he had vanished from sight, she furrowed her brow and turned to Chester's memorial and mumbled its epitaph to herself as if in question.

Then to Parker, who had begun wiping Chester's headstone of cobwebs with one of Dotty's kitchen towels, she repeated aloud. "'He was a good boy. He was my protector demon.'" She paused, then added, "I feel the key to me remembering who I am is in those words. They—and those death heads—are what have brought me back here in the first place. And Chester is the only name I remember from that time." Then gesturing to Squirrel's tent, she asked, "Who is that boy? I feel I know him. Or that I have at least seen him before."

"Peter von Brandt is his real name, but everybody knows him as Squirrel...for obvious reasons," replied Parker.

"von Brandt...von Brandt," Tilly murmured, chewing over the name meditatively before declaring, "Yes, I feel I know that name. Or that I knew it once, I mean. Is it possible for me to talk to the boy?" she said. "So I can ask him about himself."

Parker shrugged. "He obviously marches to the beat of a different drummer," he answered, and to illustrate he extended a hand toward Squirrel's tent perched precariously in the tree. "He said the name is German, and that he is named after a grandfather who was a naturalist, if that helps." When Tilly only shook her head, he changed the subject. "Well then, how long are you planning on staying here? In California, I mean."

Tilly shrugged. "I can go back to the monastery any time I like," she said. "And I was told I can use the camper van for as long as I need it. But," she appended, "if I ever do go back to Sedona, I would prefer to go back knowing who I am."

Parker hesitated a moment, then said, "I would welcome your company whenever you'd like to come here and visit with me, Yellow Dog Red and Chester."

Tilly smiled crookedly in the manner of a servant unused to being offered personal invitations, and murmured a heartfelt thank you.

"I'll call him down if you'd like," Dotty put forth, stepping forward and cupping her hands to her mouth. "Squirrel, there are lemon bars waiting for you down here!" she shouted. "Better come and get them before Danquin eats them all."

When there was no reply or movement from above, Danquin laid down a half-finished lemon bar guiltily, and pulled out his phone. He then typed Squirrel a text message.

After waiting several minutes and there was still no response, Roper spoke up. "I'll go up and see if he wants to come down," he said, whereupon he donned the tree spikes Danquin had worn, and almost as adroitly as Squirrel, ascended the tree. Standing in front of the tent on one of the two branches which it straddled, he reached out and jostled the peak of the tent gently. "Squirrel, what's the matter?" he murmured.

"Go away, Roper," Squirrel replied softly from inside.

"Why? What's wrong? Did I say something?"

"No, it wasn't you. It was that woman," he muttered, but so faintly Roper could barely hear him.

"What about her? She seems like a nice person. She only wants to meet you. Remember, she's the one who tweeted us about Chester."

A long silence followed. Then Squirrel unzipped the tent fly and peered out at Roper from within the shadows. Even through the gloom, Roper saw that there were tears glistening in Squirrel's eyes, and that his face was twisted in anguish. Squirrel's jaw moved but no words came out. Instinctively Roper reached in and rested a hand on Squirrel's shoulder; for Squirrel's expression had communicated to him for a split second the possibility that he might actually slip past him and leap off the tree.

"Are you sure you're all right?"

Squirrel shook his head.

"What then? Please, tell me," Roper coaxed, looking down uneasily at the others who had all but ceased their conversations in order to watch and listen. Another period of silence ensued, broken only by the sound of Squirrel's weeping now become rhythmic. Then finally Squirrel took a number of deep breaths and wiped his eyes, which were so bloodshot they looked to Roper to have been scorched.

"That woman," he repeated

"Tilly? What about her?"

"Her name is not Tilly."

This last gave Roper pause to glance down at Tilly, who, though forty-feet below, had overheard every word. Even from his removed vantage, Roper was taken aback by how Squirrel's assertion had ignited Tilly's expression, so that in its expectancy it reminded him of the upturned expressions of hunger mixed with expectation he had seen in person on the faces of starving children in Ethiopia when watching parachute-drops of food aid drift down with excruciating slowness toward them. "How do you know that?" he said.

"I know because I...I recognize her," Squirrel stammered, his voice clothed in certainty but oddly devoid of emotion. "Her name is...is Alice. And," he added, after several moments, "she is my...mother."

Now Roper's jaw was the one to move with no words issuing forth, as did Tilly's forty feet below them, seconds before she slumped to the ground.

When she next opened her eyes, Tilly was lying on her back on the futon sofa, under a blanket, staring up at the cobalt-blue tarp luffing in a freshening breeze that cooled her tear-moistened, scalding-hot cheeks. Blinking away the ashes of her dream—a recurring one in which a huge broom sweeps her into a dustbin in which she is naked among a collection of menacing toy trucks—she saw in profile the face of the boy whose words had sent her into a swoon. She raised herself up on her elbows. At her movement all eyes and conversation trained themselves toward her.

To Squirrel she said, "What did you say my name was?"

Squirrel's face had re-composed itself by then, so that it no longer exhibited the stricken expression of an abandoned child, but that of an adult hardened by years of isolation. "Alice. Alice von Brandt," he said matter-of-factly.

Tilly knitted her brow and, throwing the blanket aside, sat erect, with a helping hand from Dotty. "Alice von Brandt," she repeated awkwardly, as if she were juggling hot coals on her tongue. She shook her head and screwed her mouth from side to side. The words themselves had sounded like they came from a ventriloquist with ill-fitting dentures impersonating a duck.

"Are you sure?" she quailed, not letting go of Dotty's arm.

"Don't you think I would know my own mother's name?" Squirrel muttered. "Even if she was mental," he added under his breath, before snapping his mouth shut when Roper shot him a warning glance.

"You say I'm your mother?" To which Squirrel nodded and drew his expression into one in which a pound of disdain and an ounce of hope mingled like uncomfortable traveling companions. "Can you come close so I can see you better?"

Squirrel shrugged, for Tilly's words were tentative and uncertain, with little warmth, only vacuous curiosity. When he stood beside her, Tilly extended her hand, which after a moment's hesitation, Squirrel took up in his.

Several seconds passed in silence. Then Tilly, her face wrenched with uncertainty and chagrin at her inability—despite her desperate desire to the contrary—to connect Squirrel's assertion with her own experience, said in a voice made stiff with the protective armor of emotional distance, "How do you do, Peter. If I am your mother, Alice...Alice von Brandt, as you say, then I am pleased to make your acquaintance. I am also sorry. Truly sorry," she whispered. "I'm sorry for both of us, because I don't remember being a mother or having a son. But I am pleased to meet you now as Tilly Thomassock."

Squirrel nodded grimly at Tilly's formality and slid his hand from hers, which he then shoved deep into the pocket of his pants as if to shield it and him from attack. "Tilly Thomassock is the name of a dog," he muttered, gesturing with his hand toward Tilly-the-dog's grave.

His own expression, rather than being one of hurtfulness, was one of confirmation, almost relief; for it was to him a reaffirmation, a ratification of his years of living in foster homes, that he was indeed as alone as he had thought he was and, worse, now that he had met a mother who could not acknowledge him as her son, unwanted in the truest sense of the word. An orphan twice over.

Despite their frigidity toward each other, Tilly motioned for Squirrel to sit beside her on the futon, and after he had reluctantly seated himself, she said, "Tell me the name of your father. Perhaps that will help me remember you...and me."

"The same as mine. I'm named after him."

Tilly pursed her lips. "Then I am Alice von Brandt?" she said, tentatively trying the name on for size again. She shook her head when it was clear to her that the name in itself was not going to be an aperture for her to walk through, and she added, "Where did Peter von Brandt and I—we—live?"

"In the valley. On Grove Street, I think." To which Tilly again only shrugged and shook her head.

"I do not come up with those names, Peter von Brandt, or Alice, at least here in the valley," Danquin inserted, lowering his phone after quickly having conducted a name search on Google. Dotty, in the meantime, had gone over to sit beside Parker and Yellow Dog Red, while Roper examined the falcon hanging from the eucalyptus sucker. Each in their own way were trying discretely to give Squirrel and Tilly space to work things out between themselves.

Squirrel nodded. "That's because my father is not in this country anymore," he affirmed, shrugging. "He gave me up when I was seven. Three years after you abandoned us." He shot an accusing glance at Tilly, and continued. "Then he went back to where he grew up. Somewhere in Eastern Europe, I think, or even Turkey. I haven't heard from him since he left, and Child Protective Services hasn't been able to get hold of him or any relatives either, if I have any, to help with child support. I guess that makes me two-for-two with disappearing parents," he concluded with a reproachful expression twisting his face.

Tilly's face, too, was contorted; for her only wish then was that she could feel connected to Squirrel instead of projecting onto him her sadness for having abandoned him. "Is that true? I left you," she whispered aridly, matching Squirrel's tone of self-accusation.

"When I was four."

"Oh, how terrible. Why would I have done that? Was I a monster? Was I living with one?" Tilly's eyes darted from side to side, looking into the empty rooms of her memory for some familiar object to grasp. But again the only thing she saw was Chester's monument, which was itself a door that was locked against her entry to the past.

Squirrel shrugged coldly in answer; for he had quickly developed an ill-defined sense of resentment toward Tilly for putting him, still a child, in the position of having to answer such questions about adult malfeasance. "I was never told anything," he said, barely able to hide his bitterness. "I remember he brought me home from preschool one day to find that you were gone. I don't think you left because he hurt you, though, because he never hurt me. There was only a note that said 'I have to go find myself.'" Squirrel swallowed hard and averted his gaze to Weasel. "It was because of me that you left," he added disconsolately.

"What are you talking about?" Tilly said. "You were only four."

"You left because I was bad. It was my badness that made you leave."

Tilly cringed and shook her head; for Squirrel's words, despite the accusation of his own complicity in his mother's departure, also contained a note of triumph, like those of a convict who, having served his time, boasts that he is proud to have overcome his criminality. She went to put her hand on Squirrel's leg, but he drew it aside reflexively.

"Was I working?" she said, withdrawing her hand.

Squirrel shook his head. "I'm not sure. I think dad said you had a cleaning business or something like that, and I remember there were a lot of brooms, vacuum cleaners, and things like that where we lived. I remember sucking up spiders with them..." His voice trailed off.

226

"I am a good cleaner," Tilly admitted, leaning forward and tilting her head as if to get a closer view of her past through the fissure opened by Squirrel's memory. But seeing none she fell back against the futon.

"That probably explains why you could use the name of Tilly Thomassock and not be questioned about it," Parker inserted without looking at Tilly. "Because most domestics work for cash under the table and don't need any documentation."

"I don't remember doing any of that," Tilly said. "My life still doesn't exist for me before I started working in the monastery."

"I will never exist for you either then, will I?" Squirrel pounced, more than asked, sliding to the opposite end of the sofa, where Parker-the-dog was attempting to capture Weasel's attention by nudging her rope toy toward him.

Now that four feet separated Squirrel and Tilly, she found it easier to peer into Squirrel's eyes, in which she saw only burning resentment and the figment of Tilly Thomassock's reflection. Alice von Brandt was nowhere in sight, nor was her son.

"I know you are telling me the truth," she admitted finally, her eyes growing moist. "For I see no reason for you to make up any of this. But you're right. You do not exist to me as my son. Yet. But," she added, "that should not prevent us from trying to get to know each other better, because I also do not yet exist to myself as a mother, or a wife, or even as the person I once was."

"Maybe that's the way you should leave it," Squirrel said dourly. His mouth was stretched in resignation into his cheeks, which gave to him an appearance not too far removed from that of a chipmunk who had found a long hidden acorn. He then leaned over and patted Tilly on the knee in a gesture denoting farewell, which prompted Weasel to flatten his ears against his skull.

At this Tilly nodded, and her face assumed an expression of relief and resignation identical to Squirrel's, which Roper, having just turned away from Falcon, took notice of at once.

"Look at you two!" he exclaimed; for he was aware, as were the others, that in acquiescing to Tilly's problem Squirrel was only trying to staunch the loneliness yawning in front of him that her presence had reopened. Thus in an effort to bridge the gap between the two of them, he moved quickly and went behind the sofa, where he placed one hand on Squirrel's shoulder and one on Tilly's.

"If the expressions on your faces don't show you're related to each other," he said, with the barely disguised false bonhomie of a carnival barker, "then I'm Paul Bunyan, and these are the backwoods of Minnesota."

Despite Roper's overtly theatrical tone, his contact with Tilly prompted Weasel to stand and emit a warning growl. Parker-the-dog at once drew her tail between her legs and, taking up her chew toy, slunk over to Parker and Dotty beside Yellow Dog Red.

"You better take your hand off my shoulder, Mr. Roper," Tilly said, with a flattened affect meant to calm Weasel. "Weasel can get skittish when people or animals get more excited than he thinks is safe. He supposes your hand on my shoulder means you plan an attack on me," she added apologetically.

Roper raised both of his hands in the air and backed away from the sofa, and Tilly reached out to pet and reassure Weasel that everything was fine, just as a tour bus pulled to a stop down on the road and Danquin's phone rang. On the other end of the line was Angie.

"Danquin! "Where are you? How come you're not at Command Central?" she cried frantically.

"I'm in the cemetery," he replied. "Chester's owner is here, and..." His voice trailed off when he realized it was too complicated a story to tell. Instead, he simply asked Angie what was bothering her.

"There are two busses here filled with people, that's what. Dozens. And another one filled with even more people has already gone and is heading your way."

Danquin's face fell as he watched people begin to disembark from the bus. "Uh-oh. They've just pulled up," he said.

"I'm going to call for help," Angie replied. "We can't let this get out of hand."

"Don't worry. I will take care of things here," Danquin said. "What about you? Do you need help down there?"

"Yes...No...I mean, nein," she sighed, correcting herself. "I'll show them the camera feeds and tell them we are trying to be respectful of Yellow Dog Red."

"I hope they understand."

"I'm almost certain all of them are pet owners, so I think they'll understand. Good luck at your end."

"The same." Whereupon the connection was broken.

"Well," Danquin said, turning to Parker, as from out of his valise he withdrew a roll of tickets, such as are used for drawings, and a handful of pens. "Looks like it's time for the Yellow Dog Red Overlook Wine Country Cabaret to open its doors."

Parker sighed. "Let them come," he said, whereupon he turned to Yellow Dog Red and, addressing her headstone, added, "They're only coming here to see you, old girl. So, don't bite anyone."

"Mind if I stay?" Tilly put in. "Perhaps I will recognize one of the visitors. Or one of them, me."

"Like I said," Parker replied, "As long as it's okay with Yellow Dog Red it's okay with me. But Weasel will have to behave. What about you, Dots?"

"I'll stick around for awhile," Dotty said, her face coloring at Parker's endearment. "Maybe I can be helpful. And maybe I can even sell some lemon bars while I'm here."

"I'm outa here," Squirrel said. "I don't want to have anything to do with crowds of sad people. I'll go help Angie."

"How would you like to go get her and you and me a chili burger at Happy Dog? My treat," Roper said, adding, "I would rather not be stuck in a crowd of sad people either."

"I'm in," Squirrel said, letting a grin crease his cheeks for the first time. "I love chili burgers and can't stand the food I get in my group home."

"Could you get one for me," Tilly spoke up, fumbling in her pocket for money. "I love chili burgers too. And I haven't eaten in a day."

"Like mother like son, I guess," Roper quipped theatrically, raising his hand to indicate to Tilly he was buying. "Anybody else?" he said, to which Parker, Dotty and Danquin raised their hands. "Okay then, Yellow Dog Red Overlook Happy Dog Chili Burgers all around it is." A rueful grin formed on his face, and only then did Tilly let a smile escape.

D anquin met the people from the bus at the fence-line as they straggled up to the graveyard one and two at a time. Of this number half were older than fifty, and the rest ranged from sixteen to thirty, leaving a conspicuous gap of those aged in between. Many of the elderly needed assistance in making their way across the churned earth, which they received from the younger visitors with them. Danquin tore a ticket from his roll, which he handed to each of the guests with verbal instructions to fill out their names and email addresses on the back so that updates could be forwarded if they so wished, and so that plots could be held in the cemetery for their own pets in the event that it wasn't bulldozed under. Then he began letting them through the fence twelve at a time. No time limit was set for them to pay their respects, but Danquin did not allow the next group through the opening in the fence until the previous dozen had exited through it in the opposite direction. Thus an orderly and respectful procession of pilgrims made their way through the cemetery.

As had the earlier visitors, virtually all who came had their picture taken sandwiched beside Yellow Dog Red's headstone and Parker, who obliged every request amicably. And like the others who had come, they also hung pictures they had brought of their own dogs and some cats—mostly deceased—along the fence. Some sank to their knees in prayer while others contented themselves with simply looping their fingers through the chainlink fence as if by doing so they could intertwine their souls with those of their beloved pets.

Roper and Squirrel returned with the chili burgers. But in that the weather was starting to close in, Roper suggested to Squirrel, who did not want to stay in his tree alone that night for fear he would have nightmares, that he could give him a lift back to his group home. To this, Squirrel's face took on a look that told Roper Squirrel would rather be chainsawed in two than stay in his group home. Roper then suggested that, if his group home approved, Squirrel could stay in his home office on an inflatable mattress. Squirrel seized on this immediately. But when presented with the plan, the group home was reluctant to agree to the arrangement. In the end, though, they consented to it only after conceding it would be better for Squirrel to stay with Roper than for him to go and stay in his tree on a rainy night; so, after Roper signed a document accepting temporary custodial supervision of Squirrel, and Squirrel had gathered clothes for school the next day, they set off for Roper's apartment.

By early that evening a light rain began to fall. Three busloads—close to a hundred people—had come and gone, as well as dozens of other people who had circumvented Control Central altogether and had instead driven up in their own vehicles, including Wili Wallenstock who snapped a prodigious number of photos. Only then did Danquin finally relinquish his post at the fence and sit down with Parker and Tilly while Dotty went about gathering up the plates and utensils she had brought earlier in the day. As Danquin and Parker were each downing one of the German lagers Danquin insisted were needed for him to keep his wits about him, Danquin received a text from Angie informing him she would not be coming by that night, owing to the rainstorm and to the homework she needed to catch up on. She would come by after school the next day to help prepare for the delivery of the sheriff's eviction notice the day after. Danquin then escorted Dotty down to her car, and both of them departed, leaving Tilly and Parker by themselves.

With Parker-the-dog and Weasel sprawled across their laps, Parker and Tilly sat quietly on the futon sofa, listening to the rain pattering on the tarp for nearly thirty minutes after Danquin's taillights had disappeared behind the berry bushes lining the road.

Finally Tilly turned to Parker. "Why are you doing this, Parker? I mean, why are you keeping this vigil?" she said.

"To honor my friend," he said flatly, as he rolled one of Parker-the-dog's ears idly around his fingers and watched the raindrops pock the soft earth on Yellow Dog Red's grave.

Tilly nodded. "I get that. But I'm wondering," she replied. "Does your honor require memory? Can you honor Yellow Dog Red, or can I honor Squirrel if we have no memory of them? What if you were like me and you had no memory of Yellow Dog Red? Would you still be here to honor her?"

In the dim light of the solar powered lantern, Tilly saw that Parker's face went through a series of divergent expressions before it settled on one—of longing, it seemed to her—that she thought would be a fair match to her own—of longing, that is, for memories of herself. Just when she thought that perhaps he had not heard her correctly or was not going to answer her questions, Parker spoke.

"No, honor does not require memory," he pronounced, surprising Tilly with such a categorical reply. "Not in the usual sense anyway," he went on, "because, for me, honor is at its core a figure-ground issue." He then shook his head slowly from side to side as he paused to form the rest of his reply.

"Even though honor is usually understood as being transactional, in the sense that honor is conveyed through an acknowledgment by other observers of certain admirable qualities, in reality honor also implies that there is an innate worthiness of an individual's uniqueness that exists even without acknowledgment of it by others. By this I mean that the intrinsic worthiness of something or someone's unique existence is like a figure in the foreground of a picture in which memory forms the background. That is, the background can change while the foreground remains the same. Therefore honor can exist within but also apart from memory, I think."

233

Parker rearranged Parker-the-dog so that she wasn't pressing on his knees and cutting off the flow of blood to his feet. Then he yawned and stretched out whatever stiffness he could from the day's duty as vigil overseer and protector of Yellow Dog Red's integrity, knowing as his joints cracked and popped like bursting kernels of corn that neither they nor he could withstand the rigors of such an onslaught to his body through an unlimited number of days, not without succumbing to death by exhaustion. Thus, when he continued speaking again, his voice was raspy with the fatigue of having glimpsed the reality that, if this vigil persisted, his own life might indeed be in jeopardy of winding down to a stop beside Yellow Dog Red.

"It's undeniably true that the background can inform the foreground and change its outline," he went on. "After all, the two are contained and interact within a whole. But it is the foreground not the background that I am now honoring for being itself. In my case, the background is the memory I have of my years spent with Yellow Dog Red. The foreground is the love I possess for her right now. The two are connected but they are also separate, almost in the same way that an egg yoke is separate from an egg white. The yoke contains the chick and the white contains the energy the chick needs to grow.

"In your case," he continued, gesturing with his hands in a wiping motion as if to reinforce his words, "the background has been entirely erased, or at least hidden from view. Its memories no longer nourish you. But that does not mean you cannot honor Weasel or even Chester. Both are beings from whom you draw strength. Nor does it mean that you yourself cannot be honored even though you have no history, because honor, at least in the way I perceive it, does not require a detached observer to acknowledge it. It requires only a present context in order to inform its identity. A present source of nourishment..." Parker's voice trailed off.

Before replying, Tilly found herself blinking rapidly, for she had been taken aback by Parker's response, and a depth of insight she had not foreseen nor counted on; since the only thing she knew of him to that point was that he was a somewhat taciturn, ill-clothed, marginally hygienic, dimly quixotic and faintly charismatic old man keeping vigil over his dead dog's grave, while being aided and abetted by a coterie of unlikely and possibly misguided cohorts who knew how to manipulate the Internet to their and his advantage. In other words, he was a man teetering on the edge of dementia who was not unlike some of the more errant monks with a gift for gab she knew at the Zen monastery, who had gone outside the fold on their own and collected a devoted following of world-sick acolytes, based on nothing more than an unerring devotion to a worthy and seemingly hopeless cause.

"How...how do you know of such things?" Tilly stammered in amazement finally; for she began to realize that Parker's words had nudged open a door—not of memory exactly but one of worthiness—to looking at herself in a way ten years of meditation had been unable to.

Parker shrugged. "My wife died a little while ago after ten years of Alzheimers Disease," he stated, his voice flattened of emotion. "Those ten years and these months sitting here with Yellow Dog Red have given me a lot of time to think about memory and how it is related to honor, to love." He shrugged again as if to absorb and to chase away those same memories. "Plus," he added, "my occupation when I was a working man was to get to the source of people's motivations as efficiently as possible. So I guess you could say it's a lifetime of experience, all gone into the hopper."

"Have you reached any conclusions?" Tilly blurted, her voice drenched with eagerness; for with Parker's elucidation she now understood that something—an act, an event, a situation—related to honor and how she perceived it was central to the onset of her amnesia, and that Chester the dog possibly held the key to that door.

Parker smiled as he realized that Tilly expression of gloom was now eclipsed by thirst. "Other than about memory and honor, you mean?" he said.

"I guess so...that is...I mean..." she sputtered, throwing her hands up in exasperation with such volocity that Weasel stirred then growled in his sleep. "Here I am thousands of miles from the place I call home, trying to dig up memories that have been buried under...an...an avalanche of something that was probably traumatic..." Her voice trailed off and she squinted into the darkness where Tilly Thomassock's grave was barely discernible. "And all I know," she added, "is that I've taken the name of a dog, that I abandoned my son, and that I probably once had a dog named Chester who, judging by what is written on his headstone, was a pit bull."

"What I've learned," Parker replied, "is that honor lives in all of us all the time. It's a good thing to acknowledge it in others because it demonstrates respect, but it is better to acknowledge it—self-respect—in ourselves first. Otherwise honor becomes a thing—a disembodied virtue—that does not live within but lives outside of us. And when that happens, when honor becomes a tool rather than an innate virtue, it can be used by those who possess little virtue to manipulate it to their own advantage. Governments. Religions. Communities. They all bend honor to gain power for themselves. It's...it's..."

Parker fell silent, aware he was beginning to launch into a tirade about how his experience working in a government agency tasked with unearthing dishonor in its ranks had soured him permanently against the ability of organizations large and small to manipulate truth for honorable benefit.

"It's criminal, I know," Tilly acknowledged, finishing his thought for him. Then she added, "But other than that, this talk has helped me. It's helped a lot, I think. It's let me see what I guessed I needed when I decided to come see Yellow Dog Red: that I need to start here, right where I am now, to find my way back to there. To my family." Then to Parker, she said, "If you wouldn't mind, can you tell me about yours? Your family, I mean. Starting with Yellow Dog Red."

Although as tired as he could remember ever being, Parker nodded, and the mortal fatigue that had gripped him only moments before loosened its grip a notch. And with its release, memories of Yellow Dog Red and Sylvia and Tad and a lifetime's worth of people he'd known and loved poured into his awareness like sunlight breaking through the clouds after a winter rain.

"I got Yellow Dog Red from a duck hunter in the Carneros when she was eight weeks old," he set out. "She was the runt of the litter and probably wasn't going to make a good hunting dog. Sylvia and I slept on the floor with her to make her feel safe. She was the best dog I ever had..."

And thus eight hours passed, only to end when the first vein of dawn silhouetted the contused eastern hills, on what had been a long night of celebration and commiseration. As the morning sun rose, Parker finally ran out of reminiscences and tears of both joy and sorrow, and fell asleep on the futon along with Tilly and the slumbering dogs splayed like blankets atop them.

Parker was awakened a few hours later when Parker-the-dog, having slipped unnoticed to the ground sometime earlier, came trotting back and nudged him in the face. He opened his eyes to see her whole body waggling happily with what looked to be a well-chewed, half-inch-round wooden dowel clamped in her jaws. When she saw Parker open his eyes she then dropped the dowel to the ground and began to paw at it.

"Go away, Parker. It's too early to play sticky-stick," Parker mumbled groggily. But in hearing his voice, the puppy yelped. Then she picked up the stick and, with a flick of her head, tossed it into the air so that it landed against Parker's forehead.

"Oh, all right already. I'm getting up," he sighed in defeat, as he groped for the wet stick. The movements and the words had alerted Weasel, and he too awoke, as did Tilly.

The moment Parker's hands made contact with the object, he knew it wasn't made of wood. His body ached from having slept slouched over, and his eyes were still filled with dream dust as he went to toss the stick so that Parker could retrieve it and perhaps be satisfied with one throw. But the feel of the cylindrical object in his hand induced in him an awareness that it was made of some softer, almost granular material, and instead of tossing it for Parker he brought it close for inspection.

His eyes came to focus first on the yellow, barred ridges of the tube-shaped object, and from prior experience he knew exactly what he held in his hand: a bar of "one bite" rat bait. Warfarin.

Now fully awake, Parker shot to his feet, although unsteadily, for he was unused to getting up so quickly, and in the dampness his joints felt like they were packed with wet mortar. "Shit!" he murmured. "Where did you get this, Parker?" he said, and so emphatically that Parker-the-dog sat down. Then, spying Weasel snuffling in some weeds downhill from him along the fence, he shouted, "Weasel, Come!" in a commanding voice that had remarkably echoed Tilly's.

Parker-the-dog, thinking she herself had been reprimanded, slunk behind Tilly, who also was now fully awake.

"What's the matter?" she said, stretching her arms as Weasel returned to her side.

"Rat poison," Parker replied tersely, showing her the bar. "Parker gave it to me just now."

"Rat poison? How...how did she get it? Did you put it out?"

Parker shook his head. "Are you kidding? I hate the stuff. Causes rats to dry from the inside out, literally. That one," he nodded to Yellow Dog Red's grave, "got into some of our neighbor's a couple of times. She would've died from it if I hadn't had Vitamin K handy."

Tilly leaned forward to get a better look at the poison. "One of the visitors yesterday must've brought it with them," she said.

"Or dropped it off last night."

Tilly shook her head. "No, Weasel would've barked if he'd seen somebody moving around in the dark. It doesn't look like its ends have been chewed off," she observed, adding, "The only teeth marks I see are the little puppy ones where Parker had it in her mouth."

"No, it doesn't looked chewed," acknowledged Parker.

The rain had stopped and the sky was light enough by then to enable Parker and Tilly to go down to inspect where Weasel had been sniffing. They saw no new footprints in the tilled soil inside or outside the fence, although Tilly found another three-inch-long bar of rat bait lying three feet from where the other had been.

"We'd better split up and check the rest of the cemetery for more," he said, wrapping the stick of poison inside the handkerchief where he had rolled the other. "There must've been one very sick person here yesterday," he added, shaking his head.

And as he and Tilly began scouring the area for more poison, with Parker-the-dog and Weasel in tow on short leashes, they tried to picture the dozens of people they had interacted with in the hope that they could recall if any one of them had acted suspiciously. But try as he or she might, neither one could remember seeing any person doing anything that could be construed as suspicious. After they had made it around and through the cemetery without finding any poison or any new tracks, Parker was relieved that neither Parker-the-dog nor Weasel were showing any sign of the prodigious thirst or uncoordinated movements that accompanied the ingestion of Warfarin.

Nevertheless, to play it safe Parker decided to call Dotty, and after informing her of his finds and asking her if she had seen anyone acting suspiciously, he asked her to go to the emergency veterinarian clinic and bring back some Vitamin K for Parker and Weasel. Dotty could not remember seeing anyone doing anything peculiar—apart, that is, from witnessing the spectacle of having a hundred people lined up outside the cemetery as though they were awaiting holy communion.

Meanwhile, Tilly had gone down to her van to feed Weasel and to let him do his business. Parker fed Parker-the-dog and made some more quick phone calls. As Tilly approached the cemetery with Weasel she stopped and scanned the hundred and more pictures hanging from the fence. Above the spot and low to the ground where Weasel had been sniffing, one caught her attention. It was a snapshot of a gray pit bull not unlike Weasel in color. But unlike all the others it had writing on it. Tilly bent down to inspect, and when her eyes were level she realized that the dog in the picture was not some unknown deceased pet: it was Weasel. Her Weasel. And he was standing beside Yellow Dog Red's grave.

"Parker!" she gasped, and as the blood rushed from her head, she leaned against the fence and entwined her fingers into the wire mesh to keep herself from toppling to the ground. "Come look at this!"

Tilly's cry came just as Parker was holding the phone away at arm's length as though it had barked at him. Hearing the distress in Tilly's voice, he lowered the phone and moved quickly to her side.

"Look!" she yelped, pointing at the picture. "That's Weasel. That's Yellow Dog Red. This was taken only yesterday. And look what's written on it."

Parker leaned down and squinted at the photo on which the words "For every visitor to YDR 10 dogs die. krul2dbone" were scrawled across Weasel's face. Parker felt the blood drain from his own face.

"I was just talking to Danquin. He sent me this."

Parker held up his phone and showed Tilly the same quote as was on the picture, in a photo Danquin had taken of one of the tickets he had handed out.

"Who...who would think it was okay to do something like this?" Tilly said, kneeling in the moist earth and stroking Weasel's ears.

"My guess would be the Zinnis," he said, screwing his mouth into a pucker that made it look like he had tasted something rancid. "Or one of their henchmen, since they seem to be able to hire as many as they need. But I didn't see anyone here yesterday who looked like the two I've seen. And if it is them who are responsible for this," he went on, pointing to the picture, "and for the poison, those two would fit the bill..." Parker fell silent as he remembered the impression Marco and Enzo had made on him earlier.

"Why is that?" Tilly asked, alerted to the distress in his voice.

Parker frowned. "Because there have not been that many men or women I've met who have impressed me more than they did as being the kind of people who are not afraid...no, who want you to know it's them

241

you need to fear. Because they're like vultures. They loom in the background and feed off other people's fear."

"Monsters, you mean."

Parker nodded. "Evil."

Tilly shivered at the word. "I'd...I'd better be going," she murmured, turning away from Parker.

Parker saw that Weasel's ruff had gone up at her tone. "Are you okay, Tilly?" he asked, to which Weasel growled in reply.

"Yes...no...I'm not sure," she stammered. "When you used the word evil just now it reminded me of...I mean, it made me feel..."

"It made you feel like you've come face-to-face with it before," Parker said, finishing Tilly's thought and noting that she had assumed an expression of utter loss.

"Yes. But I can't remember it. I can't even say it. I can only feel it. And I only know that he," she nodded to Chester's headstone, "had something to do with it. Something good, I think. Or at least something that helped me against it. Like a...like a guardian angel..."

Parker nodded. "I know both feelings," he said. "About meeting evil face-to-face, I mean. And the feeling that there was also an opposite force, a guardian angel if you will, there to help protect me from it."

"I need to go," Tilly said, her eyes tearing up and darting from side to side as though looking for an escape route.

"Are you sure? Perhaps you should go and sit with me for awhile before you decide."

"No, it's okay. Really, I'm fine," she said, and as Weasel licked her hand she took a deep breath and her expression softened. "I've been getting these episodes more often lately. When some memory comes close and all I can think to do is run away from it. But I think you were right," she continued. "I just need time to honor myself. And I also think that just by walking this earth on my own with my best friend beside me will help me do that." She patted Weasel on the head and smoothed out his ruff.

Parker sighed. "I understand. I miss Yellow Dog Red for just that reason. A friend to walk the earth with." But then as if alerted to something, he said, "Wait a second," and went over and unfastened the baling string that tied the falcon talisman to the eucalyptus. "Here, take this," he said, placing Falcon over Tilly's head so that it hung like a necklace. "Squirrel's not here tonight, so he won't need it. And I have Yellow Dog Red and Chester to protect me."

Tilly took the woven figure in her hand. "It's heavy," she said.

"I was told there are three Liberty silver dollars in it, for luck," Parker said. "And to turn negative energy into its prey."

Tilly nodded. "I'll bring it back with me tomorrow," she said. "I suppose even guardian angels can benefit from taking walks."

Later that same morning the rain let up. Danquin, at Command Central, called Parker and then Roper, who had come by after dropping Squirrel off at school, to let them know that the Native American Studies Department at the University of California had emailed him in answer to the photographs he had sent them of the artifacts from the nut gathering camp. Their response was unequivocal and blunt: all activity that would further disturb the area must cease forthwith until further exploration could be arranged and conducted, a map made, and an inventory of artifacts cataloged. And any further activity in violation of extant state and federal historical site preservation codes, some of which Danquin referenced, would be subject to civil, and possibly federal criminal penalties if evidence were found that those artifacts had been offered for sale across state lines. In addition, all pertinent information had been forwarded to Sacramento.

Not more than an hour later, a sheriff's squad car pulled to a stop at the base of the driveway at the northeast corner of the property. An officer got out bearing red squares of stiff paper that were stapled to the three nearest telephone poles. She then walked across the muddy vineyard to the cemetery.

Recognizing the sheriff's deputy to be the best friend of his former fiancee, and a woman Roper would have dated in a heartbeat had she and he not already been spoken for, Roper greeted her warmly.

"Jordan! It's me, Roper. How have you been? It's been what? A year?"

Jordan smiled awkwardly, then let her face settle into a thin-lipped, tight-jawed business mode, despite the fact that Parker-the-dog ran up to her and began licking the mud off the toes of her boots.

"Yes, it's been awhile, and I've been good."

"You look great in a uniform," Roper blurted.

"Right. Thanks, I guess."

Realizing he had perhaps embarrassed her, Roper inserted quickly, "Have you heard from Sam?"

"Sam and Becky are fine. They like Otago. How about you?"

"Doing good. Gave the arborist business to my brother Jake, who I think you know. Got a new job, just started it, in The City, after finally getting my architects license." Then, seeing the skeptical look she cast around Parker's compound at his mention of architecture, Roper added, "And I'm helping Parker keep the cemetery open."

"Yes, of course, the Yellow Dog Red Overlook," Jordan said, and her countenance softened. "I like noble gestures, even if they are a little quixotic and...oh, yeah, illegal," she added, but without conviction.

She then trained her gaze on Roper, who saw that Jordan, whose eyes of forget-me-not-blue were electrifying, wore a pained, almost elusive expression, much in the vein of the tragic operatic heroines she had once aspired to emulate, which prompted him to ask her if she was still singing.

She shrugged. "Only in the shower."

"Lucky shower. But it doesn't pay the bills, does it?" he added hastily, realizing she might have construed his remark as offensive rather than flirtatious.

But in thinking more about the shower's fortune, Roper nonetheless found himself visualizing Jordan in the shower, singing *Mio Babinno Caro*. It was a song she had sung once when she and he were on the headlands overlooking the Golden Gate Bridge awaiting Sam, whom he had only just begun dating. As he recalled the time to mind now, the elegiacal chords issuing from Jordan had been subsumed like streamers of mist into the fog seesawing in and out through the bridge's cables, and enveloped into the wind blowing back and forth through Jordan's jet-black hair, so that had Sam not shown up shortly thereafter, Roper, whose feelings for Sam had not yet begun to crystalize beyond an early courting relationship, was

245

certain now that, given the opportunity, he could have fallen in love with Jordan instead of Sam.

"Sadly, no," Jordan sighed, and as if having read Roper's mind, she added regretfully, "It's only water under the bridge."

She removed her sheriff's cap and ran her fingers through her hair before replacing the cap again. There was something reluctant, perhaps even evasive about the motion that caught Roper's attention; as if she were either concealing something or was unsure of herself.

Noting also that she wore no wedding ring, Roper exclaimed, "You're not married! What happened to?..." Having forgotten Jordan's fiancee's name, Roper's voice trailed off.

"Arnold?" she volunteered, to which Roper nodded. "We split this past year. Just after you and Sam broke up. He ran off with a homely venture capitalist who was funding his startup. They're in Santa Clara and just had a baby...ugly as a day old mouse. But they're rich as hell."

"I'm sorry to hear that. Not about the baby being ugly, but about you and him," Roper responded clumsily, which brought a genuine smile and a further softening of Jordan's official expression.

"No, it's okay," she said, and with a theatrical wave of her hand her persona of authority faded away entirely. "Life is like police work: it's an opera. Things work out for the best. Or they don't. The good guys win. The bad guys lose. Then they change places. The curtain rises. Then it drops. The show goes on."

"I guess there's no use crying over spilt milk once the fat lady is done singing," Roper enjoined, as Jordan emitted a boisterous laugh

"Are you mixing metaphors as a way of saying I'm a Reubenesque prima donna?" laughed Jordan again.

Roper tilted his head and drew the corners of his mouth into his cheeks in a caricature of false incredulity. "You're as far removed from a Reubenesque Cleopatra as I am from a billionaire Anthony," he riposted.

Then, when Jordan glanced down at her watch, he said, "Did you come up here because you wanted to see me? Or Parker? Or both of us?"

Jordan met Roper's gaze with a flutter of her eyes and a quizzical expression that once again made Roper aware that she had come up to the cemetery with an as yet unexpressed item in her docket. When she said nothing in reply, Roper went on, "Well, okay then, let's go see what Parker is up to," he said.

Leading her around the back of the boulder in front of the water closet to the rear of the cemetery, where Parker, his back turned to them and facing uphill, was sitting on a gardener's stool, studiously pulling weeds from around the grave of a Great Dane by the name of Orix. Deeply engrossed in his activity and unaware of their presence, Parker kept to his weeding even after Roper and Jordan had drawn to a halt behind him. For her part, Jordan glanced at Roper and nodded in appreciation at the sustained intensity that Parker brought to his task. Then, after several seconds had passed in which Parker had cleared a quadrant of the grave of soap root, star thistle, and groundsel, Jordan finally cleared her throat.

"Sir?...Parker?" she murmured.

"Eh!" Parker started in surprise, craning around to see who was behind him. His eyebrows lifted at the sight of a sheriff's deputy, and he squinted against the glare of the sky behind her. Then as if to some inner directive he nodded and lowered his eyes and, barely above a whisper, said, "I'm glad it's you."

Unsure of the meaning of Parker's remark Jordan tilted her head. "Sir," she went on, "you've done a really nice job with the cemetery. But sorry to say, our department is serving you with an eviction notice tomorrow."

At this last Jordan frowned, in an expression that conveyed discomfort rather than disapproval. Seeing this, Roper realized that Jordan had come up to the cemetery not in any official capacity but, rather, to forewarn Parker of the pending action. Accordingly, when Parker hesitated in answering, Roper answered in Parker's place.

"You're not going to be the one doing it, I hope," he said, assuming an empathetic tone.

She shook her head sharply. "Oh, no...not me. I get out of processing notices of eviction whenever I can. Too close to home."

Parker leaned back and swivelled around on his stool. He blinked again against the luminance of the hazy gray sky behind Jordan, and it took several seconds for him to refocus his eyes before he could finally see Jordan clearly.

"Yes, thanks. I know all about the notice," he answered. But then he added enigmatically, "So, we meet again."

Jordan blinked against the assertion. "We've met before?"

Parker nodded. "You brought my wife back to me," he sighed. "About six years ago. She was just becoming a sundowner. Up in the tree off Carmelita. You were new to the force, I think."

"Oh!" Jordan replied, her cheeks filling with color. "Of course. The beautiful naked woman in the tree."

Parker nodded. "That was my Sylvia. You were the one who found her sitting in our son's tree house down by Carmelita Creek," Parker said.

"And all she would say to me was, 'Where's my Tad? Where's my Tad?'" Jordan's voice faded to a whisper. "That's why it took us so long to get her home. We kept looking for someone named Tad. But he was...gone..." Jordan's eyes glazed over in remembrance.

"She had a Boy Scout Backpacking Merit Badge pinned to the skin of her naked chest," inserted Parker.

Jordan nodded. "It was only when she..." But Jordan fell silent as the events of that night reemerged fully for her. Then her eyes widened and she glanced down at Yellow Dog Red's grave. "It was only when she—your dog—climbed up the ramp into the tree that Sylvia remembered where she lived." Jordan shook her head. "She cried and cried in happiness over seeing that dog. But she couldn't even remember her name...or yours," Jordan added, nodding at Parker. "The only name she remembered was..."

"Tad. He was our son. And that was only the beginning for her," murmured Parker, wincing as he remembered afresh his wife's ever-steepening descent into a forgetfulness that was a lightless forest whose unrecognizable paths led only to unremembered night terrors. "The last many times I saw her," he went on, letting his gaze rise unfocused into the crown of the eucalyptus tree, "she didn't know who I was. But she remembered Tad and, after that night, Yellow Dog Red."

Jordan's gaze too drifted up into the eucalyptus tree, where she saw Squirrel's tent, which, owing to the pool of rainwater that had formed atop it, sagged so that it looked less like a backpacking tent than a skullcap that had been flattened.

In the silence that ensued, Roper saw that Jordan's eyes had grown moist. "Here," he said, as he brought out a handkerchief from his pocket and handed it to her. Then, as she daubed her eyes, he changed the subject back to the eviction. "I hope your team is prepared when they come tomorrow," he said.

"For what? More rain?"

"It's supposed to let up later today," interjected Parker, before Roper could respond. Then turning his back on them he resumed his weeding. "So, if you don't mind, I need to freshen up a few sites for tomorrow."

Roper nodded in agreement to the weather report and, to Jordan, said, "Our estimation is that there might be some people here when the notice is served."

Jordan shrugged. "I read the papers. That Wili Wallenstock is a real whack job. And hashtag yellowdogred has been trending on Twitter. The fact is I've been impressed by what those school kids have done. They've been amazing. Speaking of which," she added, gesturing to Squirrel's tent,

"I'd like to talk to the young man who I understand spends time in the trees. Peter von Brandt is his name, I believe."

"About his living situation?"

"Hanging about in the trees, you mean? No, vagrancy is not on my mind today."

She drew out a mini-Ipad from her back pocket, and after tapping its display a few times showed it to Roper and spoke to Parker as Roper looked it over. "In a nutshell it says that lawyers for Etruscan Estate Vineyards have petitioned to lodge a domestic terrorism complaint in Superior Court against those responsible for pouring sugar into the fuel tanks of their equipment. Blah, blah, blah," she recited sarcastically. "It seems this von Brandt boy was mentioned by them as a person of interest. His group home says he is staying here in the cemetery on occasion. Do you know where he is?"

Roper's eyebrows shot up. "Domestic terrorism! You've got to be kidding. And, anyway, he didn't do it." He handed the tablet back to Jordan.

"Oh, don't worry. It won't stick. Money for vandalism crime is tight. It's just a way for the plaintiff to give the D.A. an avenue to get more resources. But," she added, replacing the tablet in her back pocket, "how do you know he didn't do it? Does that mean you know who did do it? Or did you do it yourself?"

Roper shook his head uncertainly; for at that instant he began to feel sorry for Jordan that she had been put in a position to perpetuate a charade she clearly didn't believe in.

"I just know," he replied. "He's way too sensitive and nonviolent to do something like that... Wait!" Roper exclaimed, opening his eyes wide and gesturing toward the road; for it occurred to him just then that Jordan's uneasiness had perhaps been caused by her guilt at having to manipulate him in order to gain his confidence so that she could extract information from him about Squirrel. "Is that what you were doing down on the road? Putting up...what? Wanted posters!"

"Oh good lord! Don't get your pants all in a tangle, Roper. I was just kidding. As a matter of fact those posters will probably please you. They're a cease-and-desist order for the owners of the property and their agents to refrain from disturbing the earth within a fifty-foot radius from the crest of that knoll." She pointed to the spot where Roper had found the Native American artifacts."

"Oh, sorry," Roper said contritely.

"Which means," she continued, after acknowledging Roper's apology, "that when it comes right down to it, the owners will probably be encouraged to withdraw their request for a terrorism complaint—which we all know in the office, and in the DA's too, is just a bogus harassment tactic by a fecking bloke—as a condition of compliance with the order. So, to put it another way, we're not pursuing the monkey-wrenching very actively. It's not terrorism but old-fashioned made-in-America apple-pie hooliganism, pure and square.

"But you or your compatriots must have high-flier friends," she went on, "because I was told by the sheriff himself this morning that the archeology stuff came straight out of the Governor's office."

At that moment the radio microphone that was affixed to Jordan's shoulder crackled to life, and through it a dispatcher's garbled voice could be heard, but only indistinctly.

Jordan's expression became one of disappointment. "Sorry to spoil the garden party," she said. "But I've got to go track down some green-thumb crooks. Apparently an underfinanced gardener down in the Carneros absconded in the middle of the night with five-thousand metal grape-stakes and ten miles of drip irrigation line."

Jordan rested her hand lightly on Parker's shoulder and wished him luck with the eviction. She and Roper then walked off. When they were beside Yellow Dog Red's grave, Jordan unexpectedly turned and, dropping down on her knees, ran her hands across the top of the rounded surface of dirt as if trying to smooth it of furrows.

"I remember she was a good dog," she murmured. "I used to see her waiting at the foot of the hill for her master to come back from wherever he or she went, rain or shine, day or night. She was one of those once-in-a-lifetime companions. The kind you can't believe you're worthy of. Kind of like you, Roper. Someone who makes you a better person in spite of yourself."

Jordan bowed her head, and in doing so a tiny treble clef tattoo emerged into view from beneath her collar. And Roper, who had loved that insignia on her from the first time he had seen it, had to stay his hand from reaching out to touch it.

"You know, Roper, Sam was right about you. She told me from the very beginning that you were too good a man for her." She bit her lip again as if deciding what if anything else to say, then added hesitantly, "I wouldn't be too surprised, if I were you, to hear from Sam. She told me she and Becky were thinking they might ask you if you'd be interested in helping them in…you know…in sending them down some…some, ah…some material, so that you could…you know…you could…father them a child," she managed to say, finally.

Roper was too dumfounded to say anything in response other than to repeat the word "material," and in the awkward interim that followed, Parker, unbidden but having overheard Jordan, shouted out. "You know, Roper, it's something to think about. Squirrel could use a brother!"

"What?!" Roper shot a glance up at Parker to see if he wasn't perhaps in on some very bad joke in very poor taste with Jordan. But, seeing that Parker and Jordan were both dead serious, he managed to say, "Are you—both of you—crazy? I…I don't even know if I want a child. Much less send some of my…of my…material off to New Zealand in order to father one. And," he frowned, "And Squirrel's not mine, so what are you talking about?"

"He wants to be," retorted Parker, again so categorically that Roper felt the words hitting him like an incoming roundhouse. Parker pushed himself to standing, for Dotty had pulled her car to a stop down on the road, and he was already heading down to meet her as he added, "Yours, I mean. Can't you see that?"

Once more Roper was too dumbfounded to respond, and he rechecked Parker's expression to see if there were any telltale signs of insincerity. Seeing none, he turned back to Jordan as Parker patted him on the shoulder when he passed by.

Left alone with Roper, Jordan brought her hand to her microphone and clicked it off. "You don't have to send your material to New Zealand, you know," she said, checking again to make sure the device was without power. She then reached out unreservedly and laid her hand on Roper's arm, and from beneath the bill of her cap her eyes bore into his. "I mean, if you want to become a father."

Roper's eyes opened as wide as possible, and his arms tingled with a loss of blood pressure.

Jordan was blushing so deeply that Roper thought a blood vessel in her brow might pop. "Look," she began, "I know this is going to sound crazy, but ever since I first met you, I was secretly hoping Sam would free you so that I...so that I could have a chance with you."

Roper felt an incoherent stirring in himself, and, like a leaf being drawn over a precipice, he felt he was being pulled out into the sea that was Jordan.

"What about Arnold?" he managed to whisper, knowing that he didn't give a rat's ass about Arnold.

"He and I both knew we would never marry. It was a relief to both of us when he left."

"You knew Sam was gay way back then? Why didn't you say something to me?"

"Of course I knew. I was her best friend. But what was I going to say to you? 'Roper, do you know your fiancee is a lesbian?'" She shook her head. "No, it was her life—and yours—to live. Your journey, not mine, to discover. She said she was in love with you. So, what could I say or do?"

Jordan inhaled deeply, as though she was having trouble keeping up with her thoughts. "I know this is sudden, Roper, but now that we have a chance I think we should give ourselves a try at loving one another.

At that moment Roper felt that if he were a pinball machine, he would have tilted. Or, if he were a computer, he would have crashed.

Jordan put her arms around Roper and drew him close, which he did not—could not—resist. Oddly, his awareness was drawn to the faint dirt imprints from Yellow Dog Red's grave that her hands had left on his arms, and in seeing the earthen fans of her fingers tattooed on his skin he realized he wanted nothing more than to keep those hands and this woman as tightly anchored to him as possible.

"Sure. Why not?" he heard himself say, as though from a place far away. "After all, you know me, and I know you. We've spent time together. We've talked about things we really care about. And, besides," Roper added, thinking back again to the day at the Golden Gate, "if Sam hadn't shown up when she did that day when you sang *Mio Babinno Caro*, I don't think I could've stopped myself from falling in love with you. The fact is, I guess maybe I didn't."

"Same with me. Even when I was with Arnold, I wondered what you and Sam were doing. So then," she inhaled deeply again, her voice resonant with resolve, "I know this is really weird. But here's our chance, Roper. Maybe it's our only chance. Like having a once-in-a-lifetime companion. We made choices that were right but also wrong for us. Now we have a chance to make right what went wrong."

With those words both Roper and Jordan's eyes filled with tears until their surroundings were but an impressionistic seascape.

"So, when do we get started?" Jordan asked, laughing and weeping at once as she squeezed Roper's arms. Then, wiping her eyes, she removed her cap and flung it impetuously like a frisbee across the graveyard.

Roper looked down at his watch. "Well, I'll be busy most of tonight and tomorrow with Yellow Dog Red. But I don't have anything going on tomorrow night."

"We have a deal then?" she said, her voice grown reedy and husky with desire.

"Yep. We have a deal," Roper said, and as the two lingered in a first luxuriant kiss, Dotty stepped through the fence and bent to retrieve the sheriff's hat that had landed at her feet.

"I knew I should've waited to put my cake decoration supplies in storage," she said, to which Parker nodded in agreement.

Wili Wallenstock drove up shortly thereafter and parked behind Dotty's car, followed closely by Danquin and a flatbed truck that offloaded eight portable toilets along the edge of the road. Though it was early in the day, Wili was dressed for a cocktail party, wearing a coral pantsuit, a lemon-yellow scarf, matching party shoes and a wide-brimmed straw hat. She also carried a turquoise-colored valise. After she and Danquin read the cease-and-desist order Jordan had posted on one of the telephone poles, she let Danquin assist her passage through the plowed field. They passed Jordan along the way, and, after Danquin and Jordan had introduced themselves, Wili engaged her in animated conversation for a few minutes. Danquin then deposited Wili at the entry to the cemetery before he headed back to Command Central to handle the crush of inquiries about the next day's flash-mob action. In the meantime Wili made her way over to the futon sofa and plopped herself down next to Roper, who was slouched into it with a faraway look in his eyes.

The first words out of her mouth were, "Wouldn't you swear that Deputy Simpson is with child?" to which, after Roper gave no response, Wili continued. "She was positively radiant. I told her I wanted to interview her and have her pose for a story I'd like to do on law enforcement mothers for *Vanity Fair*. What was she doing here?" she said, directing her question to Roper, since Parker and Dolly had just walked over to begin grooming the grave next to Orix.

Roper smiled goofily before sitting upright and turning to her. "She didn't tell you why she was here?" he said incredulously, to which Wili shook her head.

"Why do I get the distinct impression you're acting like the Cheshire cat who's just eaten Big Bird?" To which Roper shrugged. Seeing that he wasn't going to be forthcoming, Wili sighed and continued. "The only thing she said was that there was a break-in down-valley, and that if I wanted a scoop for a story, I could follow her. Something about agricultural supplies. But," she scoffed, "what kind of scoop is that around here? I did see the posted notice, though. But where exactly is the archeological site?" she added, scanning the cemetery.

Roper thought for a moment to ask Wili if Jordan had mentioned anything about the terrorism complaint, but judging by her tone that she was annoyed by something quite apart from today's visit, he thought better of it; no use getting Squirrel sucked into something he didn't do, and then have Wili plaster it all over her gossip column.

"The site is over there, on the knoll," he said with forced succinctness, pointing past the trailer, across from where the Gainsaid Pound house had once stood. "If you're interested, here are a few of the things that I unearthed," he said, and from out of his pocket he withdrew three arrowheads he had carried around since that first day.

"May I?" said Wili, and Roper placed the shiny black obsidian objects on her palm. "You say there are more over there?"

"Tons probably," Roper replied. "Stanley White Shadow and Thomas Ant Lake and the University of California say it might be a major harvesting site."

"Yes, so I gathered from Zand's tweets at Yellow Dog Red. He tweeted there were going to be some problems in that regard for the new owners. But who are Stanley White Shadow and Thomas Ant Lake?" she asked, while pulling out a tablet from her valise on which she began typing.

Roper decided not to correct Wili's misrepresentation of Zand as being a man, and said, "They're representatives from the Northern Paiute tribe. "They told us that Falcon, who they say has the power to perceive negative energy and make it its prey, was..." His voice trailed off as he

257

glanced to where the talisman had hung. And, seeing that it was gone, he called out to Parker. "Hey, Parker, what happened to Falcon?"

"Tilly Thomassock has it," he called back. "I gave it to her. For luck."

"Another odd name," Wili said, keying in Tilly's last name, while phonetically mouthing it and then typing in, "who has the power to perceive negative energy and make it its prey."

"It's a dog's name," Roper said, pointing to Tilly's grave. "Tilly—that's not even her real name—said she took it as her own, not knowing where it came from, after contracting some sort of amnesia a decade ago. According to her, after seeing Zand's tweets, she realized that her dog Chester is buried here. But that's all she remembers. She doesn't even remember that Peter—Squirrel—is her son. She traveled here from a Buddhist Monastery in Sedona, she says, where she's worked as a housekeeper for ten years. By coming here she hopes she can find out who she is and where she's from."

Wili lowered the tablet to her lap and tilted her head. "You're making this up, aren't you?" she charged, "to punish me for my last story."

Roper shook his head and raised his arms in the air to proclaim his innocence. "No, I swear. Tilly was here. I met her. We all met her. She told us of this only yesterday."

Wili too shook her head, but contrary to Roper's action, hers communicated disbelief mixed with deflation. "You know, Roper, I have a confession. That last story wasn't entirely my own doing. Especially the nutty and, frankly, meanspirited stuff I—we—wrote about Parker. The truth of the matter is that it was a hit piece that my editor-asshole-in-chief wanted me to throw in for some extra controversy, in the hope he could stir up enough interest in the nursing home market to boost circulation before he attends the regional meeting of small-market newspaper publishers in Reno." Wili paused a moment, then nodded as if to an inner judgment before going on.

"He wants to go strutting into the MGM Grand with his new Thai hooker slut girlfriend hanging on his arm so he can brag to all the other hacks about how well he's surviving the onslaught of online publishing, and boast to those limp-dicked bastards about fucking his whore."

She paused again and her mouth formed into a scowl, as, oppositely, Roper's went slack, in shock at both the tone and the salty vocabulary that Wili had spewed so unexpectedly. "As far as I'm concerned," she continued, "he can go fuck himself. But," she added, suddenly brightening, "I do have something here that I thought might help me make up for at least part of the hit piece."

She blinked demurely as though the forgoing tirade had never happened, and opened her valise, in which she rummaged around before pulling out a manila folder. Then with a self-deprecating nod, she said, "You see, here I was only a week ago bedding my boss, thinking I was a movie starlet and fancying myself a great regional reporter a la Barbara Walters, figuring this dog vigil thing here was going to be another boring and witless story about yet another crazy, simpleminded toothless banjo-playing back country hick grieving for his lost coon-dog. But I'm beginning to see how wrong I was."

"Don't be so hard on yourself, Wili," responded Roper, after Wili fell silent. "We all have things we need to work on."

He paused after his own words fell limply in his ears, like the self-improvement pablum Sam had once tried to get him to ingest. He turned to Wili, and seeing her slumped beside him looking like a wilted bouquet vainly defying its deterioration, he reconsidered his earlier decision to not confide in her.

"You know, Wili," he offered, "I guess I might have a couple of scoops for you if you're interested."

Wili perked up and she straightened her hat, which had tilted forward onto her forehead as she slumped. "Go on. I'm all ears," she murmured.

Roper swivelled to face Wili, and tailoring his words to what he thought would be most newsworthy to her, he said, "The first thing is that the owners of this property—the Zinni's—are throwing their weight around with the DA, trying to get the vandalism of their equipment designated as an act of terrorism. The second is that someone left rat poison here, clearly intended for my—I mean Parker's—dog Parker."

Wili met the first scoop with a noncommital expression and slow shakes of her head as she typed dutifully into her tablet. But upon hearing the second, her head snapped up and she stopped typing. "Actually," she said, "the rat poison thing is the reason I'm here." Whereupon she pulled out two photographs and handed them to Roper.

"I was looking through the pictures that I took the other day," she explained, "and out of the two hundred or so, I noticed these two," she continued. "Mostly because one of the people in them looks like a toad at a wedding. But, tell me, what do you see?"

Roper looked at the two photos that were of a clumping of perhaps ten people who had come to pay their respects to Yellow-Dog-Red. Among this group was an older, overweight, gray-haired woman in a floral day dress, carrying a small handbag and wearing an orange and black Giants baseball cap above oversized aviator sunglasses that were themselves framed beneath bushy eyebrows. She did indeed look out of place—like a toad at a wedding. In one of the pictures the woman appeared to have just removed her hand from her handbag, in which there were two yellow bars, about four inches long, clearly visible in the grip of her partly closed palm. In the other picture, the woman is bending down and the two objects are lying half-hidden amid the weeds atop two yet-to-be-groomed graves.

Roper lowered the picture to his lap. "Goddamn! That's the Warfarin we found."

"Rat poison. That's what I thought too," replied Wili.

"That woman is the person who left the poison," he muttered. "Do you know who she is?"

Wili shrugged. "Well, yes and no. But that's the thing. "Here," she said, as she swiped her screen and typed in a name. "Look at this." She handed the tablet to Roper. "I thought I'd seen those eyebrows at Advisory Commission hearings."

Roper saw that the tablet presented a picture of three men identified as Rocco, Enzo, and Marco Zinni. They were standing outside a vineyard in front of an ancient tractor below a weathered sign reading "Etruscan Turlock Vineyards." The one named Rocco was wearing oversized aviator glasses and a Giants baseball cap. The same as the woman in the picture. Bushy eyebrows and all.

"It's her," Roper answered. "Except she's a man."

"Dressed as a woman," Wili concurred. "I called Animal Control before coming here," she continued, "To find out if there is a law against putting out rat poison in a pet cemetery. I was told it was perfectly legal. But, of course, the questions I have go straight to motive. That is, Why would the owner of this property want to do something like that to control rodents, knowing that he wants the people living on it to go away? The only thing I can come up with is—"

"Intimidation," Roper and Wili said simultaneously. Then Roper shouted, "Parker!"

Parker came over to the trailer and, after putting on his reading glasses, perused the photos. As a retired intelligence analyst his first inclination was to check to see if the photos had been doctored. Seeing no evidence of this, nor able to ascribe any obvious operant motive on Wili's part for applying such an artifice, he was in general agreement with Wili and Roper that the woman in the pictures did indeed look toad-like and, by the eyebrows alone, a lot like Rocco Zinni. He then asked Roper to phone Danquin and Jordan and to email but not tweet others about their finding; so that they could organize themselves into teams while not tipping their hand via social media, and also be on the lookout for Zinni the following day when throngs of people were expected to show up. But this last proposal brought Parker up short; for it reminded him uncomfortably of the type of semi-warlike situation-command footings he had worked within for forty years. Thus, his next words were cautionary.

"You know," he said, "We should not get too far ahead of ourselves here. Just because that man is dressed up as a woman does not mean that he did anything against the law. We don't know what his—or her—motive was. Perhaps she saw some droppings and is the kind of person who hates rats and carries around rat poison in his—her—purse. Which leads me to ask, What if we're wrong altogether? What if that woman really is just a homely, masculine-looking woman with wild eyebrows?"

Parker glanced at Wili, who had hiked up her coral-colored slacks and rolled down her knee-high hose. He said, "Wili, would you do me a favor? Would you hold off printing anything about the Warfarin until at least the day after tomorrow?"

She shrugged. "Sure. Rat homicides are not really breaking news anyway. But Tilly Thomassock is another story," she added quickly. "Can you imagine that happening to yourself? Not knowing who you are and, even when you're told who you are ten years later by the son you didn't know you had, still being unable to remember. It's boggling. It's tragic. But most important, it's newsworthy. But, who knows," she went on, "maybe, just maybe when I put it out on our online edition, someone who knows something will come forward."

Dotty, who had begun to take the lids off the plastic containers she had withdrawn from her food basket, now laid out an array of savory-looking dishes she had cooked the night before. Having overheard earlier much of what Roper and Wili had said while she and Parker were weeding in silence thirty feet removed from them, Dotty felt her years-old antipathy toward Wili begin to dissolve, enough, anyway, to ask her if she wouldn't like to stay for lunch and, perhaps, catch up with Tilly, who they expected to come by later.

"Don't mind if I do," Wili answered, smiling broadly at the invitation, as behind her Armando arrived with four men in tow.

Wili, who had known Armando for years, stood and went to intercept him at the fence, where, blocking his path, she asked him if he knew anything about the theft in the Carneros. Armando shook his head at Wili's implicit innuendo and turned away. But then he halted and cast Wili a sidelong look, and after pausing to gather his thoughts, he answered her question.

"There are some very twisted people in this world who take pleasure in taking things they don't need only to satisfy their hunger for guilt. I know people like this. Guilt is food for them. It gives them strength to hurt others, and they gain special strength in feasting on other people's doubts. It is to them the same as having sex with a married man is to others."

He grabbed his crotch, and at this last gesture Wili almost yelped as though she had been slapped in the face. "So, if I were you, Ms Wallenstock," he concluded, "I would steer clear of those kind of people, because they will do whatever it takes to feed the beast of guilt in their belly. ¿Entiendes lo que estoy diciendo?"

Armando then tapped the bill of his baseball cap with his hand and walked over to say hello to Dotty, leaving Wili too surprised and shocked to respond. She quickly glanced around to see if the others had heard Armando or noticed his obscene gesture, and seeing that no one had paid any attention, she sighed and, leaning against the fence, began to busy herself with looking through her tablet for references in news archive sites to Alice von Brandt and Tilly Thomassock.

Dotty offered Armando and his men the expected-by-now lemon bars, and while they were indulging themselves Parker remarked to Armando that he thought he remembered him saying he wasn't going to return his crew to the field until later in the week or early the next.

Armando drew his mouth into a line that Parker took to be conspiratorial. "Zinni didn't assign me to it," he admitted, slapping the leather gloves he held in one hand against the palm of his other. "But the fumigation is over. The weather doesn't look like it'll hold off much longer, and I don't think it's a good idea to have city people walking on wet plastic sheeting. So," he shrugged, "I came on my own. I don't want me—or Zinni, for that matter—to be sued for creating an attractive nuisance."

Armando then spoke in Spanish to his men, who, after paying tribute to Yellow Dog Red, left the cemetery and went about the work of cutting and rolling the remaining sheeting west of the cemetery, leaving behind rectangles of refrigerator-sized bundles dotting the field like giant cubes of butter.

Keith's van pulled up shortly thereafter behind Armando's truck. Bahram emerged from the passenger side and, along with Keith's driver, went around to the back of the van and helped Keith disembark. Ten minutes later, Keith and Bahram were inside the cemetery. In one hand Bahram carried a pair of gloves. In his other he had a wine bottle, which he extended to Parker, who was sitting next to Dotty at the table.

"Well, what do you think?" Bahram said, beaming as Parker took the bottle from him and, holding it at arm's length so that he could see it clearly, read the label.

He squinted against the glare that made the rest of the label difficult to see. "'Yellow Dog Red'?"

"Yes! Yellow Dog Red. How do you like it?" Bahram exclaimed, while, in order to cut down on the glare, Parker lowered the bottle and saw now that there was a picture of a yellow Labrador Retriever beneath the crimson lettering.

"That's my old dog Twig," Keith inserted apologetically. He had maneuvered his wheelchair to the end of the table so that he too could see the label. "But we could just as easily put a picture of Yellow Dog Red there. May I?" he added, gesturing toward Dotty's lemon bars.

"Paradoxum and I are collaborating on it," Bahram explained. "It's Sirah I bought from Paso Robles blended with Keith's Alexander Valley Petit Sirah and a little Mourvedre from Napa."

Keith took a deep breath, and, when he exhaled, his words rushed out in a swarm. "Five percent of gross will be split. Between the SPCA and for preservation of the cemetery," he said. But when he saw that Parker was frowning, his voice trailed off, as much from concern that Parker disapproved, as from lack of air. "But only if..."

"Only if what?" Parker said gravely, and handed the bottle back to Bahram, who was wearing a crestfallen expression. Bahram and Keith exchanged uncertain gazes.

"Only if you approve," replied Bahram, then added hesitantly, "Angwin was adamant that we should not do anything to exploit your vigil that would make money for us without your approval, even if it was only to help you out."

"'You can't sully Yellow Dog Red,' were the words I believe she used," Keith said, to which Bahram nodded his head in agreement, then shook it with a mixture of disbelief and consternation at his daughter's almost preternatural wiseness.

"Let's just say that, for a girl her age, she was uncompromising."

Parker looked again at the picture on the bottle—doubtfully still, Bahram thought—which showed a lifelike rendition, in acrylic or oil, of a mischievous-looking Yellow Lab gazing out with burning brown eyes directly into the viewer's eyes while fronting a backdrop of lush green oak woodland dotted with lupine and poppies.

Turning to Keith, Parker said, "Tell me about Twig. She looks to have been in her prime in this drawing."

Surprised by the question, Keith smiled broadly, and his arm shot up. It lowered slowly as if by parachute, and when he spoke, his words again rushed to keep up with his available breath.

"She was six when that picture was taken. She was my service dog. She and I were on a nature walk. In the spring. On a paved section with my care giver. He took that picture. You can tell by Twig's gaze that she was eyeing something. A mountain lion on the ridge. Twig moved in front of me so that she was between me and the lion. She was protecting me with her life."

"Yellow Dog Red did the same for me once," responded Parker, after Keith had to come to a halt to allow his digressive lungs to regroup. "Sylvia and I took her backpacking with us to the Rubicon Wilderness. On the North Shore of Tahoe," he went on, vaguely aware that he had subconsciously acquired Keith's cadence as his own. "We came across a puma. Her cubs were feasting on a mule deer. I'm certain the cat, to protect her cubs, was about to maul us. But Yellow Dog Red stood her ground. She would have been cat food if she hadn't scared them away."

Parker's expression softened as he glanced again at Twig's picture. He then passed the bottle over to Roper to let him and the others look at it. Parker sighed at the memory of Yellow Dog Red and Sylvia.

"It was to be the last backpacking trip for us. The third night into it Sylvia stepped out of the tent and wandered off across a slab of granite beside the lake where we were camped. It was only by the grace of God and Yellow Dog Red," he added, "that we found her seconds before she stepped off a cliff into the water." Parker drew his hands down in a wringing motion over his face. "It was the first time Sylvia admitted that she couldn't trust herself to be alone," he went on. "At least without Yellow Dog Red being there with her. It was the best camping trip we ever had, though. We spent the whole time crying and laughing and swimming in the lake with Red and remembering..."

Parker fell silent. Then he turned to Bahram. "I like it," he said. But then nodding to the bottle, which Dotty was now holding, he appended, "And you have my approval to sell it. But only on one condition," he continued: "that the next vintage has a picture of Yellow Dog Red on it, and that every vintage that follows afterwards has a picture of a different Yellow Lab."

Bahram and Keith looked at each other with undisguised glee. "Great!" Bahram blurted. "Then we'll go ahead and do our first bottling next week. Five thousand cases."

"How much will you sell it for?" asked Roper.

"Around twenty a bottle," Bahram replied.

"That's five thousand dollars," Keith added. "And if it sells, I expect we'll do four more bottlings of five thousand."

"Twenty thousand dollars isn't chicken feed," Dotty said. "And I like the label too. But I'm more interested right now in knowing what the wine tastes like." She brought out a half-dozen plastic cups from her basket.

"Let's open it and see," Roper said. "Does anyone have a corkscrew?"

"In my pack behind my chair," Keith replied. "And there's another bottle and a glass for me in there too."

Three minutes later two bottles had been uncorked and seven, not six, glasses poured; since nobody had noticed until she and Weasel entered the graveyard that Tilly had walked up from the road.

Tilly was wearing faded jeans, a denim work shirt and straw hat, and she still wore the Falcon pendant slung around her neck. Like the others, she had also brought a pair of gloves. Parker introduced her as Tilly to Armando and Wili, rather than as Alice, and explained briefly to Armando that Tilly suffered from amnesia, and that she had come to this place, after ten years, when she remembered her dog Chester from shots of his grave on Zand's blog. Armando received this information with less sympathy, it seemed, than fear that Tilly's condition might be catching, and thus, after having a taste of the wine, he excused himself and walked over to the grave two down from Orix, where he knelt and began pulling weeds.

To that point Wili's internet search had produced no meaningful results, other than links to private-detective and real-estate agencies; therefore, upon Tilly's arrival, she seized on the opportunity to begin asking her questions about having lived in the valley, having had a son she couldn't remember, having worked in the area—all of which Tilly, although not wanting to be rude, answered with only shrugs as she made her way over to the table. There, Bahram, seeing the besieged look in Tilly's eyes, inserted himself between her and Wili, and introduced himself and Keith. Then, extending Tilly a glass of wine, he suggested to Wili that she leave Tilly alone for the time being.

Wili started to balk. "But this is real news..." But then, acknowledging Bahram's intimidating gaze, she relented, although not before firing off a final comment. "Tell me at least what your oldest memory is."

At this, Tilly brightened suddenly, and after taking a sip of Bahram and Keith's wine, her gaze grew distant. "The farthest back I can remember is waking up one morning at the monastery to the song

'Blackbird' by the Beatles. It was in the middle of winter, and in a way," she continued, "I see it as my birthday." Then, in an almost childlike voice she proceeded to sing the song's second verse. "'Blackbird singing in the dead of night. Take these sunken eyes and learn to see. All your life. You were only waiting for this moment to be free...'

"It was like the song was telling me how to learn to open my eyes to freedom to see my memories again," she went on. "But, even after that, I could still see only as far back as to when I was dropped off in Sedona. That was nine years earlier, so I didn't remember anything, except that I had come there in a truck, and I'm now nine years old."

She took another sip of wine and, seeing the bottle on the table, smiled at the label. She then went on as Wili typed in earnest to keep up with her. "I still didn't have any ID, and the only name I came up with was the one I gave to the nuns: Tilly Thomassock." She nodded toward the gravestone next to Chester's, where Parker-the-dog and Weasel were gamboling about in a pile of unearthed weeds. "Thankfully the nuns," she finished, "were good enough to let me stay and work there without ID for room and board. They made discreet inquiries for me, of course, but nothing came of them. And I didn't want to go to the newspaper... I don't know where I would've gone or what I would've done without those women. A few years ago the nuns suggested I go onto Facebook to see if anyone recognized me, or if I could recognize anybody else. No one friended me. There was nothing, except strangers wanting to meet me for coffee..."

Tilly's voice trailed off, and in the gap Dotty motioned for her to sit and have some of the savories she had spread on the table. Acknowledging that she was hungry, Tilly thanked Dotty and then helped herself to some cheese and crackers, a lemon bar, and to a touch more wine. Then, as she was lowering herself to the empty spot on the futon next to Wili, Falcon slipped out from beneath Tilly's shirt. Only Wili's quick reactions kept the talisman from being dunked into the wine.

"Whew! That was close," Tilly said, as Wili kept Falcon brushed aside until Tilly was settled onto the cushion. "Thanks."

Wili nodded in acknowledgment. "It doesn't seem like it would have been a good thing to let your good luck charm get snookered."

"No, I guess not," Tilly replied, inserting the strap through the top two buttons of her blouse to keep Falcon from falling free again. She then called for Weasel to come over, whereupon she gave him and Parker-the-dog crackers. Tilly sat in silence while she ate, and when she looked up from watching the two dogs skirmishing at her feet with some uprooted sorrel, she saw that three more people—two of whom she had met the day before—were approaching the cemetery. The third person, a young girl, was bounding ahead of the other two.

"Dad! Dad!" she was shouting.

"Who's that?" Tilly said, as the girl ran up to Bahram at a full gallop through the gap in the fence and with barely a break in her stride. She was holding a phone outstretched in one hand and a rectangular black object the size of a box of crackers in her other.

"That's Zand...Angie," Roper answered from behind Tilly, as Parker-the-dog squealed in delight and ran out to greet her.

"Dad! He did it! Slag did it! Listen!"

Before she could do anything else, however, Angie had to kneel to pet Parker-the-dog, who had rolled over onto her back and was pawing her legs while nibbling on her shoelace. Angie rubbed Parker's belly, then, standing, laid the rectangular device on the table. After punching a few commands into her phone, the box came to life, emitting the warbled voice of a man with an Irish accent singing a solemnly joyous ballad. The lyrics of the lead-in were a bit hard to decipher on the first hearing amid the lush instrumentation, but the words afterward came out crystal clear:

"Yellow Dog Red. At my feet. Wait in peace. Faithful. Wait to meet. Mellow Dog. Yellow Dog. Wait to meet. In the heath. Wait for me. Run. Run. Run..."

271

"It's an mp3," Angie announced, beaming with pride. "I just downloaded it from itunes for only ninety-nine cents." She paused to catch her breath, then continued. "I can't believe he did it already! Hey, Parker, come and listen to this!" she called out, gesturing for Parker, who had risen to see what all the shouting was about, to come over and join the others. "It's about Yellow Dog Red!"

"He wanted to surprise you," answered Bahram bemusedly, just as Squirrel and Danquin converged on the table. "I'm glad he succeeded."

Angie looked askance at her father. "You knew he did it?" she said, momentarily crestfallen. "And you didn't tell me?"

Bahram shrugged. "He texted a link to me late last night after you'd gone to bed."

Almost before his words had exited Bahram's lips, Angie admonished him to keep quiet and listen to the song. She then shut her eyes and swayed with the melody, which indeed proved to be the Irish lullaby that Slag had predicted he would create. Squirrel and Danquin had come up next to Angie by then, while Parker had come down to stand beside Roper.

Like Angie, Parker shut his eyes and listened to the strains of the song as they enfolded the tight circle of Yellow Dog Red's keepers within a shroud of sanguine peacefulness that was not unlike the peace of untroubled sleep. Emerging from within the cloth of this fabric were memories of friends and places Parker had known that felt to him like well-worn apparel. It was as if all of his past recollections were being worn by him simultaneously, one layer upon the other, and all his memories coalesced to form into a sort of cloak, or cocoon, that he knew, without knowing how, would protect and nourish him until the core of his being no longer needed their protection. And as the song thread its way backward to the farthest reaches of his being and beyond, to the nakedness of potentiality where breath itself was disrobed of all pretense, he would have willed himself at that moment to take his very last breath as a man had it been in his power.

The melody was reminiscent of the lullabies Parker's own parents had sung to him as a child eight decades ago, and it reminded him more than a little of those that he and Sylvia had themselves sung to Tad four decades after that. Thus, when the song's sadly heroic chords drew to a close a few minutes later neither his own nor anyone else's eyes remained dry. Only for Parker, however, did its dwindling chords frame a culmination rather than a commencement.

"My, what a lovely lullaby," Dotty, the first to speak, remarked, as she wiped her eyes.

"Ya, and many copies of it will be sold on itunes," commented Danquin, who had kept his attention half-fixed on the tweets streaming across the screen of his phone. "Maybe even millions," he added.

"I still can't believe he did it," Angie said, shaking her head. "He must really love dogs."

"He does," Bahram replied. "And even more, he loves people who are willing to stand up for hopeless causes."

Wili paused her furious typing into her tablet to respond to Bahram. "Like mongrel reporters no longer faithful to their abusive publishers," she stated truculently, then added, "Are you certain that was really Slag? He sounded so...sweet."

"I am," Bahram responded.

"Good. Then here goes," she said, and punching the "send" icon, she passed her hastily written report into the social media hinterlands.

"Yellow Dog Red was a good dog," was all that Parker managed to say; for the song's lyrics had uncannily echoed his own sorrow over the passing of loyalty and love into the night, and as the lullaby's final notes faded, he saw, out of the corner of his eye, a yellow blur appear then disappear behind one of the piles of white plastic tarp. "And she's come back to wait for me," he murmured under his breath so that only Dotty

273

heard him. But when he turned to look up the hill, no one or no thing was there, apart from a rectangle of folded plastic.

Weasel went over to Angie then and began sniffing her shoes. Seeing Weasel, Angie looked behind her father and noticed Tilly's presence for the first time. "Hi, I'm Angie," she said, reaching around Bahram while extending her hand.

"Hello," Tilly said shyly, "I'm Tilly. And that's Weasel," Tilly replied haltingly, taking Angie's hand, although, seeing Squirrel staring at her, her face grew flushed. "Tilly Thomassock."

"No, she's not. She's Alice von Brandt," Squirrel inserted bluntly. "My mother."

As she released her grip on Tilly's hand, Angie cocked her head in appraisal of Tilly, and then she turned to Squirrel. "I know that's what you texted me. But how do you know that she's really your mother if she says she isn't? You don't even look like each other, you know," she observed.

"I just know," Squirrel said, frowning. "She just doesn't remember me. But maybe that's because she doesn't want to remember me. Maybe it was because I was such a bad—"

"—Squirrel, please," Roper inserted abruptly but also solicitously. "What did we talk about the other day? Didn't we agree that Tilly's illness wasn't about you?"

Squirrel furrowed his brow as he eyed Roper. Then, seeing the authentic concern as well as a cockeyed quality in Roper's gaze, he nodded thoughtfully. "Okay, I get it. I know you're right. But like I said, try to put yourself in my place. Your mother abandons you and then comes back years later and denies you're related to her. I just think it's strange. And I don't understand it."

"I don't either, but..." Roper started to respond before Angie interrupted him.

"You really don't remember that Squir—Peter—is your son? How is that possible?"

Tilly shook her head. "I don't know. Everything beyond nine years ago is phhht...gone," she said, springing open her hand as though releasing seeds into the air. "Except my name. Which I know now is actually the name of that dog, apparently." She gestured to Tilly Thomassock's headstone.

Squirrel noted the falcon now dangling around Tilly's neck, and his frown deepened. "Did you take that off my tree?" he accused her.

"I let her borrow it," Parker inserted, adding, as he stepped forward, "By the way, welcome back, Angie. We've missed you."

Angie then saw the almost beatific look on Roper's face. "What's up with you?" she said, stifling a cagey grin. "You look...goofy. Like you've just done a Jesus flip on a quarterpipe."

"It's just this group of people," he replied, with a global gesture that took in all of them. "It puts a smile on my face, because I think, despite our differences, we've been able to accomplish something really special here. Even Slag thinks so. And, also," he added sheepishly, "I think I'm in love...and I also think I want to be your father, Squirrel." Roper shook his head, then looked at Squirrel. "I know this might seem out-of-the-blue, but what do you think? About a possible adoption, I mean."

Squirrel didn't meet Roper's gaze, but instead focused it on Danquin, whose attention was riveted to his phone. "I don't hate you any more for cutting trees down, if that's what you mean," Squirrel answered, "and I hate living in a group home. I think if I were an adult I would say we might be in the negotiation stage." Squirrel looked up then and saw that his tent had collapsed under the weight of pooled water.

"Hey, Danquin," he said, clumsily directing Roper's attention away from himself, "How come you didn't take Roper's spikes and climb up and fix my tent?"

Throughout this exchange, Danquin, absorbed as he was on the Twitter feeds, had paid only partial attention to what was being said. Thus when he looked up at the tent in order to respond to Squirrel's question, his expression was confused. But even more than expressing confusion, it communicated fearfulness.

"Judging by what I am seeing right now, I think we may have greatly underestimated the number of people who will be coming tomorrow," he said, ignoring Squirrel's question. "Look at all these tweets we are getting," he added, holding out his phone so that the others could see the continuous cascade of communications scrolling down the screen. "We may be looking at thousands of people."

Danquin then laid his phone on the table and directed his words to Squirrel. "I know you do not really want me to fix your tent," he said, "because I know you know I am a clumsy oaf and would wreck it. And I might also kill myself. So, I know that what you want to know from me is not really about why I have neglected your tent, but what I think about Roper and his proposal to adopt you." He shifted his gaze past Squirrel's shoulder, to a number of vans that had just turned off the road and were slowly making their way up the Gainsaid Pound driveway.

"I am only an academician," he continued soberly. "So I am not good at judging how people behave in real time. But in my opinion and if I were you, I think I would let Roper put me in his custody. Even if it is for you now only a business decision. Roper is a good man," he continued, catching Roper's eye, "and I think he has been a loyal friend to you. And, most important," he added, gesturing to Parker-the-dog who was shredding sorrel into a million pieces, "you both like dogs."

Squirrel's eyebrows shot up, but seeing the smile on Danquin's face he nodded appreciatively. Then, following Danquin's gaze, he also turned his attention to eight full-sized passenger vans that had pulled to a stop at the northern boundary of the property beneath the knoll and opposite the now-demolished Gainsaid Pound.

On the vehicles' sides the logo of the Red Bud Casino was clearly discernible. By then the others' attention had also been diverted to the caravan, from out of which there now emerged almost fifty men and women, of varying ages it seemed, all of whom were wearing what appeared to be traditional Native American garb. The occupants, acting as a cohesive band, immediately offloaded material from the rear doors of the vans and began distributing it methodically inside a perimeter roughly the size of that which had been the old Gainsaid Pound and attached kennel. At the more level eastern boundary, eight-man canvas camp tents began to materialize, six of which were linked together north-to-south and end-to-end to form an ad hoc lodge. Each outside aspect on each tent had a geometric design painted on it, of a bird in flight inside a circle of red buds, along with the accompanying Red Bud Casino moniker. Sleeping mats and sleeping bags, lanterns, and duffle bags were, in turn, brought out and distributed among the tents.

In the center of the circle, a round fire pit the size of a large wading pool was constructed out of field stones that had been brought to the site in the vans. Around the outside perimeter of the compound dozens of two-gallon terra cotta containers were distributed at twenty-foot or so intervals. An abalone shell was placed inside each pot, and faggots of combustible material were laid inside of these. The packets were in turn set afire with long wooden matches by four men who then blew out the flames, and as the material continued to smolder they gently wafted the smoke over their hands, eyes, ears, hearts, and heads. From these smoldering cauldrons the scents of burning vegetation quickly spread over the whole of the cemetery and vineyard.

As all this was transpiring, two burly men, both wearing headbands and beaded vests, detached themselves from the others and headed toward the cemetery. Given the men's size and age, they negotiated the overturned clods of dirt with remarkable aplomb, and when they had closed to within fifty feet they were recognizable as Stanley White Shadow and Thomas Ant Lake.

Danquin was the first to greet them upon their entering the graveyard. "Are you and your braves and squaws going to have a pow-wow?" he blurted breathlessly, and his eyes opened even wider in wonder than on their last meeting.

Thomas Ant Lake smiled at Danquin's childlike ingenuousness. "No," he said, shaking his head, "Falcon has called for us to come help him make prey of the negative energy that is keeping him and this land from breathing." He gestured disdainfully toward the rectangles of methyl bromide entrapment tarps.

Wili now came up beside Danquin. "It doesn't seem like the things you are burning are helping the land breathe any better," she said, clearing her throat disapprovingly after inhaling deeply a whiff of the acrid smoke while, oppositely, she admired the beaded headbands, vests and the leather chaps both men wore.

Thomas Ant Lake made a dismissive gesture to her observation. "It is sage," he replied. "We are smudging the area to purify it and to keep negative spirits from bothering us." Which Wili, with a skeptical expression on her face, wrote down faithfully in her tablet, while missing entirely that the explanation had implicitly included her. "We are here to protect..." But his voice trailed off as, on the opposite side of the seating area, he spied Falcon lying against Tilly's blouse. Then without acknowledging the presence of any of the others, he skirted the table and went directly up to her.

"I see Falcon has chosen his ally from the purest among you," he said peremptorily, without introducing himself, and with an intensity in his gaze that was penetrating to the point of being accusatorial.

Shocked by his severity and startled by being confronted by this curiously dressed and somewhat dapper man, Tilly leaned away from him and turned her head aside. "Me, pure? I doubt it," she replied with a nervous laugh." To which Thomas Ant Lake shrugged.

Behind him, Weasel, having heard the quaver in his owner's voice, broke off his scampering under the table with Parker-the-dog and, raising

278

his hackles and drawing his ears back, turned to confront Thomas Ant Lake with a growl.

"It's okay, Weasel," Tilly said softly, but with authority, as she held out her hand in a gesture that meant for Weasel to halt his advance. "He's a friend."

"Forgive my colleague," Stanley White Shadow said to Tilly, having just then come up beside Thomas Ant Lake. "He is a modern shaman. He is an MD who has worked many years with veterans, and like some other western doctors, he wears blinders when he is at work, and knows only how to go to the sources of power so he can cure what is obstructing them. Sometimes, though, this causes him to forget that in treating wounds and illnesses he also needs to have a good bedside manner or the patient will not accept his remedies."

Thomas Ant Lake tilted his head in acknowledgment, and simultaneously lowered his hand so that Weasel could sniff it. "My brother Stanley is right," he admitted. "Sometimes I forget where I am when I am working. So I must apologize for having frightened you."

Weasel, in sensing the shift in intensity in both Thomas Ant Lake and Tilly, let his ears flop forward and his shackles relax. He then turned his attention back to Parker-the-dog who was nipping on the Achilles tendon of his hind leg.

Tilly opened her palms to Thomas Ant Lake in a gesture of forgiveness. "It's okay," she said, easing back against the futon. "I was just startled to hear you say I was pure, that's all, when I don't even know who I am. I mean, for all I know, I could be a serial killer."

Thomas Ant Lake was momentarily taken aback by this last statement. But he responded matter-of-factly, "That is true. There is a killer in each of us. But none of us really knows who we are. All you or I can know is what the Great Spirit grants us to know. All the rest is unknown, and we can find out who we are only along the trail of our own journey, and only if we are lucky and we honor the ancestors who have come before us, and

279

follow in their footsteps so they can teach us to be wise. There," he said, gesturing toward the knoll where the artifacts had been found, "is one of the places where my own people came to gather strength and learn wisdom for their journey. We have come here to help them and to make sure the Great Spirit's strength is not spent unwisely. And I think that this place," he went on, nodding first toward Yellow Dog Red's headstone before bringing his gaze to bear again on Tilly, "is a place you yourself have been drawn to so that you can gather the strength and wisdom to find yourself."

"And by purity," he went on, "I meant only that I sensed, the moment I saw you, that something has happened to cause you misfortune that is not your fault, and that because of this lack of blame Falcon has chosen you to help him." He pointed to the talisman on Tilly's blouse. "If Falcon could speak to you," he continued, "he would say, 'If you scratch my back, I will scratch yours.' So, what I mean by purity is only that Falcon has chosen you because he wants to restore the balance of innocence between prey and predator, which is where purity is found, and he thinks you can be of some help in doing this."

Having overheard their conversation, Danquin stepped forward and, inserting himself between Stanley White Shadow and Thomas Ant Lake, addressed the latter. "Excuse me for interrupting. Did I hear you correctly? Are you saying that purity is a reciprocal transaction?"

Thomas Ant Lake nodded and eyed Danquin with a nettled yet also forgiving gaze, as one would toward a child who asked a foolish question. "Yes, purity and balance are connected," he replied. "Neither one can exist without its opposite. When there is imbalance the land withers, the fruit shrivels, the game starves, and the people suffer. It is the same with impurity. When the purity of inspiration to live in accord with the Great Spirit is no longer pure, it is replaced by greed, which also causes imbalance. The way to restore that balance is for purity to prevail over greed. It is through inspiration that purity is reciprocated."

"Oh," was all that Danquin managed to say, realizing only mid-way through Thomas Ant Lake's explanation that he had essentially dismissed his question as a spurious one. Or, worse, as a specious one. Danquin blinked his eyes as if he had just awakened from a long nap. He then shuffled away shaking his head, and after retrieving his phone off the table, he went up to Parker, who was sitting next to Dotty and across from Bahram and Angie, who were all listening to the "Yellow Dog Red Lullaby."

"Tell me," Danquin said, posing a question that Parker knew by its self-incriminatory inflection was clearly rhetorical and not meant to be answered, "How wrongheaded was I in coming here to America thinking I would be able to conduct my scholarly research as though I was inside a laboratory? when from the very beginning I should have seen that the methodology I have brought to my thesis was flawed. How could I not have seen that my theory," he sighed, while checking out the new tweets, "cannot begin to be measured objectively only? No," he shrugged, nodding toward Angie's bluetooth speaker, "by itself our Yellow Dog Red song will do more to diminish the need to resort to violence to resolve conflicts than will any of my findings. I will have to go home to Dusseldorf after we are done here and see if I can figure out a way to somehow include a subjective element in my methodology that does not invalidate my objective measurements."

Angie looked up from her phone, where she was viewing the tweets that were trending from the "Yellow Dog Red" mp3. "Don't worry, Danquin, I know you'll find a way to finish your research after we're done here," she said. "At school this month, my teacher is having us read some stories that are written by people she calls gonzo journalists. I think you might like them, because the authors we're reading add their own experiences to the facts they're reporting on, so that what they're writing in the blogs is true and it's also personal. I think my teacher is right; it's a good way to learn about how something works from the inside."

Danquin furrowed his brow.

"Think quantum mechanics combined with song," blurted Keith, who had been listening intently to the conversation of Thomas Ant Lake, Tilly and Danquin. "Or, if you like," he added hastily before his lungs ran out of air, "Wine making. It's nothing more than a combination of chemistry and care. One approach is objective, the other is subjective. And because the product contains elements of both, it reflects nature's true quality."

As he let his gaze fall to the now empty bottles of Yellow Dog Red on the table, Danquin's expression slowly brightened. "Ya, ya, science and song! Song and science. Science from the heart. Heart into science. Gonzo science maybe," he beamed.

"Yes, gonzo science!" erupted Keith, and raising his glass in the air, toasted, "To gonzo science!"

"And to Yellow Dog Red!" Squirrel shouted.

"To gonzo science and Yellow Dog Red!" Parker suddenly chimed in, having been caught up in the enthusiasm.

"To gonzo science and Yellow Dog Red!" the others pealed in unison, including Stanley White Shadow, Thomas Ant Lake, and Tilly.

After the hubbub had died down, Dotty, saying that she wanted to get some sleep so she could come back refreshed and ready to go before daybreak, started to gather up the plates, glassware, utensils, and remains of food scraps left uneaten. The others pitched in to help her, and when the camping area was cleared a short time later Parker informed everyone that he wanted them to leave him and Parker-the-dog to themselves for the rest of the day and that night.

There was some initial resistance to this idea, but Stanley White Shadow pointed out that if anything should happen, his band would be only fifty yards away and could offer Parker any assistance he would need. Angie also said her cameras and her LAN were still all up and operational, and Danquin said it would probably be best if he too went back to Command Central and tried to field as many of the incoming messages as he could that evening, and iron out any last minute snafus.

Moreover, but left unsaid, was that, to a person, each one there that afternoon recognized that the eviction notice and the planned action the next day would undoubtedly mark the end and also the beginning of something that would be different from the Yellow Dog Red Overlook as it had thus far been constituted. None could have said for sure how things would be altered, but all knew that they themselves had already been altered in ways—some known, others as yet unrecognized—that would reverberate through them for the rest of their lives. And most important, each one realized that Parker did indeed need to be alone with Yellow Dog Red in order to say his goodbyes in private now, rather than after the deluge of attention that could possibly change everything for him. Therefore, as night fell on a moonless landscape, upon which a patina of valley fog was forming layer upon layer, framing the rectangles of plastic tarp like icebergs in a misty sea, Tilly, Angie, Bahram, Wili, Armando and Keith passed through the cleft in the fence, soon followed by Roper and Squirrel, and finally Dotty, leaving Parker truly alone in the cemetery for the first time in months.

Parker had asked Angie to leave behind her bluetooth speaker and to show him how to operate it, and as his companions drove off in separate vans while Tilly, who had been invited by Thomas Ant Lake to stay in their compound for the night, drove her van up the driveway, Parker opened the mp3 song and listened to it—really listened to it closely—for the first time. What he hadn't heard when there were others around him but which came through loud and clear, now that he was alone and could let the music enter him without the filter of social interactions, was that the lullaby eerily captured the feeling Slag himself had exuded the first time Parker had seen him on the beach in San Francisco decades earlier.

That is, Slag had somehow incorporated virtually everything from that day into the song: the fog, the wind, the spray, the brine, the coldness, the ghostly bridge and, most prominently, the sense of being the loneliest person in the world. Which matched, Parker acknowledged wordlessly to himself now, exactly how he was feeling at that very moment; like there was a shadow surroundiing him so completely that it was an alien being enveloping his body.

Parker had been around enough death in his long life to recognize that this shadow was not actually death's embrace, although that is what it felt like; for in all his years he had seen that the arms of death were, for all practicable purposes, kind in their containment of suffering. Rather, the shadow Slag had projected that day, and which embraced Parker now, was actually outside death's clasp; that is, the shadow was uniquely within the provenance of the living who, in their ignorance—or obliviousness—of the cycles of life and death, could conjure forth from the actuality of sadness the superceding chimera of isolation.

It was his recognition of this sense of total but counterfeit isolation that now provided Parker the key to why the "Yellow Dog Red Lullaby" was so compelling; for its lilting yet dogged meter led Parker to recall the very thing that had managed to bring the song's creator out of himself: Yellow Dog Red trotting up to him and dropping her tennis ball at his feet. And that, Parker saw, was precisely the emotional center of the lullaby: the slow, methodically joyful yet spontaneous cadence of playing fetch at the seashore with Yellow Dog Red.

Tears welled in Parker's eyes, and he looked down on Parker-the-dog, who was sleeping peacefully with her chin propped atop one of the numerous tennis balls she had scattered at the foot of Yellow Dog Red's grave. Her paws jerked as she bounded through forests of sleep, and the rows of whiskers on her muzzle twitched like blades of grass as she sped through fields of dreams. In turn fourteen years of memories of Yellow Dog Red flowed over Parker like water lapping over a sandy shore. Concurrent with those fourteen years were fifty more years on the course of the river he and Sylvia had shared. Each inlet was a reflection captured in the sunlight of observation. Each branch was a mystery inside the dawning of love, each embayment was a profound discovery in the meaning and purpose of life. Dotty, Max, Tad, friends, colleagues, pets, parents, parents' parents—they all stretched like wave-trains in a spherical ocean into the past and on into the future around Parker. And, taken together, they were all drifting as one on the tides of an endless sea of which Parker knew he was but one of an infinite number of integral currents.

A frigid stream of air out of the north, rustling through the eucalyptus early in the morning, awoke Parker from this meander through the seas of timelessness to reveal that the hoarfrost that had been thickening since mid-afternoon had encapsulated him and the cemetery entirely. His bones ached and his nose ran from exposure to the cold breeze; thus he decided it was time for him and Parker-the-dog to repair to the trailer to weave together some last minutes of sleep to prepare them for the following day.

The next thing Parker was aware of was the bluetooth speaker, to which Angie's phone was connected, playing the ringtone she had programmed into the phone especially for him: Frank Sinatra singing "Strangers in the Night." Startling both him and Parker-the-dog from their slumbers, Parker fumbled for the phone before finally managing to swipe the screen to answer it, while the puppy barked at the voice in the speaker.

As soon as he drew the phone to his ear, Parker heard Angie's voice yelling out breathlessly from out of the speaker, "Parker! Parker! Where are you? Are you okay?"

"Angie? It's Parker. I'm okay," he responded, flipping on the bedside lantern. "What's wrong?"

"I couldn't sleep, so I got up and checked my cameras. They're... I mean, it's too foggy to actually see much, but I saw three...um...Indians, I think, running around in the cemetery. They were knocking over headstones."

"What?"

"I think they were pushing over the monuments."

Parker shook his head to clear it of cobwebs. He could hear indistinctly Bahram saying something to his daughter. "Wait," Parker said. "Slow down, Angie. Did you say you think the Native Americans are vandalizing the cemetery?"

"Yes. I dunno. Maybe," she replied hesitantly. "I couldn't really see their faces. But they were wearing headbands like the Indians were yesterday."

"Let me see if I can hear if anyone is out there now," Parker said, and moving the phone away from his ear, even though no sound passed through it, he listened closely. After ten seconds had passed, he said, "I don't hear anything."

"I don't see them now either," Angie replied. "I think they've gone. It's too foggy to tell which direction they went though."

"What time is it?" Parker said, groping for his watch.

"It's on the phone," Angie replied, then added, "4:50."

"I'm getting up," Parker said. "And see what happened."

"Dad and I are coming over," she said. "Roper and Danquin too. I just texted them. Wait, here's Dad. He wants to say something to you."

"Parker," came Bahram's voice through the bluetooth, "do you want me to call the sheriff?"

"What would be the point?" he replied, as he pulled on his boots. "Knocking over graves in a pet cemetery that's scheduled for demolition probably isn't a crime."

"Will you do me a favor then?" he asked. "Will you wait until I get there before you go outside?"

"Nobody is going to hurt me, Bahram," he said. "And anyway, if somebody does want to knock me over, I'm more than ready to go."

"Do it for Angie," Bahram said. "Stay inside for her."

"Okay," he sighed. "I'll wait in the trailer till you get here. But hurry up, I think Parker-the-dog has to pee."

Parker ended the call, then pulled on his trousers and a sweater, and waited and listened. An owl called out from Squirrel's eucalyptus. A coyote in the hills to the west reckoned the dawn. A frost-prevention propeller rumbled to life in the hollow of a vineyard to the south. From the north came the sound of tires hissing across asphalt. Ten minutes later Parker heard Angie's voice shouting his name as she ran toward him through the vineyard.

Two minutes later Angie fell abruptly silent, until a half-minute afterwards she knocked on the trailer door. Parker swung the door open to see Angie standing in a down jacket and a wool cap with a look of disbelief mixed with anger on her face. She was followed a few seconds later by Bahram, also dressed in warm clothes. Both were winded from exertion but both wore expressions that conveyed their relief in seeing that Parker was unharmed.

"It's awful!" blurted Angie. "See what they did? It's awful," she said, waving her hand toward Yellow Dog Red's grave in the light of the solar lantern on the table, which cast an eery gray light into the barrel of fog it illuminated.

"But we're glad to see you're okay," Bahram added hastily.

Parker-the-dog was the first out of the trailer. But even she was brought up short when, immediately after greeting Angie, she came across Yellow Dog Red's headstone lying askew in front of the futon sofa. Wagging her tail, she sniffed at it like it was an old acquaintance, but then she lowered her tail between her legs and whimpered as she retreated behind Bahram. Parker himself emerged with Bahram and Angie's help to see that not only Yellow Dog Red's headstone had been toppled, but also that of Chester, Orix, Tilly Thomassock and many others.

Two minutes later Stanley White Shadow appeared from out of the fog and entered into the cemetery. After making a quick appraisal, he said, "What's going on? Who did this?"

"You did!" Angie shot back. "Your people did this. I have evidence."

She held up her phone on which a camera feed showed, from above, a burly man with a feather in his hair leaning against a headstone until it slowly fell over. Such was the density of the fog and the angle of the shot, however, that no discernible features on the man's face were evident, nor was there any appreciable way to identify him through his clothing, since he was dressed all in black. Two other such figures, wraithlike behind the veil of hoarfrost, could barely be made out leaning against other headstones.

Stanley White Shadow shook his head sadly. "No, child, none of my people would dare to desecrate this ground," he murmured. "It is hallowed. This is the work of ghosts."

"Well, what about this?" Angie retorted, and flipping the page on her phone she brought up Twitter, and read, "'For every visitor to YDR 10 graves will go to dirt. krul2dbone.' I got it fifteen minutes ago," she muttered. "That's from no ghost."

Stanley White Shadow shook his head. "No, that is not from a ghost," he admitted. "It is from a person who has lost his bearing."

"Whoever they are," Bahram said, bending down and up-righting Yellow Dog Red's headstone, "they're sick, and they're keeping an eye on us."

R oper then Danquin appeared out of the fog in front of Parker to the scent of freshly brewed coffee just as the first light of day was stitching the eastern horizon with a fuzzy strand of silver wool. Despite the limited visibility, both men were stopped in their tracks by the disarray they witnessed, and both disclosed to Parker that they too had just read krule2dbone's tweet. In addition, Roper reported that he had texted Jordan about the vandalism, and that he thought she should also take a look at krule2dbone's tweet. Roper then took the cup of coffee Parker offered him and surveyed the havoc that had been wrought. As he was inspecting one of the fallen graves along the fence, Jordan called him.

"Roper," she said, her tone both serious and groggy from sleeplessness, "guess what? My office got wind of the crowds that are expected today, and I've been reassigned to crowd-control duty at the cemetery."

An awkward silence following this disclosure ensued as, through the fog, the full scope of the vandalism became evident to Roper. Mistaking the silence as displeasure with her news, Jordan hazarded, "Is that all right with you?" she said, her voice shivering with uncertainty. "I mean, that you and I see each other again so soon after...after...you know."

"So soon after...what happened with us yesterday?" tendered Roper, as he moved away from Danquin after realizing, and respecting, the source of Jordan's confusion. "You mean," he added, his own voice resonating unconsciously in a like manner with hers, "that we committed ourselves to explore a relationship with each other on the spur of the moment?"

"Yes," she murmured, then blurted, "Do you want to rethink things?"

"Absolutely not!" shot back Roper so forcefully that it startled him, and when there was no immediate reply, he added quickly, "Jordan, never in my life have I felt more like I'm doing the right thing at the right time with the right person. And I didn't sleep a wink last night thinking about you and me and how our lives could be together. Nope," he affirmed, "I stand by everything I said and felt yesterday. What's more, I think I might want to spend the rest of my life with you."

Roper had stopped walking and had entwined his fingers through links in the fence at a spot where he saw someone had hung a picture of four Great Danes harnessed to a sleigh in which a Shetland pony wearing a Santa hat sat beside the driver, a potbelly pig. "But what about you? Have you changed your mind?"

Jordan sighed and let loose a nervous giggle. "No way, Roper. But I just hope you know what you're getting yourself into, because I'm warning you, I'm not letting go."

While Roper was talking to Jordan, Danquin remained standing where he was, gazing stupefied across the cemetery, before absently taking a cup of coffee Parker offered him. But before taking a sip or even acknowledging Parker, he set off without a word, gliding across the fog-shrouded cemetery dawn in earnest as if he were cross-country skiing through a powdery snowfield. When he came to Tilly Thomassock's toppled marker, he stopped suddenly and lowered himself down onto his knees. Then resting his coffee on Chester's fallen headstone, he started to paw the earth around Tilly Thomassock's memorial as though he were a dog trying to unearth a bone.

Even though Parker was barely able to see Danquin through the murk as he struggled with the weighty stone, he had already guessed that what the other had seen had been so disturbing that it had placed him in a momentary state of disorientation, such as one which a noncombatant in a war zone who had come unexpectedly upon a field of carnage might experience. With this in mind Parker went up beside him and, after pausing to watch Danquin scuffle with the stone for a minute, and seeing the remoteness in his eyes, he very gently laid his hand on his shoulder. At Parker's touch, Danquin started like he had received an electric shock.

A moment later Parker whispered, "Danquin, isn't your job today coordinating rides?"

Recognizing the solicitude in Parker's voice, Danquin stopped grappling with the tombstone and blinked his eyes rapidly a number of times as if trying to rid them of sand. He then leaned back heavily on his haunches and took a single deep breath, as a frisson of recognition passed through him. And Parker felt Danquin's shoulders loosen under his touch.

"Yes, Mr. Parker, but this is the work of thugs," he answered, his voice reedy with the sudden release of tension. "I cannot let it stand," he went on through clenched jaws, his voice barely above a whisper, and only then did he turn to look up at Parker. "It must be corrected, or the hooligans...they will have won. I know how it happens. I have seen the camps. My family lost three in them."

"Yes, yes, I know how it happens too," Parker nodded, having guessed from Danquin's words that he had indeed seen firsthand what thugs could do to violate a people's sensibility and shake their confidence in the trustworthiness of others. "But here, drink your coffee," he said, handing Danquin the cup from Chester's toppled memorial. After Danquin had taken the cup in his hands, which Parker saw were still shaking, Parker smiled. Danquin too smiled wanly.

"Look at yourself, Danquin," Parker went on, affecting mock chastisement in order to soften his words, "you are reacting now out of indignation rather than purpose. That is exactly what thugs always want; for their victims to react with the same unthinking sightless viciousness as their own. How they win against us is by making us lose sight of our purpose." Parker diverted his eyes to Tilly Thomassock's headstone. "And our purpose, remember, is to honor Yellow Dog Red. That is the only reason we are here."

As Danquin's breathing became regular, Parker removed his hand from Danquin's shoulder and said, "There will be others here today who I think can better help us with the graves than the two of us. So, what do you say we get just old Tilly back on her feet? Then you and I can go on and do our jobs."

"Ya," Danquin nodded appreciatively, "you are right, Parker. I have a job to do."

Then he and Parker wrestled the fallen memorial back to standing. That it took the two of them to provide the leverage needed to raise the headstone to vertical attested to the shear heft of the marauders who had tipped all of them over so effortlessly in the first place.

Leaving his coffee behind with Parker, Danquin then departed the cemetery. But before driving into town he stopped at an espresso cart that, along with two taco wagons, had arrived no more than ten minutes after he and Roper had shown up. After ordering a cappuccino, Danquin engaged the barrista in idle talk as she brewed his drink. From her, he learned that the word had gone out through the local vendor grapevine that there would be a crowd-sourced flash mob at the old pet cemetery, and anyone who wanted to make a little money selling refreshments might be able to get away with it before being busted by the sheriffs.

Danquin paid for his cappuccino and started to walk with it to his car. The fog, which was a layer no more than fifty feet thick now, shown equally brilliant in all directions from the rays of the still barely visible sun, and in his haste and in the glare he nearly ran into six people walking in the opposite direction who he hadn't seen until they were right in front of him. They were three couples, all of whom, they said, were from Bonn, Germany, and members of a local wine club on an off-season tour of the wine country.

Welcoming the opportunity to speak to his countrymen in his native tongue, and recognizing them as professional people of a certain financial and kindred social stature, Danquin discovered not only had they all read

293

the sporadic tweets and blogs written in German he had posted, but they all now viewed him as an international celebrity, and they all carried gardening gloves Zand had asked them to bring. Flattered by their attention, Danquin also grew alarmed to discover that the number of Germans this group had heard from who were planning to come that day numbered in the hundreds, including members of an orchestra and choral group from Leipzig touring through the wine country.

Danquin hurried his step at the news of the expected influx of Germans, but before reaching his car he again almost ran into more people emerging like sprites out of the fog. Three men and a woman, they were a dapperly dressed group of blond, scrubbed and scorched-skinned South African gamekeepers, ranging from mid-thirty to fifty Danquin adjudged, who had altered their tour of American wild horse preserves to pay homage to Parker on his vigil, which they reported was such an inspiration to them that they were planning on doing the same sort of watch in their own country to bring attention to the poaching of elephants.

Their main interests, they told Danquin, were to meet Parker, of course, and Squirrel, in the hope that from the latter they could glean some helpful information on how to manage threatened canopy populations in the Knysna Forest. Zand was on their list as well, from whom they were hoping to address how to document poaching activities in the bush using cameras linked to local area networks. For his part, Danquin listened politely, but thought it better to not let on to them that the "experts" they wanted to talk with were barely adolescents and had no credentials other than those of youthful precociousness.

What was most amazing—and exciting—to Danquin, as he was finally able to extricate himself from the gamekeepers, was that, to a person, each of the visitors he met that morning produced a picture of a pet (or of an elephant) that they said they intended to affix, as a memorial to their own animal companions and in honor of Yellow Dog Red, to the fence along with the other pictures they had seen hanging on it online. For in their zeal,

294

Danquin realized suddenly that his flagging enthusiasm for his own research had been prematurely misplaced. That is, these people, who were total strangers to Parker and Yellow Dog Red and who had traveled halfway around the world to show solidarity with one man's loyalty to his dog, were in actuality living validations that an advanced society could utilize extended acts of primitive devotion to a pet as a way to diminish society's need to resort to violence to resolve conflicts.

The problem, Danquin abruptly realized, was not in the thesis itself, but in the significance he had attached, wrongly, to the word *primitive*. That is, what Parker was doing in his vigil for Yellow Dog Red was not an act derived from some primitive tribal or even mammalian instinct, which is what Danquin had always believed devotion to represent. Rather, it was derived from something more highly evolved in humankind; something, in fact, that could help sustain the species into the future: the need to cultivate and extend honor in and of itself to all things. And as he pulled into the parking slot in front of the laundry, where three dozen people were milling outside Command Central, he had already begun to conjure up ways to insert this new parameter of honor into his research on reverse devotion.

By midmorning the sun had gradually whittled the layer of valley fog down to less than half to reveal a landscape that was changed. The narrow country road was lined on both sides with hundreds of cars, vans, minibusses, and motorcycles that had somehow managed to find enough room to park and still leave a lane open. Other mobile vendors—a gyro sandwich truck, and a van out of which Yellow Dog Red Overlook wristbands were selling for a dollar apiece—were parked in a line with the two taco wagons and the espresso cart. Dotty, too, had persuaded her fish-and-chip restaurant's new owner to bake her lemon bars, which were selling for two dollars-a-pop from the espresso cart. Pedestrians who had parked elsewhere clogged the lane, reminiscing about their pets, sharing pictures, taking pictures. Lines of people waited at the portable toilets. An ambulance was parked outside the Red Bud Casino compound. The SPCA had set up a table from which they handed out packs of duty-bags, and, next to them, representatives from Canine Companions and Guide Dogs for the Blind gave out free scarves and collars, while the local veterinarian passed out homeopathic dog-chews. And dogs were everywhere.

At least forty of the forty-eight Native Americans from the Red Bud Casino encampment were interspersed at regular intervals around the boundaries of the vineyard, passing out free bottles of reusable metal water cannisters adorned with their logo. The remaining eight tribesmen and women either smudged their way through the crowd or asked people to sign a petition appealing to the County Board of Supervisors to amend the winery's use permit so that a condition for the winery to do business be appended to it that would keep the pet cemetery intact and open. Keith manned a table for Paradoxum Winery from which information on hiring the handicapped for kennel and winery duties was available, as well as information on where to taste and buy Yellow Dog Red wines, which, as this was not a registered site for the sale of wine, could not be sold on-site.

By ten o'clock three thousand people and seemingly half as many dogs had come to pay their respects, have a taco, or gyro, a lemon bar, and coffee, and listen to "The Yellow Dog Red Lullaby" through the dozens of bluetooth speakers that had been set up here and there by Angie and her skateboarding friends, who had skipped school in order to come to the event. Most of those who listened to Slag's song also downloaded the mp3 file into their own phones for ninety-nine cents. Virtually everyone snapped photos or held their phones aloft to record videos. Eight sheriff's deputies had been assigned to help maintain order, although not much really needed to be done early on, other than to assist drivers wend their way up and down the tight lane through the clots of pedestrians, skateboarders, bicyclists, and dog-walkers; and to help some of the elderly who were having trouble negotiating the overturned earth of the vineyard.

By noon, the chainlink fence on the eastern boundary of the cemetery had become a solid wall six-feet high and two-hundred-feet long, consisting of photographs, AKC ribbons, dog licences, notes, chew-toys, and collars. It was the gloves affixed to the top links of wire fencing, however, that captured everyone's immediate attention from afar; for with their fifteen thousand fingers extending into the hazy white sky, they were three thousand hands reaching skyward in either prayer, applause, or defiance, depending on how one felt.

Another two thousand Yellow Dog Red pilgrims had arrived by then, many of whom stayed around with the earlier arrivals to help groom the graves in the cemetery and to put upright the headstones that had been toppled. By mid-afternoon, with literally two thousand people working as gardeners, the whole of the cemetery was weeded, raked, tidied, and cleared of debris to such an extent that if one had stepped foot in the cemetery for the first time and didn't know better, they would have assumed that it was an ongoing, rather than a long-neglected and derelict, burial site.

Through it all, Parker sat stoically beside Yellow Dog Red like an unmoving hub of a giant wheel whose spokes were made of people and dogs that revolved round and round him. Many, if not most, of the people who entered the cemetery stopped at Yellow Dog Red's grave and stood in silence for a few moments beside Parker. A contingence of fourteen Buddhist monks from a Zen monastery in the mountains to the west came dressed in crimson robes and caps and spent the better part of half-an-hour chanting, banging on tambourines, and puffing into yak thigh-bone horns before departing. Another group of twenty monks came from a Carmelite monastery in Napa and stood in utter silence for two hours. Some people left dog biscuits, others left their hand prints in the soft dirt, and to a person all thanked or acknowledged Parker for his perseverance. None stayed overlong, however, honoring the privacy of Parker's personal vigil for his dog and respecting the desire of others to come through and pay their own respects.

In the effort to cast as wide a net as possible, Tilly was aided by the BBC and Al Jezeera, who interviewed and videotaped her at length. Oddly,

Wili was the only representative of the mainstream American press, written or broadcast, to show up, although a number of reporters from various animal-rights blogs did cover the event through online streams. After a time, even Parker-the-dog grew weary of all the people petting her and having her chase tennis balls. Indeed, she also tired of other dogs greeting and trying to hump her, and by late afternoon she had had enough, and retreated under the trailer, where she was able to curl up between the wheels and fall asleep.

Dotty kept Parker company for much of the day, while Angie, Roper, Keith, Squirrel and even Armando stayed busy coordinating the flow of visitors, the cemetery cleanup, and answering questions. After a time, Squirrel, like Parker-the-dog, had had enough and he retreated to his tent in the eucalyptus, unable to handle any more questions or the crush of people, or, especially, having to witness Tilly as she sat with Weasel next to her namesake's grave with a handwritten cardboard sign at her feet reading, "Do you know me?"

Like the fog, which persisted throughout the day as a luminous broth of light and mist, the crowd too began to thin and clump by the time four o'clock rolled around; as there appeared to be nothing new or flash-worthy happening other than an occasional dog-tussle or someone stumbling and falling. Krule2dbone hadn't made an appearance either, or at least identified himself. Jordan, too, had begun to wonder if the notice of eviction and the commotion it might cause had been postponed altogether for that day, owing to the size of the crowd. Although, when she called into the office to question her superiors, they advised her that it was still scheduled to be served as proposed.

Shortly after she made the call, and with things winding down without any untoward confrontations or disruptions having occurred, Jordan noticed that two mid-size tour busses had driven up the driveway toward the Red Bud Casino encampment. From out of the bus she saw a woman approaching the northeast corner of the cemetery where she, Roper, and a paramedic were tending to a man with a white cane who had sprained his ankle after tripping over his dog while it was trying to catch a gopher.

The approaching woman, in her late twenties, fair-skinned, with long blond hair, wearing a sleeveless white gown, white tennis shoes, and presenting a swan-like, ethereal air, sallied across the by-now-well-trod path from the Gainsaid Pound kennel, toting a cello and a pair of white gloves. In her passage through the mist, Roper remarked that she could easily be mistaken for an angel in a religious play. Then another person, a stout man, casually dressed and carrying a bass, two aluminum folding chairs, and a pair of blue work gloves followed behind. Unlike the woman, by his comportment and dress he could have been a knackwurst vendor or a plumber rather than a musician. Or, as Jordan remarked, a stalker. They both went up to the northeast corner of the fence and, putting aside their instruments for a moment, attached photos of pets to its links. They then affixed their gloves to the top of the fence, and after admiring the portrait wall for a few seconds each took pictures of it with their phones. Then the two sat themselves in front of the fence, facing into the cemetery.

When they were seated, another man, stouter than the first, with a bushy black beard and wearing a black, too-small, Sarah Brightman "Phantom Of The Opera" tee shirt, matching cargo pants, and a pair of black gloves, and holding aloft a conductor's wand over his bald head, strode up purposefully to stand in front of the two musicians. With his back to the fence and with an air of august roguishness, he cleared his throat and tapped his wand smartly against the leg of the bass player's metal chair. At the loud Ping! it made, those people standing close at hand turned their attention to him reflexively. And, with their curiosity piqued at the sight of the musicians and their instruments, they grew silent in expectation, and their silence, in turn, spread like a puddle of water crystalizing into ice throughout the lake of the gathered crowd.

With no further preparation, the conductor raised, then lowered, his wand with a forceful thrust, which summoned the bass player to draw his bow in a long arc across his string board, from which a baleful E-note similar to the call of a wolf spread over the crowd. A few seconds later, after virtually everyone's attention had been captured, the conductor indicated to the cellist for her to draw her own bow across the cello's strings. And thus the first resounding notes of Beethoven's plangent motif of the "Ode to Joy" radiated out from the two instruments echoing Beethoven's gallant call to musical exaltation.

Less than a minute later the bass and cello were joined by a bassoonist. Then six violinists, two violists, a piccoloist, and a flutist. They fanned out behind the original two, some in chairs they brought with them, while others remained standing. Next came an oboist, a clarinetist, a trumpeter, a trombonist, and a contrabassoonist. Rounding out the orchestra were a timpanist, a percussionist, two French horns, and two dozen choir members. Each person wore a pair of gloves. Each voice, instrumental and human, joined in and added to the progressive crescendo of musical and emotional excitement. And all the performers wore an expression that conveyed the rapture of inspiration from which their music flowed.

By the time the first of Friedrich Schiller's lyrics, "Freude, schöner Götterfunken," boomed out from one of the four soloists—an incredibly thin man awash in an ill-fitting suit, who had wandered to the front to stand beside the fence—every eye in the vineyard, every heart in the cemetery, every ear in the Red Bud Casino compound and along the road had turned to witness the musicians live out through the centuries-old music the enchantment and ecstacy of timeless adoration. In an optical trick of light and fog, and because of their disparate attire, the orchestra looked, when taken as a whole from afar, like a celestial version of angelic tourists afloat on a cloud.

Held in thrall both by the music and the vision, nobody, including Parker, noticed that one of the sheriff's deputies had broken off from the others and causally approached him. After the deputy, who Parker did not recognize as having been there from the start, stopped in front of him and inquired if his name were indeed Parker, he forthwith and with no fanfare handed him an envelope.

"You've been served a notice of eviction," he said simply, barely above the mounting voices of the choir. "You have three days to vacate the premises." He then turned his back peremptorily on Parker.

As the deputy walked away, an overweight elderly woman in a frowsy house-dress waddled up to him and nodded her head as he passed by. Then, as she cinched up her bosom, she turned and nodded in the opposite direction, toward another, equally large and busty woman in an equally frowsy dress, standing with a small group down in front of Orix's grave. The second woman did not acknowledge the first's glance, however, since her and the others' attentions were directed at that moment to reading Tilly's sign.

Tilly herself was gazing in the direction of the musicians and swaying dreamily like a channel buoy in the rolling currents of song. Just as Tilly was lifting her eyes from the source of the music to acknowledge the presence of the woman standing opposite her, the woman too lifted her eyes from Tilly's sign. Their eyes met.

Startled, the woman gasped, and she fell back against the monument behind her, which succumbed to her weight and toppled to the ground. "Fucking dogs," she grumbled.

The words themselves were drowned and fused beneath the swelling current of voices that had just then reached their zenith. But Tilly's eyes opened wide in stark recognition of the woman's vehement utterance. Then, as the woman regained her balance and saw that Weasel was snarling at her, she muttered, "What's the matter with you, you sick fucking bitch?"

Even though the music drowned out most of it, Tilly realized that she had heard those words spoken to her in that tone of voice before. Weasel, sensing Tilly's disconcertion, bared his teeth and lowered his ears. Then before Tilly could stop him he bolted forward. A split-second later he was upon the woman, tearing at her dress and growling. She, in turn, was thrown backward onto the ground atop Orix's stone, and as Weasel bared his teeth, the woman's wig came askew.

"Call your fucking dog off me, or I'll fucking kill him!" she shrieked, as, with one hand, she reached into the purse that had fallen off the shoulder of her dress, and with the other she tried to push Weasel away.

Tilly's lips moved but only one word came out—"You!"—as the face and the voice of the screeching woman—who it was clear now was a man disguised as a woman—suddenly became congruent with something long forgotten, which howled like a great wind out of the deep cave of Tilly's past: "I'll fucking kill you, you sick fucking bitch!"

The man in woman's clothing fumbled in the purse, and from it he withdrew a snub-nosed pistol. He pointed it at Weasel's skull. Squirrel, who had come out of his tent to stand on a limb and view the playing of the

"Ode to Joy," saw the gun and, reacting instinctively, leapt down just at the moment it was fired.

Unfazed by the gunshot, Weasel continued snarling and baring his teeth. For those not close by, the gunshot was muted and lost under the blanket of exultant choral and instrumental voices and the cascading drums, as the masterpiece was nearing its climax. But for those near at hand—Parker, Dotty, Thomas Ant Lake, Armando and a handful of other bystanders—the sound was like a cannon. Seeing the woman with her legs splayed out, and with the pistol on the ground, as one they rushed over to assist Squirrel.

Armando was the first to reach the two. Recognizing at once the eyebrows, he gasped. "Mr. Zinni!"

Four of the anonymous onlookers fell atop Zinni and pinned him down just as Squirrel succeeded in pulling Weasel away. With Weasel removed, and while Thomas Ant Lake retrieved the pistol, Dotty lifted the hem of the man's dress in order to assess any injuries, in case Weasel had bitten the man. Zinni, however, resisted this invasion even more forcefully than he had the dog's assault, kicking his legs and shouting for Marco.

Undeterred, Dotty lifted the hem and saw that the man was wearing tiger-striped thong underwear, clearly holding a masculine bundle. She gasped aloud, not at the ridiculous underwear and its surprising load, but at seeing a gun holstered against the man's thigh.

At that point, Zinni managed to free up an arm from beneath one of the good samaritans, and he reached for his gun, but Armando, having seen the gun at the same moment as Dotty, planted a foot on Zinni's crotch, blocking his hand and causing him to cry out in pain. Armando then reached down and unholstered the gun before Zinni could recover.

The other woman, the one who had nodded at Rocco Zinni earlier, now dashed forward. "Rocco, are you okay? Rocco?" Marco Zinni carped, in a voice that was high-pitched enough to be a woman's. He ripped off his own wig. "Are your balls okay?" he added.

"I'm alright, you idiot! And my balls are okay too!" cried Rocco, ripping the dress from Dotty's hands. "Just tell these cocksuckers to let go of me!" Then, glaring at Armando, he heaped his ire onto him. "You! You fucking bean-eating, good-for-nothing-wet-back Mexican loser! You work for me! And I want you to get these assholes, all of them, off my land! They're all trespassers!" And finally, "Give me my gun back!"

Meanwhile, Weasel turned his attention to Tilly. Seeing her leaning back on her elbows and gazing in a daze at the chaotic scene in front of her, he wrested himself free of Squirrel's grip and lowered himself to his belly beside her. Parker-the-dog, having been startled awake by the excitement and sudden movement, scampered from beneath the trailer and retrieved Rocco's wig, which had lodged against a wheel. She then trotted over to Weasel. But at an unseen signal from him, she dropped the wig and, resting her chin on it, lowered herself to her belly on the opposite side of Tilly.

Squirrel leaned down to grab Weasel's collar, but as he did so, he saw that Tilly's eyes were lidded and that there was a silver-dollar-size circle of blood on her blouse where Zinni's bullet, having missed Weasel, had found Tilly instead. Squirrel's eyes grew bleary. "Mom...?"

The slightest of smiles creased Tilly's cheeks. Then, training her gaze on Squirrel, she said, "Peter."

Armando now came over and knelt beside Tilly. Quickly assessing the slight amount of blood on her blouse as being from a bullet wound, he withdrew a handkerchief from his pocket and, after catching Tilly's eye, was about to apply it against her chest to staunch the flow of blood he expected to find. But then he halted; for the bleeding had already stopped of its own accord, and, additionally, he saw a glint of reflected light poking through the neck slit in Tilly's blouse. He reached down cautiously to retrieve the object, already suspecting what it was. Even so, he could only stare in disbelief at what he saw; for in his hand he cradled the knitted Falcon his foreman had made, in the middle of whose now-exposed three silver dollars was embedded a spent slug.

Seeing that Tilly had received only a bruise and a ring-shaped scratch beneath it, Armando lowered the talisman to Tilly's blouse. He rose and crossed himself while he placed his handkerchief back in his pocket. "You are one lucky woman," he murmured. "A half-inch in any direction and that bullet would have killed you." Then turning to Zinni, who was just getting to his feet, he added, "And you're one lucky sonofabitch that you didn't kill her."

"And you can go fuck yourself," Zinni spat, as Marco dusted dirt off the back of Zinni's dress and his own, and as the orchestra outside the cemetery fell silent at the completion of their performance.

"Looks to me like you might be able to pull that off yourself," Armando retorted, gesturing to Rocco's private parts. "And by the way, Mr. Zinni, I quit."

His words, though, were drowned out by the huge wave of applause meted out by those who had been fortunate enough to witness the "Yellow Dog Red Ode to Joy," as it became known within minutes after being uploaded to utube.

Tilly sat up now, and, seeing the head of the slug flattened into a mushroom in the heart of Falcon, she removed the talisman from around her neck. "Here, Peter, my son," she whispered, her hands shaking while extending Falcon to Squirrel just as Roper and Jordan, as well as four other deputies, all having realized that there had been a shooting, arrived on the scene. "I want you to have this so that whenever you encounter negative energy you will remember me."

"You...you know who I am? And who...who you are?" Squirrel stammered, his voice quaking resonantly with Tilly's as he took Falcon from her hand.

ngie and Danquin ran up to the foot of Chester's grave. Both were using their phones to record the moment. Wili too ambled up and planted herself next to Parker. "I got it all in here!" she said, tapping her tablet, which she held at shoulder height in front of her, aimed at Tilly. "I was videoing Squirrel on the limb listening to the music when the gun went off."

As Wili was saying this, Tilly, her tone mid-way between an assertion and a question, said, "Yes, I remember you. You are Peter von Brandt. My son. My only son. And I also remember I am...I remember I am...Alice von Brandt." Tilly's eyes shot open as the fugitive name escaped her lips for the first time in a decade. "And I am...I am your mother," she continued. "I remember we lived with your father at 3625 Grove Street. I remember it was a three bedroom house."

Tilly fell silent and blinked her eyes as if to clear them of dust; for with each remembrance her eyes had widened wider and wider in order to take in each successive recollection in its entirety. Likewise, each time she uttered the word *remember* she savored and caressed it as though it were a sweet delectable on her tongue and a perfect chord in her ear. When she continued her remembrances the next moment, however, her tone and her expression turned remorseful.

"I remember I buried Chester when you were three-and-a-half. I was so that I had lost my protector sad I couldn't stop crying. I felt like I was burying you, your father, and me. It was," she sighed, "the start of when I was not well. Not well at all," she sighed again. "I remember I had a breakdown when you were almost four. Depression. I remember walking away from your father. And you. My life. I also..." But now her tone suddenly changed again.

"*I remember you*," she said, pronouncing it as a blasphemous invective, and, with her voice trembling with rage, she turned to face Rocco Zinni. "I remember it all now. Every minute of it. You were the horrible monster with the eyebrows, smelly brothers, and cheap wine. You and your two brothers—that one, and another—took turns...took turns taking me to your barn. I *remember* everything!"

The word *remember* now slid from her tongue like a hot poker. Her gaze too flamed as it bore first into Rocco and then Marco. Only then did the latter show any sign of recognition of Tilly when, seeing her eyes glaring at him, he rocked back as if he had been hit on the forehead with a baseball bat.

"*You*, and *you*, used me. Over and over. But I escaped. Ha!" she laughed ironically, spitefully, mirthlessly. "Your wine is the only reason I'm not dead. Zinni Brothers Zinfandel. Such dreck!"

"And *you*!" she said, boring solely into Rocco Zinni with her eyes. "It was you who drove me out onto the mesa. Who congratulated yourself for having the decency to kill me out of mercy when you were through with me. Who poured that ghastly wine mixed with meth over me and up into my, my...to hide your, your..."

Her voice trailed off and her mouth was drawn into a bitter grimace as she grew silent in recognition of the horror her own words brought forth. None within earshot ventured to say a word, so stunned were they to hear Tilly's long-suppressed memories spill forth like hoary sewage. And lest any one of them had wanted to reach out to solace Tilly, Weasel's vigilant gaze and his primed-for-battle stance were such that everyone realized that to touch Tilly, even consolingly, would have been construed by Weasel as an attack. Thus they waited for her to go on.

"It was *you*," she continued finally, lifting her arm slowly until she pointed a finger at Rocco, "who told me the tribal police would find me and think I was a whore who had caught herself on fire doing meth. But you drank so much of your god awful swill you passed out. And I used the corkscrew to untie my ropes." She lowered her arm and rubbed the wrist of her other arm in remembrance before going on.

"Then I ran. I ran into an arroyo. I ran up into it for miles until it grew dark. Then it rained, and the arroyo filled with water. I waited for two days on a ledge. Then I came to a road and I followed it. It took me to the nuns. That's where I hid from you. But you never came for me. The last thing I remember you saying was, 'I'll fucking kill you, you sick fucking bitch!'," she whispered, as her eyes filled with tears.

Rocco, whose whole body was shaking with anger, now waggled his head with feigned sadness. "Poor girl. Even if what you say is true, which it is not, you need help, young lady, serious help, because you really are one sick fucking bitch."

He turned to Jordan, who had stood, stuck in place, along with Roper and the others, in amazement at Tilly's story. "Are you the one in charge here?" he sneered with mocking officiousness. "In case you haven't figured it out yet, Miss Deputy, I'm Rocco Zinni. I'm the owner of this property. These people are trespassers. They've been served an eviction notice. And I demand that you get all of them off it."

"I had your card. I found it at a rest stop. I called you for a job. You hired me to clean your office," continued Tilly, ignoring Rocco, even though her eyes were trained squarely on him. "But you took me to your ranch, and you...and you, you smelled like cabbage and mustard, and your filthy brothers, the one with bad, dog fart breath," she nodded toward Marco, "and the one with stinky, cat urine sweat...took me until I...I..."

She squinted through her tears and shook her head as each one of these memories surged forth to fill the vacuum a decade of lost time had created. But each one, though a gift of remembrance, was also a poisoned blessing; for each memory filled the crater of lost years with the carcasses of unrecoverable loss.

"That's when I forgot everything," she resumed. "I forgot who I was. Where I'd been. Who I cared about. Who cared about me. Until today."

308

She jabbed her finger at Rocco. "*It was you*. You who took my life from me. *You*. Please, Jordan," she said, her voice quivering with a mixture of rage and desperation, "take this man and his brother out of my sight. They're rapists and kidnappers. They're sick, and they make me sick."

"But you...you were asking for it," Marco Zinni blurted suddenly. "Rocco said you wanted us to fuck you till you went blind. Rocco says that's consensual fucking. Not rape fucking."

"Goddamn it, you imbecile! Shut your fucking rat-ass trap!" Rocco shouted, and slapped his brother with the back of his hand with such force that Marco crumbled to the ground.

Jordan grimaced, and she stepped behind Rocco. Another deputy stood behind Marco. Both applied handcuffs to the men before they could react. Jordan said, "I would advise both of you, and especially you," she nodded to Marco, "to remain silent, at least until we can get your lawyers to the jail after we've booked you."

"Book us? Are you crazy! For what? For wearing women's clothing?" Rocco exploded, his fleshy, lipsticked lips drawn into a sardonic grin. "For wanting to protect my property from a thousand vandals? No, you've got nothing on me. Nothing. My brother is obviously an incompetent. You heard him yourself. And she's obviously a lunatic." He crinkled his nose and drew his mouth into a pucker as though he had a bitter taste in his mouth. "It's every last one of these fucking trespassers you should book. Not me. And," he added tauntingly, while bending to bait Weasel, "I'll see to it that that fucking flea-bag mutt of a dog is put down for attacking me."

"Tell it to the judge," Jordan snapped, as she yanked on Rocco's arm and started to lead him away. But before she could go even five steps, Tilly spoke up from behind her.

"Jordan, wait. He's right. There is nothing to be straightened out. I'm not going to press charges against either of them."

"What?" Jordan stopped in her tracks and turned to face Tilly, as did the others, whose numbers had grown exponentially.

"I'm not going to press charges for what they did to me ten years ago," she said, rising to her feet unsteadily. "Look, he's right. I was out of my mind for ten years. I couldn't have said then who I was, much less who anyone else was. Any lawyer he could hire—and he can probably hire the best—would be able to prove that I am too unreliable a witness to identify them beyond a reasonable doubt, much less convict them of their crimes and ruin their lives after a decade has passed. The evidence of what they did to me long ago is long gone. And they've probably gotten rid of anything else that could incriminate them. There's the statute of limitations. And we were on an Indian reservation..." She shrugged, "So, there's no case."

"Now you're talking sense," Rocco said. And smiling maliciously at Jordan, added, "Take our cuffs off."

"Not so fast," inserted Stanley White Shadow, who had come up beside Thomas Ant Lake only minutes before. "Keep them cuffed, officers." He was holding a smudge whose column of smoke was indiscernible from the mist that still clung to the cemetery. "I charge them with criminally desecrating an historical Native American site."

Then, training his eyes on Rocco, he added, "Mr Zinni, please understand who and what you are going to be dealing with if you continue to insist on asserting your questionable rights here. Let me be clear, and listen carefully. I am Stanley White Shadow. Representing our tribal council I will utilize every last asset and avenue available to us, our casino, the state of California, and the Bureau of Indian Affairs to see that you and your brothers are run into bankruptcy, and that all three of you go to prison."

"You don't have no fucking authority here," Rocco snarled. "This is America, not Indian Bingo Territory."

"Oh, but we do have authority," Stanley White Shadow replied, brushing aside Rocco's insult. "Maybe not the authority you're used to. But, you see, Mr Zinni," he continued, pointing to Falcon hanging from Squirrel's neck, "Falcon has turned our common adversary, you, and by your own hand, into our prey. And there is nothing lawyers can do to protect you, and there is nowhere you can go to escape us, for it is you who are preying on yourself. Everything you do to escape only increases the chances you will trap yourself. You are a tragedy of your own making. And the harder you try, the harder you will fail.

"However," he added, making a pass with the smudge in-between himself and Rocco, "our code of honor also informs us that we must treat our prey fairly, or we bring dishonor to ourselves. So, if you are interested, there may be ways to mitigate some of Falcon's fury."

Rocco nodded, then said, "Are you through, Tonto?"

Stanley White Shadow shrugged. "For now."

"Good, then you can go fuck yourself!" blared Rocco, struggling against the manacles. Then, to Jordan, "If that fucking lunatic bitch is not going to press charges, then get me out of these handcuffs. Now! Or I swear I will sue Sitting Bullshit, or whatever his name is, his tribal bingo council, and this lame-dick county back to Appalachia for false arrest. Not to mention you," he said, jutting his jaw out toward Parker, "for causing this whole fucking thing to happen in the first place. And one more thing," he bellowed, "those Indians love dog meat, so you and your fucking dog are lucky they haven't gone on the warpath and turned her into dog stew... Yet."

Jordan flattened her mouth into a frown, and her voice lost any semblance of understanding. "I again suggest you keep quiet, Mr Zinni, since anything you say may and can be used against you. And I'm sorry. Truly I am. But we can't unlock the cuffs just yet, because, actually, we do have what looks to be a case of reckless endangerment with a—no, two—concealed weapons, even if it is on your own property. And, if what Tilly—Alice von Brandt, I mean—says is true, even if she won't prosecute and the statute of limitations has run out, then we possibly also have a case of attempted murder and witness tampering."

"And cruelty to animals," intoned Parker, "for planting rat poison where any of the animals who have come here could have died."

Rocco smirked. "You can't prove a thing."

"Maybe not, but we do have some videos," Angie said, "Look." Whereupon she lowered her camera and, punching in a few commands, turned it toward Rocco and Marco and brought up the video of the Indians ransacking the cemetery.

"Hey, that's us, isn't it? We look good, don't we, Rocco?" Marco boasted.

Gritting his teeth and seething with anger, Rocco muttered, "Shut up! Shut up! Shut up!"

Meanwhile, all of the musicians had placed their gloves atop the fence, and those who had brought pictures had affixed them to it and taken snapshots. The bulk of the players then came around to the opening in the fence and entered the cemetery, passing Rocco and Marco as they were taken away. All but the timpanist and the bass player brought their instruments to where their brethren had gathered around Yellow Dog Red's grave. After a prolonged silence in tribute to the memory of Parker's old dog, the four soloists broke spontaneously and unbidden into a plaintive four-part harmony to augment the "The Yellow Dog Red Lullaby," which was still playing on several of the bluetooth speakers scattered about. They sang a capella through the first verse of the song. Then they were joined by the other musicians who improvised on Slag's song for the better part of the next hour, so that, in the end, it was transformed from a somniferous Irish lullaby into an even more moving testimony to Beethoven's own grand testament to the joy of being a recipient of, and a partner to, the sacred.

By the time the last notes of the "Ode to Joy Lullaby Remix," as it became known, filtered into the waning light beneath the thickened spatula of fog mustering the evening mist into opacity, the cemetery was less than an eighth-filled, with the last two hundred or so diehard remnants of the gathering, more than half of whom were musicians and Native Americans. While there was still enough light to negotiate the uneven terrain safely with their instruments, all but one of the musicians bid goodbye and retreated to their busses, which then drove away. Only the violist, with whom Danquin had engaged in animated conversations about his research, remained behind, having sent her viola with the timpanist. Jordan, who had gone off-duty after the Zinnis were taken away and after witnesses were given preliminary interviews, stayed huddled arm-in-arm, leaning against Chester's headstone with Roper until the last people, apart from their nuclear group, were leaving. They then left without any fanfare, taking Roper's car to Jordan's house to spend the first night of their future together.

As he made the call to his group home to reiterate that he was going to stay another night with Parker, Squirrel was still trembling from almost having killed his mother. He was turning to head into his tree when he abruptly turned to face Alice. "I can't come live with you, can I, Mom?" he said stiffly, as if he were issuing an order from within a deep fissure of suppressed longing.

"Tonight? In my van?" Tilly answered in surprise, as she walked alongside Parker behind Keith's wheelchair, helping maneuver it through the narrow passage past Orix's grave.

"No, *ever*," Squirrel said pointedly, his cheeks suddenly flaring with color.

Tilly's hands slipped from the grips on Keith's chair, and she faced Squirrel squarely. To that point she had spoken hardly a word to anyone since the Zinnis left, other than to make statements to the deputies and to reaffirm to the paramedics who came to tend to her wound that, apart from a bruised sternum, she was unharmed. Moreover, none present, not even Squirrel, had mustered the courage to address her directly about any of the horrific things she had said.

Tilly did not respond immediately to Squirrel, but cocked her head to one side and flinched as, for the first time, she recognized in Squirrel and heard in his voice the part of herself which had driven both of them to retreat into the aseptic dome of forgetfulness; the part that was like scar tissue gone metastatic in its attempt to protect and heal, but which rather than rehabilitating succeeded only in debilitating.

"No, Peter. Not for now at least," she murmured softly. She blanched at the unspoken cruelty of her own words, and, seeing Squirrel nodding in confirmation at what he had expected to hear, she shook her head sadly in the knowledge that the less she said right then the better.

"Okay then, I won't call you Mom again. Ever," riposted Squirrel sourly.

"Oh, Peter, please don't. I..."

"And don't call me Peter either."

Parker, having overheard them, now almost literally jumped backward from Keith's chair so that he was standing between Squirrel and Tilly, both of whom were so startled by his sudden intrusion they were left speechless. Parker then laid a hand on Squirrel's shoulder.

"Okay, hold on a second, Peter," he interceded abruptly. "And listen to me. Please," he added, when Squirrel squirmed out from under his hand. "Because I have something I want to say to you while I still can. Be careful. Very careful. Your mother is in a fragile state of mind right now," he cautioned, then added, "As, in fact, are you too, Squirrel. And both of you need to be patient with each other. Chill out, as I think you call it. Can you do that, at least for now? For me?"

Before either Squirrel or Alice could respond to Parker's uncharacteristic intercession, Parker turned to face Alice. "I know that after having not known the truth for so long you want only to speak the truth now," he said. "That is more than commendable and, God knows, it has to be therapeutic for you. But until you recover from the injuries you've suffered, you might also think to ask yourself if sooner rather than later is really the time for either of you to speak with unfettered honesty to each other?

"In my mind the answer is no," he said, hastily answering himself. "Because to do so will likely be heard by the other as a hard fact. And in such a fragile environment, when kindness and empathy are not communicated in equal measure with truth, honesty can become brutal and cruel, depending on the circumstances, and truth can then be turned on its head by resentment into its opposite: truth that is a lie. A weapon of retaliation rather than a bridge to understanding. Do you understand what I'm saying?"

Squirrel shrugged as did Alice.

"Good." Parker said, then added apologetically, "Do either of you care if I speak my mind for just a second more? Because, as I see it, I think I am in a unique position to know what you are both facing. And my fear is that if you don't hear each other clearly right now, you may never be able to hear each other clearly again."

Once more both Alice and Squirrel shrugged and waited for Parker, who had never spoken in quite the same frank, almost donnish manner to Squirrel. Parker rolled his head around on his shoulders to help him clear his mind and also to keep out the cold and damp. He then lowered himself to one knee in order to level his gaze with Squirrel's.

"In being an old man who has seen and done a lot, I've observed what memory loss can do to people," he continued. "With my wife. With me. With people I worked with who were traumatized by violence. Try and look at it this way, Squirrel," he went on. "The amnesia that has surrounded your mother for years is like an impregnable wall, one that has kept her living a life totally apart inside it. Her mind did that to keep her from seeing what would truly horrify her. The truth. If she had seen the truth before she was ready to be healed, she would never have recovered.

"But the thing about a wall in the mind," he went on, "is that, even when the wall is gone, there is still an habitual memory of it that continues to act as a barricade. It's like a shadow wall, or a shock wave following an explosion. But instead of protecting your mother, this phantom wall prevents the future from entering into her, and her from entering into the future. In some ways it's a harder wall to bring down because it is both inside and outside your mother. I think someone your age would call it a virtual wall. Do you understand what I'm saying?" he asked again.

"That we both need time to become whole again?" Alice ventured, as Squirrel chewed on his lip.

"I guess so," he mumbled. "But I'm her son, you know. So why can't she just love me?"

"Listen to Parker, Peter. He's right...I think," Alice murmured, resting her hand tentatively on Squirrel's shoulder. "There is still a barrier between me and you, and me and this world, even though I know it's only in my mind. And yours. Here's how it feels to me right now," she went on. "which might help you and me to understand each other a little better. It's as if when I look at you I see not one person but two. There's Little Peter and Squirrel, and neither one of you is totally related to the other. There are ten years missing. Right now it's like you are distant cousins to me rather than one person who is my son. Does that make sense to you?"

Squirrel nodded his head slowly as he processed Alice's words and those of Parker. "Uh huh, yeah...I guess it does... I think... I mean...I think...I think that's sorta how I look at myself whenever I look in the mirror," he stammered, furrowing his brows in recognition of himself in his mother. "Like there is the person I see reflected in it, and then there is the other person only I can see. They're the same but different."

"That's all I'm saying," Parker nodded. "Right now your knowledge of each other is only just beginning to come into focus. It's fragmented. Someday soon, though, I'm confident that the feelings each of you have for the other will form into a whole. A family. And if you want to know what I really think, Squirrel," he went on, "it's that the reason you like being in trees so much is that you need them to see people from two perspectives, so that you can form one that's true to you. The trees have been the family that has given you the protection and the vantage that lets you do this in safety."

"Like your mother will someday," Alice replied, her gaze carefully nestling into Squirrel's. "That is, if you will teach her how to climb trees."

Having overheard this exchange, Keith exclaimed, "Exactly! I couldn't make wine if I wasn't able to resolve the same paradox at the center of the one you two are facing, of knowing that the truth you need to know is

317

unknowable, until you know the unknowable truth. The whole truth. To resolve this," he went on, "you have to recognize that knowing and truth are written in different languages. The language of wine is chemistry. The language of the family is love. One without the other makes shitty wine, or unhappy families."

For the first time since she had shown up days earlier, Alice's face was lit by an unabashedly heartfelt smile. "Would you mind, Keith," she ventured, stepping over to stand beside Keith's wheelchair, "if I park my van at your place tonight, so we can maybe talk some more about this stuff? And about Squirrel and me. Because paradoxes are all I can think of now. That is, now that my memory is intact, I wonder about how my life is connected, or disconnected, to my memory. I mean, can I even say my life is mine if I can't remember it? And if I can't remember it, then whose life was it?"

Keith loosed a grin that was transformed into a sublime smile. "It would be my pleasure, madam," he said, with a courtly flourish of his hand. "I always like good company. And heaven knows," he added, "with my mind locked inside a body like this, all I ever think of is paradoxes and of how my body is related like a very distant cousin to my mind."

During this latter conversation Bahram, Danquin and the violist had succeeded in lifting Orix's stone back to vertical while Angie, who was barely able to keep her eyes open, shored it up with dirt and rocks. As she was pushing the last buttressing stones into place, she looked up and noticed a glint of light coming from a crack near the base of the boulder at the entrance to the water closet. Suspecting at once that it was a remote camera, and knowing that it was not one that either Squirrel, Danquin or she had placed there, she went over to inspect it.

"Hey, Squirrel, Danquin," she called out, holding aloft a cube-shaped object after she had pulled it out. "Can you guys come over here and see if you recognize this?"

Danquin and Squirrel joined Angie, who held in the palm of her hand a mini-cube-camera, which was much like the ones that were planted around the cemetery and connected to her LAN. Neither Squirrel nor Danquin were familiar with the brand, which prompted Angie to pronounce, "Then someone outside our network planted this to spy on us. This is how they knew who was here, and when."

Danquin took the cube from Angie and shined his camera on it. When he turned it on its back, he saw that, apart from the name of the camera's manufacturer, another name was etched in longhand into the metal casing.

"Does anybody recognize the name 'W.C. Engineer'?" he said.

After a brief pause, Parker replied, "I do. Wine Country Civil Engineering. They're surveyors. Why?"

"It looks like they've been spying on us," Danquin said, holding the tiny camera in the air. As he did so, he tilted his head at the sound of drums rolling like foghorns through the fog from the vicinity of the Red Bud Casino compound.

"Or maybe it was put there as part of their job to survey the site," Parker said, although without much conviction, as he too listened to the thrumming of the drums and turned to Keith to say goodbye. He then gave Alice a hug, saying he hoped he would see her the next day, which she promised. But then as Keith started to roll away, Alice stopped abruptly and, gazing back at Squirrel, who was now inspecting the camera, she said to Keith, "Please don't leave without me. I'll be back in a few minutes."

Alice came up next to Squirrel, just after he had handed Parker the cube, to hear Parker say, "Looks like all the other ones to me."

"It's not," Squirrel said, eyeing his mother rather than Parker, for she was looking intently at his face. "It's totally different. See," he went on, breaking his gaze away from Alice and pointing to the name of the manufacturer and then to several other physical features that were meaningless to Parker.

"What should we do with it?" Angie said, taking it from Squirrel's hand.

"Leave it," replied Parker. "Maybe someone will come to get it, and we can ask him why he's doing it. After all, the surveyors were here legally, and this is the Zinnis' property. And, anyway," he shrugged, "if it's on right now, it's filming us, and whoever owns it knows we know it's here."

Bahram, who had come up to Angie, nodded in agreement. "Yes, it's good to keep your friends close and even better to keep your enemies closer," he inserted. "And you, young lady," he said, draping his arm over Angie's shoulder, "need to come home with me. Right now!" he added hastily, when Angie started to protest. "You have school tomorrow, and don't forget, you need to get up early so we can Skype Slag about his song."

"Tell him thanks for me," Parker inserted, "And that I think his tune captured perfectly how I feel about my dog."

"We'll do that," Bahram said, as he gently tugged Angie to his side.

"Wait, before you go," Parker said, "Yellow Dog Red and I want to say thank you, Angwin, for all the things you did to make this happen today. It was beautiful. You put Yellow Dog Red on the map. You deserve all the credit. And if I was an executive at Google or Twitter, I would hire you in a heartbeat. You, too, Squirrel," he added.

Angie and Squirrel lowered their eyes and smiled, but when neither said anything, Keith, who had remained where he was, interjected, "If Google and Twitter don't want you...Paradoxum wants you...to make and run our media presence...on the web."

"And will you tell Slag for me," Alice blurted to Bahram, "that his song helped open my eyes and my heart to my son, and to my new life, in ways I can never fully express?"

"I will do that. I'm sure he'll appreciate it," Bahram said, leaving with Angie under his arm. "And don't forget, Keith, we have a lot of Yellow Dog Red wine things to talk over."

Alice turned and recaptured Squirrel's gaze. The rigidity that had resided in her eyes and in his was gone now and she threw her arms around Squirrel and pulled him close. "Thank you, Squirrel," she whispered. "You are everything I could have wished for in a son. Everything. Remember, I love you. Don't ever forget that." She then sniffled and almost giggled at the preposterousness of her own words.

"I won't forget," he said, wrapping his arms around his mother. "And you can call me Peter."

Parker now heard Wili Wallenstock's voice rise up in a shrill "Whoopee!" that sounded almost like a war cry above the steady drumbeats. He hadn't seen her since Stanley White Shadow had invited her—and anyone else who was interested—to attend the purification ceremony on the Gainsaid Pound property they were conducting to rid the land and themselves of the Zinnis' poison.

Wili's war cry was among the last voices Parker would hear that night as, left alone finally, he sat "conversing" with Yellow Dog Red. To say he spent one hour or five conversing would be to diminish to the span of an atom's trek across a pinhead the temporal reality Parker experienced that night, for as the evening wore on, time lost all meaning for him while it both shrank and expanded in the blink of an eye that, accompanied by the resolute drumbeats, stretched longer than eons to encompass the passing of the entire universe. One moment he was sitting in the pet cemetery beside Yellow Dog Red, with her on her side wagging her tail, eyes closed, and breathing softly while he scratched her back. The next moment he was on the windswept Mongolian steppes traveling in a camel caravan with a guard dog he knew to be Yellow Dog Red. Next he was but an impulse on the shock wave of an exploding star, fully aware that the nova's stellar dust was part of Yellow Dog Red, himself, Sylvia, Tad, Dotty and everyone else he knew. Then he, and Yellow Dog Red, and Tad, and Sylvia were tromping barefoot along an infinitely long strand of white sand in Baja

California, picking abalone shells up off the beach and seeing the same nacreous stellar core mirrored in the mother-of-pearl galaxies at their feet.

On and on it went. From infinitely short to infinitely long. From infinitely small to infinitely large. From infinitely weak to infinitely strong. Yet, through all these manifestations and transformations, Parker was aware that no matter how far removed or how close at hand, how minute or how gargantuan, there was always the presence of those he loved in both the waking and the dreaming, the living and the dying. Yes, he thought finally, as he made his way to the trailer: I have found love. It is everywhere. And I am ready for it to take me.

The purification ceremony went on until morning the next day. Before heading home, Wili, her step surprisingly light for someone her age having stayed awake all night, stopped on the way to her car to see Parker and, if possible, grab a cup of coffee. As she came to the opening in the fence, Squirrel, like a spirit emerging from the fog, passed her silently on his way down the hill. He eschewed stopping to talk to her, however, as there was a van on the road, blaring its horn, awaiting his arrival to take him to school.

Finding the door of the trailer ajar, but with no coffee or Labrador puppy in sight, Wili, thinking that Parker may have gone somewhere already, peeked inside. She was surprised to see that he was still asleep in his bed, with Parker-the-dog curled up between him and Dotty, who was also asleep. Hearing the door squeak as it opened, Parker-the-dog raised her head, and, seeing Wili, wagged her tail happily and leapt over Parker, waking him abruptly.

"Oh, I'm so sorry to bother you two," Wili said, trying to shut the door that Parker-the-dog, greeting her with wiggles and licks, would not let her close.

Dotty was awake now too. Both she and Parker were in the clothes they had been wearing the night before, and both, in seeing Wili, assumed sheepish expressions as they sat up. Dotty, rubbing her eyes of sleep, was the first to speak.

"This is not what you think it is, Wili Wallenstock. We..." she began.

"Oh yes it is," Parker countermanded. "It is exactly what you think it is. Two people who are old friends who love each other, sleeping in the same bed after a long day. And you can print that."

Dotty poked Parker with her elbow, and Wili waved her hand in dismissal. "Whatever," she said blandly, adding, "I'm sure it's fine." But then drawing out her tablet from her purse, her tone grew energized. "This is the real reason why I stopped by," she said, almost breathlessly. "I wanted to show you something I caught last night when I was filming. May I?" She motioned with her eyes as she let Parker-the-dog out the door, inviting herself to sit on the bed next to Parker.

"Sure," Parker said, as he scooted closer to Dotty to make room for Wili. "What did you get?"

"You won't believe it unless you see it with your own eyes," she said. "And, if I don't get the Pulitzer Prize for all of this... Alice's awakening. Marco's confession. The 'Ode to Joy'..." She shook her head and her voice trailed off as she swiped her finger across the tablet's screen until she came to the portion she was looking for. "Here, check this out." And she extended the tablet to Parker to hold on one side while she held onto the other and manipulated the screen images.

In a second, the bottom half of the tablet's screen was filled with a video of Weasel on top of Rocco Zinni. Above and behind them was Alice. And above Alice in his tree was Squirrel. When the scene came to the point when Rocco pulled his gun out of his purse, Wili stopped the film and pushed it into a closeup of Squirrel and the foliage surrounding him. Then she let the film continue playing, but now in extra-slow motion.

"When I saw it last night at the purification ceremony I couldn't believe it," she yipped. "This is what I want you to see. Look! right above Squirrel's tent. See it? In the tree."

Parker had to hold the tablet farther out from them for the image to come into focus. But then they both saw it: a very large brown-and-red-winged, hook-beaked bird perched atop a limb of the eucalyptus.

"Is that an eagle?" Dotty said, as Wili tapped the screen and homed in on the bird for an extreme closeup.

"It looks like a...a falcon," Parker said, as he shook his head to clear it; for not only was the size of the bird dumbfounding, but so too was its plumage, which shone with gem-like iridescence from within.

"*It is a falcon*," Wili confirmed in elation. "But now, watch what happens next," she said, and again she started the film in extra-slow motion and kept the focus on the falcon.

Now Squirrel fell from the bottom of the video frame and disappeared as he leapt from the tree. A second later came the retort of gunfire. A second after that the falcon also disappeared.

"Did either of you see the falcon fly off?" she said, to which both shook their heads. "I didn't either. Neither did Stanley or Thomas. So, I'll run it back." And Wili now looped the five second segment so that it ran continuously in slow motion.

"It's there. There's a gunshot. And then it's not there. But I didn't see it fly away. I can't find any images of it flying into the tree either," she went on. It's just there in the moments before the bullet hit the totem around Alice's neck. And then it's not there. It just disappears into thin air."

"What did Stanley and Thomas say about it?" Parker said.

"Stanley said it was Falcon doing his job. In any case, I'm off to get a cup of coffee and see my publisher. He said he thinks we can get my video on 'Sixty Minutes' or 'Dateline.' And," she added with a shrug, "he said he's thinking again about leaving his wife..."

She rose to her feet and took the tablet from Parker. "By the way," she said, squinting out the open door into the halo of mist hanging over the outstretched hands ringing the cemetery. "I want you—both of you—to know how much I admire you for what you're doing here. And I'm truly sorry, again, for what was published about you earlier. I'm not really a dog person, as you might have guessed," she went on, "but I can see now that

Yellow Dog Red means so much to you because she saw faithfulness in you. She knew you were as good a dog as she was."

Parker nodded. "Thanks. She was a good dog."

"And a lucky dog," Dotty added.

"We're all lucky," Parker replied. "But there was never a better dog than Yellow Dog Red."

CNN didn't take Wili's tape, at least initially, nor did "Dateline" or "Sixty Minutes." However, a local independent television station did, and within a week the mainstream news media ran with it both in this country and abroad. Likewise, it went viral across all the social media platforms, one of which was viewed by the county District Attorney. He then invited Alice and Jordan to talk with him the following week, after he had received 115 sexual harassment complaints against Rocco Zinni, from women who had either been sexually assaulted while in his employ, or who had been sexually harassed as a condition for obtaining employment.

Another viewer was the Governor, who, being an eighth Paiute herself, requested that formal judicial inquiries be launched into Zinni's excavation of Native American artifacts, as well as into his apparently illegal use of methyl bromide. Moreover, since Zinni could find nobody to work the land after word got around about Falcon, operations on the vineyard and even on the planning of the winery facilities came to a standstill. The SPCA, emboldened by all the publicity, also brought suit against Zinni for his disregard of the covenants that had created the pet cemetery in the first place, alleging that only they, not Zinni, had legal standing to evict Parker. And thus, under a clouded title and negative notoriety, the county rescinded without prejudice Parker's eviction notice.

As she had indicated, Alice von Brandt did not file charges against the Zinnis for rape and kidnap. However, because Rocco was charged by the D.A. and later convicted of attempted murder, reckless endangerment, and with carrying a concealed firearm without a permit, Alice's deposition detailing her ten years of amnesia after having been raped by the Zinni brothers *was* admitted into evidence, but only for the sentencing phase of Rocco and his brothers' trials.

But it was the class-action sexual harassment suit brought by the 115 woman against the three Zinni brothers that bled the Zinnis dry financially, and proved to be their ultimate undoing; for the cost of procuring legal representation to defend themselves—of going to trial in court, and of defending the guilty verdicts through the protracted appeals process afterward—forced them to offload under duress virtually all of their real assets at fire-sale prices. In the end though, none of their money or assets did them any good; for on top of Rocco's multiple sentences, each of the brothers were also convicted of various counts of sexual assault, battery and rape. In sum, the Zinni brothers were looking to spend the next 120 years in prison, which none of them expected to survive.

One of the salutary outcomes of the proceedings against the Zinnis was that Keith and Bahram, with the help of the Red Bud Casino's holding company, were able to purchase the Gainsaid Pound Vineyard property at a convenient price. They changed the property's name to Yellow Dog Red Vineyards, which was incorporated as a nonprofit subsidiary of Paradoxum. In turn, the profits from Yellow Dog Red Vineyards were dedicated solely to supporting educational programs, the SPCA, and to programs for abused women. Another beneficial outcome was that the Native American archeological site on the knoll, other than being a seasonal gathering place for the local tribes, was also identified as a burial ground and, therefore, designated sacred land, and the knoll was subsequently allocated protected cultural status in perpetuity.

As part of their corporate filing, Paradoxum Vineyards agreed to place the cemetery, which retained the name Gainsaid Pound Pet Cemetery, in an unbreakable trust with the SPCA, whose Yellow Dog Red endowment was funded initially by $300,000 from Slag's mp3 lullaby sales. Additionally, ongoing sales of Yellow Dog Red wines, and annual summertime performances in the vineyard by the Leipzig Philharmonic in subsequent years augmented the fund well enough so that it was able to rehabilitate derelict pet cemeteries in other states, as well as to provide funds for training a hundred people a year with disabilities to work in the wine industry, and a hundred per year to work in veterinary medicine.

Danguin returned to his university in Germany the following month, where he refined his research, to whose original postulation—that an advanced and highly developed society can utilize extended acts of reverse devotion to a pet as a way to diminish that society's need to resort to violence to resolve both inter- and intra-societal conflicts—he added modules derived from chaos and fractal theory and, most telling, from animal whispering practices. He got married the following spring in Germany, and he spent his honeymoon on zip-line explorations of the canopy of the Amazonian rain forest. On the first leg of their return trip, he and his new wife made a stop at the Yellow Dog Red Vineyard to celebrate the double marriage of Alice to Keith, and Roper to Jordan, and to meet up with the Leipzig Philharmonic, which was launching its second American tour there.

The marriage ceremony was held at the site of the old Gainsaid Pound kennel overlooking the cemetery, now surrounded by budding vines. The chainlink fence had come down, and the fence that had been erected to replace it consisted of interlocking five-foot-tall stainless steel gloves into whose palms the pictures that had been affixed to the original links were held by metal clips. In addition, hooks for animal control licenses lined the perimeters of each and every hand, and during the wedding, in which a light breeze swept across the vineyard, these emblems of devotion glittered like thousands of points of light. Like Danquin, Roper and Jordan too honeymooned in the trees, only in their case they chose to keep their feet on the ground and spent their time hiking through the bristlecone pine forests in Eastern California.

Alice and Keith spent their honeymoon at the guesthouse of the Buddhist retreat where Alice had been the housekeeper, in Sedona, and

329

after a week's stay, Squirrel joined them and became enthralled with rock climbing. He also became brother to Axel a year later and, after legally changing his name to Squirrel, moved in with Keith, Alice, Axel, and Weasel to the house in town that Parker had vacated. A year after that, Squirrel was able to make contact with his father, who was living in Turkey. The two have yet to meet. Squirrel eventually went to Stanford on a scholarship, where he studied Geology. He later emigrated with his Australian wife to Australia, where, she assured him, there were far more rocks to climb than trees. As far as is known he never climbed another tree.

It took Roper and Jordan less than a year to give birth to identical twin boys: Jessie and Parker. Two years later, as a surrogate to Sam and Becky, Jordan gave birth to their girl, who they also named Parker. Roper, among other commissions, was hired by Keith and Bahram to design and oversee the building of the Gainsaid Pound Winery complex, and Jordan gave up her job as sheriff's deputy to manage the Yellow Dog Red Trust, which sent her and Roper to New Zealand and Australia at least once a year.

Angie traveled with her father to Ireland that summer for a conference on animal rights, where they met up with Slag outside Sligo in a castle on a lake filled with swans. As it happened, Slag confessed he had actually been at the cemetery the day of the flash mob disguised with a beard and blue glasses as a barista, and not wanting to steal Yellow Dog Red's thunder, he hadn't told anyone. He had, however, gone on to produce a CD on which the lullaby was included with eleven other songs, most of them inspired by that day's people and events. It went platinum the first month it was released and, incorporating footage from Angie's videos, won the music video of the year award.

Four years later Angie was admitted to MIT's Artificial Intelligence Program, from which she graduated at the top of her class. Later still, she and Danquin collaborated for the United Nations on a film project, whose genesis was his research on the Yellow Dog Red Overlook. It later won a documentary award at Cannes.

Wili did not win the Pulitzer Prize. She did, however, win the heart of Stanley White Shadow, as well as winning a job as the casino's fashion consultant and their media coordinator. She also wrote a book about her experience. Its publication earned her an appearance on "The Today Show" and "Ellen," but it was the inclusion of her original critical newspaper article about Parker, which she had incorporated as an appendix in her book, that brought her unlikely but lucrative speaking engagements at conferences around the world that dealt with providing meaningful activities for people with dementia.

Even after the legal title and the security of the cemetery property were settled, and there was no compelling need for him to stay in the graveyard, Parker continued to reside there nonetheless, in a 32-foot motor home that belonged to Dotty, which replaced the teardrop trailer. And as had been his routine from the very beginning of the Yellow Dog Red Overlook, Parker awoke and had coffee and cereal with Yellow Dog Red every morning. Sometimes Dotty, who began to spend half her nights there and the other half at her house, would breakfast with him before going about her day. Often they would then drive off together on their errands. Always though, Parker, along with Parker-the-dog, insisted on returning to be at Yellow Dog Red's side before nightfall.

On a hot August morning two-and-a-half years after Parker's vigil had begun, with the vineyard in full leaf, Dotty emerged from the motor home to see Parker sitting motionless in his chair with his head down, his trunk leaning forward in anticipation, and his hands gripping his armrests firmly as if he were stuck midway in the process of standing. She saw that his eyes were closed and that his right foot was planted on the margin of Yellow Dog Red's grave. An empty coffee cup lay on the ground next to Parker-the-dog, who was curled at Parker's feet.

Parker-the-dog's eyes were directed not at her or at Parker, but at the eucalyptus tree Squirrel had once inhabited. It was then that Dotty saw, in the soft dirt at the center of Yellow Dog Red's grave ahead of where Parker's foot lay, that there were actually four sets of faintly indented and newly formed footprints—a child's, a woman's, a dog's, and what looked to be the imprint Parker would have made had he stood and taken a step forward. The prints led side-by-side from there to the base of the eucalyptus twenty feet away.

Dotty reached out to nudge Parker awake with her hand, but she was certain even before she made contact with his shoulder that he was gone. When Parker did not respond to her touch, Dotty let out a mournful whimper and slumped to the ground beside him, prompting Parker-the-dog to grab the tennis ball and jump to her feet in preparation for playing fetch. The dog's attention, however, was again fixated not on Dotty but on the lower branches of the eucalyptus.

"Goodbye, Parker, my friend," Dotty murmured, as her eyes filled with tears.

At the mention of Parker's name, Parker-the-dog bounded over to the side of the eucalyptus. She then stood on her hind legs and began to hop and whine while she simultaneously pawed the bark with her front feet as if trying to climb into the tree. Dotty shifted her gaze upward to where Parker-the-dog was directing her attention: to the branch on which Squirrel's tent had once rested. There, in the clear bright white light of the hot summer morning she saw four distinct figures—three human, one canine—standing on that same limb. No words were exchanged but Dotty recognized by their shimmery likenesses that they were Parker, Sylvia, Tad, and Yellow Dog Red.

The next moment the leaves of the eucalyptus became feathers affixed to two immense wings, each one at least a hundred feet tall. The tree trunk split in two to become two legs. The roots, huge talons. A deafening keen came from everywhere and nowhere at once, renting the air of movement and a silence so vast that Dotty felt she was herself but a single leaf trembling in a windless void. The wings drooped down. They draped themselves around the family. Then Parker, Sylvia, Tad, and Yellow Dog Red disappeared into the enfolded wings that had gone back to leafage.

Parker-the-dog lay down with her ball at the base of the eucalyptus. "Parker, come!" Dotty called out to her, her voice trembling. But Parker-the-dog remained, motionless, where she was. And so she remained for the rest of that day, and for the rest of the following month, moving away only to do her business. Weeks later, Parker's ashes were spread atop the grave, conjoining with Sylvia's and Tad's (and with Dotty's two years later).

Roper and Jordan took Parker-the-dog as theirs. They were loving owners, but notwithstanding their attempts to keep her at home Parker-the-dog preferred to spend her days not with them but in the vineyard at the top of Memory Road by the side of Yellow Dog Red's grave, where she lay all day long by herself, or sometimes sitting with Armando, beside the grave, chewing meditatively on the tennis balls that were left by visitors, or sitting beneath the eucalyptus tree, gazing to the spot where she had last seen Parker, until it was time for her to go home for dinner. Her grave is located kitty-corner between Yellow Dog Red's and Chester's.

Finally, beginning three years later, after the fourth annual performance of the "Ode to Joy" by the Leipzig Philharmonic at the up-and-running Yellow Dog Red Winery, there could always be a set of foot prints found leading away from Yellow Dog Red's grave to the eucalyptus Squirrel had once inhabited. A family of falcons now calls the tree home, coming back every year to build a nest on the same limb where there had once stood a young man's tent.

ABOUT THE AUTHOR

Patrick Moran has been writing stories for forty years. He has written eight novels and a dozen or so short pieces, some, or all, of which defy easy description. Suffice to say, the stories all resemble to one degree or another in prose that quaint historical curiosity known as the Mohole Project, which was an attempt in the mid-20th Century by misguided and misdirected under-employed engineer types to bore a hole through the outer crust of the Earth, to the mantle and, thence, to the outer reaches of its core, in the hope that by descending to the center of the physical world they would learn where it (and therefore we) came from, and where it (and we) were going.

In other words, schooled in Geography, he has tried to use his word processor much like a drill bit, boring with it through the outer layers of that crenulated over-flap of under utilized gray matter we loosely term self-awareness, into the core of the neuronal root ball beneath it that we call consciousness, in the hope that the mysterious core at the center of all things would reveal itself. Whether he's succeeded or not is not for him to say. He only knows that in these forty years there is just one indisputable thing he's learned: that pointing is still the best tool that anybody can ever use to explain any one thing and all things.

When he is not writing, he is throwing sticks for his Labrador Retrievers, and using hammers to pound nails into the various out-of-plumb structures he builds with his wife and life-partner on their five acres of wildly overpriced oak forest, and then using crowbars to unbend the same nails. Likewise, he made a living working with people whose luck in life can be measured by the degree to which their minds and bodies, bent by the nails of genetic inequity or just plain shitty luck, can be straightened by the crowbar of social equity. All in all, in other words, his is a good life he wouldn't trade for anything, except, perhaps, for a deeper understanding of this one.

Other books and writings by Patrick Moran

Blue Boxes: A novel that seeks to answer the question: What is sacrifice? A gray whale is caught up on an offshore oil rig in Southern California. A 30-year-old Butterfly Diary written in 1959 by girl dying of cancer ties the characters together in ways none could have imagined. Available now in ebooks.

Tsunami Sundog: Set in the late 21st Century, this novel follows a net-stretcher named Tali Rosen as she is swept up on colliding waves of organic, electronic and spiritual energy that transcend the boundaries of life and death. Their collision catapults Tali into a landscape of recombinant after-death bardos, where in order to remain among the living she finds she must undo a scheme to make the land of death a profit center. Available now in ebooks.

Harvesting Rosa Sweetnail: A novel set in the Wine Country of Sonoma County, in Northern California, in which the surgeon emeritus owner of a nearly bankrupt winery, Griffin McXain, covets the heart of his neighbor, Rosa Sweetnail, to replace the failing one in his beloved wife's chest. Through the strength of her art as a sculptor and her Indian heritage, Rosa discovers that a heart is not the only thing that is inherited from dust. Available now in ebooks.

The Tibetan Book Of Dina: A tale told by a dog, named Dinasaur, whose master unwittingly gives his pet the Buddha's rice bowl, stolen from a lamasery in Tibet. Dog and man learn they must return this very special kibble dish to its rightful place, sending them on an adventure that begins in San Francisco and ends in Tibet, where the dualities of life must be reconciled to a timeless perspective before the bowl can be returned. Available now in ebooks.

a'a: A coming-of-age story set in Hawaii, it centers on the Ironman Triathlon, in the mid-eighties. A young man, Tyrone Clancy, learns through the death of an Hawaiian eeler—caused by Tyrone's father's rigid adherence to his training schedule—that life is more about the responsibility of sustaining the spirit than about beating the clock. Available now in ebooks.

That Which Bends: This is a novel that reflects on the nature of fortune, in which an expatriate American businesswoman adrift in the world, and a San Francisco restauranteur on a final journey look beneath their reflections in the timeless waters of Venice to find that which bends the world is love. Available now in ebook format.

Swimming in Stone: Set in Venice and Asia Minor, this is the sequel to That Which Bends. It tells the tale of Dusty Rhodes after she and her lover, Bodie Bloom, have won forty million euros in the Italian Lottery, only to see Bodie die shortly afterwards. Heartbroken but rich beyond her wildest imaginings, Dusty embarks on a voyage of hope with Bodie's estranged family in order to split Bodie's portion of the winnings in accordance with his last wishes. In the end Dusty and Bodie's family learn the truth that real fortune is measured not in the currency of exchange but in the currency of hope from which redemption may be wrung. Now available in ebooks.

The Hard'n-Back: A sports fantasy about a planet whose water-borne peoples must compete in globe-girdling rowing races in order to win the right to reproduce. Failure to win means facing the "Long Death" of extinction.

Rootbound: Rhianna's lifeless body lies splayed atop a salt spire on the south shore of Mono Lake. A sapling oak rises from inside the young woman's abdomen. Murder by tree hugger? Or something more complicated? On the eve of his arrest, the confessed killer walks up to an aspen tree and disappears into it. Heed is his name. A genetic interloper between flora and fauna. A shape shifter. Thus begins the mystery confronting Rhianna's ex-husband Marlyn, a transgender man, to uncover how a murderer could take the life of his beloved, and how he can bring himself to rationalize those same choices as his own. Available now in ebook format.

Place of Promise: Set in Los Angeles right after WWII, this is the story of Daniel Rose, the idiot-savant, homosexual scion of a Hollywood movie studio mogul. Recently dishonorably discharged, Daniel is used by his family to secretly funnel money to Israeli A-bomb development.

Holognosis: The Knowledge of Wholes: Holognosis is a concept I have developed that tries to provide a structure for building a bridge that ties together the shores of rationality to those of faith. Holognosis expands on the ability of systems to orient themselves, through a process resembling homeostasis, in the center of surrounding fields of all sorts, beginning with but not exclusive to, gravitational fields. In being an extension of the function of equilibrium, Holognosis encapsulates the process of centering, which we call self-awareness, in which the barriers between physical and metaphysical are seen to be discreet spherical membranes delimiting degrees of wholeness through which the stuff of life ebbs and flows.

patrickmoranbooks.com: The website of Patrick Moran and all things Holognostic.

Made in the USA
San Bernardino, CA
30 October 2017